PYROMANTIC

PYROMANTIC

LISH McBRIDE

SQUARE
FISH

HENRY HOLT & COMPANY | **NEW YORK**

SQUARE
FISH

An imprint of Macmillan Publishing Group, LLC
175 Fifth Avenue, New York, NY 10010
fiercereads.com

Our books may be purchased in bulk for promotional, educational,
or business use. Please contact your local bookseller or the Macmillan Corporate
and Premium Sales Department at (800) 221-7945 ext. 5442 or by e-mail
at MacmillanSpecialMarkets@macmillan.com.

Library of Congress Cataloging-in-Publication Data
Names: McBride, Lish, author.
Title: Pyromantic / Lish McBride.
Description: New York : Henry Holt and Company, 2017. | Sequel to: Firebug. |
Summary: "When a mysterious illness starts to affect the magical community, it's up to
Ava, who can start fires with her mind, and her team to stop its spread . . . or else one
of them might be next"— Provided by publisher.
Identifiers: LCCN 2016006415 | ISBN 9781250104298 (trade paperback) |
ISBN 9781627795494 (e-book)
Subjects: | CYAC: Fantasy. | Magic—Fiction. | Fire—Fiction. | Adventure and
adventurers—Fiction.
Classification: LCC PZ7.M478267 Py 2017 | DDC [Fic]—dc23
LC record available at https://lccn.loc.gov/2016006415

Originally published in the United States by Henry Holt and Company
First Square Fish edition, 2018
Book designed by April Ward
Square Fish logo designed by Filomena Tuosto

1   3   5   7   9   10   8   6   4   2

LEXILE: HL750L

For Martha Brockenbrough—
I wouldn't have made it through this book without you.
Thank you for being an excellent and silly human.
(Ficus.)

PYROMANTIC

1

SOME THINGS MEND MORE EASILY THAN OTHERS

FIREBUGS ARE CREATURES of flames and heat, sibling to the phoenix and dragon. Not genetically, but in spirit. So why was it that all it took was a hot summer day in Maine and a stuffy loft to make me want to stick my head in the freezer? If an ice cream truck went by right now, I'd melt the tires and tackle the driver. Not that we had ice cream trucks in our town. Too small. Sylvie said she saw one once, but I'm pretty sure she was just hallucinating. I fanned myself with the papers in my hand and tried to listen to Cade.

"'I told you, Ava—you can't go out if you didn't finish your...' I'm sorry, does this say *embroidery*?" Cade glanced at Sylvie, a dubious expression on his face, and for very good reason. The likelihood of me sitting down to work on some stitchery is about up there with seeing a walrus skydive. No, that wasn't quite right. Make that an entire herd of skydiving walruses in matching spandex doing a synchronized aerial routine as they plummeted toward the earth. Firebugs and cloth-based handicrafts don't really go together well. Sylvie ignored Cade, the click of her knitting needles pausing as she counted rows.

"'But, Papa, the dance is tonight! If I miss it, I won't be able to hold my head up in polite society all season!'" I crossed my ankles, my bare feet resting on the paint-splattered drop cloth covering the couch. I wiped sweat off my forehead with the heel of my hand. Maybe if I shaved my head, I'd be cooler.

Cade knocked my feet down. "As if you're fit for polite society now, Rat." I stuck my tongue out at him.

"Stick to the script, please," Sylvie responded, her voice a singsong. The clicking resumed as she returned to her work. I couldn't quite tell what she was making. Knowing Sylvie, it could be anything from a cape to a life-size Dalek cozy.

Since we'd had to rebuild Broken Spines after it was burned down, we'd expanded upward. The bookshop now had a kitchenette and employee lounge, as well as a spare room that we were probably going to use for storage (if you listened to Cade) or a deluxe napping station (if you listened to me and Sylvie). We were going to win, especially after Cade saw the badass bunk beds I'd had the dwarves install already. I'd always wanted bunk beds.

My new boss, Alistair, had decided that even though he wasn't part of the Coterie when all this happened, the organization should help foot some of the rebuilding costs. I was grateful for this generosity, though I didn't tell him that. Because even with our insurance money and the back pay Alistair had given me and my team, we couldn't afford dwarf builders. They're the best, and quite frankly, we can't afford the best. We can't even afford the second best. I'm not sure we could swing the top ten.

Cade put his set of pages on the counter. "I now regret encouraging you to read Jane Austen."

I gently rested mine on my chest, letting my hand hang down. Sylvie had worked hard on the script, so I didn't burn the pages, which was tempting. Since Sylvie didn't know I was a firebug, I couldn't burn them right that minute anyway. Not without my secret getting out, and only two humans knew what I was— Cade and my ex-boyfriend, He Who Must Never Be Mentioned Ever If You Don't Want a Fiery Reckoning Brought Down Upon You. I needed to keep it that way.

"I guess I should be happy you didn't demand we put a pianoforte up here." Cade picked his pages back up.

"I considered that," Sylvie said. "But it would ruin the flow. And I couldn't find one within the budget." Sylvie had taken over the organization and decoration of the upstairs space. Everything was purchased and positioned for maximum efficiency. I'm not kidding. She'd used graph paper and a scientific calculator and read some interior design books that had come into the bookshop.

Sylvie is plagued by extreme cuteness. Today she'd braided her hair into a crown and placed tiny blue flowers in strategic places. Her purple, girl-cut T-shirt featured a glittery kitten with a jet pack. Her voice is cute, her smile is cute, and her disposition is sunny. Even I had the urge to pat her head occasionally. In contrast, I was wearing a tank top with a tear at the bottom. My jeans shorts had seen better days, and about all I could manage with my hair was a loose ponytail. There were no strategic flowers, nor would it have occurred to me to use any. My clothes leaned toward the darker end of the color spectrum in general, and the only glitter I had on me had come off Sylvie's shirt when she'd hugged me earlier—something she'd gotten in the habit of doing ever since I came back from my battle with

Venus. Not that Sylvie knew anything about what had happened. We'd told her that I'd fallen victim to an aggressive stomach flu. Whatever the cause, seeing me emaciated and worn out had scared her. So now I had to put up with random hugging because I was Sylvie's friend.

I hadn't exactly sought out the relationship. Since I grew up on the run with my mom, people my age, especially normal human people, mystify me. I haven't had much contact with the completely human world. I wouldn't have known how to make friends with Sylvie even if I'd wanted to, but for whatever reason, she'd decided she liked me. And you don't argue with Sylvie.

Sylvie was an employee, yes. She was young. But she also ran the bookshop with a tiny iron fist when she was around, and we didn't argue. Sylvie was damn good at fixing problems, and she'd recently decided that Cade and I needed to be fixed.

"What are you making, anyway?" I asked.

She didn't look up from her project. "Don't change the subject, Ava. You two need help easing from ward and guardian to father and daughter." Cade crossed his eyes at me at the same time I stuck my tongue out at him. "I can see you, you know." We both got a stern glare from her before she continued. "*Role playing* is a proven tool that psychologists use to improve communication and rebuild relationships. I still think it's a good idea."

"It's not the role playing I'm objecting to—" At Cade's snort, I amended my statement. "Okay, I don't *completely* think role playing is ridiculous, and I appreciate your help, Sylvie, but if I'm having a difficult time with the D-word, what makes you think I can manage an unscripted *Papa*? Or would want to?"

"I love it when you call me Big Papa," Cade said, taking a

sip of his iced tea. He frowned. "That sounded less disturbing in my head."

"Well, it sounded super creepy outside it." Sylvie had her back to Cade, so I flicked my fingers and the remnants of his iced tea went up in steam. I pretended to look at my nails so I wouldn't see his disapproving look. I wasn't supposed to "play" with my powers. (He calls it play. I call it practice.)

Cade grabbed the pitcher of iced tea out of the fridge and poured himself another cup.

Sylvie held her glass out to Cade, shaking it in case he hadn't noticed it was empty. "So what word would work for you? *Father? Pa? Daddy?*"

"I rather like *Cade*, actually." I shook my own glass for a refill. Cade very pointedly looked at me while he put the pitcher back. That's what I got for evaporating his drink.

Sylvie shot me her own version of the disapproval look. Apparently I was just racking up the censure points with everyone today. "Don't be like that," she said. "Cynical and whatnot. You've been calling him Cade your whole life. You're denying him his title—one he's earned. It's a respect thing. You have a chance now that you never thought you'd have—you get to call someone Dad. Don't toss it away."

"Daaaaaad, she's making me talk about my feelings. Make it stop." I really threw the whine into the last word, then grinned at Sylvie. "There. Is that better?"

Sylvie dropped her knitting in her lap with a motion that was part pout, part exasperated sigh. "You're deflecting."

"And I'm going to hide all your books on psychology. Clearly you can't use your powers for good."

"This is for good!"

Cade sighed. "Children, stop." He held up a ten-dollar bill. "If I offer this money on the altar of the ice cream gods, may I have a few minutes of peace?"

Now that was a plan I could get behind. I bounded to my feet and snatched the ten out of his hand. "Mine." I one-armed him into a hug and kissed his cheek. "Thanks, Dad."

Sylvie huffed. "You did that on purpose to mock me and my script."

Cade shook his head. "No, she just wasn't thinking about it because I offered her ice cream. Food is a large motivating factor with my daughter."

I scrunched up my nose and squinted my eyes, a face Cade likes to tell me will stick one day. "Nope, still feels weird." I ignored Cade's sigh and grabbed Sylvie's arm. "Come on. Ice cream beckons. You can come back to your meddling later."

She pulled back. "But—"

"Ice cream, Sylvie. Did you hear that part? The knitting can wait. It's wicked hot. Surface-of-the-sun hot. Besides, I'm sure there are about five other things you can try to change about me on the way there."

Sylvie reluctantly came with me, her face still pinched. "Eleven, not five. I've made a list."

"I'm offended."

Cade's voice floated down the stairs after us. "No you're not. You're surprised it's only eleven." Damn it, he was right.

We got frappes, then sat on a bench in the sun playing Spot the Flatlander.

"I spot a couple from away. Notice their khaki plumage and her full face of makeup. If those aren't summer people, I'll eat my shirt. Fifteen points." Sylvie was from here, so she pronounced it "summah people." It was easy to spot the people from away. Locals were working. They didn't have sweaters knotted around their necks, nor were they driving ten miles under the speed limit to gawk at our "provincial" village. Driving can be a real pain this time of year. You find yourself organizing your whole life around avoiding left turns.

"Damn, I missed them." I scanned the crowd, trying to catch up. Sylvie was winning. I was a little distracted by my phone, which kept buzzing with incoming texts. "Hey, there's one. He forgot to take off his lobster bib. That's worth twenty points at least." The man was also overdressed, and I was willing to bet that if we got closer, we'd smell bug spray.

"Either his family hasn't mentioned it, or he's wearing it on purpose. That's got to be worth at least twenty-five." She grabbed my arm. "Children in matching 'I Heart Maine' T-shirts! Three kids, that's ten points each, plus a five-point bonus."

"Bonus?"

"That boy is over twelve and his parents managed to get that shirt on him. That's worth a bonus. I am slaughtering you." She was almost bouncing with glee.

My phone went off again, the change in my pocket making the vibration extra loud.

"Are you going to respond to him?"

"Who?" I asked, but it was a stupid question and Sylvie treated it with the dignity it deserved—a scowl. "I'm busy."

"He didn't do anything wrong."

"I know," I said, holding my frappe against the back of my neck. I'd done my best to hide from Sylvie that Lock had asked me out. She'd always had a huge crush on him. But somehow she'd pulled it out of me, in all its embarrassing glory. After a

7

lecture on my initial boneheaded handling of the whole thing, she hadn't missed a single opportunity to point out my continued poor approach to fixing the rift.

The rift seemed like it would be pretty hard to fix, though. Bianca, Alistair's right-hand girl and general pain in my ass, had asked Lock out shortly after our debacle. Bianca is a caulbearer, and everything I'm not. Her power isn't flashy like mine—she can throw a veil and hide people or things. She's calculating, mindlessly loyal to Alistair, and pretty in a pixielike way. According to the rumors that had filtered back from Lock through Ezra and eventually Sylvie, the date hadn't gone well and they'd decided they were better as friends, but somehow that was worse. I could easily have stepped aside and been noble if he'd dated Bianca. It would have hurt, but I could have managed if that's what would have made Lock happy.

Bianca as a friend, though, was a lot harder to deal with. It felt like Lock had instantly replaced me in his life. For years it had been me, Lock, and Ezra. Quite frankly, I didn't know how to deal with a new person coming in and screwing up the dynamic. And since I didn't know what to do, I ignored the problem, which meant ignoring Lock.

"He thinks you're punishing him."

"I know," I said, my exasperation thick.

"So talk to him." I couldn't see her eyes behind her sunglasses, but I knew Stern Sylvie was talking.

"It's not that simple." I finished my frappe, the straw making an undignified sputtering noise. "And why aren't you mad at me, anyway? I thought Lock was your one true love."

Sylvie shrugged. "The fickleness of youth."

I shoved my sunglasses back onto the bridge of my nose. "It's almost your birthday. You're only about a year younger than me, and you don't have a fickle bone in your body."

She tossed the remnants of her frappe into the trash and helped me up. "Friends don't fight over boys, Ava. Lock likes you and you're both important to me, so I've moved on." She linked her arm in mine. "It was really very big of me and quite dramatic, and your continued refusal to talk to him is ruining the effect. So stop digging your hole deeper, and text the poor boy back."

I grunted in a noncommittal fashion, which she seemed to take for a yes. "What?" I asked when she wouldn't stop staring at me.

"You know you can trust me, right? That you can tell me anything?"

I quashed the urge to fidget. The thing is, I did trust Sylvie, but that didn't mean I could tell her my secret. Bottom line, Sylvie is human. To tell her about my power and the Coterie would endanger us both, and I like my friend too much for that. "Of course," I lied, fixing a fake smile to my face.

I thought I saw a flash of disappointment cross her features, but it was so fast, I barely caught it.

"Okay," Sylvie said. "Well, we'd better get back. That shop won't organize itself."

I snorted. "You know Cade is perfectly capable of setting up a little bit of furniture, right? Especially since you already gave him a diagram."

Sylvie patted my arm. "Sure he can. But if your dad sets it up, then I'm just going to have to fix it, so I might as well do it the first time."

"You're awfully charming for a despot, you know that, right?"

"I resent that. It doesn't have to be my way, it just has to be the right way." She stepped carefully over a line of ants.

"Which just so happens to be your way."

"If you can find a more efficient manner of doing things, then I will happily apply that method."

I laughed, giving up on the argument. We were occasionally able to convince Sylvie that she wasn't right about something, but it happened so infrequently that it seemed like never. If Cade hadn't started writing down these triumphs in a small notebook in the back office, I wouldn't believe those events ever occurred.

We were busy when we got back to the shop, and then it was dinnertime. Cade ordered pizza for us and the dwarves. It had been impossible to hide the dwarves from Sylvie. She was at the shop even when she wasn't scheduled to be. Cade and I had come up with all kinds of explanations for her but hadn't used any of them so far. She had lots of questions for them about their work, and the dwarves seemed endlessly patient with Sylvie—far more than they were with anyone else. But it was odd that she hadn't said anything.

Between the work and the pizza, the night flew by, and before I knew it, I was at home and in bed and it was too late to text Lock back. At least, that's what I told myself when I ignored my phone yet again.

ALISTAIR'S VOICE sounded tinny and far away when I answered the phone the next morning. "I need you in Boston," he said without preamble. I readjusted my cell, which was pinched between my shoulder and my ear. My hands were full of books. I guess I could have gotten one of those hands-free things, but then I would've had to punch myself in the face. I hated the people who came into the bookshop with them on. They looked like they'd had the bits of plastic surgically implanted into their ears, and I always wondered if the people ever took them out, even to sleep. Sylvie was convinced that those customers were secretly cyborgs.

I slid a paperback onto one of our brand-new shelves. Broken Spines would reopen in record time because of the dwarves. We could have simply moved into a new building—it certainly would have been cheaper—but we all liked the original location. So Alistair fast-tracked all the permits in addition to furnishing a motivated group of builders. And if my small town of Currant, Maine, had thought it was weird that we had height-challenged builders who worked through the night, well, no one said anything.

The new building was gorgeous. Brick on the outside, beautifully carved wood on the inside. I traced a finger along the thin wooden vine cut into the shelf next to me; the veins of each leaf stood out in amazing detail. You couldn't find work like this anymore—not by humans, at any rate. It was worth every single penny. They even built a cat tree for Horatio that looked so much like a real tree, I expected a dryad to take up residence. Gnarled roots sank into the floor, making it appear as if the trunk were growing out of it. Branches twisted up, the stained-glass leaves shining a brilliant emerald. A new skylight sat above it, and when the light hit the tree, it cast a fractured green pattern on the floor and walls, making you feel like you were caught in a constant Technicolor leaf fall. The dwarves said the leaves would shift color when it came time for autumn. I couldn't wait. I was almost glad that Venus had burned the other building down.

On the phone, Alistair cleared his throat. "Did you hear me?" He was almost shouting now. The Inferno, the restaurant and club that the Coterie operated out of, was also getting an overhaul. Probably because I had blown up large chunks of it. Allegedly.

"Yeah, sorry, I got distracted. What's so urgent?" I only asked this as a formality. We both knew I'd go. Although Bianca was Alistair's real second in command, we were pretending that I was, for the sake of appearances. Bianca did better work if she could use her skill set, which was sneaking. Whereas I was a loud, mouthy distraction with a known history of playing muscle. Basically, I seemed scarier than Bianca, so I was on display. This would lead to more treks to Boston, though I suspected that lately he'd been fobbing some jobs off on other teams to give me time to heal. He'd glossed over that, however.

"Shouldn't be too big of a deal—just something I want to nip in the bud, so to speak. I'll send the files to your new tablet—" I must have made a sound, because he stopped and sighed. "What happened to the new tablet, Ava?"

"It's not my fault!" The words came out rushed, no doubt confirming to Alistair that it was entirely my fault. Alistair was trying to whip the Coterie into shape—running it like an actual business instead of something out of a supernatural *Goodfellas*. And as part of that, he'd given me a fancy tablet and a new phone to "facilitate communication." He was supposed to send me files and stuff on it. I'd tried to learn how to use it, and Sylvie had talked me into dipping my toe into social media. Some nonsense about me being more like a normal teenager and less like a deranged technologically challenged hermit. So I did. Naturally, the first thing I did was friend Lock. Which meant that the very first image I saw on my tablet was one Bianca had posted on his page. Her and Lock cheek-to-cheek at some café. The camera had caught him midlaugh, the corners of his eyes crinkling, his entire face alight. I hadn't seen him laugh like that in weeks. In fact, I barely saw him at all. Only for work, and then he was all business and so was I because we were both auditioning for the Most Awkward Person Ever Award. It made my stomach clench. I felt bad for Ezra, who was stuck in the middle. So to see that smile with Bianca rubbed salt into an already raw wound. Then the image crashed, and I noticed the smoke and the burned-plastic smell. I'd melted the casing. Luckily, Sylvie had been busy shelving and hadn't noticed me peeling the brand-new tablet off my hands and throwing it away.

I could almost hear Alistair rubbing his face with his hand out of frustration. "Is it repairable?"

"It has gone to see the great tablet in the sky." I squeezed my eyes shut, waiting for him to yell at me. Venus would have threatened me until I pretended to lose cell coverage and shut off my phone. And then she would have carried out those threats. "I'm sorry?"

"No you're not. Not really. Look, this is probably my fault. I should have taken your ... issues into account. We'll get you something else. Something warded for someone of your particular talents. In the meantime, if your phone happens to follow in the footsteps of your tablet, please go get a new one. In fact, you should carry a backup in your bag. Top of the line—no bargain-basement stuff, Ava. Keep the receipt and I'll reimburse you."

"My phone is a business expense? Does the Coterie have an accountant now?"

"It had one before. An underutilized hobgoblin named Zet. Venus wasn't even keeping receipts. How she ran this place . . . Anyway, you'll be seeing a lot of Zet. Don't lose your receipt. He bites."

Of course he does. "So . . . tonight?" I asked, shelving another book.

"I'm sending someone to pick you up. Don't worry—it's someone you like."

There was a click as he ended the call. Didn't anyone say good-bye anymore? And who was he sending—Lock? If he sent Lock, did that mean Bianca would be coming, too? A spark flitted from my left hand, and I jerked it away from the shelves. They were heavily warded and spelled against fire, but the books weren't. Bookseller probably wasn't the best job for a firebug. But I liked it a hell of a lot better than the job my talents actually qualified me for. I shelved the rest of my stack, then went to find Cade to tell him he had to call in Sylvie. I needed the night off.

The Coterie is more clandestine crime family than employer. I don't get performance reviews, there is no time clock, and I can't quit. Being a firebug makes me an impressive and efficient enforcer, and the last boss couldn't pass that up. To stay alive and to protect what little family I had left—Cade—I signed a contract with a hired blood witch, handing myself over to the Coterie. I am essentially an indentured servant for them until I die, or until I find another blood witch willing to cross the Coterie to break my contract.

I'll probably die first.

We used to joke that it was a crappy job but at least we had nonexistent benefits. We couldn't make that joke anymore. Alistair signed us up for medical, dental, and vision insurance.

14

I think 401(k)s are next. So far Alistair is a best-case scenario for new boss, but I keep wondering if that's an act. He certainly seems to be keeping to his word that I'm going to be more of a threat than an out-and-out assassin, but he could just be trying to pacify me. Power corrupts, right? Alistair has power. How long until he's ordering me around the way Venus did? Pushing with my feet, I spun the chair at the front desk around until I was dizzy. I kept thinking about this like it mattered. Like I could actually do something about any of it. I flopped back into my chair and watched the ceiling spin.

The doors chimed, and Sylvie bounded in. Sylvie always bounded. I'm pretty sure she is part puppy.

"Ava! Look what I made to go with the fancy new store." She continued to dance about as she brandished something in front of me.

"Sylvie, it's awfully hard to be sufficiently in awe of your skills when you're bouncing around too much for me to actually *see* what you're holding." She stopped and put her hand in front of my face. She had knitted a cat collar. With a little bow tie.

"Bow ties are cool," she said, her tone solemn.

Horatio would absolutely hate it. He hated collars of any sort. "Good luck," I snorted.

Undaunted, Sylvie went off to find our resident feline. Her voice filtered in from the back. "So you've got a hot date tonight?"

"Yup, that's me, social gadabout."

Sylvie walked up, Horatio a purring mass of orange fur in her arms, his bow tie firmly attached. Apparently Horatio thought bow ties were cool, too.

"Ugh, that's disgusting. I bet he didn't even scratch you. If I tried to do that, my arm would be mincemeat."

She smiled at me, her cheek snuggled up against his fur. "You should try asking him nicely. He's a very well-mannered feline if you treat him with courtesy." She scratched under his chin, and he stretched out further to give her better access. "So, no date, then?"

"None. *Nyet.* Negatory, milady."

"Thanks for your freakishly thorough answer."

I saluted her from my seat.

She put Horatio gently on the floor. "You act like it's a crazy question. If you're not careful, you'll miss your opportunity with Lock. Or is this a Ryan thing? You can't stew over that mess forever." She flopped into the chair next to me.

"Who says?"

"I say. The honorable and much beloved Queen Sylvie has decreed it."

"You're not royalty," I said.

"Yet," she said firmly. "I'm not royalty *yet.*"

What Sylvie didn't know was that I wasn't really mourning the loss of Ryan—I was grieving the *idea* of Ryan. As it turned out, our entire relationship was based on lies and betrayal and make-outs, and I only liked one out of three of those things. Before that, though, he'd represented the possibility of a normal life for me. Now that ideal had died a whimpering death. No white picket fences and whatnot for this girl.

And yet I couldn't help feeling a little sorry for what Ryan had lost. Once, he'd been bright, cheerful, popular, and smoking hot. He'd had what I thought was a perfect life that I envied to my inner core. Now he was more of a hot mess. I tried to avoid him as much as I could, but Currant was a small town. The awkward bump-into-each-other was inevitable.

Sylvie rolled her chair into mine. "Any minute, some nice boy will walk through those doors, and a whole new chapter to your life will begin." We both stared at the doors, waiting for her words to be prophetic.

"I don't know what annoys me more," I said. "That you're an optimistic romantic, or that it appears to be contagious."

Horatio leapt into Sylvie's lap, telling her quite plainly that she wasn't done petting him. "I'm not sure if I'm either of those things, but I don't think they're as bad as you think they are. All I'm saying is that we deserve as much of a shot as anyone when it comes to matters of the heart." She batted her eyes at me coquettishly.

"Please never do that again."

The growling rumble of a motorcycle cut off whatever response she might have had. Sunlight glinted off the chrome as the rider parked. Though the motorcycle itself gleamed, with its black paint job setting off the silver accents and making it look new, the riding leathers and saddlebags were broken in and worn. This was not a new toy, but a seriously loved bike. Once the motorcycle was parked, the rider dismounted, his body turned away from us. On the back of his jacket was a logo I recognized—a beat-up cartoon jackrabbit with the stub of a cigar in his mouth. I wasn't surprised to see shaggy brown hair when the rider took off his helmet and tucked it under his arm. Apparently my ride had arrived.

Sid turned, taking in the new storefront with a grin. There's something mischievous in Sid's grin. I can't quite place what it is exactly, but it's like he's always thinking of something funny at your expense. He looks like that all the way up until he knocks your lights out, too. There were probably several blades hidden

on his person; there usually were. He didn't exactly look dangerous, though. Especially now—brown eyes squinting against the
light, his wiry frame lined in leather and jeans. He looked boy-
ish and friendly. And he was, to a point.

Sylvie looked at me, her eyes hooded. "I thought you said
you didn't have a date tonight."

I blinked at her. "What—Sid?" I laughed. "He's too..."
What? Old for me? How old was Sid? "He's too Sid," I finished
lamely. His grin widened when he caught my gaze through the
window, and he gave a little wave as he hopped up the steps. I
gave a weak wave in return.

"Well, if it's not a date, that's a travesty. He's cute." Sylvie
tilted her head, considering. "Is he single?"

The bell chimed as Sid pushed the door open and came over
to lean on the counter we were seated at. "I hope I'm not
interrupting."

"You're not," I said. "Sylvie here was just talking about
how cute you are. And I had to agree—cute as a soft, cuddly
bunny."

Sid lost all his humor, and his right eye twitched. Were-hares
are incredibly sensitive about what they turn into, and I knew
Sid especially took offense quickly if he thought you were making fun of him. The funny thing is, I like Sid. So why was I going
out of my way to annoy him? Maybe I'd been sort of hoping
my team would show up, Ezra and Lock, just like old times, and
the fact that they didn't chafed. Still, not Sid's fault.

I took a deep breath, blowing it out my nostrils. "Sorry, sorry.
Don't know what got into me."

"You're just being your natural, charming self," Sid said with
the appropriate amount of disdain. "Maybe it's a defense mech-

anism? You know, the lady protesting too much? You can't deny that there was a little *spark* between us in the past, hmm?"

Geez, you accidentally set a guy on fire *one time*, and he never lets you hear the end of it.

Sylvie looked between us, trying to figure out the subtext that was obviously there. I could see her filing it away mentally to chew over later. "Yes, well, I was just asking Ava if you were single." She scratched Horatio but kept her gaze on Sid. "Are you?"

Sid blinked. "I guess I am. Why?"

Sylvie placed Horatio gently on the floor. "I've had to retire my recent crush, which means I have a position open. It's a big spot to fill, but you might be a possibility."

"Don't you dare turn any of that into innuendo," I said, jabbing a finger at Sid. "The only person allowed to corrupt Sylvie is me."

Sylvie handed a bemused Sid a card. "Here's my calling card. Text me and we'll talk."

He tucked it away carefully in his pocket, then grabbed her hand and kissed her knuckles. Somehow Sid can manage to be both courtly and impish at the same time. "As my lady wishes." He stepped away with a flourish before turning to me. "Ready, you harpy? Your chariot awaits."

"You're a terrible human being," I said, snagging my jacket from the back of my chair. "Let's get this freak show on the road. Thanks again for covering for me, Sylvie."

She pulled out a large tote bag from under the counter. "It's cool. I brought my knitting."

Sylvie had been knitting sweaters for a charity. She was a fair knitter, but it had seemed to me that the cardigans she'd been churning out were sized a little oddly. When I'd commented on it, she'd said quite curtly that they were done to very particular specifications. Since I didn't really care, I'd let it go. I gave her a final thank-you, and then we were out the door.

Sid handed me a helmet and a leather jacket that had the same logo on the back as his did. "I brought Ikka's spares for you," he said. "The jacket might be a bit big. You can stow yours in one of the saddlebags for later." He put on his helmet. "Is she always like that?"

"Sylvie? Yeah. I mean, the calling cards are new. She's been reading a lot of Jane Austen. And what's wrong with my jacket?" I loved my beat-up old army jacket. Not stylish, no, but amazingly functional. I had all kinds of things in the pockets and sewn into the linings.

"If we take a spill, do you want to be in leather or in that?"

"Is not crashing an option?" I asked, but I did as instructed and put on Ikka's leather jacket.

Since my butt was not accustomed to long rides on the back of a motorcycle, Sid pulled off at a diner halfway through. Sid and I both eat like binging termites. Like many weres, Sid has an incredibly fast metabolism. I don't, but I do burn fuel when I make fire, and calories are fuel. Once I run out of that energy, my body will start burning fat, and then muscle. If firebugs don't watch their food intake, and if they're not careful with their fire, they will literally burn themselves up. So, if at all possible, I keep a few extra pounds on at all times. I'm probably the only teenage girl in America not trying to slim down for swimsuit season. To be fair, I don't think I'd be that kind of girl anyway. If people don't like me because I don't meet some sort of skewed body measurement, they are welcome to find different company. I even have a list of suggested activities for them, starting with "suck it" and ending with "nude alligator wrestling."

Sid and I each ordered appetizers and entrees, and he pre-ordered dessert for us, even though it was clear that the waitress thought he was being optimistic. Or she was just having a bad day. Four loudmouthed guys—either drunk or just obnoxious— were keeping themselves busy yelling at one another and her. Judging by our waitress's generally frazzled demeanor, she was not having a good time. Sid offered her his wide, devil-may-care grin, which is a doozy. I don't think anyone is immune to it. She wasn't. A hint of a smile flitted across her face in return as she tucked her notepad into her apron pocket.

Once she was in the back, Sid quietly got up and walked over to the boisterous table. I couldn't hear what Sid said to them because he was talking softly. The ruckus from the table was cut short as if someone had suddenly dialed down the volume. I looked up just in time to see Sid coming back, the same grin on his face, the same attitude. Huh.

"I don't know what you did," I said, "but I'm glad you did it. I can now hear myself think."

Sid shrugged nonchalantly at me as he slid back into his chair. "I just gave them their options, is all."

The waitress went back to the now-quiet table, and by the time she came over to us, she was beaming.

"You guys need anything," she said, staring at Sid, "anything at all, you just let me know."

Sid propped his elbows on the table and rested his chin in his hands, his expression too innocent to be believed, at least by me. The waitress totally bought it, though. She dropped her gaze, filling up our water glasses as she did. Her cheeks were rosy, and I could see the pulse in her neck flutter. Just like that, Sid had earned her worship. It's amazing what one nice gesture will do.

My phone buzzed. I ignored it. It buzzed again.

"Aren't you going to answer that?"

"It's rude to check your phone at the table." I believed that. But I was also being a filthy, filthy coward.

"Still ignoring Lock?"

I slid down in my chair. "How would you know? Are you guys best buddies now or something?" I tried to keep the jealousy out of my voice, but it didn't work.

Sid picked up his butter knife, spinning it in his fingers. "Hardly. I've nothing against your boys, but we haven't picked out our matching tattoos yet. We're at the Inferno a lot, though, and people talk."

"Can weres even get tattoos?"

"No. Our bodies reject the ink as foreign matter. I figured I'd tell Lock after he got his."

"Sneaky. I like it." I straightened back up in my chair. "Why are you at the Inferno so much?"

Sid flipped the knife and caught it in his other hand. "We've been working so well with Alistair, I think he decided that he didn't want to mess up a good thing. He's worked out some sort of deal with Les."

"You guys are Coterie now?" I couldn't imagine the drove permanently handing themselves over to anyone. The drove, the were-hare's answer to the werewolf pack, only had one boss, and that was Les.

"No, we're just doing some contract work." He smirked at

my obvious discomfort as my phone vibrated again. "Which you'd probably know if you ever looked at your texts."

Our food appeared, and I finally gave in and checked my phone, if only to get Sid to stop smirking at me. Damn smug bunny. The first was a text from Lock to see if I was on my way to Boston. The other two were from Ezra, who wanted to know if I was going to ever answer Lock or if perhaps my fingers were broken. As I was reading, Ezra sent me a selfie with the message *Because I know you're going through withdrawal. You can't go cold turkey on this kind of hotness.* I took a moment to admire Ezra Sagishi in all his glory because who wouldn't? It's not my bias toward him as a friend that makes me call him gorgeous. Where it concerns Ezra, beauty is not subjective. If my phone could speak, it would expound on Ezra's amber-gold eyes and flawless tan skin. Sonnets would be written about his cheekbones, and I'm pretty sure you could pick another body part at random and find someone who's written a dirty limerick about it. His features are a perfect meld of his Japanese and fox heritage, and if he smiles at you, you're doomed. He is, in essence, a total knockout. I sent back an emoji of a smiling pile of poo, because someone has to keep his vanity, however well deserved, in check. Hopefully that would keep him off my back for a bit. I typed and deleted three responses to Lock before I settled on *Yup.* With my strong grasp of the English language and obvious wit, it was no wonder I was doing so well in my relationships. Stars and sparks, what a mess.

Despite my focus, I still saw the waitress slip her phone number to Sid.

"Was our waitress grateful for her knight in shining leather, then?"

He took a bite of his pie before pointing the fork in my direction. "Ava, I am insulted. Do you really think me the type of man who would take advantage of such things?"

"You did keep her number."

He stabbed at his pie again, an irritated twist to his features. "Yeah, well, I'm not. But I'm not going to throw away her number in front of her, either. There is a fine line between charming rogue and jackass, and I prefer to land on the side of the former."

"Okay, well, as soon as you're done with your pie, we need to head out. Alistair will have kittens if we're late. I'm still posing as his scariest weapon, so he can't start without me. If you need to say good-bye to anyone, now is the time." I couldn't help my grin. "Just be quick. You know, like a bunny."

Sid didn't talk to me again until we reached our destination. Totally worth it.

2

THE MORE THINGS CHANGE, THE MORE I HAVE TO REPLACE CLOTHING

THE MAN WASN'T WHIMPERING, but he would be soon. He crouched on the floor, a line of bloody spit connecting him to the oh-so-white carpet Alistair hadn't replaced yet. Sid hovered over him, fists at the ready to give the guy another good thump. I stood next to Alistair as he relaxed on his chair as if it were a throne. His face impassive, like he didn't have a care in the world, a glass of whiskey dangling dangerously from his fingertips. The scene reminded me so much of Venus and Owen, her pet firebug, that I felt my stomach lurch. Standing next to Alistair didn't make me Owen. I would never be that deranged or depraved. A small voice deep inside pointed out that I was already standing by watching someone get pummeled for crossing the Coterie. What made me really sick wasn't what I was doing but that I agreed with Alistair on this one.

Matias was a mid-level thug out of Philadelphia. He was some flavor of shifter, though I couldn't remember what kind. He was part of a steady stream of idiots we'd caught trying to carve a piece of Boston for themselves. Alistair was still cementing his rule, and they saw that as a business opportunity. And while I didn't agree with a lot of the Coterie's business principles, I could see that Matias was dangerous. Selling drugs to humans was bad. Selling them to other creatures like us was dangerous beyond belief. Control and the ability to blend into humanity kept us safe. Matias endangered that safety, which meant he was endangering some people I held very dear. So I stood by and watched Sid get his hands dirty. Literally. His knuckles had split and bled and then healed, but the blood was still there, drying as I watched.

Matias spit, leaving a bright red smear on the carpet. "I can give you a cut."

Alistair held up his glass, swirling the whiskey in the light while pretending to think about what Matias was offering. Alistair wouldn't take more than a sip or two while this was going on. Like many things about him, the whiskey was a part of the image he wanted to present. He wouldn't actually drink while he was busy. Losing any kind of control didn't appeal to him. "I don't think you understand the situation, Matias. Money is not the problem. You are." The amber liquid in his glass caught the light as he brought it down and took a sip. "And I think perhaps you aren't taking this seriously."

Matias spit again, this time aiming at Sid's feet. "Your bunny can work me over all he wants. You think I'm a stranger to pain? That I can't take anything he can dish out?"

Alistair sighed, handing his glass off. To everyone in the room, it looked like the glass disappeared. In reality, he'd handed it to Bianca, who was hiding behind her veil.

"The problem is, Matias, I don't want to kill you." He rested his chin in his hands, bored and immaculate, like the lazy god of *Esquire* magazine. "Well, that's not entirely true. I don't care enough to actually kill you. It's a lot of work, you understand. Hiding bodies and all that—it's a heck of a mess, and I'm not fond of mess. Ideally, you would just slime your way back to Philly, but then that leaves me with a problem. I have to convince you to leave in a way that doesn't seem like weakness on my part and will sufficiently impress upon you what a mistake it would be to return. Unfortunately, you're so stupid that a beating won't work. Pain isn't enough. You need nightmares."

Matias laughed. "You think your bunny is capable of that?"

Sid's mouth tightening was the only sign that Matias was getting to him. Knowing how touchy the drove could get with this kind of thing, I was strangely proud of his restraint.

Alistair sat up. "Oh, most certainly, but I think you're going to need something a little flashier."

I knew a cue when I heard one, so I stepped forward. Matias was really laughing now, spit spraying from his busted lip. I was close enough that I'm sure some got on my jeans. This is why I wear dark clothing to Coterie soirees. Matias relaxed, thinking Alistair was playing a joke.

Now it was my turn to get my hands dirty. I started slow, sparks flowing from my fingers like a cascade of fireworks. By the time I stood over him, my arms were bathed in flames and his laughter had dried up. Orange flames turned to blue as I kicked the temperature up. Matias lurched backward a foot before he caught himself, the effect of his sneer ruined by the sheen of panic sweat on his brow.

I crouched down so we were on the same level. "Forgive me, but I spaced out during the interrogation, and I can't remember what you are. So before I get started, there's something I need to know."

A fine tremor shook his body as he croaked out, "What?"

Our noses almost touched as I leaned in. "Exactly how much damage can you heal?"

THE EVENING ended as many of our Coterie get-togethers ended, with me throwing up in a Coterie bathroom. The door creaked open, and I turned my head to see a glass of water and a washcloth. Alistair handed me the glass and draped the damp washcloth over the back of my neck, the cold instantly making me feel a little bit better.

"He'll heal," he said.

The water soothed my scratchy throat as I drained half the glass. "I know."

He made an exasperated sound that I knew meant *Then why all the fuss?*

I grabbed the washcloth and held it against my flushed face. "I'm not into torture."

Alistair leaned against the door of the private bathroom, his arms crossed. "You met him. He's an idiot. It was this or death."

"Then why not kill him?" I asked. Venus would have slit his throat and then complained about the stains it left on her beautiful carpet.

Alistair dropped his arms, his gaze softening. "Before I answer you, let me ask this—did you ever get sick after meetings with Venus?"

"Sometimes."

"But not every time?" He asked the question but already seemed sure of the answer.

I shook my head.

He crouched down, easing himself to the floor, his face close to mine. "I think I know why. Because of the position I've put you in, you feel more responsible. With the structure Venus had, you didn't feel as guilty. With her you didn't feel like you had a choice. I've changed the dynamic. Let me guess—you're starting to feel like you're turning into Owen, and that both frightens and disgusts you, doesn't it?"

I didn't answer. I didn't have to—he could see it on my face.

Alistair sighed. "Ava, you're not Owen, and I know you won't believe me, but I'll say it anyway. I'm not Venus." He rested his arms loosely on his knees. "I know exactly how she would have handled today—she would have slaughtered Matias in front of a select audience, who would have told everyone, thus reinforcing that she was not to be messed with." Alistair always looked in control, cold and calculating, but as I watched he let that facade drop, and I realized how young my new boss was. I'd have been surprised if he was much past thirty. He rubbed the heel of his hand across his forehead, a weary and habitual-looking gesture. "Believe it or not, I'd rather not kill people if I don't have to. I'm sorry you had to burn Matias."

"I can still smell singed hair." My throat tightened. "I know he's not screaming anymore, but I can still hear him."

For a second, I thought Alistair might reach out to comfort me, but he never moved. "Terrible, I know. But I can't let some street thug come into my city and push his poisons. He would have no problem peddling drugs to Coterie kids. And if I can't protect my people from threats like him, what's the point?" Sounds of rushing water moved through the plumbing, breaking the quiet as we sat there. "He will heal his burns eventually.

Then he will go home and tell everyone not to come here. He will wake up screaming for the rest of his life."

"So will I," I said, turning my head slightly so we looked each other in the eye.

"That's the price we pay to keep our people safe." He looked at me, not with pity but with understanding, which somehow made me feel worse.

"I know," I said, closing my eyes.

"You agree with me," he said, his voice hushed. "And that's why you're getting sick."

Again, I didn't have to answer. Alistair's clothes rustled as he stood up. "Rest until you're ready to come out." I heard him pause as he reached the door. "The difference, Ava, is that Venus hurt people because she wanted to. She might have dressed it up in different ways, but that's what it boils down to. We're not doing that. We have to be ruthless, yes, but it's to protect the people who belong to us. As long as we're doing that, we're not going to be like them."

The faint scent of bleach wafted up from the toilet, and my stomach clenched. "And if we lose sight of that lofty goal? Lots of evil in this world happens because of some greater good, Alistair."

"Then we'd better not let that happen, Ava." I heard the door rattle as he rested his hand on the knob. "Besides, I've already thought of that. If we start to act like our predecessors, Bianca has orders to murder us in our beds."

I couldn't help but laugh at that. "And you're sure that plan will work?"

"I trust Bianca implicitly—with my life and with my death."

With that cheery thought, Alistair left me to gather myself in the empty bathroom.

Once I'd calmed down, I scrutinized my reflection in the mirror behind the sink. Not so much to check my hair or anything like that. No, I needed to make sure I'd removed all evidence of Matias. Dried blood freckled my face. I used the washcloth to scrub it off. Just as I'd thought, you couldn't see any blood on my clothes, but I still had a faint whiff of burning human flesh about me. There wasn't much I could do about that. Sure, I could take a shower, but I'd have to put my clothes back on. I settled for washing my hands up to the elbows in citrus-smelling soap and then headed out in search of Sid.

Normally I would have grabbed something to eat before I left, but I didn't want to run into Lock or Ezra. They weren't working restaurant shifts anymore—now they got their pay exclusively for Coterie work—but that didn't mean they weren't around.

And because I have the worst luck ever, there they were, at a table with Sid and Bianca. Lock was seated next to Bianca, their chairs close and their shoulders touching. It was like they'd been friends forever. I felt a firm jab of jealousy before I crushed it. This was my fault, and I was just going to have to learn to take my lumps with a smile. Ezra and Sid were on the other side of the table, each one doing what he could to annoy the other. A stylish black cane rested against a fifth chair that sat empty at the end of the table. Ezra had stepped into a silver bear trap and was still healing from the ordeal. The trap had torn into skin and muscle and left him on crutches for weeks. Because of the high silver content, Ezra had healed slowly. Not quite as slowly as I would have if I'd stepped into a bear trap, but definitely not at his usual clip. Mostly he managed with a slight limp now, keeping the cane around for when he got tired. In a few more days, the limp would probably be gone.

I took my seat at the head of the table, wishing I could disappear into the wood of my chair. Ezra nudged a plate in front of me—my favorite burger, served with roasted veggies instead of fries. The vegetables were Lock's idea: I'd put money on it. Convinced that Ezra and I didn't eat well enough, he did his best to make us healthy.

The burger was still warm, which meant the boys ordered it knowing I'd be in the bathroom for a while. I don't know why, but that thought more than anything else tonight made me want to break down sobbing. As I ate, I waited for Lock and Ez to start in on me for avoiding them. No one said a word. They all chatted and let me wrap myself up in their aimless conversation and laughter and didn't give me any shit. It didn't feel like shunning or an angry silence. What it did feel like was understanding and support, which made me more ashamed of my behavior than a shunning would have. I could be angry at a shunning, but I couldn't be mad at this, which took away the only defense I had. I didn't know what else to do, so I ate quietly. Once I was done, Sid excused himself from the table and pulled on his jacket so he could take me home. Only then did Ezra pull me into his arms. He stuck his nose behind my ear, loudly breathing me in, and I couldn't help but smile. His nose was cold. Like a dog's. Bianca nodded at me, knowing that all I expected of her at the best of times was a lack of animosity. Lock fiddled with his cloth napkin, only looking up at me at the last second. Everything we'd been leaving unsaid was in his face. I looked away first. I don't think I've ever left their company so fast. If I'd been a cartoon, there would have been a little cloud of smoke where I'd been standing.

When I was zipping up Ikka's jacket, I felt something sticking out of the pocket. I pulled out a scrap of paper, rolled up and clutched tightly in a vine, a tiny purple flower blooming near the end. My fingers trembled as I unrolled it. *We miss you, little dumpling.* Though unsigned, I knew the note was from Ezra. The flower, from Lock.

Sid wordlessly handed me Ikka's helmet, and I shoved the flower and note back into the jacket pocket. When I was properly suited up, I climbed onto the bike. I spent the first part of the ride crying, and Sid spent it pretending not to notice.

3

FIREBUGS AREN'T GOOD
AT PLAYING IT COOL

MANAGED TWO GLORIOUS days to myself before I got another assignment from Alistair. I hung out with Sylvie and Cade, putting the bookstore together and pretending to be a normal person. We were going to reopen in a few days, a week ahead of schedule, because dwarves freaking rock.

Early on the morning of the third day, my phone beeped, indicating that I had an e-mail. I wanted to ignore it. I just wanted to keep basking in the bookstore's normality. But ignoring it wouldn't make it go away, so I left Sylvie to finish cleaning the windows by herself as I opened the case file Alistair had sent. The more I read, the more my stomach began to feel like a leaden pit. Sid was on his way to pick me up, and we were headed to Portland. Alistair wasn't going to wait for this problem to come to him.

Elias Johnson, rogue werewolf, and Luke Baker, siren, had been making noise in our territory. In mythology, sirens were female. Though female sirens outnumber males five to one, males do exist. They just aren't as popular, mythology-wise. My theory is that most sailors didn't want to admit that they'd crashed their ship into a bunch of jagged rocks because pretty men had tempted them with their song. The reality is, it doesn't matter if the siren is male or female—if they sing and you listen, you're toast.

Elias and Luke were hiding out in an old warehouse down by the water that was so derelict, it should have had a sign out front that said CREEPY BAD GUYS LIVE HERE. Surely there must be a cheerful-looking warehouse somewhere on this planet, but I have yet to see one. It's like they propagate a universally seedy atmosphere.

We didn't bother to sneak in—we weren't there for that kind of show. My role was to be a bogeyman, which meant I had to go in big, loud, and scary. So I had Sid kick the door down while I walked in bathed in flames, my feet leaving smoking footprints behind me. It turned out even better than I thought and undoubtedly would have been very impressive to all of those involved if they hadn't been really, truly dead.

And from the smell of it, they'd been dead for at least twenty-four hours. We'd had a few abnormally warm days, and the warehouse's only air-conditioning was a handful of small open windows set up high. The whole place smelled like salt, seaweed, and rot, with a baseline of offal. I gagged, dropped my flame, and yanked my shirt up to cover my mouth. I'd left Ikka's leather jacket on the bike, Sid being uncomfortable with the idea of me setting it on fire.

Sid must have been having a worse time of it because of his heightened sense of smell, but he wasn't showing it. He sauntered over with a whistle and examined the bodies. There were more than we thought there would be. From where I was standing, it looked like there were two males and three females. We knew the exact number based on the heads lying on the floor. The men were reasonably intact, though not in the best shape.

"Those our boys?" I asked through my shirt.

Sid examined the bodies, pulling wallets off the two men. The women didn't appear to be wearing much, though I think they'd arrived that way. Maybe they'd come from a club, but I doubted it. My gut said these were escorts, which I didn't know much about, but even prostitutes carry purses, right? I reluctantly walked over and started searching for them so I could at least *look* useful.

"These are definitely our boys," Sid said. "At least, the photos on their IDs match. Well, would match if their faces weren't so . . . puffy." Elias, the werewolf, had been able to heal some of what had happened to him, but he was still covered in blood and worse. Luke was almost . . . pulpy . . . in parts. And the women? They were a puzzle best left for a medical examiner—a puzzle with some pieces missing.

Sid stood up, wiping his hand on his jeans before pulling out his phone. "Alistair? Yeah. The job was easier than expected. In fact, you might want to get up here." He nudged one of the corpses over with his boot. It was putrefying already, and I couldn't help notice the brown goo all over it. Something was helping the corpse along its road to Breakdown City. "And you should probably be quick about it."

WE WAITED outside for Alistair. The drive from Boston to Portland takes two hours without traffic, and there was no way I was spending that time hanging out inside the warehouse.

There's not a lot to do while you wait next to an abandoned building. I tried counting all the lobster buoys in the water, but Sid kept shouting out random numbers and messing me up. I really wish I'd brought a book with me.

When Alistair arrived, I expected him to storm in all red-faced and blustery, yelling about us dragging him up here, but he didn't. I kept waiting for Alistair to act like Venus, but he hadn't yet. That didn't mean he wouldn't, but strangely his nice demeanor was putting me on edge. Where were the tantrums? The crazy demands? He was ruining my mental picture of how a Coterie despot should act.

Alistair looked cool and unruffled, as usual. His brown hair was neatly styled, his sunglasses pushed up in such a way that they were more of a fashion accessory than something he actually used. And he was wearing an honest-to-goodness polo shirt. With *slacks*. I couldn't tell if Alistair was ruining the Coterie's image or classin' it up a bit.

Bianca drifted in behind him as usual. Everything about her was a study in pale—blond hair that barely qualified as blond it was so light, pale skin, and the lightest gray eyes I've ever seen. I wasn't sure if she darkened her eyebrows or if they were naturally darker. We weren't friendly enough for me to ask. Most days, we were lucky if we didn't try to throttle each other.

To make up for all the pale, Bianca usually wore all black. Today was no exception—black boots, black jeans, black hooded sleeveless T-shirt, eyes thickly ringed with black eyeliner so that the ghostly gray of her irises jumped out at you. I considered buying her a Hawaiian shirt for her birthday. She would love that.

Alistair and Bianca both examined the bodies, as well as the rest of the warehouse. They didn't look too pleased that the situation had taken care of itself.

"I thought you'd be a little happy. Why aren't we doing cartwheels of joy?" I asked after Alistair had glared at the bodies for a few minutes.

"Because before, it was a tidy package. Come in, show them who's boss, leave. Now it's a mess," he said, scowling. "I dislike messes."

Bianca used a pen to lift the shirt off one of the bodies to peer at the torso. It made a wet sound as it unstuck. She didn't so much as pause. "Before, we knew the enemy. Now we have to wonder if these deaths are unrelated to us or a play for territory or if it's another unknown group eliminating competition and sending Alistair a message."

"You make it sound like we've been dealing with a lot of this," I said. "We've had a fairly light summer, though."

She let the shirt drop and moved on. "No," said Bianca, drawing the word out as she examined what I think was a finger. "*You've* had a fairly light summer."

I looked at Alistair for confirmation. He continued to scowl down at the bodies. "We've been dealing with a lot of people who saw the change in Coterie leadership as an opportunity to make their own play. I figured I'd get proactive with this one."

I knew I wasn't getting called in for every little thing, but I hadn't realized they'd been cutting me out to such an extent. How much had everyone been working as I whiled away my days in the bookstore?

"Instead," Alistair continued, "I get this muddle. Extra work and a waste of life. Not to mention that no one here will be getting a proper funeral." Alistair looked at the corpses of the three women with some pity. "I'm afraid their families will never know what happened to them."

Bianca eyed one of the tables, which was covered in a dusting of fine white powder. "Something tells me that the families are expecting that kind of fate."

"Doesn't make it any less sad," he said.

"And why aren't the families going to hear?" I asked.

Alistair held out his arms, shook his fingers like he was limbering up, then spread them wide and concentrated. "Because," he said, "after we get everything we can from them, you're going to honor them with a Viking funeral. In the meantime, though, we need to preserve the scene." Frost crept across the ground, covering the bodies; the temperature in the warehouse dropped several degrees and kept going. Sid found a long pole to close the windows, and then Alistair left us all, including Bianca, to guard the warehouse. I couldn't tell who was less thrilled, me or her.

"Where are you going?" she asked, indignant, as he walked toward the door.

"To find us a necromancer," he answered without turning around. "We need to ask these corpses some questions."

No one wanted to hang out in the warehouse. One, it was so cold, you could see your breath, and two, it smelled like human Popsicles in there. So we took turns walking around the perimeter or sitting by the door. Sid had to prop it back up, since he'd kicked it in so dramatically.

We ordered pizza, and if the delivery driver thought it was

weird to deliver six pies to three people sitting outside a run-down, semi-abandoned warehouse, he didn't mention it. After two hours of sitting around, Sid decided to try to take a nap while Bianca and I took turns keeping watch. I'll say this about the caulbearer, she doesn't slack on the job. If I was sitting, she was walking, and if she sat down, she glared at me until I got up.

At the next walk/glare rotation, I finally said something. "I get it. You don't like me. You don't have to pretend you're all business. Just say you want me out of your face." I dusted off the back of my jeans as I stood up.

Bianca gave a sharp exhale of disgust. Her face looked like she smelled something foul. "Believe it or not, Ava, not everything is about you." She leaned against the warehouse, hands in her pockets. "Alistair left us here as guards. When he shows up, we are going to hand over this warehouse in *exactly* the same shape as when he left it. Because that's what he wants and that's all that matters. Just because you don't take your job seriously doesn't mean the rest of us don't."

Ah. I was the disgusting thing she smelled, then. I felt my cheeks burn and I knew if I glanced down, sparks would be slam dancing all around my fingers. "You think I don't take what I do *seriously*?"

She gave a half shrug. "You whine. You bitch and moan and do the woe-is-me thing, and it's boring. You're a firebug. So what? Get over it and do your damn job. Nobody is interested in holding your hands as soon as you're done wringing them." She looked away, like I was dismissed.

Oh, that was *it*. I flicked my hands wide open, enthusiastic flames licking my fingers. Bianca pushed away from the wall, fists at her sides, ready to go.

Before we could get any further, someone grabbed my wrists.

"That's about enough of that, children." Sid's warm breath brushed my ear.

Bianca and I both opened our mouths to argue, but Sid shushed us. When we both opened our mouths again to complain about the shushing, he laughed. I don't know what he found so funny.

"While you two are hissing and spitting, someone could be breaking into this nice warehouse we're guarding. Tell you what—I'll take a little stroll around the premises. In the meantime, Ava, you go inside and make sure everything is as it should be. Bianca, guard the door."

Before I could even get the words out, Sid answered, "You pulled inside duty because you were about to throw fire at our ally here. She's not the enemy. I don't care how much you guys want to bicker, but your control should be better than that. You don't get to spark in public just because you're pissy." He dropped my wrists and disappeared around the building.

My cheeks still burned as I stomped to the door. I wanted to argue and pout, but damn it all, Sid was right. My control should be better. I wasn't a new bug anymore. Bianca opened the door, smirking, and I stopped so hard my boot heel almost squeaked. As nice as it would be, I couldn't act like a child, which meant doing things I didn't want to do. I took a deep breath.

"Sorry," I said, not looking at Bianca. "Sid is right. I was being a brat." Before she could do more than blink at me, I walked past her into the makeshift freezer.

41

If Alistair ever got bored of being a crime boss, he had plenty of career options open to him. The warehouse was still cold enough that I could see my breath as I moved. My boots left patterns in the frost as I walked around the edges of the room. Except in the spots where the frost wouldn't go. A film of sticky goo coated that part of the floor. Now that I had noticed it, it was easier to see. I followed the goo up the wall to one of the windows. Then down by where I was standing, which was currently behind a pile of rotting crates. Something had waited here and left an oozing puddle. I edged around it, not wanting to step in the mess. Nothing good oozes—slugs, businessmen, infected sores. Things like flowers, kittens, and adorable ponies hardly ooze at *all*. In the natural world, the more dangerous or disgusting something is, the higher its goo factor. Believe it or not, monsters like myself are part of the natural world—the same law applies to us. Which meant that whatever left this mark probably wasn't friendly, and the likelihood that it would, at one point, try to digest me was pretty high.

I took out my phone and snapped some photos for later just in case. We might need them to identify the creature, or to figure out what happened here. On a whim, I sent the photos to Cade to see if he could identify the slime trail. I took some plastic sandwich bags out of my pocket and carefully took a sample without touching the goo. My phone vibrated with an immediate reply from Cade, saying he would hit the books to see if he could find anything like the goo, but suggested I send the photos to Alistair as well, since the Coterie had better resources than he did. A few texts from Lock had come in without my noticing. Nothing special. Just *Bianca said you were on a job—why didn't Alistair call me?* Followed by *Why didn't you call me?* I wondered if he'd noticed that it was the first time he'd texted me since yesterday morning. Next was a text from Ezra: *Text Lock back before he implodes.*

I ignored them both.

I STOPPED counting Alistair's absence in hours and started going by deliveries. By the time he came back, we'd had Thai, tacos, and sub sandwiches. I was taking advantage of being in a city (Currant had only one stoplight—we did not, at this time, warrant a Thai restaurant), and Bianca was stuck somewhere between awe and disgust at Sid's and my appetites.

Alistair wasn't alone when he returned. His passenger climbed out of the car, pulling a pack of cigarettes from her thin jacket. Without a word, she fished a lighter out of her green cargo pants and lit up. She glanced around, and I could see her eyes assessing us. I bet she didn't miss a thing, either. Her brown hair was pulled back from her face, and her body was lean, like she was prepared to fight or run, depending on the situation. Her heeled boots added an inch or two to her already impressive height, and her white tank top set off the deep gold of her skin. I wouldn't call her pretty—something about the way she held herself negated that. Striking, maybe. Or terrifying. Yeah, that was closer to the truth. I could see her being worshipped as an Egyptian goddess, and not a friendly one. She was the kind that you left a sacrifice for and hoped she didn't notice you too much.

The woman looked down at the empty food trash and waved her cigarette hand, leaving a trail of smoke. "At least one of them is a were—probably two."

Alistair leaned against his car. Whenever he did that, he

43

looked like a TV ad for an upscale cologne. "You haven't even touched them yet." He sounded defeated.

She nodded toward the garbage. "You called me as soon as you locked down the scene. That's a lot of food for three people." The cherry end of her cigarette flared as she took a drag, her eyes still moving. "You." She pointed at Sid. "What do you turn into?"

"Not telling," Sid said, his voice flat.

She grinned, clearly enjoying the game. "I can see three knives from where I'm standing. Only a few weres that I know of bother with weapons. Too scruffy for a mongoose. Not prissy enough to be a swan. Cocky." Her grin widened and took on a decidedly wolfish quality. "Hare."

Sid slumped. The woman moved on to Bianca but continued almost as soon as she took her in. "Obviously your pet caul-bearer." Bianca stiffened, but the woman either didn't notice or didn't care. "That just leaves you," she said to me. She got close to my face, her brown eyes inches from mine. "Not a were, though you obviously eat like one."

"Hey!" Just because she was right didn't mean I couldn't get huffy about it. "How do you know that food wasn't Bianca's?"

"Mustard on your shirt here, sriracha on your pants there, and you smell like pepperoni." She jabbed at the offending spots with her cigarette but was careful not to touch me.

"How do you know that's sriracha?" Sid asked.

"Sriracha and I have met. Repeatedly." She pointed to a faded stain on her cargo pants before she took another quick drag of her cigarette. "You're not a careful eater, and you have a high metabolism, but you're not a were." At my surprise she said, "You're not twitchy. Weres have a hard time sitting still when

44

being approached by a stranger. They growl, they pace, they posture," she said, ashing her cigarette in Sid's direction, "but they don't just stand there."

The air was still as we continued to stare at each other. She stepped back, circled me, made me lift my feet to show her the soles of my boots, but never laid so much as a fingertip on my person. Finally she was back around to my front. With great ceremony she dropped her cigarette and ground it out with her boot. She pulled a fresh one from the pack and held it up. "How about you light this one for me?"

Alistair sighed and I knew that, whatever game we'd been playing, he'd lost. "You didn't touch her—I watched. How did you know?"

She winked at me and put her new cigarette away. "She eats like a were but isn't one. All her buttons are metal. There are scorch marks on the bottoms of her boots from stomping out flames. I can see embroidery peeking out from the inside of her jacket cuffs—my guess is runes, mostly the ones to do with fire and protection. And every time I took a drag, her eyes followed the ember."

Had they? I didn't notice I was doing that. Sloppy. She held out her hand, and I hesitated to take it. I'd heard things about touching necromancers, all of them warnings against it. But then I saw a flicker of disappointment in her eyes and said the hell with it. I shook her hand.

"Nice to meet you, firebug."

"Likewise, necromancer." Her grip was firm and warm, and I didn't vomit bees or turn into dust or anything. It was just a handshake, and a good one. With a start, I realized that I liked her. Weren't necromancers supposed to exude evil and walk around covered in human blood? She was wearing a necklace with a little Eeyore charm on it, for heaven's sake. "Are we going to keep this all supersecret superhero codenames? Do I have to start calling Bianca 'the Veil' or something?"

The woman laughed.

"We could do that, sure, or you could just call me June." She looked at Alistair. "Now how about we get to the dead things?"

4

BRING OUT YOUR DEAD

JUNE WALKED STRAIGHT over to the scene, suddenly all business. She gave the corpses a thoughtful frown before digging some chalk out of her pocket. "All right, little miss, come on out. I'd like you here before I start making circles."

Nothing happened. Was there a ghost around that I couldn't see? Were the bodies supposed to get up and sing us a Greek chorus? June obviously expected something to happen, but the warehouse was quiet and the only thing moving was our breath steaming in and out. She tapped her foot. I didn't think June sat still very well, either. "I don't have all day," she said to the air.

There was a rustling noise and the soft scuff of shoes as a little girl came out from behind the box pile. She didn't look like much—shorts, a faded Batman tank top, and flip-flops, her inky hair held back in two ponytails. Little pink heart-shaped sunglasses covered her eyes. That didn't stop us all from going into defensive mode. Sid dropped into a crouch, knives appearing almost magically in his hands. A large fireball flared to life in front of me, and Bianca disappeared. Only June and Alistair didn't react.

The little girl propped her sunglasses on top of her head, both eyebrows going up with them. "Whoa there, cowpokes. A little high-strung, are we? Chill your knickers. I've been invited."

None of us twitched until June confirmed what the little girl, introduced as Ashley, said.

"What did you think I was going to do?" Ashley asked, clearly amused.

I shrugged. "I don't know. But we're stuck in a warehouse with several dead bodies and you appeared out of nowhere. Not everything looks dangerous at first. You could have been wearing glamour. Better to be prepared and alive than assume you're not a threat and get added to the human Popsicle pile."

Ashley turned to June. "I like her. Can we keep her?" She clasped her hands like she was praying. "Maybe we can send her up to Seattle to keep Dipshit McGee out of trouble?"

"No one can keep that boy out of trouble," June said absently as she drew a circle around us in chalk. She closed herself inside with us. Only Ashley was left out. "No one break this line until I say, no matter what you see or hear. Got it?"

June pulled out a small knife and sliced into her forearm. Blood welled, dripped, and hit the ground. It felt like the temperature dropped down even lower. Each breath burned like frost coating my lungs.

She started with the women. They pieced themselves together—arms reattaching, holes filling, bones knitting together with sickening pops. It became less pleasant from there. Once they were whole, June started questioning them one at a time. The first just started . . . screaming. The shrill sound felt like a physical assault. It raked at my eardrums and my heart. June did her best to calm her, but in the end she had Ashley give her a little tap, and the woman collapsed and went still. The second girl didn't scream, but her eerie silence was almost worse. The only sound she made was this pathetic bleating noise when she sobbed. Other than that she just rocked herself and stared off into space.

Ashley put her back down the same way. I'm no expert, but I think their traumatic deaths had torn holes in their sanity. Even their dead selves couldn't cope. Which, by the way, was absolutely *spectacular* news for us. Because I'd have to go out and hunt down whatever this thing was.

"So far all I can tell you is that they were human. Literally torn apart—probably by the were." June's wound had stopped bleeding. She flexed her arm, starting the flow again.

"Are you sure?"

"From the way they went back together and the general scene, I'm pretty sure. This was not a nice death, Alistair, and not a quick one."

"Is that why they're acting like something out of a Japanese horror film?" Sid asked.

June nodded. "Between what happened and the drugs, I think that's a fair assessment."

The third girl wasn't much different from the other two.

"Do you think the guys will be more of the same?" Alistair asked.

June pursed her lips in thought, her arm dripping blood onto the floor again. I wonder if she even noticed. "Probably," she said, finally. "But I can't be sure. Do you want me to do them both at once?"

"If you think it's safe."

"Alistair, I'm raising the dead. It's never safe," she said. "That's why we have the circle. But I think I can handle it." June flicked her hand, making a thin line of blood drops hit the floor. The room temperature dropped again and I shivered.

The boys snapped to life, and I can honestly say it was nothing like the girls. Elias reached over and grasped Luke by the arms, hurling him into the warehouse wall. Before Luke even hit the floor, Elias was running toward us at full speed, only stopping when he smacked into June's circle. He flew backward, skidding along the warehouse floor. Before I could blink, he'd rolled up onto his feet and was back, stopping just short of the circle. His face twisted in a snarl of rage, spittle flying from his lips. He clawed at the circle. When that didn't work, he began throwing himself at it, over and over, testing different spots for any possible weakness.

We were all so focused on him, no one noticed when Luke got to his feet. I didn't spot him until he'd halved the distance between the wall and our protective bubble. He didn't thrash against it like Elias. Instead, he opened his mouth and everything went white. Blinding. I couldn't see anything or hear anything. The pain was excruciating. Every nerve ending hummed with electricity, shocking me down to my core.

Then it cleared and it felt like I was floating. The world was a dream and Luke was its center. All I wanted was to be near him. If I didn't go to him right now, I would wither and die. He was my water, my air—

I'm not sure who broke the circle. One minute, my head was stuffed with fluffy clouds and angel song; the next I was staring at Luke's collapsed body on the floor. Ashley stood over him, her hand out. She'd tapped the siren back into the realm of the dead, and that's why my head had cleared. Stars and sparks, he could have killed us all.

That's when Sid screamed.

I turned in time to see Bianca grab Alistair and throw a veil over him. They popped out of existence. She must have spread it out over the rest of us, too, because I could only see Sid and Elias grappling on the floor. Sid was an experienced fighter, but it doesn't matter how many blades you have and how fast you are when the person you're fighting is already dead. Elias was tearing into Sid with clawed hands until gashes bled from his chest, his leg, and his face. Sid stopped screaming when Elias cracked a rib and punctured his lung.

Ashley left the safety of the veil and tried to jump in, but Elias dodged her advance, grabbed the back of her shirt, and tossed her across the warehouse. I couldn't get a clear shot from where I was standing, and I didn't want to throw fireballs and hit Sid. Besides, flesh wounds meant nothing to Elias. Nothing short of debilitating was going to work on him. So I did the only thing I could and hurled myself onto Elias's back. Even with my arms around his neck, he didn't register me as a threat. He continued to wail on Sid, who was still doing his best to defend himself, but each block was a little slower. He was losing a lot of blood, and his breath was wet and labored.

I'm not the biggest or the strongest person around. I don't carry weapons. But there's a reason I don't have a knife or spend a lot of time on my right hook. I don't need a weapon because I *am* a weapon. I held Elias tight and let myself burn. No fireballs, no concentrated bursts. Just flames from the crown of my head to the tips of my boots.

I could live a thousand years and never get used to the smell. It was all I could do to not gag. I tightened my grip. I could fall apart later, but there was no time for indulging in weakness. Elias's skin and hair started to blister with the heat before I moved to fat, and soon muscle.

He was so far gone that he didn't notice right away. My nostrils filled with the stench of hot, rancid fat, and I squeezed tighter. Elias spun around and tried to grab me, but I hung on like a barnacle. I wouldn't last two seconds if he managed to dislodge me. I was getting dizzy from the spinning before Elias figured out that what he was doing wasn't working. He skidded to a stop and grabbed onto my arms, his claws digging into my flesh. I felt a warm wash of blood as he tightened his grip and I screamed, but I kept burning.

It's not the easiest thing to burn a body quickly. The average human body is 75 percent water. And I had to go deep with Elias. He wasn't feeling pain, so a light burn wasn't going to affect him. I needed to burn him to ash and bone, and that takes a lot of heat, somewhere between 1,100 degrees and 2,000. I've never stuck a turkey thermometer in someone, so I don't know exactly. But I'd looked it up online—I wanted to understand exactly what I was capable of doing to a person.

It's not the cleanest process. The soft tissue vaporizes. Skin becomes waxy, blisters, and splits. Muscles and tendons tighten around bone as they char. It's not something even I'm usually up close and personal with. I sent fire into Elias's entire body, but I focused on the brain in the hopes that every zombie movie ever was right: destroy the brain, destroy the zombie. Eventually he dropped to his knees. He swayed there for a minute, his grip on my arms loosening. Then he fell forward in a puff of ash.

Despite what you think you know about cremation, people don't actually turn into powder. Vampires, well, that's a whole different situation, but the human skeleton doesn't burn very well. Crematoriums have a separate machine they use to grind down the bones. So while some ash puffed up into my nose, eyes, and mouth, there was just as much leftover charred flesh and bone beneath me to cushion my fall when Elias finally disintegrated beneath me.

I stayed on the floor for a moment and tried to breathe, thinking about the amazing shower and the gallons of mouthwash in my future. For future reference, charred werewolf ash tastes *awful*. Like singed hair and oily fat. I gagged.

June had to pull me up, my arms still death-locked around what was left of Elias's neck. She dragged me over next to Sid. He was at least breathing normally again. He'd twisted into a partial push-up and was spitting up blood to clear his lungs. We made a neat pair.

"Try not to get blood on me, okay?" I asked.

He reached over, his chest dragging into the ash, and smeared blood down the front of my shirt with one hand.

"You did that on purpose," I said.

He nodded, then spit one more mouthful of blood onto the floor.

"Well, you're now covered in Elias, so we're even."

"This is why we're friends," he said, then collapsed onto his back. He held out his fist so we could bump knuckles. "Thanks."

I reached over and tousled his hair, making sure to really smear the oily black ash deep into the roots. It would be a bitch to get out. "You're welcome, hoss."

Sid laughed, though I could tell it was painful for him.

We were all sitting in a rough oval, a smoldering werewolf in the middle, and not the sexy kind of smolder, either. Bianca had dropped her veil and everyone had reappeared. Ashley bandaged a dazed-looking June's arm while Alistair pressed a folded handkerchief to a gash on her forehead. Bianca sat close by, a stunned look on her face. I'd have to clean my own wounds. Lock usually did that for me. I felt a pang of loss for my friend.

"So that was fun," Sid said, using the edge of his shredded shirt to wipe the blood off his face. Some of the smaller gashes were already closing.

"What on earth happened?" I asked. "Was he rabid or something? Can werewolves get rabies?"

"Not that I'm aware of, no." Alistair had a grim look on his face.

June took a cigarette out of the pack in her pocket, but her hands were shaking too hard to light it. I sparked it for her and she mumbled a thank-you.

"I've never seen anything like that," she said.

Alistair lifted an edge of the handkerchief to check June's wound. "Bianca, can you fetch the first-aid kit from the car? This could use a few butterfly bandages. And grab the camera. I want better definition than our phones can offer." Bianca snapped out of her reverie and jogged out of the warehouse. The look Alistair gave June was stern. "I shouldn't have asked you to raise two at once. I didn't think it would be that risky." His words took the blame, but his tone implied that she should have known, too.

Ashley knotted the end of the makeshift bandage. "It shouldn't have been that dangerous. June always has control. That guy . . . It shouldn't have happened." She poked Alistair in the chest. "So don't grouch at her. You may be the boss up here, but you're not the boss of us." Venus would have cut her finger off for that. But Alistair merely raised one hand in surrender.

"My apologies, mighty Harbinger. I didn't mean any harm."

Ashley scowled but stopped poking him.

"I should have had control," June said, watching the smoke drifting up. "It was like his mind was . . . gone. Just gone."

Bianca returned, first-aid kit and camera bag in tow. She handed the kit off to Alistair, then proceeded to take pictures of everything in the warehouse. The camera was large and professional and looked comically huge in Bianca's small hands, but she clearly knew what she was doing.

"Has that happened before?" Sid asked, grabbing some alcohol wipes, ointment, and gauze from the kit. "The mindless revenant thing?"

June shook her head. "When I raise people, even weres, they usually come back as themselves. It doesn't matter if they've rotted down to bones, flesh re-forms—they look whole. If a piece was removed before they died and wasn't buried with them, that's a different thing. A severed head won't regrow the body. It has to be, you know, together."

"So whatever happened to him," I said slowly, thinking it through, "happened before he died. Whatever it was ate his brain so that there wasn't enough for him to fully regenerate when you raised him. Is that what we're saying?"

June mashed her cigarette into the warehouse floor, earning another reproving glare from Alistair, who was trying to apply the butterfly bandages to her head wound.

"Stop moving," he snapped.

She ignored him. "Yes, Ava, I think that's exactly what we're saying."

"You forgot something," Sid said, tearing open an alcohol wipe from the kit so he could clean some more blood off himself. "What do weres do best?"

I looked at the skin he was wiping clean. "They heal."

"Exactly." Sid winced as the alcohol hit an open wound. "So not only did it eat his brain, it did so in such a way that either his body didn't have time to regrow the damage, or it couldn't." He motioned at me to hold my arms out so he could dress the small punctures in them. They weren't bleeding much anymore, but with what was in the warehouse, cleaning them was a good idea. It hurt like hell, but it was a good idea.

"What could do that?" Ashley asked.

Sid threw the wipe on the floor, his grim look highlighted by the occasional flash of Bianca's camera. "I don't know. Silver, maybe. But in his brain? I wouldn't even know how that could happen." He carefully smoothed on ointment and opened the new roll of gauze.

"Secret experiment?" I offered. "You know, like Wolverine and the adamantium. Maybe we should bring back just his head and get someone to run tests on it."

"No," Alistair said firmly. "We don't know what happened, but it happened to the siren as well. We can't take the risk that it might be a contaminant or a virus. Something passed by contact. I won't jeopardize our people. Remember what I said, Ava. After Bianca is done with the photos, you're going to have to burn the whole place down."

I started to protest about the loss of evidence, but he cut me off. "I said no. We burn it all. After what I've seen, I don't want even the lowliest protozoa crawling out of this building alive when you're done."

"Kill it with fire?" I asked, already feeling weary from Elias.

"Exactly. Kill it with fire, then we head to the Inferno. Everyone showers. Thoroughly."

Sid snorted. "You don't have to tell me twice."

"I'll get someone to bring us new clothes. Everything—and I do mean everything—on your person will be bagged and burned. Whatever this thing is, I'm not bringing it into my home."

Sid and I both grabbed our respective jackets.

"Yes, even your jackets. Ava, I know yours is warded. I'll get it replaced. Ashley, what about you?"

"My clothes are technically a projection. I'm corporeal—I can affect things on this plane—but I'm not *here* in the same way that you are. I could snap my fingers and change my outfit if I wanted."

Alistair made me leave my carefully collected bag of mystery ooze in the warehouse. He wasn't taking any chances. Once everyone was a safe distance away, I was asked to do my thing. I felt a twinge of sadness for everyone inside, that no one would really know what happened to them. But Alistair was right. So I burned everything down to ash and bone.

I was shaky by the time I finished. Between Elias and the warehouse, I'd been burning not only hot but also for a sustained amount of time. Sid fetched me a bottle of water from the trunk of Alistair's car, and I swallowed a few electrolyte pills. Hopefully they would hold me over until I could rest or get something to eat.

"All right, then. Everyone is headed back to the Inferno," Alistair said when I was done. "Ashley, are you staying with June?" June, cleaned and bandaged, looked like nothing had bothered her today, until you caught sight of the faint tremble in her hands.

"I'll stay for a while yet," Ashley said. She hovered close to June but gave the necromancer her space.

"But that's way out of the way for Sid and me." Not only did I not feel like going back to Boston tonight, but that drive in these clothes, smelling and feeling like they did . . . I shuddered.

"I know it's a long haul, but we need to contain this as best we can." Alistair examined us carefully, ending with me and Sid. "June can ride with me, and we can clean her up enough to be passable, but you two . . ."

"Look like a murder scene," I said.

"Which means you're going to have to ride close to us the whole way home, and Bianca will have to veil you."

Sid rubbed a dirty hand over his face. You can only clean yourself so much with tiny wipes. "Because it isn't difficult enough to ride a bike on a busy road where some of the drivers can't see you, now we get to actually be invisible."

"Where's your sense of adventure?" I asked.

"I think the rabid werewolf ate it."

5

DON'T TRY THIS AT HOME . . .
OR ANYWHERE ELSE

IT TURNS OUT THAT RIDING on an invisible motorcycle when you are also invisible is incredibly dangerous. Makes me wonder how Wonder Woman manages in an invisible plane. Being a superhero clearly has its advantages.

We tried to follow Alistair's car, but people kept attempting to merge into us, thinking we were an empty space. Since Bianca's veil also managed sound, people couldn't hear the motorcycle right next to them. I clutched Sid and gave thanks for his excellent reflexes. Things did get a little less terrifying when the roads had enough of a shoulder for us to drive next to the car, but that wasn't always possible.

By the time we reached the Inferno, I wasn't shaking from electrolyte withdrawal anymore, but from pure terror. Sid was ghostly white and not in much better shape.

I climbed off the bike, barely able to pry the helmet off my head, my fingers were shaking so bad. "Let's never do that again."

"Agreed. Would you think less of me if I vomited over by that car?"

"I couldn't possibly think less of you than I already do."

"Will you hold my hair? I don't want to get any puke on it. There might be some lovely ladies in there, and I'm not really into the kind who can sign off on puke hair." He grabbed both the helmets. Alistair had assured us someone would come out to disinfect the vehicles. At least Sid wouldn't lose his bike.

"Yes, because blood, gore, and ash are cool, but you draw the line at vomit."

He offered me a friendly arm as we followed Alistair. "I do have some standards, you know."

I couldn't help it—I laughed. Maybe my usual team wasn't with me, and something ached at the absence of Lock and Ezra, but Sid was good backup, too. And I had to give Bianca some credit. It couldn't have been easy holding a veil for that long. I didn't have to like her, but I was going to have to respect her. It was the adult thing to do. Damn it. Being an adult sucks.

Alistair led us in through a back door and down some stairs into a tiled room that stank of disinfectant. Showerheads lined the wall, each one surrounded by a flimsy vinyl curtain that really only concealed what absolutely had to be covered. Not quite prison-shower bad, but getting there. I really didn't want to know what the original use of this room was.

Alistair had us each take a stall, pull the plastic shut, and strip. We threw our clothes and our bandages into the middle of the room, and when I peeked around the curtain, I saw someone in a hazmat suit come in. Sid was very upset when he was forced to hand over all his blades and a bracelet that apparently doubled as a garrote. He settled down once he heard that he'd get them back after they'd been disinfected thoroughly. Dr. Wesley, the woman in the hazmat suit, would be stitching, inspecting, rebandaging, and examining all of us after we were clean, or so Alistair said.

Again, I didn't want to know why Alistair even *owned* a hazmat suit. Our clothes were collected and taken to an incinerator. The liquid soap I had to use had a hospital smell to it—all medicine and no love. Not the kind of thing you purchased in the store. Despite the chemical-warfare-grade cleaning agents, I still had to wash my hair several times to get all of Elias out of there. I'm not sure I managed.

"Any more and you'll go down the drain, my wrinkled dumpling." Ezra grinned at me from around one side of the vinyl. He handed me a fluffy towel. I didn't shrink away—Ezra's seen all I have to offer.

"You never texted us back." He handed towels to Sid and Bianca, who were on either side of me, but barely looked at them. I guess they got privacy. Probably strict orders. Ezra's not the best at understanding boundaries. Because he's charming and heart-smashingly gorgeous, he gets away with a lot.

"I was a little busy." I traded the towel for a soft white robe, the kind people steal from luxury hotels.

Amusement lit up Ezra's whiskey-colored eyes. He clearly wasn't buying my lame-ass excuse. "I'm not *new*, Ava."

"Sorry," I mumbled.

He gave a head tilt of acceptance before grabbing robes for the others. At least it was just a huffy Ezra I was dealing with, although he was clearly not too upset. I wasn't sure I could

61

handle Lock right then. Between the bike ride and the earlier fun, I was whuped. All I wanted was some detangler for my hair and a nap. Neither seemed likely.

Alistair led us all through a few hallways and up a stairwell that I was pretty sure I'd never seen, into an unfamiliar set of rooms. The Inferno is the acting headquarters for the Coterie. The building has three levels, but the public only knows about two. Purgatory, the restaurant, sits on the ground floor. They serve the best burger I've ever had, and there's usually a line out the door—reservations are a good idea. It toes the line between comfortable and swank, and it's a place people go to be seen.

If you go through a pair of gilded elevator doors, you can reach the dance club, Heaven. If people go to Purgatory to be seen, then they go to Heaven to be seen with less clothing. The staff wears wings, and everything is ethereal and beautiful. I hate it. To be fair, my only experience with Heaven was a tainted one. My charming ex-boyfriend who will not be named roofied me when I was in Heaven. Lock had to carry me out almost unconscious. Not my favorite memory. Plus, it reminds me of a roller disco for some reason.

The bottom floor, which is underground, is aptly named Hell. Under Venus's reign, it was the last place you wanted to be, and frequently became the last place some people were seen alive. I hated it more than Heaven, but at least Hell didn't pretend. It was large and labyrinthine, and used to be white from ceiling to floor. Venus liked the contrast with blood. Alistair had been remodeling, and this area had obviously already received treatment. It was a bit of a forced remodel. I burned a lot of Hell down during a firefight. The sprinklers and the fire department managed to shut the fire down before it reached the upper floors, so they only took on a little water damage and some smoke.

The room we were in was put together like a hotel suite—soothing pale green walls, warm colors on the couches and carpets, and a well-stocked minifridge.

Everything about the room beckoned you to relax—all except one very irate-looking half-dryad. Judging from the plaster dust in the air and the new Ezra- and Lock-shaped dents in the wall, we'd interrupted a disagreement. Ezra's face was flushed, and he was midshout. At the sight of us, Lock dropped his hands from Ezra's throat and they both put on a serene countenance. From the guilty look Lock threw my way, I could only assume the quarrel was about me. Great.

Lock is a very even-keeled kind of guy—usually. Forgiving, gentle, and everything you'd expect from a nature spirit. But people sometimes forget that nature is multifaceted. On one hand, you have idyllic meadows, gentle breezes, fluffy bunnies, and calm seas. On the other? Tornados, earthquakes, monsoons, and sharks. Lock spent most of his time in fluffy-bunny mode. Today was not one of those days. Every muscle in his jaw was tense, and one of them was twitching. His gray eyes were like granite. We stared at each other, and it was like the only people in the room were me, Lock, and his pissy attitude.

I looked down at my shaking hands and realized that all of this, well, it just *sucked*, and I didn't want it anymore. Then Bianca gave him a light kiss on the cheek and the spell broke. Because I was trying to be mature, I didn't even make a gagging sound. Lock seemed to notice then what state we were all in. He shook the plaster dust from his hair and handed out clothes to everyone.

Alistair examined the room with chagrin. "The contractors just finished this room. The paint has barely dried. If I didn't need you both doing other things so badly, I'd make you fix these walls yourself, understood?"

Ezra was unconcerned, his attention already somewhere else, but Lock appeared repentant.

Bianca and Alistair and the other Coterie regulars like myself had our own spare clothes on hand. Alistair had called ahead with sizes for June, who grabbed hers and hit the bathroom. Sid took a separate bedroom. And lucky me—my clothing came with a firm hand on my wrist as Lock dragged me into the other bedroom.

"If you're going to lecture me, at least turn around so I can get dressed while you yell."

He dutifully turned around, even though, like Ez, he's seen it all before. But Lock has good manners and didn't point that out. If we were going to fight, I didn't want to be naked. It's incredibly difficult to fight in the nude. It's actually a little disturbing to realize how many times I've actually had to do just that. Lock was silent as I got dressed, and he looked more relaxed than before, but I know him. He'd gone into slow-simmer mode. I hadn't seen him this mad in a while, and I couldn't decide if I should tiptoe around him or get defensive.

Ezra slipped in, shutting the door again before anyone could get a peek of me in my unders. He cradled a fire extinguisher in his arms.

"You here to break up the fight?" I asked. I said it lightly, hoping to decrease the tension in the air. As much as I didn't want to argue, I also wanted to get it over and done with. It felt weird to have this disconnect between my best friends and me.

It was like half my family had packed up and left town, only I knew for a fact that it was my fault and it was not a vacation. Ezra wasn't mad at me. Frustrated, yes, but not angry. I understood that. He was stuck between Lock and me, though, and trying really hard to not be. It was a crappy position for us to put him in, but I couldn't see a way out of it.

Ezra set the fire extinguisher down. "Not today, my little apple fritter. If I thought it would help, I would park my beautiful self in that chair with some popcorn and watch the fireworks. Instead, I am going to be right outside that door, and I'm going to make sure you're not interrupted."

I yanked on a pair of jeans that were still a little loose and grimaced. I'd gained back a lot of the weight I'd lost while fighting Venus, but clearly I wasn't quite back to myself yet. I fiddled with the zipper, buying myself a few precious seconds. Of course I knew I had to take my medicine, but that didn't mean I would like it. Ezra came over and cupped my face in his hands. "I refuse to let you two destroy what we have." He squeezed my cheeks until I made a fish face. "So I'd better hear yelling. Alistair says whatever you break will come out of your pay, just so you know."

I spend a lot of time hurting the people I love. Not on purpose. It's like there's a radius of pain around me, and the closer you get, the more it sinks into you. Cade had been kidnapped and beaten last spring, just for being the most important person in my life. *Dad*, I corrected mentally. It was easier to say *Cade* than it was to say *Dad*, and I realized that I was doing it for the same reasons that I was avoiding my friends. This thing with Cade was new and fragile, and I was afraid the wrong move would crush the fledgling life we had.

Lock and Ezra had been hurt at the same time as Cade, Ezra

more so than Lock, at least physically. And just like with Cade, I knew that I shared some of the blame for his injuries with Venus. And that sucked, but I knew they were all healing and soldiering on. I'd been too chickenshit to face up to what I'd done to Lock, which was totally different, I know. Yes, Lock had been roughed up in the fight. And that hurt me, of course. Emotional pain, though—I didn't know what to do with that. Lock had been brave. He'd put his heart out there, and I'd panicked and crushed it. That pain was all on me, and I didn't know how to fix it.

Ezra rested his forehead against mine, his eyes inches away. "Try not to do more damage to him, Ava." He said it softly enough that I wasn't sure Lock could even hear him. I was too close to peer around him to see if Lock still had his back turned.

"All my fault and all that?"

Ezra tweaked my chin. "He got this talk already. If you'd been answering your phone or texting me back, you would have had it, too. The fault is shared, though you both will try to claim it." He gave me one more reproving look, then sauntered over to Lock, smacked him on the ass, and headed for the door.

"You're supposed to say 'good hustle' or 'good game' after you smack any of our asses," Lock said. "It's a rule."

Ezra popped his head back in before he shut the door. "When have I ever followed rules? Remember—yelling. Happening now. Not letting you out until a peace treaty has been reached." Then he shut the door with a soft click.

I yanked on a tank top and sat on the bed. I didn't want to start the yelling. I wasn't angry like Lock was. Okay, so sometimes I was, but mostly what I felt was a hollow dread low in my stomach. How something so empty feeling can also be so heavy at the same time I'll never know. Heavy, empty, and delicate. I was afraid that in taking out the problem and examining it, I might break everything.

"You can turn around now." I folded my hands in my lap. "I'm ready."

Lock turned around and didn't say anything. He tried. He opened his mouth, then shut it. He turned and stared at the wall, as if the words he needed might show up there. His eyes shone and his hands were fisted and I could see that Lock wasn't just angry, either. He was hurt. I did that. I put that pain there.

Before I could think too much about it, I got up from the bed, crossed the room, and threw my arms around Lock's neck. "I don't want to yell," I whispered. I closed my eyes and held tight. At first, Lock didn't move. His whole body was rigid, but I didn't stop hugging him. "I am so, so sorry."

I hate apologizing. Not that I don't need to do it often, but it always feels like it's not enough. Even though the words are like glass as they come out, they just don't quite cut it. It's like handing a starving person a piece of gum.

Lock sighed and his shoulders softened. He put his arms around me and squeezed me to him. "I don't want to yell, either. I hate yelling."

"I make you yell a lot."

"You really do." He rested his chin on my shoulder. "You just... you do some really dumb stuff. Brave, but dumb, and it scares the hell out of me."

"It's my superpower. I even make Cade yell sometimes." He laughed, and it was a startled sound, wet like he'd been crying. I closed my eyes. "I've really missed you. This whole thing. It sucks. You've been trying to talk to me, and I shut you out. It's not that

I didn't want to, but what would I say? 'Sorry for being an ass' doesn't really seem to work."

"I didn't exactly make it easy on you. I . . ." His voice trailed off as if he couldn't quite make the words happen. But I knew. He'd had to hole up and lick his wounds. I guess we both did, but when you're the wounded party, you at least have the sense of being wronged to cling to. You know that you didn't really do anything. But when you're the one who put all the terrible into action? Nothing to cling to except regret, and let me tell you, regret does not know how to cuddle.

"We were both kind of assholes," I said.

"But you still take the prize," Lock added. And I didn't argue, because he was right. He pulled back and looked me in the face, and it finally clicked in just how close my friend was, how wrapped around each other we were, and I felt compelled to run and to lean into him at the same time. Lock didn't seem to notice.

He rested his hands on my hips and looked down, and I could have counted every long eyelash if I wanted to before his gray eyes met mine again. "It might take me a while," he said. "It's not that I don't want to forgive you, it's just . . ."

"It's hard," I said. "And I kind of have a lot to make up for."

"The rejection hurt. It's your answer to give, but it still hurt. But the radio silence afterward . . . that hurt more." He let go of me and walked over to the bed but ended up sitting on the floor, his back against the mattress. He rested his arms on his knees and tilted his head back. "Maybe I overreacted. I don't know."

I sat down next to him, my head resting on his shoulder. "Don't do that," I said.

"What?"

"Try to take all the blame. You make the problem all yours to keep me from having to deal with things, and I appreciate it, but this one is on me."

Lock took my hand in both of his, absentmindedly massaging the pressure points. "How about we split it thirty–seventy. Then we can both be sorry but you can really torture yourself over it. And that way you'll have to make it up to me by not throwing yourself in front of every terrible and dangerous situation, and also maybe make me some wacky cake."

"You want me to bake? Are you sure you're not still trying to torture yourself?"

"Wacky cake is pretty simple—"

"Do I need to remind you of the great pudding fire?"

"But—"

"It was instant pudding, Lock."

He dug gently into the padding around my thumb. "How about we have Sylvie make the cake and you can buy ice cream."

Ezra opened and shut the door quickly. He walked over and frowned. Then he pushed both of our legs down until they were flat. Lock let go of my hand, but Ezra shook his head, grabbed our wrists, and reconnected us. "You can hold that one." Then he sprawled out over us, belly up, his head snuggled into my stomach. "You didn't yell, which was disappointing. No, you had to talk it out. Like grown-ups. Fine. But you have to at least let me take part in the cuddling." He took my other hand and cradled it on his chest. "And the ice cream. I'm definitely in for the ice cream. Maybe some apology foot rubs. I mean, don't limit yourself."

I kissed the top of his head, pulling back only enough to speak. "What makes you think you get any of this?"

Ezra snorted. "I should get more. I had to deal with *both* of you. The whining and the hand wringing. It was unseemly. . . . And you weren't much better, Ava."

I sighed and rested my cheek on his hair. "I love you, Ezra."

"How could you not? You're only human. Now tell me something I don't know. Like why you went on a job today without us. We're a unit. A team. You don't go out without us. The hare is adequate, but he's unaware of your ability to get into trouble. You need experienced Ava handlers around at all times."

Leaning over was uncomfortable, so I sat back up and propped my head on Lock. It felt good to be around my friends again, even if they could both be suffocating know-it-alls sometimes. "First of all, I didn't go out alone, I had backup. Second, I didn't know who Alistair was sending to me."

"You could have requested us," Ezra said.

"And you could have called," Lock added. "I had to find out what was going on from Bianca."

I frowned. "Bianca told you?"

"Yeah," Lock said, holding tight to my hand so I couldn't pull away. "She called us from the warehouse. Turns out they have these things called cell phones now. You can call people from all over the place."

Yep, I still wasn't out of the doghouse with Lock. Well, what did I expect—instant forgiveness even when he'd told me it would take time? "If you know everything, why are you talking to me, then?" I couldn't quite keep the hint of recrimination from my tone.

"We still need to hear your side. Walk us through, because now that we're here, we're jumping in."

Like they would do anything else.

I'd mostly caught them up by the time Alistair called an end to our minimeeting. I could have gotten mad because he cut us short, but Venus wouldn't have given us any time at all. It's good to put things in perspective sometimes.

6

MINIVANS REALLY ARE
QUITE PRACTICAL

FOOD HAD BEEN ORDERED, and a veritable banquet met us when we entered. Sid was already sitting down with a heaping dish of fried chicken, potato salad, and his own basket of rolls. Mouth full, he nodded at a similar plate he'd already heaped with food for me.

Sid and I were going to be best friends.

Alistair tipped the cream pitcher into his coffee. He carried the mug back to his seat and set it aside to cool. Then Alistair stared off into space for a moment, like we weren't there.

I didn't want to push. With Venus, you didn't badger for more info. She told you what she wanted to tell you, and that was it. Most times, you didn't want to know more. But I was starting to understand that wasn't the way Alistair functioned. When he took over, he said he prized curiosity and intelligence, and at the time I thought they were just words he said, not words he meant. People usually say they want ingenuity and independent thought in their staff, but really they just want obedience.

It would be foolish to think that Alistair didn't want that, too, but he appeared to want it tempered with judgment. Which, sadly, I tend to lack. As it was, it took all my energy to not set fire to the furniture. Between exhaustion from earlier and the emotional runoff from my discussion with Ezra and Lock, I was a bit out of sorts.

Alistair blew on his coffee before taking a sip. Despite all the horror today had held, Alistair was still in firm control of himself and of us. I couldn't quite decide if I should admire that or fear it. When he was finally ready, he spoke. "We'll need to see if Elias and Luke were an isolated event or not."

"What makes you think it's going to happen again?" Bianca asked.

Alistair tapped his fingers along the side of his mug. "I don't know. A feeling, perhaps. Or maybe it's just preparation. It's something none of us have ever seen. I don't like that. It makes me uneasy, which leads to me wanting to understand the problem more, which means we need more information."

He turned to June. "Are you able to stay?"

June shook her head. "I have my own people to take care of. I'll be on the next plane I can catch."

"Fair enough. I appreciate you dropping everything to come here. If I may impose a little more upon you, could you reach out through your contacts to see if anyone has seen this before? Ashley, please do the same, if you can." He turned to Bianca. "I want you to keep your ear to the ground and your veil up and see if anyone is making noise on this."

It was my turn. "Ava, I'd like you to call Cade and check in, let him know Lock or Ezra will be driving you home." I opened my mouth, but before I could say anything, he said, "This is nonnegotiable. You've expended a lot of energy today and you need rest. The boys are fresh. I'm sending all of you back to Currant. Sid and Bianca included. If my feeling is right, I'll have a team I know and trust farther out in the field. If I'm wrong, you spend a few days getting paid for sitting around. Sid, get in touch with the drove. See what they can drum up and if they can spare your sister. And I'm keeping your bike another day or two. I want to make sure it's clean."

Sid winced. "Not my bike . . ."

"It'll be thoroughly cleaned and decontaminated by Mick and his team. I'm waiting for them to handle it because I know you want it back in one perfect piece, right?"

"Right." He returned to his food, a mournful aspect about him. "You know that where Ikka goes, Olive is likely to follow," Sid said through a mouthful of food.

"I'm aware that you three are somewhat joined. Normally I would hesitate to include anyone as young as Olive, but I think she defies normality."

Sid nodded. "She'd just stow away, so might as well give her permission. Keeps you from looking foolish when she shows up anyway."

Alistair gestured to the cart. "Everyone help yourselves to as much as you wish. After we finish up here, I want you to head out. I need you ready."

Alistair stood and set aside his now-empty mug. "I'll send along a runner with various other supplies you might need. Now eat." The door shut behind him as he left.

We ate our food quickly, then geared up to go. After putting his dishes on the cart, Lock went over to talk to Bianca. I tried really hard not to watch. That way I wouldn't have the vision of Lock smiling at her, and Bianca touching his arm in a familiar fashion. Nope, not burned into my retinas at all. I feigned a need for the bathroom and stuck my hands under the faucet, hoping no one but me had seen the sparks.

We said our good-byes to June. She would be staying the night at a Coterie hotel before heading out in the morning. I found myself wishing June could stay. She threw Alistair off his game, and it was nice to see him rattled.

Lock got his new van from the lot and pulled it up to the curb so we could all load in.

"A minivan?" I asked as he hit the unlock button. "You taking the kids to soccer practice after this?"

Lock snorted. "That joke was beneath you. And yes, a minivan. How many times did we wish we had a bigger car before? Like that time we had to haul away that half-conscious orc."

"Or the time we had to move that entire colony of gnomes across state lines." Ezra snapped his seat belt shut. "I, for one, approve of Lock's new mom car. Obviously I wouldn't be caught dead owning one myself, but I like that we can transport a body *and* have enough cup holders for all of us."

"Besides," Bianca added, sliding into the seat next to Ezra, "no one pulls over a minivan."

"I stand corrected, Lock. Your new car *rocks*."

THOUGH THE SUN had set, the humidity was thick when I called Cade as the van pulled up to a gas station. He wasn't happy, but after what we'd encountered earlier, I don't think he was surprised.

"I really wish you could have had that sample analyzed, Rat."

"Yeah, me too."

Sid leaned closer to my ear. "Did you tell him about what happened at the warehouse?"

The problem with having a phone conversation in a car with weres, be they bunny, fox, or anything else, is that they have excellent hearing and eavesdrop whether you want them to or not. I hadn't been planning on telling Cade about our near-death experience. Since Sid didn't get any elbows or glares from the other people in the car, I assumed Lock and Ezra approved of me telling Cade everything, which was no surprise. I didn't much care what Bianca thought.

"Well, I'm going to *now*," I said, wishing I'd waited to call until I was alone.

"Tell me what?" Cade asked, his voice getting that strange parental tone telling me quite clearly that I would spill all or face wrath.

"It wasn't a big deal. Really. We're all fine."

"Ava . . ."

I sighed. How does Cade manage to get an entire lecture into one word like that? It was no use. I told him the whole thing, Sid occasionally chiming in by shouting next to my ear. I scowled at him. "Do I need to put him on speakerphone?"

"No, I'm done. Besides, I hate speakerphone."

The phone was silent on Cade's end, and I could picture him pacing and frowning, turning everything over in his head. "As much as I want you home, I wish Alistair had kept you there for the night. You have to be exhausted. That aside, at least he seems to have your general safety in mind. Keep me updated along the drive. And take care of the boys." He hesitated. "I'm glad you worked things out with them."

I grunted.

"You did work things out, yes?"

"Mostly. I don't want to talk about it," I said, looking at Ezra. "Big ears."

"I see. Call Sylvie—see if she can cover your shifts. Watch yourself, Rat. Love you."

"Love you, too."

I texted Sylvie to avoid the listening-in factor, but Ezra tried to peek at my screen anyway. He's nosy. He can't help it. It's a fox thing.

Me: *Can you cover my shifts for a few days?*

Sylvie-tron 5000: *Ooooo, so it was a hot date! I am so proud of you. My little girl is all grown up. . . . :)*

Very few people are listed under their given names in my phone. Ezra's number came up as Superfox and Lock's was Flower Power . . . or at least that's what his contact was after Ezra got ahold of my phone one day.

Me: *What? No. I told you it wasn't a date.*

Sylvie-tron 5000: *That's a crying shame. That guy was ruggedly handsome. Like Han Solo. Or a scruffy Mr. Darcy.*

Sid leaned over my phone with a grin. "She thinks I'm a looker, eh? And what date? Did you tell her I was your date?"

"No." I yanked my cell closer, tipping it away from him. "And mind your own business."

Me: *And full of himself, too. Besides, I thought Lock was your one true love.*

Sylvie-tron 5000: *He was the Zelda to my Link, but that doesn't mean biker boy couldn't be the Princess Peach to my Mario. I have two hearts, like the Doctor.*

Sid snatched my phone, cradling it away from me. A scuffle

ensued, and before I could get my phone back, Sid had called Sylvie. He held me back with one hand.

"Hello, is this Sylvie?" Sid grinned and continued to slap away my hands until I gave up. If I thought it would be a short conversation, I was wrong. I didn't get my phone back until we'd gassed up and gone on our way. I'd even had time to get beef jerky and a slushie from the gas station. And, yes, I know we just ate. Firebug. Don't judge me. Actually, go ahead and judge me. I don't care.

"She said she can cover your shifts as long as Cade lets her work on her clandestine knitting project at the same time."

"Clandestine Knitting Project would be a good band name," Bianca said.

"But you could only do one album, and then you'd have to break up, or you'd become the Knitting Project, and that's not as good." Sid dug into his pocket for his own phone but paused. "Why would a knitting project be steeped in secrecy?"

"You and Sylvie sure got cozy fast," I said with a huff. "She didn't tell me about her knitting project for days, and I had to pester her to get that much. She's knitting cardigans for charity or something. Don't know what kind, only that the sweaters look kinda funky to me."

"She's funny. How old is she?"

"Too young," Ezra and Lock said at the same time. I knew that protective tone well. Defensive shield up—must keep the women-folk safe.

"She'll be seventeen in a few weeks." We were planning a movie marathon—Sylvie was still picking the theme—and Cade was going to make a cake.

"See?" Lock said. "Too young for you, lover boy." He turned in his seat. "Did she ask to speak to me?"

"Nope," Sid said with a grin. "Besides, she's not that young. I'm only eighteen."

"She didn't mention me at all?" Lock said at the same time I said, "You're only eighteen?" Sid didn't look that young. Some guys at eighteen still look half formed, like they haven't quite filled out and grown into themselves yet. Not so much our hare friend.

I punched Lock in the arm. "She probably didn't know you were with us." My phone beeped.

Sylvie-tron 5000: *You should invite Sid to my party.*

Me: *I bet he'd dress like the Tenth Doctor for you.*

Ten minutes went by before I got a reply.

Sylvie-tron 500: *Sorry, I got excited and dropped my phone into my frappe. My phone is sticky now but somehow still works. It's a Christmas miracle. Do you really think Sid would dress as the Doctor?*

Me: *You're so easy.*

IT WAS LATE when we pulled up my driveway. We had made good time back to Currant, though, stopping only at the gas station and, later, for Dunkin' Donuts. I don't know if the world runs on Dunkin', but me and the weres sure do.

It had been a strangely pleasant drive. Not back to our usual level of comfort, but getting there. Bianca and I barely snapped at each other at all. I was doing my best to remember that she was Lock's friend now and I needed to make nice. Which was hard because she had the uncanny ability to drive me right up the wall. Luckily I seemed to have the same mystical ability.

Now, as the minivan came to a stop, Bianca turned around in her seat and frowned at me. "Your cabin is two bedrooms, right?"

"Indeed."

Bianca made a face. "I bet we're supposed to share a room just because we're both girls."

Normally I would have made a face right back and told her we could sleep anywhere we damn well pleased. But then I thought of her sharing the living room with Lock and had to shove my hands in my pockets before the sparks gave me away. Unfortunately, I'd forgotten that my normal clothing had been destroyed, and these pockets weren't warded like my pants usually were. I may or may not have singed the tops of my thighs.

I shrugged, pretending to be nonchalant. "That might be for the best. Sometimes Lock snores, and Ezra prefers to sleep naked. He usually crawls into the wrong bed, too." He claims to be sleepwalking, but I don't buy that for a second. "And who knows what weird thing Sid does."

Bianca grimaced. "Fine." She sniffed. "Hey, anyone else smell that?"

"Smell what?" I asked.

"I don't know. Like smoke."

A quick look down showed that my pants were the source. I pressed the sweating cup from my slushie against my pockets. "I have no idea what you're talking about."

7

SLAYER WOULD
BE SO PROUD

OUR CABIN became headquarters. Cade and Sylvie would be manning the bookstore during the day, so we would generally have the place to ourselves. Sid's sister, Veronica (Ikka), and Olive joined us about an hour after we arrived, bringing sleeping bags and food. I was still a little fuzzy on how Olive was related to Sid and Ikka. I was fairly sure she wasn't a sibling, but she never talked about her family, and any inquiries were met with silence or direct threats. But whether she was actually related to them or not, she'd made Sid and Ikka her kin. So we all just treated them like siblings and left it at that.

We were still trying to figure out sleeping arrangements when Cade walked in carrying two deluxe dog beds.

"What are *those*?" Ezra said, his eyes narrowing. "You don't have a dog."

"No, but I do have a house full of people and only a few

places for said people to sleep. So we're going to have to get creative."

If Ezra had hackles, they would have been up. "I'm still not seeing why you have beds for dogs. There are no dogs here."

Cade shook his head. "I understand how the label might upset you, but really, I couldn't leave these in the pet shop for dogs to use. They're way too nice."

Ezra perked up. "Nice?"

Cade settled the beds by the log stove. "Sure. Stuffed with goose down. Thick, quilted fleece top. I guess I could see why you wouldn't want to use them, though. I'm sure a sleeping bag on the floor would be much better than something like a dog bed." He surveyed them, hands on his hips. "You're right. What was I thinking? I'll take them back tomorrow."

Ezra examined the beds. "Down, you say?" He stared at the hardwood floor and the pile of sleeping bags and the soft, cushy dog beds, considering. Comfort won over pride. "Let's not be too hasty. One night. That's it. But we're renaming them fox beds. I don't want to hear any more mention of the D-word."

Sid grabbed the second bed. "I don't know what you're talking about. This is clearly a deluxe bed for hares."

When I went up to my room that night, there was one russet fox sprawled on his new bed, his small booted feet in the air. In a few minutes, he'd curl up into a ball and go to sleep. A few feet away, two large brown hares roosted in the middle of their own bed, with a smaller gray-brown leveret tucked between them. One of Olive's feet was white. It was cute, which I'd have to mention to her in the morning, but only if I was outside stabbing range. Bianca was still down on the couch, quietly reading, and I assumed she'd come up later.

It was probably the weirdest sleepover in the history of sleepovers.

I climbed up into my loft to find Lock in his pajamas, half-asleep on my bed, like the past few weeks had never happened.

"Shouldn't you and Bianca switch places? Gotta protect my reputation and all that."

He opened one eye. "That's a great idea. You and Bianca sharing a room. Because you get along so well. After you freeze each other's bras, I'll have to break up the fistfight and your dad will have to use the fire extinguisher on the new drapes. I'm too tired for such shenanigans." He flipped a corner of the sheet up so I could climb in. My comforter was folded at the end of the bed. Maine summers tended to stay on the warm side. "No, I figured this would be better."

"You could always take the floor," I said, turning off my light and climbing in next to him.

"Except you pitch a fit when I do that. I'll probably end up there after you hit me a few times anyway."

"You know I have nightmares. And you snore."

"Nobody's perfect, cupcake." The bed creaked as he flipped onto his back. "And you snore, too. Like a congested buffalo sometimes."

I slapped his shoulder.

"You're so abusive," he said, shoving me back. "Now get some sleep."

I stayed awake, listening to the night noises. Ezra yipped in his sleep a few times. Bianca muttered, and I thought I heard the thump of one of the hare's feet. I lay there and waited, unsure if I was nervous that Lock might turn toward me and start something, or if I was really hoping he would. But of course, being

Lock, he respected my space and went to sleep, just like he'd told me to do, and I wondered why I'd even considered that he'd do anything different. I listened to his breathing even out as he drifted deeper into sleep, and thought about how much I cherished that honesty and forthrightness and yet was kind of annoyed by it at the same time.

Hey, I never claimed to make any sense.

WE MANAGED what could generously be referred to as a nap before all our phones started to go off. Bianca cursed, and in my haste to get up, I fell out of bed.

"We would make terrible firefighters," I said, peering out of my loft. "I'm too clumsy and the hose would knock you on your ass."

"Get up and get dressed or I'll show you how I can handle a hose," Bianca said as she sat up on the couch. Apparently Bianca didn't wake up bright eyed and bushy tailed. I didn't, either, so I couldn't blame her. Ezra had changed back to human and was trying to navigate putting on trousers. His foot kept missing the hole. Sid and Veronica were already dressed and doing their best to persuade Olive to stay at the cabin. Cade, his hair sticking up and his pajama pants and T-shirt rumpled, was making coffee.

"Olive, I would appreciate it if you stayed with me." He adjusted his glasses so they sat more comfortably. "We can act as home base. To be honest, I need someone around who knows how to secure a location." Olive looked torn. She wanted to go with Sid and Veronica, because she always wanted to go with them. That's where the action was. If she stayed with Cade, there was less of a chance of that, but she would be in charge of his safety and, in her mind, in charge of a mission. She pushed her bangs out of her face with a small, tan hand. "Will you leave the Taser? I only have the blades I usually wear."

"No, I think we learned that lesson last time, but I will leave the collapsible baton," Ikka said, pulling on her jacket.

Olive scrunched up her face. "Are we still talking about that? He's fine now." She took the baton from Sid before studying Cade. "Will you make cookies?"

Cade got out some travel mugs for us. "Might as well. It's not like I'm going back to sleep anytime soon."

"Then your proposal is acceptable," Olive said, slipping out to walk the perimeter.

We were all dressed and out the door five minutes later. There were three hot spots that Alistair wanted us to check out, and he wouldn't let any of us go alone. Bianca went with Sid, Ezra paired with Ikka, and I went with Lock. Alistair had sent only a few short sentences about what was going on.

Lock and I were given the address farthest out, somewhere deeper inland than Currant. You know how sometimes farmers decide to raise alpacas or emus, or seemingly random creatures, even though they're not quite in farm country? They buy a little plot of land, and if they're responsible, they do their homework and learn about the animal they're raising. If they're irresponsible, they're just in it for whatever cash might be available and don't care too much about the animal they're raising.

When we pulled up to the house from the long, winding driveway and I saw the wooden fence accompanied by a secondary electric fence, that's what I thought we were facing—hobby farmers. Emus, maybe turkeys, or I don't know what. It wasn't immediately clear what it had to do with Alistair and the Coterie. Maybe this was a family of sweet, nonhuman farmers that had been set upon by crazed weres or something. I thought of our earlier confrontation with Elias, and Alistair's feeling that it was just the beginning, and prayed that we were facing something mundane. Or at least mundane for us. All I knew was that when we climbed out of the minivan and stood before the old Victorian farmhouse, the front door already stood open. When the nighttime breeze floated by, I smelled blood.

The house was isolated, so we didn't have to worry too much about neighbors seeing or hearing anything. That didn't mean the neighbors were safe from whatever creature was about. The front mat told me this was the Jeffersons' house, and I wiped my feet even though I didn't think the Jeffersons were going to care about the state of their floors anytime soon.

We made our way through the downstairs quietly. While it would have been nice to call out to the family to see if they were home and okay, we didn't know if we were the only invaders or not. So for our own safety, we kept quiet.

The Jeffersons' house was well put together; clearly someone cared about appearances. The paint looked new, and the wood floors gleamed. A large white area rug protected the floor and the furniture was spotless, a quilt nicely folded on the back of the couch. Big sliding doors led out to a patio, a smaller entryway led off to what was probably the kitchen. Family photos graced the walls: Mr. Jefferson holding up his catch of the day from some fishing trip. Mrs. Jefferson rock climbing with her husband. And a girl I assumed was their daughter smiling and holding up a second-place 4-H ribbon in one hand while hugging a fat, lop-eared rabbit in the other. She looked like her mother—dirty-blond hair, bright green eyes, her skin a light tan. From the pictures, the Jeffersons looked like a normal, happy, middle-class family. Which made the blood spatter on the carpet between the sliding doors and the kitchen all the more worrying. I knew, though, that being normal and happy didn't keep you safe from violence. Somehow that made it seem worse.

I grabbed Lock's sleeve and pulled him with me as I followed the drops into the country-style kitchen with gingham drapes, canisters with roosters on them, and bright yellow cabinets. Normally I'd have said it was a quite cheery kitchen. Except normally Mrs. Jefferson wouldn't have been sprawled facedown on the floor in a pool of her own blood. Lock felt for a pulse, but I knew that wasn't necessary. The smaller drops already looked tacky. She'd been here for a while. A blood-soaked towel was clasped in her hand. She'd probably been using it to staunch the wound, which was why we only found drops in the living room and not a more extensive blood pool.

"What do you think did this?" I asked, burying my nose in my elbow. Mrs. Jefferson, through no fault of her own, didn't smell very good.

Lock turned her over gently. A ragged gash tore through her shirt and into her torso. I don't think it took her very long to die. I could see a few spots of blood on her surprised face, one right below her chin like a beauty mark.

"I don't know. It doesn't look clean, like from a blade. From the ragged edges and the direction, I would say she was mauled by some sort of animal." I handed him a towel so he could wipe the blood off his hands. "She has a smell, too. Something beyond the normal death smell. It's almost..." He shook his head. "I can't place it. I wish we had Ezra with us."

"I don't know what it is, either, but then, I'm working really hard to not smell stuff right now."

Lock stood up, his gaze back on the blood. "Well, we know she wasn't attacked here. We're going to have to follow her trail of bread crumbs."

I looped my arm through his. "You shouldn't make Hansel and Gretel references. It reminds me of that one assignment we had at the gingerbread house." Even so much time later, my stomach still lurched at the thought. "All the tiny bones."

Lock shuddered. "That witch had lost her mind. To this day I want to throw up when I smell burnt sugar."

We left the kitchen, letting ourselves out the sliding doors and onto a small patio. There was a modest yard and a rickety shed off to the left. At the edge of the grass, I could make out more of the fence I'd seen before, and what looked like a gate. Lock pulled a small Maglite out of his pocket, and we headed over to the fence. It didn't take us long to determine that Mrs. Jefferson had come through here. The latch had blood on it. So whatever had attacked her was probably out in that pasture.

"I feel like we should take bets now," I said. "What are you thinking? Mad cows? Killer were-sheep? Chupacabras?"

Lock swung the flashlight beam out into the field. "We're too far north for chupacabras. They prefer warm climates."

He flipped the latch.

"Do you ever stop and think we're becoming like soldiers who've seen too much? I mean, you didn't even blink when I mentioned chupacabras or were-sheep."

Lock grabbed my hand. "I've never met a were-sheep. Met a were-goat once. Nice lady. Lived in my mom's woods one summer." Lock kept swinging his flashlight, but we weren't spotting anything.

"Wait," I said, stopping him. "What was that? Over there. I thought I saw a blur." Lock dutifully swung his flashlight to the left. At first all we saw was the reflection of eyes. Just a glow of green when the beam of the light hit. Then more eyes. Lock tilted the light, and we finally got a full view of what we were looking at.

"Is that what I think it is?" I whispered.

"Were you thinking that we're looking at a herd of peryton?"

"Well, I was thinking winged deer, but that was because I couldn't remember the actual name." I'd never seen a peryton live before. They aren't very common and usually only breed in remote locations. It's pretty difficult to keep a herd of winged deer hidden.

The body of the peryton is deer-like, but it's closer to an elk in size. They have big, broad chests, and the males have impressive antlers that would make a hunter drool. I'd only ever seen pictures of a typical North American peryton, which has the coloring one would expect to see in, say, a white-tailed deer. The wings and trailing tail feathers resembled those of an eagle. They were majestic, serene creatures.

These peryton didn't look like that. Based on their plumage, I was sure they were imported. They were stunning—closer to parrots or peacocks than eagles. The male nearest to us had a brown speckled chest, but his sides and wings were a smear of blues and greens with the tips a deep iridescent purple. He spread his wings out in warning as he hissed our way. Lock turned and looked behind us. We hadn't noticed the second fenced-off area when we came in, but I could see it now. It held a handful of does, their coloring much more subdued.

"Ava, do you see that large oak off to our left?" Lock held my hand tightly.

"No," I said. Being half dryad, of course Lock knew where all the trees were. But all I saw was darkness. "What else do you think is out here? I mean, what attacked Mrs. Jefferson?" I didn't know a lot about peryton, but I knew they were herbivores. They ran or flew to avoid predators, and they didn't fight unless attacked. The only time they were remotely dangerous was during rutting season, and that was in the fall.

"You're looking at it," Lock said, his voice low.

"You're kidding me."

"Nope. I don't know about the does, but the bucks aren't acting right. There's definitely something wrong. So when I yell 'go,' I want you to haul ass for that tree. I'll be right behind you, okay?"

"Still don't see the tree," I said, starting to back away from the peryton. They were all hissing now, their heads low like geese, their wings spread wide to make them look even bigger. I couldn't remember if they had claws or hooves for feet. I wasn't sure which would do more damage.

Lock pointed into the dark. "Just run that way. We'll get to high ground and reassess." He pulled a handful of seeds out of his pocket and tossed them at the peryton. "Go!"

I ran like, well, like a herd of giant deadly peryton were chasing me. I could hear Lock's footfalls behind mine, so I didn't worry about leaving him behind. Moonlight was minimal, and I couldn't see the ground very well. Which is how I tripped over

Mr. Jefferson. I screamed as I fell, catching myself with my hands as I toppled, my legs awkwardly draped over the gutted, bloated corpse of Mr. Jefferson.

Lock dragged me to my feet. "Puke later. We're almost there." He glanced back. "*Haul ass*, cupcake."

Unlike me, Lock actually jogged on a regular basis. I do a fair amount of running, but usually it's away from things that want to kill me, or toward things that I have to kill first. I'm not what one would call athletic. I don't jog unless Lock makes me, and I don't do hurdles or climb ropes for fun. And since I hadn't been around Lock for weeks, I hadn't been running *at all*, and it showed. I got to the tree and I had nothing left. I looked up at the trunk and said, "You've got to be shitting me."

"Nope." Lock grabbed my waist. "Alley-oop." I shrieked in surprise but managed to grab on to the lower branch. Lock could toss me because he also did things like lift weights. But there was no one left on the ground to lift him up. Luckily for my companion, trees are overly fond of him, and this one was more than willing to dip a branch for him to climb. He scrambled up like a monkey, urging me to go up a few more branches. The peryton milled about below us, staring up and hissing. Except a few on the outside who were strutting, their chests out, their tail plumage spread and shaking for all to see.

I held on to the branch with a death grip. "What the hell just happened?"

Lock put his hands over mine. "First, I'd like to remind you that when you get stressed, your body has a certain response." His voice was low and soothing. "And that you're currently holding on to a tree, which is the only thing between us and a certain, antler-filled death. Do you understand?"

I nodded and tried to think calm thoughts. Kittens. Puppies. A nice, well-done peryton steak, fresh from the grill.

"How did we manage to outrun them?" I asked.

Lock adjusted his perch on the branch so he could get a better look at our pursuers. "I threw some heavy-duty vine seeds at them and did a fast grow. It didn't slow them down much, but it got us here."

"Thanks," I said. "I don't fancy becoming peryton chow."

They milled below us, hissing and strutting. As I watched, two of them reared up and hurled themselves at each other. Their antlers crashed together, the noise making me want to inch back.

"Something is very wrong with them," Lock said. "They're acting like it's rutting season, but it's not. And I got the sense that they thought we were standing between them and the does. Peryton are smart—they must have seen people open the dividing fence before, and they're pissed that we aren't doing just that."

"So they killed the Jeffersons because they were keeping them separated? Harsh." A few more of the males lost interest in us and started doing their very romantic head-butt thing. "Well, we'd better think of something before the mosquitoes eat us to death." That made me think of something. "Wait, why aren't the peryton up here gnawing on us? They have wings."

"I think they're clipped." The clouds moved, and a little more moonlight crept in. I couldn't see Lock, but I could make out a faint outline. "What could screw these guys up so much? They're acting unnatural."

"We'll figure that out later," I said. "Right now we have to work out how we're going to get away." I dug my cell phone out of my pocket, but the screen told me there was no service to be had. "Crap. I guess it's just us, then. Do you think Alistair wants us to try to contain them for later, or is this a mission of destruction?"

"I don't think we have much choice," Lock said. I could hear the regret in his voice. Nature spirits really don't like destroying nature. As we watched, one of the males hurled itself at another one, but instead of ramming his horns, he lashed into the other's chest. The injured peryton screamed in pain. I couldn't tell in the low light, but I was willing to bet that the wounds on that peryton matched the ones Mr. and Mrs. Jefferson had. "I don't think they're coming back from this."

"Suggestions?"

"You take one half. I'll take the other." Lock dug through his pockets, no doubt digging for seed packets.

I see a lot of things in my line of work that I wish I could unsee. If I made a physical list, I would need a ream of paper. My brain isn't going to run out of nightmare fuel anytime soon. But I can honestly say I've never blown up deer before. I guess it was more like spontaneous combustion, really. Lock threw seeds and grew plants that captured, twisted, and crushed the peryton. It sounds torturous, but we didn't have a more humane option, and I could tell Lock was throwing in as much energy as he could so the process would be as quick as he could make it. Mine wasn't much better. The peryton screamed while they burned. As the internal pressure built, a few of the cooking peryton exploded. Bits of flesh and blood flew through the air, covering us and the tree in fat, muscle, and skin.

When it was finally over, we climbed out of the branches. I rubbed Lock's back as he threw up next to the tree. It was one thing to hunt someone down for the Coterie, but a whole different thing to be forced to messily put down a whole herd of animals that didn't know any better. When he was finished, he straightened up, and I used the sleeve of my jacket to wipe the tears and what might have been brain matter off his face. Totally romantic.

"This is the second time in the last few days that I've been covered by cooked fat and flesh. I'm beginning to question my life choices." That got a hint of a smile from Lock, but it was weak.

He brushed my cheek with the heel of his palm. "Looks like blood, too."

"Huh. So it was literally raining blood? Slayer would be so proud."

We kept an eye out as we walked, doing our best to stay alert. There was no guarantee that all the peryton were gone. Lock swung us by the does' pen. They appeared a little agitated, which made sense. Even if they couldn't see what had happened, the smell and noise of our peryton cook-off would have made any creature wary. Apart from that, though, they acted normal. Lock made sure they had water; then we left them for the moment. Since they posed no immediate danger, Alistair could decide what to do with them.

We trudged back to the house. I made us take a moment to ruin the guest bathroom by cleaning ourselves up. Those lavender towels would never be the same, but Lock and I couldn't walk around with gore-covered faces. Lock found a tube of toothpaste and did his best to clean the puke taste out of his mouth. Back in the kitchen, I draped a quilt over Mrs. Jefferson before I filched a banana and sat on the counter to eat it. Seems heartless, I know, eating next to a body like that. But the phone was in the kitchen and I needed to eat after all the energy I'd expended blowing up peryton. After being with the Coterie so long, you get used to a certain amount of callous-seeming practicality. Lock called the situation in to Alistair using the Jeffersons' landline. Definitely not something we should have done, in case the human police became involved later and decided to take a look at any outgoing calls, but we needed to check in on this, and our cells still didn't have any service.

"Cleaning crew is on the way out," Lock said as he hung up. "We're supposed to see if we can find the daughter, then get out." He rummaged through the cabinets until he found two glasses and poured us some water. "Drink." He handed me a glass.

"Shouldn't we search for the girl?"

"While I hope she's alive, I doubt it, and either way we won't be much help if we collapse. I don't know about you, but I'm wiped." Without thinking, I put my empty glass down and pulled Lock closer so I could examine his face. His eyes were tired, and the area underneath them looked smudged with bruises. He hadn't had time to shave, and his dark stubble made his face appear pallid. He'd missed a spot of dried blood by his ear, so I grabbed the dishcloth dangling from the sink next to me and wiped it off.

I ran my thumb along the edge of his chin, moving his face to the side to see if I'd missed anything, and he swallowed. In a breath I realized how close he was. I'd pulled him against the counter so that he stood between my legs. His hands were on my thighs for balance—I hadn't even noticed him putting them there. This is how it always went with Lock—one minute, everything was fine and it was just me and my best friend, and the next there was this sudden awareness of each other. I could feel the heat of him under my fingers and smell the scent of his skin, and I wanted nothing more than to close the distance between us. Instead we stood, paralyzed, each of us either too afraid to move and break the moment, or too worried that if we moved, we would follow our own gravitational pull into each other.

A few months ago, I would have made a joke, pulled away, sliced through the tension, and put up a comfortable wall. But after being away from him and feeling the sharp ache of his absence, I realized that the last thing I wanted to do was to put up anything that would make him go away again. At the same time, I'd tasted what it was like to lose him, and I was even more afraid to do anything that would jeopardize our friendship than I had been before. My apology was still fresh and the hurt I'd caused probably still raw. Now simply wasn't the time to stray from comfortable paths. I also didn't want any first-kiss kind of stories to involve the phrase "a few feet from a fresh corpse." I'm particular that way.

I pulled my hand from his chin.

"We should go look for the girl," I said.

Lock nodded and stepped back, offering me a hand to help me down. My stomach sank, and I would have traded that feeling for another peryton bloodbath any day.

8

FINDERS KEEPERS

WE WENT UP a set of stairs and found ourselves in the middle of a landing. Off to the left were two closed doors, while there were three to the right of us. More family photos dotted the walls, but there was nothing on or around the doors to indicate which room had belonged to the girl. Splitting up would have been faster, but we had no guarantee that the house was safe, so we explored as a team. In Coterie life, the buddy system often saves you from certain death.

The doors on the left revealed a bathroom and a large office and craft room. Nothing tried to eat us in either, so we decided they were clear.

The first door we opened on the right was a linen closet, and the scariest thing in that was the floral print on the sheets. After that we found the girl's room. It was as immaculate as the rest of the house. I don't trust people with clean houses. I don't mean tidy houses, or that I like filth, but when nothing is out of place? No laundry on the floor or the occasional dust bunny?

That's when I start to worry. It's not normal to live like that. Even the craft stuff was in neatly labeled bins. We kept our house pretty organized, but if you walked into my room, it looked more like something was trying to nest there than like a human dwelling.

"Even her posters are framed," Lock said.

"I know, it's kind of freaking me out." I checked under the bed and found nothing. That's right: *nothing*. Not even a rogue dirty sock or a stack of overdue library books. "I'm beginning to think these people were aliens."

Lock checked the closets and confirmed that they were not crammed full of junk, but also neatly organized. Moreover, the girl wasn't in them. That left the last door. The master bedroom.

I didn't really want to see the Jeffersons' bedroom. It's terrible to glance into the private part of someone's life, their inner sanctum, and know that they won't be coming back to it. It feels like an invasion. Since we were physically going to walk in there, I guess it was an actual invasion. But we didn't have a choice.

Lock rapped softly on the door with his knuckles. "Hello? If you're in there—you don't know us, but we're here to help."

Silence.

Lock splayed his hands as if to say, *Now what?* I knocked this time, a little louder. "Hi. This is Ava. My friend Lock was the other person who just talked to you. We . . . we know what happened downstairs. Well, we know what happened to your parents."

"We're really sorry for your loss," Lock added.

"Yes. Very sorry." I nudged him with my elbow. Either he was going to let me talk or I was going to make him take over again. "We're hoping you're okay, and we'd like to take you to safety so someone can . . ." I couldn't think of a nice way to say, *Clean up this awful mess.* Sweep her parents' slaughter under a rug? Cover up the peryton snafu in the backyard? I settled on "fix things."

The corner of Lock's mouth twitched, clearly mocking my word choice. I flipped him off. "Anyway, we're going to open the door, okay? Please don't throw stuff at us." I reached down and turned the knob slowly, the metal chilly in my grip, then gently pushed the door open. Cold air wafted out at us, and I tightened my jacket. The Jeffersons liked their air-conditioning.

The master bedroom was much like the rest of the house. Immaculate, cute—right out of a catalog or the set of a TV show. Large four-poster bed with a plaid cover and a hope chest at the foot of it, probably holding all the winter blankets. Reclaimed-wood picture frames on the walls—a parade of their life from wedding to baby to now. The plush carpet softened our footsteps. Again, I wished we had Ezra—he would have been able to listen for breathing or slight movements. Lock and I were somewhat limited by our human senses. It would have been useful if the girl had left some sort of trail. A bloody handprint or a closet left ajar.

Lock stayed by the door in case she tried to bolt. Just because we knew we were friendly didn't mean she'd come to the same conclusion. If I were her, I'd be hiding somewhere with a weapon. Despite all the fishing photos, I hadn't seen any hunting paraphernalia, so it appeared that Mr. Jefferson had stuck to fishing. Since he was raising livestock, he might have some sort of rifle about, though. Best to be careful.

I opened the closets first. I stood to the side, reached over, and flung the door open while keeping myself out of the possible line of fire. But the closets were empty. That left the hope chest and the bed. I checked the hope chest first—just blankets and the sharp smell of cedar. Which left the bed. I couldn't think of a good way to sneak down and peek without putting myself in danger. Except maybe crawl on top of the bed, but surely that would alert the person probably under the bed. . . .

"I'm going to look under the bed now. I'd really like it if you didn't shoot my face off or hit me with anything, okay? I like my face." I crawled onto the hope chest and flipped the edge of the blanket up. When nothing happened, I moved slowly onto the floor. The girl was wedged down toward the head of the bed, curled into fetal position, her hands tightly clasping a pair of large scissors, probably pilfered from the craft room. Her eyes were wide, and I could see her trembling from where I was. Even in the semidarkness, I could tell she was in shock. Well, couldn't exactly blame her. She was looking at me but wasn't *seeing* me, not really. Too busy being locked into her own private little hell, I imagine.

I don't consider myself an unfriendly person, but I'm not exactly warm and fuzzy, either. At least, I'm not the kind of person that people automatically open up to, or little kids smile at. I'm not sure what I do that instantly marks me as suspect, but there it is. My guess was that, having been raised on the run and not really throwing down roots anywhere, I was missing some key social cue. I was fairly good at blending in, but I didn't give off the welcome vibe. It just wasn't one of my strengths. Still, I smiled and tried to not look off-putting. "Hey there," I said, while waving Lock over with one hand. I wasn't the right kind of person, but Lock was. He was one big ball of warmth and comfort—the human equivalent of chamomile tea.

Sure enough, as soon as Lock eased down and started talking, she perked up. He introduced us again and offered our help. The girl was still out of it, but I could tell she was actually hearing Lock, whereas my voice had all been white noise.

She let out a shaky breath, and I saw it mist out into the shadows. I looked closer and realized that the bed frame around her was covered in tiny icicles. There are quite a few things, believe it or not, that can create cold and icicles out of nothing, but— factoring in the current summer season—very few of them were mundane. And since the effect was centralized around the girl, then odds were good that she was either the cause or the target.

Alistair could manufacture cold like this, since his element was weather. Ice elementals, yetis, and other creatures could as well, but very few of those actually look human. In fact, for a lot of them, human was a valid meal choice. The girl breathed again, and this time frost wound out from underneath her. I pushed my hand down on the carpet, and it crunched.

"I think we've got ourselves a Jack Frost," I said, lifting my hand off the icy carpet.

"More like a Jill Frost," Lock said. "Don't be sexist."

"I always thought the term encompassed the whole race, like firebugs, or how we stopped using the word *actress* and just use *actor* now."

Lock gave the girl a gentle smile while continuing to argue with me. "*Jack* implies masculine. You know a lot of girls named Jack?"

"No, but I'd like to."

The girl watched us now, her eyes focused, though she was still shaky. "You're not police." Her voice trembled, but she gripped the scissors tighter. She was a fighter. Good.

"No, we're not," I said. "We're Coterie." She now had the scissors in a stranglehold, her knuckles white. Smart girl.

"Mom made me call the phone number. For emergencies only." She licked her lips. "But I got a restaurant. I hung up."

Likely she had called the Inferno, gotten the switchboard, and panicked when she didn't know who to ask for. Alistair would have had someone investigate the dropped call. "I doubt you'll take my word for it, but we're not here to hurt you. Someone sent us. The place you called? The Inferno? It's Coterie owned."

Lock opened his hand and the girl flinched, but all he had there was a tiny seed, which she probably couldn't even see. The seed split, a thin green shoot appearing out of it. The shoot unfurled and grew leaves, curling like a vine around Lock's hand and onto the floor. "Dryad. We're not known to be killing machines."

The fact that Lock was part of my team, which under Venus's reign had indeed been, essentially, a killing machine, was neither here nor there. If it made the girl feel better, so be it. Her hand eased on the scissors, but she didn't let go. Then she shifted her attention to me. "What about you? Are you a dryad, too?"

"No," I said. "I'm not cool like that. I'll show you what I can do, but I want you to remember that's all I'm doing—showing. Not here to hurt you, okay?" She didn't nod or anything, but I decided that she'd heard me. I mimicked Lock's open hand, but there was nothing in mine. I called a flame into my palm—just a little one—and attempted to do a flower. It would have been better to do it slowly, but I hadn't been practicing that kind of control lately. In fact, my lifestyle tended to encourage the opposite. Instead of a delicate flower, I got a monstrous lily that rock-

102

eted up and met with the ice on the bed frame, causing it to hiss and steam. The girl flinched and leaned back.

"What are you?" she whispered.

"Firebug." I killed the flower.

"I've never heard of a firebug." Her face became pinched and tense. I wasn't surprised. When it came to frosts, they either vilified firebugs because we were their opposites and they feared that we would have some sort of extra power over them, or they chose to believe we were a figment—a made-up story their parents told to scare them. If the frosts hadn't spent much time with others like them, the story didn't get passed on. I thought about the house, with its neat, and somewhat off-putting, catalog charm. Mr. and Mrs. Jefferson had been playing human. They'd wanted to fit in but probably hadn't spent enough time with actual humans to see how they lived. So they'd built their camouflage from data mined from magazines and TV. If the girl had gone to school, she'd be much better acclimated simply due to the day-to-day interaction with people. The parents could have avoided such contact.

My guess, based on experience, was that the parents had probably immigrated in, most likely from an even colder climate, and then done their best to erase all vestiges of their origins. Accents would be ground out, old recipes forgotten, local habits and customs adopted. Whether or not the girl even knew about this transition was a toss-up. She might have been too little when it happened, or not even born yet. And with customs went religion and folktales. So no ingrained fear of firebugs.

"Well, until tonight, I've never considered a peryton to be deadly, so I guess it's a day for new discoveries." My neck was starting to get a crick from holding my head up to talk to her.

"Look, this is starting to get really uncomfortable. If I'd wanted to hurt you, I could have already. But I haven't, because we really are here trying to figure out what happened and to get you out. So, please, do me a favor and rejoin the outside world? My neck hurts and I kind of want out of your house. You can keep the scissors if it makes you feel better."

Lock shot me a glare for being so blunt, but he should have known better. I'm not a negotiator. To our surprise, the girl crawled out from under the bed, though on the other side. I respected her for keeping the scissors.

"Do you have any family?" Lock asked. "Anywhere we can take you where you'll feel safe?"

The girl shook her head. "Mom said all her family were dead and Dad didn't talk to his. A falling-out."

"What's your name?" My neck cracked as I rolled it to get the kinks out.

"Kat."

"Is that short for something? Katherine?" Creatures can give up a lot of things, but names . . . names were difficult. I was willing to bet that they'd had to change their last name to Jefferson, but when it came to naming a baby, old habits died hard, as they say.

"Katya." Her eyes tightened as she glared. "Call me Kitty and you die."

My money was on Eastern European descent. I nodded, then left Lock to deal with Kat while I popped back into the kitchen to call Alistair from the landline. Funny how I had always done everything I could to avoid contacting Venus but didn't have that problem with Alistair. I didn't entirely trust him yet, but I couldn't deny that he was preferable to my old boss.

"Alistair," he said instead of *hello*.

"Hey, boss."

"Ava. I hope you have some good news for me."

"That entirely depends on your definition of *good*," I said. Even though I had no evidence, I was willing to bet that Alistair was pinching the bridge of his nose in that "give me patience" gesture I brought out in so many people. Taking pity on him, I gave him my report. As succinctly as I could and almost entirely without snark, sarcasm, or any of the other things I was known for. I must have been tired.

"The cleanup crew is on its way. I'll have to remind his tech people to clear out the phone log. At this rate, Mick is going to have to hire more people."

Mick, from Mick's Sparkle-Time Cleaners, was the guy you called when a situation had to be taken care of in such a way that it wouldn't show up on human radars. He was expensive but usually timely. "That bad, huh?"

"I've been putting out metaphorical—and occasionally actual—fires all night. Boston has been doing what we expected. Some extra squabbles due to regime change, but out in your neck of the woods from Portland and up the coast, we've had a spike in activity. Katya seems okay?"

"Yeah. No visible injuries. She was doing better when I left."

"You left her alone with Lock? Out of sight?"

"No cell coverage."

"Then you should have either waited to check in or brought them with you."

"Sorry, I wasn't thinking."

"Clearly," Alistair said, and although there was some censure in his tone, he left it at that. Even though I deserved a good talking-to. We were pretty sure everything had been caused by the peryton, but there was still a small chance that Kat, disarming and young looking as she may be, might have been the real culprit, and I had just left my partner alone with her. Stupid. The phone was a portable one, so I dashed back upstairs.

Luckily for me, all they were doing was talking when I slipped back into the room. I must have made a relieved sound because Alistair said, "All is well, then?"

"Yeah, fine. What do you want us to do?"

"Have Katya pack a bag. Quickly, please. She'll probably want to linger, but I want you guys out of there ASAP. I'm going to call Cade and see if she can stay with him tonight until we can get something else set up for her. Then I'm afraid you're going right back out. I'd have you wait for the cleaning crew, but it's going to be a while and I want you guys out of that house."

My stomach dropped. "Right back out? Really?" Lock looked over at my tone, but I waved him off. I'd fill him in later. "So it's as bad as you guessed, huh?"

Alistair didn't answer for a moment, and when he did, his voice was gentle. "I'm afraid, Ava, that it's looking much worse."

"Do we even have time to drop Katya off, then?" I could feel the tight grip of panic closing around my chest.

"Yes. Sid and Bianca aren't in immediate danger. They've backed off for now."

"Okay." I twisted the phone away from my mouth and told Lock to help her get a bag packed.

"But, Ava? By no means should you dawdle."

"You got it, boss-man."

9

WON'T YOU BE
MY NEIGH-BOR?

WE PACKED KAT UP and dropped her off at the cabin. And no, we didn't just toss her on the front porch. We actually walked her in and introduced her to Cade. Olive patted her down and searched her things, taking her job as security enforcer very seriously. Katya looked taken aback, but then Olive wordlessly handed her a cookie and patted her cheek before disappearing outside to do a perimeter check.

"Believe it or not, but that's about as nice a reception from Olive as anyone outside the drove has ever received," I told Katya. I snagged a cookie and kissed Cade on the cheek.

We promised we'd be back later. Lock gave her his cell number. Having a lifeline to someone, even a near stranger, seemed to ease her anxiety over staying in a new place.

New directions and terse instructions in hand, we got back in the car. Well, Lock had those things. My hands were full of water bottles, a thermos of coffee, sliced apples, and sandwiches. Despite our gory state, Alistair advised against changing our clothes. Something about how "it could only help," which wasn't reassuring. So wherever we were going, it was going to be messy, and being covered in a fine spray of peryton blood and guts was going to be a plus. Excellent. At least our faces and hands were clean, so we could eat in the car.

Lock drove and I stuffed my face, pausing to feed him the occasional apple slice or bite of turkey and cheese. I, of course, had bacon on mine and three different kinds of cheese, because fat and grease are very important food groups to me. Lock didn't feel the same way, which made me wonder about him sometimes. His food preferences definitely leaned toward his dryad heritage, though he did eat some meat, which was clearly a trait handed to him from his human father. You didn't hang out with the dryad crew unless you planned on being basically vegan. Protectors of the forest don't like it when you eat animal flesh and keep animals as food-producing slaves. I could see their point sometimes, but man, I love cheese. So much.

"If I could marry cheese and have dairy babies, I would."

"Well, until the day the government recognizes that love, you'll just have to keep living in sin with cheese. But I support your strange ways." Lock leaned over and took a bite of the sandwich I held out for him.

"Do you think Katya will be okay?" I asked. Just because I wasn't the warm and fuzzy one didn't mean I wasn't concerned. I knew what it felt like to have your world implode, suddenly having to take care of yourself. Not something I really wished on anyone.

Lock swallowed his bite, considering. "I think so. I mean, it will depend a lot on whatever actually happened out at her place. But she's a frost. They're a tough lot."

This time we were headed out to the Androscoggin Riverlands State Park, which was about a thirty-minute drive from Currant. Whatever situation Sid and Bianca had been sent out into, it hadn't gone well. So we were riding cavalry. They would have to catch us up when we got there.

Androscoggin Riverlands, being a state park, is not technically open after dark. So we couldn't just pull up and leave the car in a lot. We had to hide the van a ways off and head down a path that led to the river.

Hiking at night is kinda creepy. Hiking through a forest preserve at night when you know your cohorts are having trouble with some sort of beastie is much, much creepier. We found Sid and Bianca on a picnic table set back from the water's edge. Or I should say, they found us. They blinked into sight as we started to walk past them. Bianca had been holding a veil around their table, which meant they were hiding. That didn't bode well.

Sid waved us over, Bianca grabbing Lock's arm and dragging him next to her on the bench. I clambered up on the table next to Sid. He held up a finger in silence until Bianca could put up another veil.

"Talk softly if you can—it will make my job a whole lot easier." Bianca said it to all of us, but I'm pretty sure she was aiming that comment at me. Apparently she thought I had a hard time with "inside voices."

"What's going on?" I asked. Usually when we got sent in as backup, people were in trouble—either trying not to get eaten by something, or halfway to being eaten by something. That's how these things tended to go. I was glad my friends—or, at least, my friend and Bianca—were safe, sure, but it was still a bit of a surprise.

"Kelpies," Sid said, nodding to the water.

"Do they usually come up the river?" Lock asked. I could hear the frown in his voice.

Sid leaned closer, his elbows propped on his knees. "They like being closer to the coastline. If they came upriver, either it was because they were following a food source, or something in their environment changed and they didn't like it."

Kelpies emigrated from Scotland with early settlers, and they can be very nasty. "If something is scaring them out of their environment, I don't want to meet it."

"I think we're all in agreement there." Sid perked his head up, listening. My ears aren't as good as his, obviously, and sadly neither is my night vision, but I didn't see anything around us right then. And kelpies are kind of obvious. When you first see them, they look like adorable shaggy ponies. Until you get up close, you'd swear that's all they were. But then you touch their coat, and it's damp, with the stench of brine and mudflat coming off them in a powerful scent, even if they are nowhere near either. Their mane is actually made of a very delicate seaweed, and some of the older kelpies have bracken and moss on their fine coats.

If you get even closer and stare them in the eye, you see a malevolent intelligence. It's not that kelpies are evil per se, it's just that they find people to be especially delicious. Which is why their teeth are another dead giveaway. They don't have flat, broad, herbivore teeth like normal equines. Kelpie teeth are jagged and serrated, like a shark's, perfect for tearing flesh.

Kelpies spend most of their time in the water. Once they're submerged, their "hooves" open and spread, revealing webbed, fingerlike appendages. The hard outer shell that looks like a hoof splits into talons. Perfectly formed for swimming *and* the rending of flesh.

When I first joined the Coterie, we had to go after a guy who had managed to capture a few kelpies with enchanted bridles. The moron had been using the kelpies for pony rides. Might as well cover the kids in steak sauce and strap them to a hungry lion. We didn't really have to do anything to that guy . . . except remove the bridles. The three kelpies he'd captured returned to human form and dragged him into the ocean. He never got the chance to be a repeat offender.

Sid faced the river the entire time we talked, unwilling to lose his focus on it. "They are incredibly tricky beasties."

I was starting to see why Sid and Bianca had waited for us. Unfortunately, I was also starting to understand why Alistair thought it a bonus that Lock and I were covered in peryton. We smelled extra tasty—we were bait. "Has food been scarce?"

Bianca shook her head, her hair looking white in the moonlight. "No. In fact, it's been a great year for fishing and such. They should be full and happy."

"That's not all," Sid said, running a hand through his hair. "Kelpies are usually solitary hunters."

Lock straightened. "You've seen more than one?" Even in the faint light I could tell he didn't quite believe Sid.

"What?" I asked, looking between them. "Is that bad? Why is that bad?"

"You think I'd make something like that up?" Sid's tone was light, but I could tell he was a little put off by Lock's question. I'd been around Sid enough to know that he took his job seriously. He approached things carefully but didn't back down from danger, either.

"I didn't mean that I didn't believe you, just that I'm surprised." Lock let out a breath and finally answered my question. "If you were swimming and you saw a tiger shark, how afraid would you be?"

"Fairly terrified. They're aggressive, aren't they?" I asked.

Lock nodded. "Now imagine that you're swimming and you look down and see a bunch of tiger sharks."

"Ah," I said. "Got it."

Bianca stood and pulled Lock with her. "It will save a lot of time if we just show you guys. Walk slowly and softly. No matter what, stay together. If you bolt, it will tear the veil if I'm not expecting it. Try not to talk until we get back to the bench. It's less work for me, and I don't want to waste any energy in case we need it later." With that, she laced her arm through Lock's and walked off. Sid jokingly offered me his elbow, and I took it. Just a lovely stroll along the kelpie-infested riverfront. You could almost smell the romance.

They led us around a bend in the river to a marshy area. Lock stopped so suddenly in front of me, the only reason I didn't bump into him was that Sid jerked me back. Not that I could blame Lock. An entire herd of kelpies was grazing along the water. Well, it looked like they were grazing, but as I peered closer, I could see that they were munching on small fish and frogs.

"It boggles the mind," Sid whispered. "Kelpies do not herd. They might share territory, but for the most part they avoid one another except during mating season. But I count ten, all close together." They moved skittishly, tossing their heads and snorting, two kelpie colts in the middle of their group. Restless kelpies protecting young. Great. I squinted. It was dark and we weren't close, but it seemed like some of them had strange algae patterns on their coats.

After we got a good eyeful, Bianca led us back downriver to the bench. We waited to speak until she gave us the go-ahead.

"I don't even know what to say." I plopped down onto the bench, suddenly exhausted.

"You can see why we didn't barge in," Bianca said.

"I can't see why you didn't run screaming," I replied.

Lock stared up at the sky, his hands on his hips. "Okay, so we have kelpies acting strangely. Grouping, coming farther inland than usual, but not acting aggressive. Or at least not more aggressive than usual. Has there been an escalation in human deaths around the river?"

"I looked into it on our way out here," Bianca said. "No one's reported anything."

"So what does their behavior tell us?"

I shrugged. Hell if I knew why kelpies did anything.

"Something is scaring them," Sid said slowly. "When an animal leaves its territory and there hasn't been a food shortage, then that seems the most likely reason. An influx of predators, something's gone wrong in the environment—there's always a factor. I just didn't think kelpies were scared of anything. Usually they break down other creatures into two groups: *food* and *that thing I can head-butt to death.*"

"They had the colts in the middle where the herd protection would be the greatest," I said. "So I'm banking on predators." While that was great to know, it didn't actually help us out a lot. After our discussion, it was clear that kelpies usually *were* the apex predators. With the exception of humans poisoning their environment, there wasn't much in the ocean that was scary enough to take on a kelpie and was also willing to come that close inland. "Did either of you try talking to the kelpies?"

Sid and Bianca looked at me like I'd grown donkey ears.

"Talk . . . to kelpies." Bianca spoke slowly, carefully enunciating the words for me. "The very creature we learn not to talk to because they spend their free time trying to drown us and eat us?"

"Yes, those kelpies," I said. "Dangerous or not, they're part of the community and the local ecosystem. If they aren't actually attacking anyone, then we have to consider them the victims of whatever is going on until we know otherwise."

"You're insane," Bianca said, her eyes wide.

Lock crossed his arms. He was used to my crazy. "All right, cupcake, but I'm going in as backup."

Despite her arguments, I had Bianca drop the veil. If we suddenly appeared in front of the kelpies, they'd bolt. Or stampede us and eat the pulpy flesh that was left over. Neither option really worked for me. I took the lead, with the moon lighting our way. It wasn't bright enough to fully avoid the mud and marsh water. I was beginning to wonder if my current outfit was going to have to be burned as well. I was really hard on clothes.

As we got closer, we slowed our pace. The herd raised their heads, their nostrils flaring and taking in our scent. I got as close as I felt comfortable, and waited. After a few seconds, a shaggy gray female stepped forward, flanked by a slightly larger male. His coat was more of the traditional greenish-black you see in depictions of kelpies. Not that I could see their coats well. They appeared to be covered by . . . something. I squinted.

"What do you want of us, fire creature?"

Kelpies may be deadly and tricky and all that, but their voices are something from a dream. *Musical* doesn't even begin to cover it. The female kelpie's voice was like standing on the shore during the sunset and listening to the waves. It was the heady smell of summer sun on the grass and the warm feel of sand between your toes. It was everything good and natural. A voice you could trust. That's how they get you.

"I'm not here to cause trouble," I said. "We haven't had any reports of an upswing in missing humans or that you've been poaching where you aren't supposed to hunt. Since that would call attention to us all, we appreciate that." Also, it was gross, but hey, as part of the target food group, of course I thought it was disgusting.

"Then why are you here?" the male rumbled. Where the female had been a soft breeze on the beach, his voice was a thunderstorm over the ocean. The crash of waves against the rocks and the bracing feel of sea spray on your face. Just as beautiful, but in a different way. Though he must have been a newer import. She sounded like Boston and a trace of something else when I could concentrate past the magic of her voice, but he definitely had a Scottish burr to his words.

"Yes," she said. "Why? Have you come to offer yourselves up as our meal?" She tipped her head, and I swear an amused look flitted across her horsey face. "That would be quite delightful, I must say."

"We are not on the menu," Lock said, his shoulder against mine.

The male kelpie's nostrils flared again. When he spoke, he sounded a little disappointed. "A green man. Eating you might cause trouble, but I suppose that would simply give you the flavor of forbidden fruit."

It's not like I wasn't scared. But the thing about a job like

115

mine is that after a while you get a little blasé about things threatening to eat you. After the two hundredth time, it loses its zest.

"Can we skip the part where you posture and threaten to eat us, and go right to the part where you tell us what has you upriver and together as a herd? My feet are wet from all the water and I'm not getting any warmer."

The kelpies' ears flattened back and they bared their teeth. I guess they didn't care for my approach. "Look," I said, holding my arms out. "It's been a long night full of creatures acting out of character. I had to blow up several peryton earlier because they . . . well, they started to act like you guys, actually. It was weird. And I'm covered in gore and I'm tired, so believe me when I say I'm not trying to offend you. We just want to find out what's going on, and then we'll be out of your hair or kelp or whatever."

"We can take care of ourselves," the female said.

"You are small and weak." The male flicked his tail. "What could you do that we could not? You are food. That is all."

"Then help us out so we can protect the creatures that aren't strong like you," Lock said.

It was a tactic doomed to fail. You don't appeal to the better nature of kelpies. They don't have one. Or at least, they don't have one for anything that isn't kelpie.

"If you don't tell us," I said, "we'll just keep coming back. Only next time there will be more of us. And we'll be noisy, scaring off all the fish and game."

The male snarled. "You wouldn't."

I shrugged. "I don't want to. I'm basically a lazy person. But our boss wants to find out what's going on in his territory, and to be honest, I'm not comfortable ignoring anything that could flush out the mighty kelpie." When all else fails, flatter.

The kelpies stepped away to confer, and I finally got a good look at their coats in the moonlight. I tipped my head closer to Lock. "Is it just me, or are some of them wearing cardigans?" Lock looked, but his eyesight wasn't much better than mine.

Sid angled in between us. "They are. Those kelpies are definitely wearing cardigans."

"You didn't notice that before? It's stranger behavior than all the other things put together," I said.

"We didn't get this close before," Bianca said in Sid's defense.

Sid slipped his arm around my shoulders. "Believe me, it's something I would have mentioned. Each one is like a tiny horse version of Mr. Rogers." He stifled a guffaw.

"What?" I was almost afraid to ask.

"I was just imagining them as a scary movie poster: *Night of the Kelpies: Won't You Be My Neigh-bor?*" And then he couldn't stifle the laughter anymore and he had to step away. At least one of us was having a good time.

The kelpies returned from their discussion. "Do what you must, but the kelpies will not help you."

They'd called my bluff, and there wasn't really anything I could do. "Okay, I understand. Can I ask about the cardigans, though? How? Why?"

"The reasons we have them are our own." Then the kelpies left. There was nothing to do but hike back to our cars. We were leaving with more questions than we'd had when we walked up, but at least we were still in one piece. Which, when dealing with kelpies, is a definite victory. Still, I couldn't help but think that whatever was bothering the kelpies was eventually going to bother us, and I needed to find out what that was. Soon.

10

COMING OUT—IT'S NOT JUST FOR DEBUTANTES

BY THE TIME we got back to the cabin, I was exhausted. The blood and other bits of peryton had dried, leaving my clothing stiff and scratchy in places, and I smelled. My boots were covered in mud, so I'd had to leave them outside. Veronica and Ezra weren't coming up roses, either.

"Crazed nixie," Ikka said, her nose scrunched up in distaste.

Sid snapped his fingers. "That's the smell I was trying to place." He handed her a laundry basket for her clothes.

"Mean, vicious, rabid nixies," Ikka said, dropping her shoes into the basket. They squished. She was sopping wet.

I went into my room and had to literally peel off some of my clothing. I think a fine layer of skin and hair went with some of it. Bianca, now in my robe and waiting for the shower, had to help.

"Ow!" I glared at her, but she didn't look the slightest bit repentant. "You could be a bit more gentle. Try not to enjoy this so much."

"Yeah, I love touching dried animal guts. Best thing ever." She finished yanking my shirt off. "Don't be such a whiner. It's better to do it fast, like a Band-Aid."

We glared at each other, and for some reason that made us both bust into giggles. After we were done, I shucked myself out of my jeans, throwing them into the laundry basket she held.

"Don't take that the wrong way," Bianca said. "I still don't like you."

"You like me enough to touch animal guts."

"I just don't want the cabin to stink."

"Fair enough." My underwear went into the basket, and I put on Cade's robe. I had found a fragment of antler and bits of feather in my unders. I shuddered. Shower soon. "It can't get worse than this, right?"

Bianca flopped onto the bed. "I'm hoping Alistair is wrong and it slows down."

I rested the laundry basket on my hip, wondering if I should just dump the clothes in the trash. "Is Alistair often wrong?"

"No," she said with a sigh. "Never."

"Great."

THE MORNING arrived too quickly, as it does when you don't get much sleep, and it was met with much grumbling and a side of blueberry pancakes. Sylvie showed up at nine, a container of berries in hand and a smile as big as her face. If she was surprised to find a cabin full of grouchy, bruised, scraped, worn-out people, she didn't show it. Instead, she joined Cade in the kitchen and started making pancake batter while he got the coffee going. We have a decent-size kitchen table, but it wasn't quite big enough for everyone we had over. Ikka and Olive brought in some of the folding chairs from our sugaring shack so we could try to squeeze in. Sid handed out coffee mugs while Sylvie, ever the morning person and happy hostess, began to pour.

Katya, her face wan and her hair in a messy bun, held out her mug wordlessly.

"It's hot," Sylvie warned. "So if you're not going to add cream, I'd give it a minute."

Kat was so tired and out of it, I'm not even sure she heard Sylvie. She huffed a gentle breath over the top of her cup. Frost whirled through the air, and the surface of the coffee froze into a thick layer. Kat set it down, hard. "*Damn.* Overdid it." She grabbed a butter knife and began to chip away at her now-iced coffee, a few quiet tears moving slowly down her cheeks. I remembered this stage of grief. When everything was so raw you cried over the stupidest things, sometimes without even realizing it was happening.

The room became unnaturally quiet, the snap of the bacon and clink of the knife on the ice the only noise as everyone stopped, looking from Sylvie to Katya and back. Even the unflappable Cade sat there, spatula in midair, his mouth a thin line as he thought furiously of a way to spin this. Kat abandoned her knife and glared morosely at her cup.

Sylvie patted Kat's arm. "That's okay. It's just coffee. Ava can fix that for you, can't you, Ava?" My friend hit me with a do-it-now-or-we're-not-friends kind of glare. I hesitated. She couldn't mean what I thought she meant. I looked to Lock for his take, and he shrugged one shoulder, Ezra resting his head on the other as he tried to sneak in a nap. At least I think he was napping. He had sunglasses on.

"I suppose we could..." I trailed off. We could what? We didn't own a microwave.

Sylvie pointed at the offending mug. "Now is not the time for subterfuge." She wiggled her fingers. "So just do your thing and fix it."

"My thing?" I said slowly.

"The fire thing. I don't know what you call it. I tried looking it up. At first I thought it might be pyromancy, but that's used for divination and I don't peg you as the seer type. So you're not exactly pyromantic, which I don't think is a real word anyway. Pyrokinetic maybe? Most of these terms come from video games and D&D, which isn't much help, but it's not like I can do real research. People don't study these sorts of things, I suppose because you all want secrecy, which I get, but it's vexing, you know? And I did try to respect that, or at least give you some opportunities to confide in me, but you were taking your sweet time." She patted Katya's head. "In the meantime, this girl is crying, and I just can't abide that—I can't. So fix her damn coffee or you're not getting any."

Sylvie finally stopped for a breath. Her cheeks were flushed, her eyes narrowed, and she was mad. No, she was frustrated, and Sylvie didn't handle frustration well.

"I don't think I've ever seen you mad," Ezra said, not moving from his spot.

I looked around the room for some kind of help. Everything in me screamed to keep this hidden, to throw Sylvie off the scent, even though it was clear that it was too late for such things.

"And don't go looking to your Super Friends here for assistance. I may not know what they all are, but I know that they know what I know."

Cade gently took the coffeepot from Sylvie. While I had seen Sylvie upset before, it was rare to see Sylvie *this* upset. She didn't anger easy, being the fairly happy-go-lucky type. My instinct may have been screaming at me to hide, but cool logic was telling me two things: One, the jig was up. Two, if I wanted to keep Sylvie as a friend, it was time to come clean. I handed Katya a cloth napkin with one hand, and with the other I tapped the frozen surface of the coffee. The heat released slowly as the ice melted and turned to steam, the coffee warm once again.

Sylvie lowered herself primly into a chair. "Thank you."

"How long have you known?" Lock asked.

"I'm not sure. A while? Her hands sparked once after she had to deal with a customer who yelled at her when we wouldn't buy any of his books. Not a big spark, but I saw it. At first I thought I'd imagined it or something. I read this study once that talked about how when your brain is confronted with something it can't explain, it will make crazy connections and draw false conclusions. Like the people in the 1600s who believed in the spontaneous generation theory—there was this guy who thought you could wrap cheese in rags and it would spontaneously produce mice, because he never saw the mice climb into the rags. As far as he was concerned, they just appeared. It's also why we connect black cats to bad luck. Superstition is brought about by our brain skipping over missing information and building a hypothesis based on that faulty data—"

"Sylvie." Cade had gone back to flipping pancakes and cooking the bacon, but I'd heard him say her name in that tone often enough to know it meant that she needed to get to the point.

"I paid attention after that, and I saw it happen again. Not a lot. You're good at hiding. I thought about taking notes but figured I shouldn't without your permission."

"You're right," I said. "Notes would have been bad."

"Once I realized what was going on with you, it wasn't such a leap to figure out that the rest of your friends probably have something going on as well." She tented her fingers around her mug. "There was just always this intangible wall, this separateness that you kept between me and the rest of your group. At first I thought it was because I'm younger, but that didn't really seem to bother you, and besides, I'm not that much younger. Then I thought maybe you were the kind of girl who wasn't really comfortable with other girls, but then you made more girlfriends. . . ."

Sylvie turned to Lock and said something, but I could no longer hear what she was saying. I felt a hand rest lightly on my shoulder. I was not surprised to see Bianca beside me.

"I've thrown up a quick veil," she said. "No one is paying attention to me—they can still see you, but they can't hear or see me, so don't say anything. Okay?"

I gave a slight nod, disguising it as taking a sip of my coffee.

"You're going to have to call this in to Alistair," she said. I tensed, and I knew Bianca felt it. "Don't panic. Really. I think it will be okay. We all like Sylvie, and whether you believe me yet or not, Alistair is not a monster. I don't think he'll do anything to her, but he does need to know there's a potential security issue."

Another minute nod from me. I didn't like it, but she was right. Alistair had to know that I'd screwed up. I excused myself to use the phone.

The call was short, and once I'd hung up, I returned to my

breakfast. My heart wasn't much in it. I ate, but I don't remember what the pancakes tasted like or how many of them I consumed. After that, the morning was relatively quiet until Alistair arrived with Les and Duncan.

Duncan gave me a bear hug in greeting, something he's been doing my whole life, but for the first time, I hesitated before I returned the hug. I'm not sure he noticed. Or maybe he did and understood. I still hadn't quite forgiven him for his part in the confrontation with Venus. How long would it take me to trust him again? He was the closest thing I had to a grandfather in my life, which made me realize that I did want to forgive him. Someday, hopefully soon. But my heart wasn't quite there yet.

Alistair took Sylvie aside to talk to her while Les and Duncan introduced themselves to Katya. The plan was that she would go live in Duncan's cabin for the moment. I could see that she quickly warmed to the two men, even though they were gruff.

Les was a thick man, short but slabbed with muscle. Black hair hung to his shoulders, and he had either an extreme five o'clock shadow or a very tightly cropped beard. A fine tracery of scars wound around his throat and trailed into his shirt. I'd always wanted to ask about them but had never quite felt comfortable doing so. He wore the leather vest most of the drove wore, the emblem of a scrappy jackrabbit ready to rumble on the back. In short, Les perpetually looked like someone who could start some shit. Still, he had Katya smiling in short order.

Worried about Sylvie, I tuned out the conversation and didn't realize I'd been staring at Les's scars until he said something.

"It's killing you, isn't it?"

"A little."

I could tell Les was trying to decide whether to end my suffering or let me twist. He finally took pity on me. "Becoming
the head of the drove means the old leader must be removed.
Sometimes the leader will step down or die, but mostly leadership shifts because someone challenges the old regime."

"And you had to fight?"

"I had to fight."

"It's all brute force, then?" The drove didn't strike me as the
kind of group to rely only on strength. They were too wily.

He shook his head. "Not really. After the fight, there's a ceremony. If the drove accepts you, they step forward and blow
silver powder into the wounds. It burns like nothing you've ever
imagined, and it isn't a quick thing. It lingers, as it should, so
you don't forget what you just went through—you remember
the cost of what happened. The scars will never fade."

"It's a mark of station?"

"And a mark of acceptance," he said. "Every time I'm challenged, the scars build."

"What happens if they don't accept you?"

Les's voice grew soft. "If you're lucky, they shun you."

"And if you're not lucky?"

"Then there won't be a big enough piece left to bury."

I wanted to reach forward and touch them, to see if I could
feel the heat of the silver. Was it still in there? Did it still bother
him? "Does it still burn?"

"Sometimes."

"Was it worth it?"

"Yes," Les said without hesitation, his voice firm.

It made me wonder what the old leader had been like, for
Les to have gotten that cold, hard look. But I'd already asked

enough personal questions. If on another day Les wanted to tell me, that would be up to him. So I did the mature thing and thanked him, then left to check on Sylvie.

When I entered the kitchen, I found Cade talking to Ikka, his newspaper and coffee forgotten next to him on the counter. Sylvie was gone, off to the bookstore. In a move that I found to be somewhat premature, Cade was talking to Ikka about getting someone from the drove to temporarily handle my workload at the bookshop.

Lock, Bianca, Ezra, and Sid already sat around the table. I plopped down into the seat next to Ezra. To the untrained eye, Alistair looked like he always did—perfectly coiffed and ready to sail his yacht into the sunset. I'd spent enough time around him, though, to see a few telltale signs that the last day or two had been rough. His smile was just a hair tired, his shoulders not as square as they usually were.

"You think it's going to ease up?" Lock asked, his chin resting in his hand. Bianca nudged his shoulder with hers. A tiny childish part of me wanted to shove her out of the way, but I squashed the urge. Lock was allowed other friends. I had to get used to sharing my favorite people. This was the trade-off for getting more friends in our group. Our circle was expanding, and that was great, but it also gave me a flutter of panic deep in my gut. What if all our new friends made Lock and Ezra see that I wasn't that necessary? That I was a burden? Let's face it—I was a bit of a pain in the ass. Would all these new people make them realize they didn't have to deal with the hassle that was my friendship?

Alistair shook his head. "I wish I could say yes, but from all reports it seems to be escalating. We're in a lull right now, but I don't think it will last."

"What reports?" Sid asked. "We didn't get sent any this morning." A hand appeared from below the table, the palm held out flat. Without looking over, Sid placed a cookie into Olive's waiting palm. The hand and the food disappeared. I peeked under the table to see Olive sitting cross-legged, half the cookie already gone. She glared at me, twisting away like I might crawl under the table and take her snack away from her.

Alistair reached into his pocket, removing his phone. It had been vibrating off and on since I walked into the kitchen. He frowned at it before setting it to silent. "You were all spent. I brought in some volunteers from the drove, and Parkin is helping out." That was reassuring. The drove knew what they were doing, and Parkin was a were-rhino. Nobody in their right mind argues with a were-rhino.

"Why outsource?" Cade asked, handing me a small plate of cookies.

"Yeah," I said, sitting back upright. "Doesn't the Inferno already house a lot of people?"

"We still don't know how loyal they are. For all we know, they could be helping whatever's going on," Bianca said.

I frowned. "Is it that bad?" Ezra tried to swipe a cookie from my plate, and I smacked his hand without taking my eyes off Alistair. "Next time, I burn that hand."

"I don't really know," Alistair said, glancing at his phone again. Although it was still in silent mode, even from here I could see that the screen kept lighting up. "We haven't really had time to fully vet everyone. I believe most of the staff we have left is loyal except for a small handful who are pretending. Those people are marked and can be expected to do exactly what's best for them and nothing else. That doesn't mean I would trust any of them with our lives, which is essentially what I have to do with my teams right now." He folded his arms, probably to keep himself from grabbing his phone, though the move looked non-chalant. "Basically, we're still recovering from the shift of power from Venus to me. Repairs are presently being made, but people were lost, and though we've gained some, we're still not a strong and unified force."

"We're afraid someone will use this turmoil to try to stage a takeover," Bianca added.

Ezra yelped, cradling his hand.

"What did I tell you?" I didn't feel too bad singeing his fingers. He would heal.

Alistair reached over and grabbed a few extra cookies from the container on the counter and put them on a plate, sliding them over to Ezra. Far from thanking him, Ezra just stared at the cookies, a thoughtful expression on his face. Alistair's eyebrows tilted up in surprise.

"He thinks it tastes better when he steals it," I said. "So right now he's trying to decide if he's hungry enough to eat what you gave him or if he should keep going for my cookies." I solved the problem by tipping his plate onto mine. Now he'd have to steal them back and he would be happy.

Ezra grabbed my hand and kissed my fingers, holding the hand to his chest. "You really get me."

"You'll still be punished if I catch you," I said.

"If he gets caught, he deserves it," Olive said from under the table.

"Exactly," Ezra said, stuffing a cookie into his mouth. I hadn't seen him take it.

"Fascinating." Alistair settled back into his chair. "To be honest, we don't know if what's happening right now isn't part of someone's, or several someones', various plans to take over. We haven't been able to figure out if this has been an orchestrated attack or if things are just hitting all at once."

"Have we found any common thread between the incidents?" Sid put his arms on the table and rested his chin on his wrists.

Alistair shook his head. "Not yet. Then again, we haven't had much free time to really analyze things, either. For now, rest up. We need you fresh."

ALISTAIR'S PREDICTION rang true. He didn't even make it out the door before his phone went off, and this time he couldn't ignore it. So we were being sent out again. And again. Though the timing of the events appeared random, a vague pattern began to evolve in our days. Sleep—not enough. Fight some things. Burn your clothes. Eat. Nap. Fight more things. Eat. Gag when you find . . . something . . . encrusted under your nails. Shower until the water runs clear instead of green or brown or red, depending on your injuries or what you were covered in. Get so tired, you find yourself actually laughing at Bianca's jokes, followed by surprise that Bianca actually makes them. Rinse. Repeat. Cha cha cha.

We followed this pattern for a solid week. Suddenly Cade's decision to get someone to cover me at the bookstore didn't seem so crazy.

"It's like the entirety of the coast between here and Portland has decided to implode all at once," Lock said, holding an ice pack to his eye. He was going to have a shiner. Ezra finished changing a bandage on one of Bianca's arms while she ate trail mix with the other.

Sid poured coffee into all our empty mugs. "C'mon, every-one. Mug up."

I grumbled, my head resting on the table. "I never thought I'd say this, but I am tired of coffee. Contrary to my earlier hypothesis, it is not, in fact, a replacement for sleep." ·

"You shut your lying mouth." Ezra covered the lower half of my face with his hands. "Such scandalous talk, Ava. I won't have it." I shoved his hands away.

"Well, it's as good as you're going to get anyway." Sid refilled his own cup before replacing the pot.

"We can't keep on like this," Lock said.

"You said that two days ago." Ezra collapsed into a chair, his head lolling back against the top. He looked to be ten seconds from passing out.

"I meant it two days ago." Lock set his ice pack on the table before he put his face on it.

"What are you doing?" Ikka asked, propping herself up with the kitchen counter.

"I'm icing my eye," Lock said. "This way seems much more efficient."

Alistair walked in without knocking, a tube of paper in his hand. All of us except Bianca groaned as he ushered us into the living room. She was just that dedicated to Alistair. Even she made a face, though. We had started to associate Alistair with work, misery, and bad news. Not his fault, I know, but if some-one always shows up during flu season, you start to connect them with chicken soup and throwing up. It's just how the human brain works.

Alistair ignored our complaints. There was a squeaking

sound behind him, and I turned my head to see Olive rolling in a big whiteboard.

Alistair unrolled the paper, which turned out to be a map, and pinned it to the wall. Olive got out numbered pushpins and a sheet of lined paper covered in Alistair's precise and elegantly looping handwriting.

"Are we going to school now?" Ezra asked. "Because I'm almost certain that I graduated."

"You didn't graduate so much as they passed you to get you to leave." Lock sat up, the ice pack left on the table until Bianca scooped it up and made him put it back on his bruise.

"What are you talking about? They loved me there. I was king of the school."

"More like the god of chaos."

Ezra sprawled in his chair, a satisfied look about him. "So you admit I'm a god?"

"Give up, Lock." I tipped some more cream into my coffee.

"I brought this in to help us visualize what's been going on," Alistair said, taking the prudent course of action and ignoring us. "The numbered pushpins correlate to that paper there, which tells us the when, where, and what of each problem." He gestured to the whiteboard. "This is for any notes, ideas, or thoughts."

"Notes?" Ikka asked, pulling herself up straight on the couch.

"What kind of creatures we are dealing with, what their dominating elements are, numbers of victims, and so on." Alistair rubbed the back of his neck. "I've been poring over the information as it comes in, but I still can't see the connection. So I decided some visuals and some new—trusted—eyes would be welcome."

Olive continued to put pins into their respective spots. Alistair grabbed a black marker and started a column for creatures, another for elements, and another for numbers. The kelpies we'd dealt with earlier belonged to the element of water, because that was where their strength lay. Lock, being half-dryad, was earth based. Some creatures were aligned with more than one element. I spent my time on land, but clearly my element was fire as well, which made me a little harder to classify.

We filled in the board, shouting out details as we thought of them. Despite the visuals Alistair was providing, I still wasn't seeing a connection. The creatures were all different. The places seemed diverse. The numbers varied. In fact, the only thing the board seemed to accomplish was the headache I was getting staring at it.

When we were done, Alistair stepped back, hopeful. "Anything?"

"I now hate whiteboards," Sid said.

I grabbed my hairbrush and started on my hair, thinking that I could at least do something useful while we floundered. Ikka got up without me asking and gently pushed me to the floor so she could sit behind me and braid my hair. When Ikka was around, she often took over like this, and it was simultaneously comforting and strange. I was fine watching her throw knives, kick people in the solar plexus, and take on her share of dangerous creatures. But no matter how many times she did it, I was still surprised that she hummed softly and braided my hair with kind hands.

Everyone stared at the board and offered their theories, most of which sounded vague and wrong, but Alistair scrawled them on the board anyway. Ikka had made two braids this time and was pinning them to my head like a crown. It's relaxing, having someone groom you. I can see why monkeys are so into it. I let myself sink into that soothing feeling and let the jumble of information float before my eyes. What did it all have in common? On the face of it, nothing. But maybe I was thinking too specifically. I needed to widen my range, think in a more general fashion. As soon as I did that, a few things emerged.

"Humans," I said.

Alistair turned to me. "What do you mean?"

"Are they having the same problem?" I asked. "I mean, when I look at the board, all the information is so disparate. The only connection is something Lock said earlier—it's like everyone from here to Portland has lost their damn minds."

Alistair tapped the dry-erase marker against his slacks and looked at the board thoughtfully, trying to see what I was talking about.

So I pushed forward, hoping I could make some sense out of it. "But that's not true. Not everyone has lost it—just us. So we're either missing some vital information—like what's going on with the human population—or we're so busy focusing on what's there that we're forgetting what's not there. You know, like Sherlock Holmes. Or the curious incident of the dog in the nighttime."

Everyone blinked at me, and rather surprisingly, Olive spoke up. "The dog didn't bark. That was the clue. Sometimes it's what didn't happen that's important." She'd been quiet this whole time, unobtrusive. When she caught everyone staring at her, she blushed a little. "Ikka read it to me."

Ikka patted my head, letting me know she was finished. Sid was already behind her and taking the brush. I would have offered to help, but Sid was faster. In the drove, everyone helped with everything, and labor wasn't divided so much on gender lines as by whose hands were closest. And they were apparently big on storytime.

Alistair continued examining the board. "You're right, Ava. Either we're missing information, or there's none to miss. My guess would be that there's none to miss, as we haven't stumbled upon any humans in our incidents save for a few that I think can be categorized as in the wrong place at the wrong time, like those bodies we found in the warehouse. I haven't caught anything in the news. It pains me to admit I haven't been focusing on the human world as much as I normally would, so while I think you're correct, we need to look into it. Which means I need to tap some different contacts." One side of his mouth quirked up. "I knew the board was a good idea."

Alistair's phone beeped. All the joy he'd found in the small step forward our session had afforded him leaked out. His features took on a grim cast as he read the text. "Looks like our break is over. Everyone get ready to go." He jotted down notes on two scraps of paper, handing one to Bianca.

The caulbearer was frowning at our paper like it had insulted her mother. "A bar fight? It's ten in the morning! What kind of person gets a buzz on at ten in the morning?"

Alistair smiled at her. "I believe that particular bar opens for brunch, and I'm not sure if the incident actually involves alcohol."

Bianca tucked the paper into her pocket. "It's a fight in a bar. When don't those involve drinking?" Grumbling, she went back to the living room, and I followed. I needed to grab my freshly cleaned boots and my jacket. The weather was supposed to stay in the seventies, but I usually stashed emergency supplies in my jacket. Or at least, I had before Alistair made me destroy that jacket. Well, I would take whatever was hanging in the closet and make do. Alistair had been true to his word on most things, but I was still surprised to see a new light jacket in the closet for me. I fingered the runes on the inside of the cuff. It was warded against fire. For some reason, I found my eyes tearing up as I held the jacket.

"Did you find your new jacket?" Bianca had her head down as she laced up her shoes. "It should fit. Lock gave him your measurements and told him what you liked to have stocked in it, so it should be close to the one we had to get rid of."

The inside of the jacket held several small pockets, and I found electrolyte pills, emergency cash, energy bars, a thin folded knife, plus a few pockets that were open for me to fill. It was even the same army-green color as my old one.

When Bianca came up behind me, I realized I hadn't answered her. "He tried really hard to get it right, Ava, but if you don't like it..." Her tone made it clear that if I didn't like it, I was an ungrateful jerk.

"No, actually. It's perfect." I slipped it on. Why was I getting so emotional over a jacket? Clothes were just there to keep you from the elements and indecent-exposure fines.

Mollified, Bianca grabbed her own summer jacket, which was, shockingly, black. Just like everything else she wore. "Good. He said that if you like it, he could get a few more made. You know, extras and then a few for colder weather."

It wasn't until the jacket was on that I figured out why it was affecting me so much. The jacket made me feel cared for. Venus had always treated us like chattel. We were protected in that we were assets and she didn't want us damaged—the same way you sharpen and oil a good knife. Respect the blade and it will last you a long time. But other than that, she didn't care. Alistair didn't have to replace my jacket, and he didn't have to make sure it was so much like my old one, but he did. Yes, it would help me work more efficiently, and I'm sure he'd thought of that. It wasn't a one hundred percent altruistic gesture. But having it ready and stocked told me that my comfort and safety were also factors for him. And I wasn't sure how I felt about that. The Coterie had always been something to escape. Something to run from. So why didn't it feel like that anymore?

11

WE'LL TAKE OUR
ORDER TO GO

CROUCHED IN A BACK STREET in Portsmouth, the Blue Moon was hard to find if you didn't know where it was. You couldn't tell what it was by looking at it . . . if you could see it at all. We had to go down an alley, through a gate, and then into an open courtyard, and after all that you had to knock on the correct door. Once inside, you were greeted at the hostess stand, which was curtained off from the main area so you couldn't see into the bar. This was done on purpose. Every once in a while, humans found it. They would be told that the establishment was full and then politely encouraged to leave. Since they couldn't see the seating, they couldn't argue. I asked the owner, Manny Ruiz, what happened if the person argued. He said then they were not-so-politely encouraged to leave, usually by one of the bouncers. I eyed the bouncer with us. He looked like someone had tried to make a mountain out of flesh and bone. I certainly wasn't going to start a fight with him.

The bar wasn't usually open for brunch until eleven, but it had opened up early for a special party. The Blue Moon was nice—lots of smooth honey-colored wood, a central fireplace for the winters, and large skylights giving it a bright, open atmosphere. At first glance it looked like any other high-end establishment, but in reality it catered to our kind of crowd, mostly weres. None of the waitstaff was human, for one, and they had a fairly unorthodox menu. Bloodtini, anyone?

"Do you get any humans here at all?" I asked Manny as he ushered us in.

"Not a lot of them," Manny said, throwing a bar towel up on his shoulder. He looked delicate compared with the bouncer, but Manny was probably close to six feet tall. With a runner's build and black hair that was longer on top and slicked back, the sides shaved short, he looked professional and also very young to be running his own establishment. "Most people, if they bring a human in here, it's someone who's like family, someone who's personally invested in keeping our kind under the radar." He grinned then, and though I didn't know what flavor of creature Manny was, he was definitely a predator. His teeth were just a little too sharp. "Besides, the first time they come in, I have a nice chat with them. You know, give them the ground rules. Make sure everything is crystal."

"Does that chat involve you dangling them out a window headfirst or anything like that?" I tried not to smile, but Manny was one of those people who made you grin.

He tilted his head. "You know, it's never really come to that. I just use very small, precise words and give them a warm, friendly smile, and that's about all it takes."

Right. I'd seen that smile. And I bet Manny had Colossus

here with him when the chat happened, too. Most likely they didn't have any problem at all.

While we were making nice, Bianca and Sid were busy scoping out the bar. It was laid for service. Napkins neatly folded. Fresh flowers in vases on the tables. Silverware out. It didn't look like a bar fight had happened. Even the staff was in order.

"Mr. Reynolds," Bianca said to Manny, "we don't want to take up all your time. We know you have to open soon."

Manny took the hint. "Right. That." He tilted his head to the right. "C'mon. I'll show you." He led us into a private dining area. Now *this* looked like the site of a bar fight. The very large, very nice, and probably quite heavy wooden dining room table was upended. The bottom of it was scored by thick gouges—claw marks, from the look of them. The chairs were tipped over, the floor covered in broken glass. Shattered vases and trampled flowers were over by the windows, one of which was broken.

I pointed to the wall. "What's that?" It looked like wrought iron whatever it was.

Manny squinted at it. "I believe that is the handmade stand we use for the champagne bucket."

"I see." The room had probably looked wonderfully elegant this morning. Everything I could piece together in my mind added up to a setup for a rather classy fete. In fact, maybe I could talk Alistair into taking us to a celebratory brunch here after this whole mess was done. And, you know, after they'd cleaned up all the blood. There were spatters on the white linen tablecloth, on the walls, and on the floor. No large pools or anything, just a lot of spray, like someone had nicked an artery . . . or been airborne at some point.

"Any casualties?" Sid asked.

Manny shook his head. "We had to call in a doctor. Coterie approved, of course. Lives up the road apiece. Lots of serious injuries. But we locked the guy down pretty quick. Still, it was crazy."

"So it was only one person?" Bianca asked.

"Yeah. Name's Howie. Nice guy. Been in a few times. Usually quiet. Never been a problem."

Sid's eyes followed a particularly fine spray across the ceiling. "Looks like he's a problem now."

Manny dug his hands into his pockets. "Yeah." He sighed. "Everything's stove up. You know, I can't get Mick's out here for a week? A whole week of lost income. This room was booked solid. People aren't going to like rescheduling. Can't risk bringing in a human crew, though."

Sid borrowed a pen and paper and wrote down a number for Manny. "You don't really need a cleaner if there are no residual spells or anything and no bodies to dispose of. Just a discreet construction crew. Call this number, ask for Felicity. Small crew from our neck of the woods. They won't be booked out like Mick is right now. They're not as high-profile. Quick, solid work. Tell her I sent you." He handed the pen and paper to Manny.

He took it, folding the number neatly and putting it in his pocket. "She like you?"

Sid stiffened. "Yeah, she's like me. In fact, she's my cousin. And she's wicked good with a hammer. You give her any shit, she'll bring it down. Then the rest of the drove will descend to clean up what's left, you get me? So watch your manners."

Manny's smile was slow and lazy. "I like you guys. Funny." He shook his head. "No one said you guys were funny. Don't worry. If she can clean this mess up fast, I'll kiss her feet and call her a queen." He kicked a piece of broken chair. "Come on, I'll show you Howie."

The boys led the way back into the hallway, and I hung back, making eye contact with Bianca. "Cat?" I mouthed, making little finger ears.

She nodded slowly, mouthing back, "I think so." Then she snorted. "It would explain the attitude."

Manny led us into the kitchens. Even though the bar wasn't quite open yet, the kitchen was busy. Prep cooks were chopping and making sauces; the head chef walked around with a clipboard, checking inventory. Waitstaff darted about, grabbing this and that. Everyone made sure to stay out of Manny's way.

We stopped in front of an industrial-size freezer that was flanked by two more gigantic bouncers, one of them the tallest and strongest-looking woman I'd ever seen. Where did Manny find these giants? Did he have them imported from some huge country, or were they clones of some sort? I noticed that the freezer had dents in the door. Dents pointing out.

I pointed at them. "Were those here yesterday?"

"Nope," Manny said, grasping the handle. "That's all Howie." He paused before he opened the door. "Seems to have calmed down a little. At least, he stopped punching the walls. Ready?" He cracked opened the door without waiting for us to answer and swung it open slowly.

I'm not sure how Howie looked earlier, but he didn't look good now. When weres have been fighting, you can't tell the way you usually would with people. They heal too fast. You have to look for secondary signs. Torn clothing, bloodstains, and so on. Howie was a mess. His clothes were torn and bloody. His hair was wild, like he'd been running his hands through it. The skin around his knuckles was pink and fresh, so he hadn't stopped punching the walls until fairly recently. Manny had more to worry about than just his dining room. Howie had gone on some sort of spree in here. Grated cheese dusted the floor. Boxes were turned over and ripped up. Whole chickens and turkeys were tossed around, their pale carcasses eviscerated.

"Glad I didn't put him in the fridge," Manny said. "We just got a shipment of Kobe beef in there."

Howie was hunched in a corner, surrounded by torn-open boxes of butter pats and freezer jam. He looked feral and moderately hypothermic.

"I think the cold slowed him down." Bianca cupped her hands by her face and blew into them for warmth. I could see my breath even though we were by the open door.

I poked Sid. "He remind you of anybody?"

Sid moved to the side, watching Howie. Then he moved to the other side. Howie may have been half-frozen, but his eyes tracked Sid. Mad but aware. "He reminds me of our warehouse friend."

"He does look a bit peaked." Bianca pulled out her phone and dialed. "Which means that despite our care, this problem followed us from Portland."

"Or it was already here," I said.

Bianca shook her head. "Either way, Alistair isn't going to be happy."

Alistair didn't want us to bring Howie back to the Inferno. If Howie had caught or been infected with whatever had driven Elias Johnson to Crazy Town, he didn't want it that close. But he didn't want Howie destroyed, either. With the hypothermia,

Howie's frenzied state had been slowed. He was an ideal specimen for Dr. Wesley to study. We had an opportunity to bring him in safely, or as safe as we were going to get, and we couldn't pass it up.

So we shut the door and waited for Alistair's people in plastic suits to show up. It was tempting to sit down and rest, but it didn't seem right. And I knew that if I sat down for too long, I'd curl up and take a nap. So we left the bouncers in charge of guarding the freezer door, warning them not to open it for anyone but the people in hazmat suits, no matter what. We also had to make sure that the food the cooks had been preparing was not from the freezer or that it had been removed before Howie had been tossed in. The chef assured us that he'd check in with the prep cooks and make sure.

That done, we headed back to the dining room to clean up. Manny gave us gloves, and Sid found a shovel and some brooms. We righted the table with the help of a few waiters and then started stacking the furniture that looked salvageable in one corner. Bianca and I swept up the glass and bigger debris, while Sid shoveled it into a garbage can. We managed to make a small dent in the mess before the hazmat team showed up. Unfortunately, all that the cleaning really did was reveal more damage. The wood floor had been scraped to hell under the table. It would have to be refinished, and we discovered more wall dents and a few broken fixtures.

Once Alistair's team had sedated and collected Howie, we were free to leave. We piled our tools by the door in the ruined dining room and got ready to leave.

"Sorry we didn't help much," I told Manny.

He dried his hands on a bar towel and flipped it back onto

his shoulder. "You got that guy out of here and helped clean up the dining room. And your boy here got me in touch with Felicity. She's already on her way with her team." He clapped me on the shoulder. "You guys did good. Never met a Coterie team that would help with the dirty work, you know? We're grateful." One of the waiters came out with to-go boxes. "I'm sending some food home with you guys as a thank-you." Manny shook his head. "You're welcome here anytime. Tell your boss that, too. Never thought I'd see the day that I'd be saying *that* to a Coterie team."

We thanked him for the food and promised to pass on his invite to Alistair. Manny was right. I never thought I'd see the day when the Coterie got that kind of welcome, either. A few months ago, we were a necessary evil called in when the crap you were facing needed the biggest weapon you could muster. Had Alistair really changed the organization that much, that fast? Or was it all an illusion? A false sense of calm to coax in the reluctant mouse?

IT WAS NICE getting back to the cabin and not feeling like I needed two showers and the utter destruction of everything I was wearing. I had to wipe some plaster dust off my face and do a quick washing-up, but that was it. Sid spread the food out on the table and texted everyone to let them know we had a feast waiting. We were the first team back. Either that or the other teams had already been back and then sent out again. With just Sid, Bianca, and me, it was quiet.

I kicked off my boots and collapsed on the couch to watch TV. I was too tired to read, though I missed it. TV's nice, but there's just something about a book.

Sid nudged me over, sprawling out on the other half of the sofa. He had an untouched chicken leg in his hand.

"Shouldn't you be vegetarian?" I asked. I prodded him until he gave me more room. "You know, being a hare and all."

Sid took a big bite out of his drumstick. "You forget. Human. Omnivores." He took another bite, tearing the chicken with his teeth.

"You'd better not be on my bed," Bianca yelled from the kitchen. Since she'd been sleeping on the couch, she'd become a little proprietary about it. I heard her enter the living room, but she didn't come over.

"C'mon, Bianca. Joooooin us," Sid called.

"Yeah, what are you doing, anyway?" I asked. I didn't particularly care if Bianca joined us or not. I had to admit that my bone-deep dislike of her had been waning the more we worked together, but that didn't mean I wanted to hang out all the time. Still, I could be friendly.

"Adding our info to the board, you lazy bums."

"I'm not a bum," Sid said.

"You live in a tent." The marker squeaked as she wrote everything down on the board.

"I live in a caravan," Sid corrected with a superior lilt to his tone.

I snorted. "You live in a trailer with your sister on someone else's land. That's not much better."

Bianca twisted away from the board, her smile so big, I could see a dimple in one cheek. "You live with your sister?"

Sid frowned, clearly not liking our tone. "Look, it's different for us. The drove likes to stay together, and until recently we lived on the go. Works better for our kind. Think of it as a cultural lifestyle choice." He scooted over to make room for Bianca, pushing me to the edge of the couch. It was my couch. Why was I getting squished? But I didn't complain. Sid was used to a lot of people and a lot of companionship. This week had probably been difficult for him. Whereas I was used to a lot of alone time, so my stress was in the other direction.

After a brief hesitation, Bianca joined us, though she chose to sit rather than sprawl. "Okay, but if I'm going to join you, we have to find something we all like. No reality TV. And I hate laugh tracks."

I grabbed the remote and found a nature documentary on bats. We took a vote and all decided that bats were cool, so we stayed on that channel. Less than five minutes passed before Bianca was stretched out next to us. Sid leaned forward, placing his chicken bone on the coffee table, promising to dispose of it as soon as he got up. No one talked as we watched, and it was one of the most relaxing moments I'd had in a while. I hadn't realized exactly how keyed up I'd been. First with the Lock and Ezra tension, then the Sylvie thing, followed by all this mess. With the exception of passing out the second I hit the mattress for naps, this was the closest thing to resting that I'd had in over a week.

So of course it couldn't last. We were right in the middle of a disturbing part where the commentator was talking about white-nose syndrome, a fungus killing off millions of brown bats. It was spreading so fast, they were having a hard time dealing with it. Which meant a lot more bugs in my hometown, without the bats to eat them, and a fading good mood in our room, because we were all so fond of the little flying fuzzballs. That's when Bianca's phone went off, followed quickly by mine and Sid's. I have to be the only person my age who would love to not have a cell phone. Sure, they're convenient at times, but the problem with them is that someone can always find you. Bianca was the first up, as usual. Always ready and willing to jump to as far as Alistair was concerned. Sid and I were understandably less enthusiastic.

The plight of the brown hat would just have to wait.

12

CARELESS WHISPERS—
PLANT EDITION

WE WEREN'T GONE LONG. Alistair just sent us out to burn down a building that wasn't worth the cleanup costs. Apparently the insurance was worth more than the building would have been even after we'd cleaned it, and with everything going haywire like it was, he had to cut some of his losses. Plus, there was no way we could explain away those kinds of bodies.

Back at the cabin, I kicked my boots off and watched as Lock added more info to our board. "Who imports ushi-oni? What possible reasoning could they have to do such a thing?"

"Maybe they're cute as babies," Ezra said, removing his own shoes.

"They have the head of an ox and a spider body. There is no way they have cute babies." I tugged at one of my laces, then realized I'd melted them together and that I'd have to cut my way out of them.

"Even possums have adorable baby possums, and the adults

are hideous. It's possible," Lock said, intent on the board as he added notes.

If this kept up, we'd have to get another board. My phone beeped with a text from Sylvie. It was a photo of the whoopie pies that she'd made and brought into the bookstore. Whoopie pies that I would be eating if I were at work like I should have been.

I slumped in my chair. "I hate everything."

"What I love about you, cupcake, is your undeniable optimism."

"I'll show you optimism right up the side of your head."

"So violent," Ezra murmured. He stretched his legs onto my lap. "I don't think I've ever been this tired. A stunning creature was giving me the eyes earlier, and I couldn't even be bothered to flirt back. I think I might be dead. Ava, my little plum blossom, I want to be cremated. Remember that."

"If you die on me now, I'll scatter your ashes in the Playboy Mansion." I grabbed his leg, the one that had been injured, and rubbed it down for him.

"You wouldn't dare."

Sid lay spread-eagled on the floor because apparently a bed was simply too far away and he was too tired to shift into a hare and curl up by the fireplace. "I would think you'd like the Playboy Mansion."

Ezra sniffed. "The dream of frat boys and men with no imagination. Not interested. I plan to go out with some class."

I patted Ezra's leg. "Not to make you feel worse, but Sylvie just sent me a picture of the whoopie pies she made." I'm not sure what Ezra's favorite thing in the world is, but whoopie pies are high on the list.

He sat up quickly and held out his hand. "Give me your phone."

I leaned away from him. "Get your own phone." You don't hand things over to Ezra if you expect to ever get them back, though the way things were going, I was severely tempted to give it to him.

Ezra snapped his fingers at me a few times. "It's charging. C'mon. It's an emergency."

Knowing I'd probably regret it, I handed him my cell. He immediately typed in my key code (which I hadn't told him, by the way) and hit a few more buttons. "No, this is Ezra. How many did you make? And can you describe the smell to me?" I could hear the murmur of Sylvie's voice on the other line, but not what she said. "Look," Ezra said, cutting her off. "That's great. Here's what you need to do. Drive to Ava's right now. I'll pay you. Cash. And gas money. My soul. I *need* them, Sylvie!"

I could hear her laugh. Then Ezra went back to wheedling.

"If she's smart," Lock said, "she'll wait until he offers her his car."

"Even Ezra's not that desperate."

"I will give you my car!" Ezra shouted into the phone.

"Great, Lock, now you're giving him ideas." I shoved Ezra's feet off of me, forcing him to sit up. Lock capped the dry-erase marker and put it away. I stared at the info on the board and knew I'd forgotten something. What was it? I was sure that if I stopped thinking about it, I'd be more likely to remember, but thinking that always makes it that much harder to stop thinking. Something about . . .

"Sylvie, come on! You're killing me."

Something about Sylvie. Sweaters! I snatched my phone from Ezra, then smacked his hand as he reached to grab it back. I'm afraid the slap fight went on longer than it should have. Lock had to intervene by sitting on Ezra.

"Sylvie," I said, slipping off the couch to get away from the boys, who were now wrestling.

"Ava! Are you coming back soon? It's not that I don't like the extra money, but I'd also like a day off."

"Didn't Cade find a few helpers to come in?"

"Fine, I'm just bored and I miss you guys. Also, this is not how I saw my summer unraveling."

"Ugh, sorry, Sylvie. I'm kind of stuck for now. I owe you big-time."

"Yes, you do. I see a lot of puppets in your future as you help me make *Godzilla, the Musical!* a reality."

"I don't think the third act is ready." (It wasn't. Godzilla's roaring soliloquy went on way too long.)

"I've been working on it."

"Sylvie, I kind of have a weird question for you."

There was a scraping noise as she switched the phone to her other ear. "Weird questions are my absolute favorite."

"It's about those cardigans you were knitting."

"Cardigans?" She sounded cagey, and I knew instantly that my suspicions were correct. I wouldn't have considered it a few days ago, not really. But now I knew that Sylvie had some insider knowledge. Add that to her bizarre knitting project, and it was just too much to be a coincidence.

"Yes, your secret knitting project for charity."

"I'm afraid I can't disclose any information on that particular venture. Ava, I think I hear my mom calling me."

"No you don't, Sylvie. I know you're at the store. The thing is, I met some kelpies the other night."

"Kelpies?" her voice squeaked.

"Yeah, you know, murderous creatures that look like harmless Shetland ponies? They were wearing cardigans just like those odd-shaped ones you've been knitting. It's kind of weird because they were on creatures you weren't supposed to know about. But I'm starting to think that you know exactly what I'm talking about." Silence greeted me on the other end.

I had her. I could tell. And I was thinking now would be a good time to get someone to cover Sylvie's shift for once. "I'll explain when I get there, but for now I need you to tell your mom you're coming over to stay at my house for a few days. Summer sleepover, okay? We'll pick you up in half an hour. You can borrow clothes from me."

"Your clothes won't fit me," she argued, a note of desperation evident in her voice.

"Then we'll make a pit stop at your place."

Ezra raised his hands in prayer, and I took pity on him. "And would you please bring some whoopie pies?"

"I don't know." Sylvie didn't sound completely comfortable with my idea. "That might be a strain on the bookstore. All those new people . . ."

"The bookstore will survive. Cade's there, anyway. And don't worry, I promise this is a mission for good. Oh, and pack those cardigans and your knitting stuff, just in case."

She hesitated before she finally said, "You sure this is a good idea?"

"About as sure as I am of any of my ideas, which means not really, but you should do it anyway."

"Fine," Sylvie said. "I'll do it. For science. Also for you, but mostly for science." We said our good-byes, and then I hung up so I could set everything else into motion.

Ikka called her cousins to make sure the bookstore would be covered. As I suspected, it didn't take much more than that. After the big blowup in the spring, Cade had been spending time with Duncan. And since the drove was almost fanatically devoted to Duncan, and Cade was like a son to him, they'd opened up their family umbrella to include my guardian. I mean dad.

After that, I called Alistair and caught him up. I could almost see him—hair slightly askew, maybe a few buttons on his dress shirt unbuttoned and his slacks wrinkled. He sounded that tired. Or at least, tired for Alistair.

"You want to run that by me again?"

I went over the kelpie information again and the connection I thought was there. "Look, when I asked her on the phone, she got evasive. That's not normal Sylvie. The kelpies were really attached to those cardigans. I'm not sure what's so special about them or what they do, but I think they're more than a status symbol. Kelpies aren't concerned with appearances. So those sweaters must be handy to them."

The silence that greeted me meant Alistair was actually listening to what I said. After years of Venus, it was still so weird.

"So you're thinking that you can barter with them. Trade the cardigans for info."

"Yes."

"You want to try to make a deal with deadly fairy horses that eat people." He said it slowly, like he wasn't sure I understood what he was saying. Or as if I had lost my marbles.

"You got it, hoss."

"It is a sign of my desperation that I am even considering this."

"Alistair, we're worn out and things aren't slowing down. If we don't do something to get ahead of this . . ."

"Yes, I know. My reign will be shorter than that of the Spanish king Louis I."

I hesitated. "Yes?"

"He was king for about seven months before he died of smallpox."

"Oh. Okay, yes. Shorter than that, but with less smallpox."

"Take someone with you. Someone Sylvie knows. Ezra or Lock. Whoever needs the break more. Tell the rest I'll be sending assignments soon. And, Ava? I know you'll be tempted to dawdle, and it's not that I don't understand . . ."

"But you need me to haul ass back to base."

"Yes, that, exactly. But I would say it more politely."

I waffled between who to take. Riding with Lock might be awkward, because he might want to talk about *feelings*, and to be honest I was kind of worn out on the whole emotions thing. But if I took Ezra, he would want to talk about whoopie pies the whole time. Which is cute for about three minutes, and then I would want to shove him out of the car at full speed.

I took Lock.

It's not a long drive from the cabin to the store. It's longer if you're able to sweet-talk the driver into stopping at the Freeman's Dairy Barn stand for ice cream because, hey, a firebug's got to eat and Lock can stand my puppy dog eyes for only so long, though I know that when he caves I'll be on the receiving end of such glares as "that is not proper nutrition" and "even though you don't have to worry about weight gain, think of your arteries." He'd slowed down on those looks after our battle with Venus. I'd overextended my reach, and if Lock hadn't stopped me, I would have gone nova. You don't want to be around a firebug when one of us goes. We destroy not only ourselves but also everything in a fairly large radius. It's not pretty. So when I got a double scoop, sprinkles *and* jimmies, he kept his comments to himself.

I'd burned a lot of fat and muscle in the process of fighting Venus. I could see my collarbones and hip bones when I came to afterward. So for a bit, he paused the discussion of my poor eating habits until I put the weight back on. He was really worried, and Ezra was so anxious about it, he even offered to share some of his lobster roll with me once. It's not that Ezra doesn't share, it's just that he expects you to snag some without asking. It's the fox way. So if he was actually offering, then that meant things were quite dire.

I neatly avoided talking about anything of import by passing out in a sugar-induced haze. Hey, it had been a long couple of weeks. I didn't wake up until we reached Broken Spines. Sylvie was waiting for us, sitting under Horatio's tree with her knitting.

Cade greeted me when I came in, emerging from the back of the store. He handed me a handful of paperbacks. "These came in while you were gone. I thought you might like them. I know you've read the first two, but sometimes rereading can be soothing." He held them out to me, and I took them and set them on the counter, right before I tackled him in a bear hug.

"You've been worried."

"Out of my skull," Cade said. "I know you have a team of people around you to protect you, and I know you can take care of yourself, but, well, you're still my girl. Somewhere in my mind, I think no one can protect you like I can, even though I know that's ridiculous. What good would I be in a fight?"

I hugged him tighter. "You'd be plenty good. I can tell."

"Thanks, Rat," he said, letting me go. "But I'm a reader, not a fighter."

"You could throw books at them," I said, tucking one of the smaller paperbacks into my jacket pocket. "Big, thick hardcovers. Those would smart."

After we made our good-byes, we escorted Sylvie out to the van. She'd talked her dad into dropping off a duffel bag with her toothbrush and some clothes so we wouldn't even have to stop by her place.

It was a little uncomfortable seeing her after the big firebug reveal. I leaned on the car door while Lock helped Sylvie with her bags. We stared at each other, unsure what to say. Then she lifted up a Tupperware container. "I brought whoopie pies." Her cheeks pinked. "And the knitting stuff. Ava, I . . ." She hunched her shoulders.

I took the container from her. "Thank you for doing this. It really will help. And I'm glad I don't have to hide from you anymore." Her eyes lit up, but I covered her mouth with one hand before she could open it. "And I know you have questions. We have a short drive ahead of us. I will answer a few, but I don't want the ride to turn into an interrogation. We have more important things to focus on." She mumbled something into my palm. "I don't care if it's for science or not." She scrunched her nose up in irritation.

We climbed into Lock's minivan, Sylvie sitting behind me. I looked in the rearview mirror and saw her eyes light up again. "So what can you do, Lock? Can I ask? I know you can do something. Don't hold out on me. Ava's being her usual stingy self, but I know you'll talk to me." She cracked open the container and handed him a whoopie pie. He ate it one-handed while he backed out of her driveway. "I'm not above bribery."

"Hey! I never got offered a bribe," I said.

She squinted at me. "You never gave me the chance."

Lock laughed. "Good to see you, too, Sylvie. Wait until we get to the cabin, and I'll show you." I caught the twinkle in his eyes—he knew this would drive her crazy. So out of pity I spent the entire ride distracting Sylvie by giving her a quick overview of what had happened with Venus.

"Okay, so let me see if I've got this straight. You, Lock, and Ezra have been working for Alistair's group, the Coterie. Only, it used to belong to Venus, who was an evil bloodsucker. Ryan, your pretty but clearly deranged ex-boyfriend, spied on you and tried to hand you over to Venus. He was, in fact, dating you on her orders." Her fingers tapped the seat as she spoke. "Which makes him *a bad man*. Venus kidnapped Cade, and you all went to rescue him, burning down most of an island and nearly killing all yourselves in the process. Would you say that's a fairly accurate summary?"

"I would say, yes." I poked the air-conditioning vent so that it blew directly into my face. I was really starting to love Lock's new mom van.

Sylvie's fingers stilled. "There's one thing I still don't get."

"And what would that be?" I asked as Lock growled at the driver in front of us for going ten miles per hour under the speed limit. They were busy getting an eyeful of the landscape. If Sylvie and I were playing a game of Spot the Flatlander, I could have claimed five points.

"I understand why you broke up with Ryan and everything else, but if Lock saved your life and all that, why were you guys fighting?"

The air in the van instantly became weighted. My throat went dry, and I was suddenly as into the landscape as the summer people were.

Sylvie touched my shoulder. "Wait, is this because he asked you out and you said no?"

Lock turned his frown on me before swinging his attention back to the road. "You told her I asked you out and that you said no?" He glanced back at Sylvie in the rearview mirror. "Is that what she told you?"

Sylvie tipped her hand in a "kind of" motion. "She said you asked her out but that went poorly. Ava was pretty vague."

Lock snorted, relaxing. "Went poorly. Yeah, you could say that. Ava became the human avatar for panic."

"I wasn't that bad!"

Lock's expression said otherwise. He opened his mouth, and I jabbed the button for the stereo. "You know what? We're going to listen to the radio now." And then I turned the volume up so high, the van started to vibrate.

I couldn't hear Lock now, but he said something to Sylvie anyway, and I'm pretty sure it was "Just like that."

That's when I noticed that in my haste to turn on the radio, I'd melted the knobs and it was now stuck on NPR. You haven't really heard Garrison Keillor until you've heard him at an ear-splitting decibel.

By the time we made it to the cabin, I had a slight headache. Lock paused outside our door. A shrub squatted to the side, wilted and dry from our lack of rain. It had been a dry summer so far. Lock held a hand out and spoke to it in a coaxing voice. It stretched out to touch him, swaying in a phantom breeze. New shoots unfurled and a few buds opened. Lock fetched it some water from our almost empty rain barrel.

Sylvie's face was aglow, like she'd just witnessed Hercules fighting the Hydra. "He's a plant whisperer!"

"He's a dryad," I corrected. "At least, he is on his mom's side. And before you ask, if Ezra wants to do the reveal for you, that's up to him. In the meantime, why don't you harass Lock with twenty questions." She skittered off, shouting questions as she went. Lock, for his part, seemed good-natured about the whole thing.

13

WHEELIN' AND DEALIN'

THE CABIN WAS EMPTY when we entered, but there were signs of occupation everywhere. Various-size clothes hung from the line strung in the backyard. Extra boots and shoes were drying on the porch. The dreaded whiteboard took up a great deal of space as well. I couldn't wait until this was all over and I could get my territory back. Growing up, I'd never had a room to call my own, and now that I did I'd found that I was very territorial over it.

Sylvie was already so spun out on new information that she was practically vibrating. I had to make a deal with her, lest she drive me to distraction and make me do something I'd regret. So we decided on a trade of information. She could ask us a few questions, and Lock or I would answer to the best of our ability. If it was a question we couldn't answer because we didn't know or because it involved someone else's secrets, then that question didn't count. As a gesture of goodwill, I let her ask a bunch of questions first. Not only did this make Sylvie happy, but it also had the added bonus of getting her focused. If I'd tried to ask my questions first, Sylvie would have been all over the place because she'd have been too busy thinking of the questions she wanted to ask. That's just how Sylvie and her giant brain work.

Surprisingly, most of her questions were Lock based. Well, not too shocking, because she thought Lock was ultra dreamy (her words, not mine), but that wasn't why. She simply thought my power was kind of boring, which was new. People are usually excited by what I can do. Fire is like that. Start a bonfire and watch people flock like dazed moths.

But Sylvie was pretty much over it. "So, do they call you a green man, like in all those hippie pagan books my mom has? Are you actually green? Do you have your own tree? I read somewhere that dryads can't leave their trees. Is that true? If it is, how come you can leave yours?" Lock politely answered the first twenty before he started to shoot me looks of desperation.

I took pity on him. "Sylvie, give Lock a break. It's our turn anyway."

She folded her hands and waited expectantly.

"First, about you figuring me out. I mean, even if you heard or saw something, most people would have shrugged it off or decided it was sleight of hand. Not many would take the leap to firebug."

"I suppose not." She twisted the ring on her finger while she decided how to answer my question. "I've known about the hidden world for quite a while, though, if that's what you mean. My uncle Tim married a siren. Well, half-siren, I guess. I think her dad was human. I'm not sure it matters anyway. She's really nice, though she can never join us for caroling, and there was that one unfortunate incident where she sang the happy birth-day song and no one remembers the last two hours of Grandma Hildy's birthday party. Do you know how unsettling it is to not know whether you had cake or not? I had another piece just in case and got a stomachache."

"Can't say I've ever had that problem." I could see Lock strug-gling not to laugh. It's hard to keep up with Sylvie sometimes.

"Well, it's really weird. Anyway, she's pretty awesome. She was terrific help during the marine biology unit at school. I've met some pretty neat people through her. Only I'm sure not all of them are actually people. They wear things to help make them appear human. Aunt Fiona has a necklace that she wears, kind of like the ones you guys have, only the symbol is different."

Lock glanced at me. Lock and Ezra both wore anti-fire charms around their necks. Silver for Lock, platinum for Ezra due to weres' silver allergy. They were small—about the size of a Scrabble tile. The boys were usually good about hiding their wards, but apparently not good enough. Or we hadn't been wor-ried about it around Sylvie. Not that it mattered now, but it was a security breach, and one we'd have to watch in the future. Not everyone took things as well as Sylvie did.

"And that's how the knitting thing came about."

I must have spaced out and missed some of what she said. Then again, maybe not. Sylvie was pretty handy with the non sequitur. "How was that?"

"Aunt Fi was having kelpie problems. One had moved into the stream she liked to frequent. Kelpies eat a lot, and one mov-ing into your ecosystem can be rough if you share the same dietary needs. So she, my aunt Fi, thought it might be good if the kelpie spent less time in the water hunting. But they dry out, you know? And so they have to return to the water pretty frequently." ;

"Skip to the end, Sylvie."

"I'm putting 'skip to the end' on your tombstone, cupcake," Lock said.

"I just don't like to dawdle, conversation-wise." I motioned for Sylvie to speed it up.

"So like I was saying, kelpies need to stay damp, like frogs, only with more fur."

More fur? Were there furry frogs?

"So this kelpie, it was eating up all my aunt's favorite snack. Which made her grouchy. I guess I would be upset if someone did that to me—like when my dad finds my stash of chocolate and eats it all. But then I thought, well, kelpies are sort of like sharks—they scare people and eat a lot, but they're still a necessary part of the ecosystem." Sylvie pulled her knitting bag onto her lap. "I overheard my aunt talking about the problem with one of her friends—a witch, I guess." Sylvie paused and thought for a moment. "Are there different kinds of witches?"

"Yes," Lock said. "While some powers overlap, they tend to specialize in the magic that is strongest in them."

"Can they specialize in symbols? Like your necklaces?"

I nodded. "So your aunt's friend was like that? A rune witch?"

"I'm not sure. Just a guess. But they were talking about creating something for the kelpies to help them stay moist so they could spend more time on land. They'd been experimenting with a charmed necklace, but it wasn't working well. So I asked them if it had to be jewelry." She held up a skein of yarn. "The thing about this cotton is that it's absorbent. It already wants to hold on to the water. So I asked if we could make something out of this. The witch spelled the yarn and made up a pattern for me to follow that had runes in it, and I tweaked the pattern so the kelpies could easily wear it. Since the cotton naturally absorbs, there was less stress on the spell." She showed me the cardigan she was working on. "They can wear it in either form and they can spread farther onto land so they have longer to hunt. It means less stress on the water resources and my aunt gets to eat her fish in peace." She put the stuff away. "So why the sudden interest?"

"There's been some trouble. Lots of creatures acting weird. We met some kelpies who had formed a herd, which was strange. Your sweaters appear to be working, though. They were all out of the water and feeding when we met them." I would have to point that out to Alistair.

Lock opened up some windows to let the air in, making sure the screens were firmly in place when he did. "Ava noticed that some of them had sweaters on and thought they looked familiar. We were hoping to maybe trade one or two of your cardigans for some information. Something has the kelpies spooked, and we need to know if that thing is what's been causing all our problems."

"At the very least it could rule some options out."

Sylvie pushed to the edge of her seat so she could see us better. "I don't know how much help I'll be. I've already handed off any completed ones. There's the half-finished one I'm working on. I think I can persuade my aunt and her friend to part with it, but it's still a lot of work, Ava, and time consuming. I'm not sure you're going to have much to offer."

"I'll think of something. We're pretty good at winging it."

Lock closed his eyes and gently smacked the back of his head against the wall. He hates when I wing it.

Kelpies are nocturnal. It's not that they're always asleep during the day; it's just that hunting is better at night. It's harder to look closely at the adorable pony in the dark. Humans have poor night vision compared with a lot of things out in the evening, and by the time they notice the jagged teeth, the seaweed mane, it's too late. If they notice at all. Also, from what I know about kelpies, I'm pretty sure they hate morning people, except as a breakfast food.

BIANCA AND EZRA joined us and we met Alistair at Androscoggin Riverlands. The kelpies had moved farther inland, munching their way through the buffet that was the marshland by the river.

Lock was worried about that. "This many kelpies converging here, it's going to trip up the local ecosystem. We need to get them back to their habitat."

"Yeah," I said, stepping delicately around some rotting wood. "So they can ruin that ecosystem."

"That's not nice, Ava." Sylvie tromped behind us, her knitting bag clutched to her chest.

"Nice or not, it's true. They came over from Scotland— whether they hitched a ride on a freighter or whether some dumbass smuggled them over, no one knows. But they're invasive, Sylvie. There's nothing out here that eats kelpies." Lock caught Sylvie as she stumbled over something and helped her right herself. "The only thing keeping us from being neck deep in killer sea ponies is their low birthrate and territorial fights. The biggest danger to a kelpie is another kelpie. Until now. Whatever is going on, it's bringing them together. And honestly, that's not good."

"Did my sweaters make them herd like this? Would the runes change their behavior?" Sylvie asked. "Is this my fault?"

"No, Sylvie," I said firmly, stopping as I startled a frog. "While your sweaters have made it easier for them to gather on land, you didn't make them gather in the first place. Something is scaring them. That's our guess, anyway."

We found Alistair waiting on the trail, looking like he engaged in clandestine meetings in the woods every day. I guess he probably did. Ezra was complaining about the walk, the bugs, the temperature, and whatever else he felt like complaining about. He is, at heart, a woodland creature, but only when he's in fox form. In human form he prefers a more lounge-ready atmosphere.

"You sound like the summer people," Sylvie chastised Ezra. She held out her hand. Being a bright and sensible creature, she had brought a single whoopie pie with her, which she immediately shoved into Ezra's hands when the whining hit peak levels. His eyes glinted in the moonlight. He flung one arm around Sylvie and picked her up, swinging her around. She let out an "eep!" and lost her knitting bag. Ezra gave her a big kiss on the cheek.

"You have brought me manna from heaven, and for that I am eternally grateful." He finally let Sylvie find her feet. I handed her the discarded knitting bag. He doesn't do it often, but when Ezra does thank someone, he does it properly.

As we walked over to where the kelpies were feasting, Sylvie explained the cardigan thing to Alistair. I wasn't really listening to what she said, letting her excited words flow over me and occasionally smiling at her wild hand gestures. Sylvie gets very excited about new ideas. Sometimes her brain spins so fast, I feel like the hamster wheel might become unhinged and fly out of her skull.

The moon was fat and bright, so the thoughtful expression on Alistair's face was easy to catch. I wondered how much of it was aimed at the sweaters and how much was for Sylvie herself. Alistair didn't waste good resources. He wasn't going to run around telling humans about us for recruiting purposes, but he certainly wasn't above taking advantage of a human who was already aware. Not to mention that Sylvie seemed to take it all in stride. Heck, she reveled in it, enjoying the new information and possibilities. I wondered if Sylvie was going to get recruited away from Cade at some point. Something to worry about later, when we weren't almost in range of the aforementioned killer sea ponies.

Again, we approached openly. There were fewer of them this time. Only the ponies with cardigans were on land. Their foals were conspicuously absent. Bianca was there to throw a veil so we could escape if the kelpies turned on us, but we hoped it wouldn't come to that. We stopped about fifteen yards away, giving them time and space to come to us. I was cool with talking to them, but that didn't mean I wanted to crowd them or offer myself up as an appetizer. The gray female stepped forward, flanked by the same green-black male as before. She took the lead. Since we didn't normally see them in groups, and no one was stupid enough to get close to them during mating season, no one knew which gender, if any, was dominant with them. I couldn't really base any findings off this group since they were acting abnormally to begin with, but it did seem like they were deferring to the female gray as their leader.

"We told you that we would speak no more. Why are you here?" Even though her tone was ominous, my ear focused on the soft sound of the sea trapped in a shell, and I smelled the salt and brine of it all. That detail helped me snap out of it. The river is freshwater. I shouldn't smell brine. Even knowing that, I wanted to strip down and dive into the water, followed by a long nap on the sand. But it was late at night, the water was frigid, and I would most likely be eaten. I had to remind myself that this would be the outcome. That's one reason kelpies are so dangerous. A few words and you'll happily walk right into their open maws.

"So my associates told me, but we've brought you something—something we think you'll like more than a meal." Alistair's tone was polite and cordial, but a sharp breeze swept through the meadow, bringing the smell of the river. Maybe it was natural, but I thought it was most likely Alistair letting off a little nervous energy, and perhaps combating some of the kelpie-induced sensory overload.

The gray kelpie snorted in obvious disbelief. "And what do you think we would find so precious?"

Sylvie stepped forward and held up a half-finished cardigan. "He thought you might like this."

I hadn't been aware of how much the herd was moving until they stilled. All their bottomless black eyes focused on Sylvie and her sweater. I'm not an expert at reading pony faces, but I've seen naked longing before, and that's what was there in their eyes. They wanted that sweater *bad*.

"I think I have your attention." Alistair's tone was desert dry.

"How did you get that?" the gray kelpie asked Sylvie.

I couldn't tell in the moonlight, but I think Sylvie blushed.

"I made it. It's hard to tell in the light, but I probably made yours, too." She frowned. "The witch could have asked another knitter, but as far as I know, I'm the sole source." She put the sweater back in the bag. "That's why each one takes so long."

I caught the slight frown on Alistair's face when she said that, and I was pretty sure I knew why. If Sylvie, a human with very little connection to our world, was the sole source of something that was clearly benefiting the kelpies, why hadn't the witch sought more help? What exactly was the witch's angle here, anyway? That bothered me. Yes, there are altruistic souls in the world, people like Sylvie who just want to help. But I didn't know this witch and I am not a trusting person. I very much wanted to track that witch down and ask him or her a few pointed questions.

One of the ponies in the back, another green-black male, but with a white starburst pattern on his forehead, pushed his way forward. "If you make them, does that mean you can fix them, too?"

"That depends on what needs fixing," Sylvie said.

At once, the ponies rushed her, which meant we all sprang into defense mode. I flicked my hands out, ringing us in fire. Lock and Ezra leapt in front of Sylvie while Bianca threw a veil over her, making it look as if she'd vanished. Thunder rumbled above our heads where no clouds had been, courtesy of Alistair.

Sylvie dropped her bag and threw up her hands. "Wait, wait. Calm down!"

At the same time, the ponies were casting their heads about wildly, indignant cries becoming an unintelligible mass of noise.

"I think they're just trying to show me the things that need fixing!" Sylvie shouted. She pushed Lock and Ezra aside. I dropped the wall of fire right before she walked through it. It didn't all go out right away, and I had to do some quick stomping. It had been a fairly dry summer. Sylvie marched up to the kelpies and tried to get them to line up, quickly becoming frustrated when they wouldn't listen to her.

"They can't hear or see you," Alistair said. "Bianca, drop the veil."

Bianca hesitated. "Are you sure? They could be clamoring for a Sylvie-course meal."

Alistair put a hand on her shoulder. "Let's see how it plays out. I'd like you to be somewhat careful with your person, however, Sylvie."

She nodded, not looking at him. Bianca dropped the veil, and the ponies stopped shouting. They surged forward again, only to be halted by Sylvie's imperious "Stop!" She clasped her hands in front of her. "Thank you, that's much better. I can't see if you're all trampling me." She pointed at the kelpie with the starburst. "You, what's your name?"

"Fitz," the kelpie said, drawing himself up to his full height. I doubted Fitz was his actual name. Kelpies belonged to the fae, and as such got weird about giving out their names. They believed that knowing someone's true name can give you power over them. And for certain practitioners, it was a definite possibility.

"Nice to meet you, Fitz. Now, how about you stand here, and the rest of you that need help line up behind him? I can only do one thing at a time, but I promise I'll try and get to you all."

I groaned. She had to deliver now. Fae put a lot of stock in promises.

She waved her hand at me. "Ava, stop being so negative. Ezra, Lock, fists down, please. Does anyone have a flashlight?" Lock, being the always-prepared Boy Scout type, had a small one in his jacket pocket. He held it while Sylvie examined the first sweater. There was a tear, only about an inch long, but it was dangerously close to one of the runes.

Sylvie crouched down to get a better look at it. "I can fix this. You might want to take it off, though. I don't want to stab you with the darning needle. It's not sharp, but no one likes to be jabbed."

I'd never seen a kelpie shift, or even heard much about it. People who had witnessed a kelpie in human form didn't generally live to share details about the experience. A pulsing green mist enveloped the pony, surprising Sylvie and making her fall back on her butt. When the mist faded, a thin young man stood where the pony had been. I would have assumed that their coloring would transfer, but if I hadn't seen the change, I couldn't have guessed this man was Fitz. His skin was pale and his hair was a thick, curly black. His eyes had changed shape, but the pupil and iris were the same bottomless black as before. He was naked except for the now-oversize cardigan. He quickly unbuttoned it and presented it reverently to Sylvie. Kelpies are much easier to read in human form. We were all still getting suspicious looks, but the one Fitz threw Sylvie was one of polite devotion.

She stared openly back at Fitz. I'm not sure she'd known about the kelpies' shifting ability. I cleared my throat, and Sylvie blinked, snapping back into reality. She considered the sweater, turning the garment in her hands. "I wonder if that witch has a spell that can make the sweater adjust with you," she said almost to herself. Placing the sweater on her lap, Sylvie dug through her bag. She pulled out a pouch that held her darning kit—I only knew this because she'd made the pouch herself out of some Doctor Who fabric she'd bought on the Internet. She hadn't stopped talking about it for weeks.

Fitz sat cross-legged in front of Sylvie, his hands on his knees, his attention on her as she worked. Though the temperature had dropped and it was fairly chilly out, it didn't seem to bother Fitz that he was buck naked in a field. I wondered if the fae run warmer than humans.

Sylvie had Lock adjust the light so it was directly on the tear. She threaded her needle with darning yarn and went to work. Sylvie worked quickly but carefully, wanting to make sure the stitches would hold. She tied off the yarn and handed the cardigan back to Fitz. "Be gentle with it if you can. I'm not sure how it tore in the first place. My aunt said the witch put something on them to keep that from happening. They're not indestructible, but it should take a lot to do that kind of damage." She slid the darning needle back into its place. "That's what I was told, anyway."

Fitz held his cardigan delicately, his black eyes wide. "You are a maker of miracles." I hadn't noticed it before, but there was a slight Scottish burr to his words. He'd definitely emigrated. We all tensed as he leaned in and grabbed Sylvie's hand and pressed her knuckles to his lips. "You do not know how much this means to us."

Sylvie extracted her hand politely, as if people kissed her like that all the time. "I don't mind. It's been fun."

Fitz turned his attention to Alistair. "You wanted to know what has drawn us together? There is something in the water. Something . . . bad."

An explosion of silver sparkles off to my left made me turn just in time to see the gray mare shift, her change coming much faster than Fitz's had. She was dwarfed by her sweater and had to push up the sleeves while she walked. She looked much like Fitz, only her skin was a pearlescent white, and her long black hair tumbled down to her waist. Even with the moonlight washing out most of the color, I could tell that in the sun her lips would have been a deep and pouty red. Right now, those lips were curled in a snarl.

"Fitz! What do you think you're doing?" She stomped her foot like a bratty child. "No one said you could talk to them. We agreed!"

Fitz leapt to his feet. "Gwenant—"

She stomped again and started tearing into him in another language. It wasn't one that I recognized. A lot of rolling r's and gentle "th" sounds that I wasn't familiar with. Gwenant was waving her arms now, her voice growing louder with each arm wave and hand flip.

Fitz was growling right back at her, though his language sounded different from hers. Was it just the way he spoke, or was he actually yelling at her in a language other than the one she was using? He kept pointing at Sylvie and waving the cardigan.

Sylvie grabbed onto my shoulder. "I think she's speaking Welsh! That is so cool," she whispered, her voice full of glee.

"Is he speaking Welsh, too?" It was funny—I couldn't understand a word, but I could tell from the tone and some of the body language what was going on. Fitz was carefully breaking down his logic to her, and Gwenant's arms were crossed as she looked to the stars for patience. It looked so ridiculously human that I wanted to laugh. But I didn't. Because you don't laugh at creatures that can eat you, not even if they're having naked hissy fits in a marsh.

"No, that sounds more like Scottish Gaelic."

"Then how can they understand each other?" I asked.

Sylvie considered this. "Scotland and Wales aren't that far apart, and it would make sense that they would learn neighboring languages. You see that a lot in other countries, especially if the country is small and close to those other countries. It would be necessary for them to learn it for trade."

"We don't do that here," I said.

"Well, America is large, and so many of us don't worry about it. I expect if you or I lived close to the southern border, we'd learn Spanish. But to be honest, I think the way we approach languages is a bit backward. We should learn them early and be more diligent—"

I cut off her lecture. Gwenant's arm gestures were calmer now, but she was still not buying Fitz's arguments. "How do you even know what they're speaking?"

Sylvie gave a quick half shrug. "I really want to visit that area someday. The cultures, the languages, the history. Fascinating."

After a final command, Gwenant crossed her arms. Fitz gave her a curt nod and put on his cardigan. Personally, I thought the idea of putting a cold, somewhat soggy sweater on while standing out in the crisp night air sounded hellish, but Fitz didn't seem to mind. In fact, he looked relieved to have it back on.

"We will help you," Gwenant said, and from the way she spit the words out, I could tell she wasn't happy about it. "In exchange, the girl will fix our sweaters and our foals will be put at the top of the list."

Fitz held out a hand and helped Sylvie up. "But what if I can't fix them?" Sylvie asked. "I haven't seen all the sweaters yet. I don't know what kinds of repairs are even necessary."

Gwenant's face grew thunderous. "Are you trying to trick us, puny creature?" Fitz scowled at her but didn't say anything.

Alistair stepped up, putting himself to the side but ahead of Sylvie, not quite blocking her but making his position clear. "She is merely putting down some ground rules. If she doesn't, you will run roughshod all over her." He stared down at the petite kelpie, his face a mask. "Kelpies have a certain reputation for keen dealing, so I don't think the comment was off base. We want to make sure everything is clear. We will hear your terms and then negotiate. Ezra, in my car there is a blanket. Fetch it, please."

Ezra didn't much care for the word *fetch* but didn't argue for once. I think the way Gwenant and Alistair were staring at each other, their eyes shrewd, their faces blank, was giving him the willies.

"Lock, can you convince some of the plants to move? We need a circle, something big enough for Ava to make a bonfire. Which means we'll also need wood. It's only going to get colder, and not all of us are comfortable." Alistair smiled blandly at the kelpies.

Lock and I went about our tasks quickly. Alistair wasn't just thinking of our well-being. A pleasant, crackling bonfire would be a consistent reminder to the kelpies of what I could do. If that didn't work, I could always go over my peryton story again with more graphic detail.

14

JUST DARN IT

EZRA STRETCHED an old picnic blanket out off to the side for Alistair and Gwenant to sit on so they could began their negotiations. Lock persuaded the plants to climb out of the ground, their roots marching them along to safer land. They were reluctant at first, but then Lock told them why he was moving them and they hopped to. I swear one of the ferns gave me a dirty look.

I glared back at the fern. "Surely there was an easier way than moving all of them."

"Faster and more efficient, yes. You could have razed the plant life down to the ground or I could have only evacuated a ring of plants to act as a firebreak. But there's a lot of endangered flora around here. I'd rather take a few extra minutes and move them safely."

I grimaced, following him to gather some wood. "I guess that's the big difference between your powers and mine. Your first thought is life and maintaining ecosystems. Mine's all destruction."

Lock grabbed my wrist, the movement fast, but his hold was gentle. "You're oversimplifying again, cupcake. Power is a tool. Don't want to use yours for destruction? Be more creative. I could just as easily tell the plants to wither and die. But that's not what I want to do. Don't get stuck in the idea that your power is a single-purpose weapon. It's lazy thinking, and you're better than that." His hand slid down and he squeezed my fingers gently before letting go. "Besides, forest fires have an important role in nature, too."

We gathered wood in silence after that. Lock had said his piece, and I needed to think on what he said. Soon enough we had a bonfire going, Bianca casting a large veil over all of us so that some nocturnal river enthusiast didn't spy a large group of ponies and a strange impromptu knitting circle of one.

Sylvie didn't want to waste time, so she started in on the line of kelpies with sweater related failures. If our respective leaders didn't come to an agreement, then she would stop, or most likely we'd have to make her stop, but until then, she just wanted to get going. I spread my jacket out on the ground to give her somewhere slightly more comfortable to sit. Rather surprisingly, Fitz stood behind her like an overprotective big brother, directing the ponies as they shifted and handed over their respective garments.

I didn't want to pass up the opportunity to learn more about the kelpies, but I don't think I gathered much info. There really didn't seem to be any correlation between the coloring of the pony form and the human form. White ponies were just as likely to be black, brown, white, and every shade in between when they shifted. I couldn't always tell the males from the females until they were in human form, either, unless they spoke or I got a flashlight and did some creative leaning, which would make what I was doing fairly obvious.

Sylvie had used toggles instead of buttons, which the kelpies would still be able to maneuver when they were in kelpie form. Some of the sweaters had lost their toggles, others had tears like Fitz's sweater did. Most were reparable. Sylvie singled out three or four that she could do a temporary fix on, but she knew they wouldn't last long. Basically, we were going to have to find another knitter. Sylvie couldn't keep up with the demand. I could tell she was fighting it, but there was a defeated cast to her features.

So she stitched and worked, and Fitz stood guard.

"Looks like Sylvie made a friend," Lock said.

"Only Sylvie could inspire protective feelings in a kelpie." I really wasn't that surprised. Sylvie was just one of those people. She was like the personification of an adorably hyperactive kitten. You had to love her.

"It's more than that," Bianca said, linking her arm through Lock's. I did my best to ignore the gesture. Arms. They were just arms. Bianca and Lock were friends, and that's what friends do, or at least that's what you do when you have touchy-feely friends like Lock and Ezra. At least his arm was all she was touching. It could have been worse.

"How do you know, Bianca?" Ezra gave my shoulder a reassuring squeeze. "You speak Welsh now?"

"No, but I overheard some of the negotiations. Since Fitz was the one who stepped forward, he's responsible for us now. If we mess up or act in bad faith, it's his job to fix it."

I leaned into Ezra. "And by 'fix it' you mean slaughter the lot of us and turn us into pony chow?"

"Pretty much." Bianca went back to Alistair, who was beckoning her over. Negotiations seemed to be over. Alistair didn't look happy, but he didn't look angry, either.

"Gwenant will allow her fellows to talk to us and will, should the time come, provide aid in this endeavor, and this endeavor only." A few of the kelpies were getting uneasy waiting, their eyes casting back toward the water. Alistair flicked his wrist, and a small cloud appeared. With a gentle push, he sent it over to the upset kelpies and had it mist them with rain. They looked at the cloud, stunned, but quickly got over the miracle of it and simply enjoyed the rain. Who knew that kelpies enjoyed frolicking and prancing in the rain? One of them was chewing on a frog while prancing around, which kind of ruined the image, but I chose to ignore that.

"And what are we giving them in return?" I asked.

Alistair twitched his other wrist and sent another cloud over. "Sylvie is going to fix what she can. If the sweater can't be fixed, it will be replaced, but only after she provides them with two junior sweaters and another regular-size one."

I winced. "Alistair, she's already identified four that won't keep their patch for long. The ward and the yarn took too much of a hit. Sylvie is amazing, but she's not a machine." I watched as Sylvie stitched, her concentration fierce as Fitz maneuvered the flashlight to shine on the right spot. "And you know she didn't keep the fact that those fixes were temporary to herself. The owners of those sweaters are aware."

Alistair rubbed the back of his neck. "Nor should she. Any sign that we're crossing the kelpies and Gwenant will rain

179

hellfire down upon us. I'll have to get ahold of Sylvie's aunt and her witch friend. We need to know if the ward pattern is enough or if there are steps we aren't aware of." He let his hand drop. "And we're going to have to find more knitters."

We were there until almost three in the morning, and oddly enough it was Fitz who called the halt. Sylvie had poked herself a few times with the darning needle because she was tired and her fingers were getting cold. Darning needles were too blunt to break skin, but it was indicative of how worn out she was getting. And despite the flashlight, she was squinting, and I think she was getting a headache. She'd pause occasionally to rub her temples.

Fitz told the remaining kelpies they'd have to wait until the next day for their patches, even though there were only a few sweaters left to fix. Two of them shifted to argue, but Fitz held his ground. "If you force her to keep working, the stitches won't be as good. She's exhausted. You can wait one more day. I'll make sure she comes back tomorrow." The other two were much bigger than Fitz, but when he stuck out his jaw, they backed off. Apparently you didn't mess with Fitz. I couldn't tell if that made me feel better that he was sort of on our side, or worse. What did it take, exactly, to be scary to the other kelpies?

Ezra was rubbing warmth back into Sylvie's hands, keeping an eye on the kelpies as he did. Just because we'd come to an agreement didn't mean we trusted them.

"I'll come back tomorrow when the light's better. The work will go faster then," Sylvie assured them. She packed her things and stretched.

We watched as most of the kelpies dispersed. Fitz talked softly to Gwenant a little ways off. She was much calmer now, or maybe her arms were tired from all the waving she did earlier.

"I thought they were going to talk to us." I shook out my jacket and pushed my arms through the sleeves.

"We are," Fitz said, coming back to us, his accent thick with his own weariness. Gwenant left without so much as a good-bye. "I'm to go back with you."

"Won't that be difficult for you physically?" Lock asked. "What with us not being by the river and all?"

Fitz adjusted his cardigan. We were really going to have to get him some pants. "Your boss and Gwenant worked something out. There will be some minor discomfort, I'm sure. Gwennie will have seen to that. She does not like it when she doesn't get her way." It looked like Fitz was used to putting up with such things, too.

And that's how we ended up carpooling with a kelpie. He sat in the back with Sylvie, while Lock and I rode up front. I drove, since Lock had done the lion's share of the driving so far. He liked to drive and I was somewhat indifferent, so usually I let him. I adjusted the rearview mirror and pushed it too far down, accidentally catching a good, long look at Fitz's legs. "Gah. Okay, first things first. When we get back, we're getting you some trousers."

"You have a problem with the natural state of the body?" Fitz had curled himself into the back seat so that his back was to the door.

"No, I mean, I hang out with Ezra, who's naked a large portion of the time. I'm pretty used to that."

"Why, is Ezra a nudist?" Sylvie asked as she buckled her seat belt.

"It has to do with what he is," I said, "which you'll have to ask him about. But maybe don't ask him about nudity specifically, because it's Ezra, and you don't really want to get him started." I turned the key and the engine sputtered to life. "It's just weird to see a naked dude in a cardigan, Fitz. You're Porky Pigging it. And that's not right."

Fitz closed his eyes. "Who's Porky Pig?"

"He's a cartoon pig who only wears a jacket, but no pants. We can show you videos later," I said. "Just trust me on the trousers. Now are you going to spill what you know, or what?"

Fitz gave me a tight-lipped smile. "I told your boss I'd wait until we're all together. Makes sense to only be telling it once." There was no budging him, so we didn't bother trying.

BACK AT the cabin, Bianca veiled Fitz so that if one of our neighbors was taking a late-night stroll in the woods, no one would see a pantsless guy walking about and call the cops. We all found it unnerving to have an invisible kelpie walking with us, so she dropped the veil immediately once we were inside the house, and I dug up a robe until we found him something else. Fitz didn't think the robe made much of a difference. Trust me when I say that it did. Alistair got him a big glass of water, which would help the kelpie put off the discomfort of being on land a bit longer.

When we were all gathered, Fitz started talking. And the thing he started talking about was snails.

"They are very big." He held his hands out until they indicated something about the size of his head. "Never seen a snail like that. At first we thought it was a boon. Snails can be quite tasty." He took a sip of water. "Only, it turned out that they weren't so good to eat. The kelpies that did, well, it was a last supper."

"They're poisonous?" I asked, sitting next to Sylvie. She had put on her pajamas and curled up in a blanket on the couch. After being outside so long and sitting on the ground—even with a bonfire—she was having a hard time getting warm, so she'd cocooned herself in one of the comforters. I thought I heard a strangled squeak come out from the pile, but wasn't sure.

"Not exactly. I saw a harbor seal eat one, no problem. Other things can eat them, but we can't. We tried to avoid them, but they seem to be drawn to us. There is never just one snail. That's why we've been spending so much time on land. The snails can't survive long out of the water."

"You can't be near the snails at all?" I asked.

"We don't know." Fitz kept glancing around our living room, though not in a nervous manner. I don't think kelpies spent much time indoors. This was probably an experience he wanted to file away. "After what happened to the ones who ate them, none of us wanted to be near them. But they chased us. So we left."

"What happened to the kelpies that ate one?" Alistair asked.

Fitz cast a concerned glance at his water glass. "They drowned."

"Kelpies can't drown," Lock said from his seat on the floor. "They're water creatures. That's like finding a dryad that can't climb trees."

Fitz scratched his forehead. "Aye, that's the thing of it. It's like whatever makes a kelpie a kelpie was gone. Without it . . ." He spread his fingers wide. The room was quiet as we all digested that. What did it mean when something took away the thing that made us different? If something took my fire away, could I manage without it? Or was it too wrapped up in my physical makeup

183

for me to survive without it? A few years ago, I would have jumped at the chance to find out. When my mom and I were on the run, outcast and hunted because of what we were, trading my fire away so I could be normal would have seemed like a miracle. I wouldn't have even had to think about it. But now? Psychologically, it was too much a part of me, the way I saw myself.

Humans can cope with this kind of thing—the quarterback that blows out his knee, the ballerina who breaks her femur. They can always do something else. Not being able to throw a pass doesn't make them less human. But a firebug who can't throw fire, or a kelpie that couldn't swim, that was a different story. I had no idea what would happen to me on a physiological basis. And I was nowhere near as magical as a kelpie. I, at least, was basically human, but with a bonus. But kelpies were all magic. They lived and breathed it. What could take that away?

"It's like those locusts," Lock said. "The ones Ava, Ezra, and I had to deal with a few months back. They swarmed and devoured any magic in their path. I've never heard of magic-eating snails, but I don't see why they couldn't exist."

"That would explain why we're not seeing any problems with the human population," Bianca said. "If the snails are like those locusts, they only attack things with magic. Humans would be left alone."

"How did that affect the sweaters?" Sylvie asked, all but her face swathed in blanket. Her voice sounded high and tight.

"The snails think they are delicious. Sometimes they would manage a bite or two before we could get away. We are fast swimmers, but we must stop to eat, and the snails, they swarm. That's why so many of the sweaters are damaged."

"That would tear at the wards and the material," Lock mused. "Though I'm not sure how snails could tear yarn."

"Oh, that's the best part," Fitz said. "These snails have teeth."

"Like a mouth?" I asked.

"Snails don't have mouths," Sylvie said. "They have these hard organs that are kind of like tongues covered in teeth. They use those to rip, tear, and grind food. It's pretty fascinating."

"Well, right now they're using that fascinating organ to tear up your handiwork," I said. "And you sure do know a lot about snails." I heard another muffled squeak. "Did they go after kelpies without sweaters?"

"Aye. They went after the ones without sweaters, but they swarmed the ones with them," Fitz said grimly.

"More magic, more snails?" Ezra asked.

Fitz nodded and then picked up a candle and sniffed it, recoiling from the smell. He put it back quickly. I had a feeling that before he left, Fitz would touch every item in this cabin.

Alistair stared at the whiteboard. "So, we have magic-eating snails chewing up warded sweaters and killing kelpies and driving them out of the water, as well as another mysterious something causing aggression and madness. Great. Two problems. Are they both natural, or is someone causing this?"

I heard a muted something from Sylvie's cocoon. "Oh, this is ridiculous, Sylvie. You can't be that cold." I yanked the blanket away from her face. And that's when I discovered that the muted something was Sylvie crying. "What the hell, Sylvie. Are you okay?"

She shook her head, her hair sticking a little to her wet cheeks. "You don't have two problems, you have one. I think."

Her face twisted. "And it's just...it's very upsetting!" She buried her face in the blanket and sobbed, her shoulders heaving.

"Well, that was unexpected," Ezra said, blinking at our hysterical friend. "Right. Lock, get her some hot chocolate."

"That's very thoughtful, Ezra," Alistair said. I agreed, but I knew to wait for the rest of it.

"And while you're at it, make me some."

Ah, there it was.

Alistair sent Bianca for a cold washcloth, which he applied to the back of Sylvie's neck. He didn't say anything, just sat there, waiting for her to pull herself back together. Only when Sylvie had hot chocolate in her hands and the sobs had become hiccups did Alistair press her.

She gazed into her hot chocolate for a long time, and I could see Rational Sylvie taking over again.

Alistair sat on the coffee table so he was at eye level with Sylvie. "What do you mean, you think we just have one problem?"

"I think it is statistically unlikely for two new things to appear in an area at the same time—two things that affect the same specific population no less, and not have them be related." Sylvie's hands trembled as she held the hot chocolate.

I thought about what Sylvie said. Both problems had reared their nasty heads at the same time. We hadn't found any evidence of overlap, but that didn't mean there wasn't any. And it wasn't just two things that were new. "I keep coming back to Sylvie's project. The snails and the violent outbreaks aren't the only things that were new. Those warded sweaters are pretty fresh and shiny, too."

Alistair folded his arms, his face grim. "We need to find that witch. I can take care of that. Everyone get some sleep. At least a few hours. Sylvie, I need the witch's contact info. First we'll find out what we can about the magic used on the sweaters. I have a feeling the witch's cooperation will vanish when we bring up the snails. Then we can see about rounding up some knitters. And that is honestly something I never thought I'd say."

Bianca got up and stretched. "Sid can knit."

We all turned and stared at Sid.

"What?" he said, somewhat indignant. "A man can't knit? I happen to like it, and I'm good at it, so there."

"I think it's less of the man thing and more of the biker thing that makes it so unlikely," I said. "But right now, we're all just grateful."

Alistair nodded. "Yes. Though I hate to lose a fighter, I need you more on this. So I'll talk to you and Sylvie as soon as I get in touch with the witch."

We were dismissed. Sylvie bunked with us. I have no idea where Fitz ended up sleeping. I was so exhausted, I fell asleep almost immediately. Sylvie, though, was restless. She kept tossing and turning, waking me up. Finally, sometime around four in the morning, I made fire fishes for her. They swam lazily through the air, giving her something to focus on. Then a long, thin dragon flamed in, snapping up the fishes in his giant whiskered maw. I let the last fish get away. The dragon tried to get him, but the fish was too quick. Eventually they both got tired and curled up together, friends instead of predator and prey. I let the image fade slowly into smoke. Then, with a happy sigh, Sylvie curled up and went to sleep.

15

YOU THINK IT'S KINDA FUNNY... BUT IT'S NOT

I WAS CALLED OUT again a few hours later to deal with an ogre. We'd started sorting the events into two categories after Alistair's talk last night—creatures who'd lost their minds, or the snails did it. I think it spoke to our lack of sleep that these categories made sense.

The ogre, unfortunately, fell into the first category. We found him at a were's house. The homeowner, a polite werewolf named Nora, had tried to escape the crazed ogre by hiding in the sailboat her husband had dry-docked in an old barn. He was in the middle of restoring it. I think Nora normally would have taken on the ogre, but she was five months pregnant and home alone. So she hid and the ogre beat the crap out of the sailboat.

The ogre was too big and too dangerous for us to contain. By the time we got there, he was almost rabid—totally mindless and violent. Viscous, pink-tinged sludge dripped from his bulbous nose, and dark red blood oozed from both his ears. Lock and Bianca got Nora out while Sid and I distracted the maddened ogre. Bianca slid back in to help just in time for the ogre to let loose a monster-size sneeze. I had just shot a great blast of fire to herd the ogre back, so I only got hit by a few charcoaled lumps of...something better left unnamed. Sid and Bianca weren't so lucky. They were both covered in the thick pink sludge.

Once Nora was safe, I set fire to the boat and the structure around it, trapping the ogre inside. At that point, it was damaged beyond repair, and we figured it would be easier for Nora and her husband to claim insurance on the scorched remnants. Or, at least, it would be easier for them to explain that than try to feed the insurance company a plausible reason for why their sailboat became a busted-up wreck in dry dock.

Though I knew there was no feasible way for us to save the ogre, that didn't exactly make any of us feel better as we listened to him burn. Even Sid and Bianca, who really weren't feeling charitable due to their mucus bath, looked on grimly while I kept the fire going. The ogre screamed, an unholy bellow. Bianca threw a veil of sound over it, drowning out the noise so that no one would call the cops. And so we didn't have to listen. Which somehow made it worse. He was crying out the last of his life, and no one even heard it.

For the first time in a while, I found myself retching after a job. I leaned against the side of Nora's house and tossed up my cookies. It's not like the ogre was the first creature I'd had to burn to death, and it's not like I had a choice. Alistair didn't pass out those assignments as often, not like Venus had. But something about his cries got to me. Crazed Elias aside, I'd grown used to not snuffing out the lives of others.

The air was still and quiet, thick with heat. A blackfly buzzed around my head, and I waved it away. I couldn't even hear the snap and crackle of the flames as it ate away at the structure. A freshly hosed-down Bianca came around the side of the house with a glass of water. I was done throwing up, but I still felt wobbly. I'd managed to stumble a few feet away from where I'd been sick before I slid down and rested against the wood siding. Bianca sat next to me and handed me the water.

"Has he stopped screaming?" I croaked.

"Yeah."

"Thank you." I downed the water, enjoying the soothing cold on my ravaged throat. The blackfly buzzed by my head again. Annoyed, I flicked my fingers and it disappeared in a poof of ash. I didn't feel bad about the blackfly. I've been on the biting end of one before. No, thank you. "Sorry about your snot bath."

"Me too." She took off one of her shoes and attempted to squeeze some of the water out of it. "There's nothing we could have done, Ava."

"I know. It's just . . ." I didn't know how to end that sentence.

"It's like they're rabid." Bianca tipped her head back against the house. "Whatever is going on, it destroys their brains. There's no coming back from that. It might help to think of it as a mercy killing. Because they can't be feeling good with that kind of damage happening."

I set the glass down in the dirt. "I know. Has Alistair learned anything yet? From the peryton or Howie?"

Bianca sighed. "We had to destroy the male peryton at Katya's house. Too dangerous. The females are quarantined somewhere. So far they aren't showing signs of anything. It seems to strike quickly, so maybe they're fine? I don't know. There's not enough data. We don't know if it's a virus or a chemical or what. And Howie, at least as of this morning, is being kept sedated and sectioned off. Heavily sedated. Or he loses it. So it's not like he can be questioned. We have someone running tests on him. We tracked down his boss at the marina, and he didn't have much to tell us except that Howie was a mellow guy, always came to work, well-liked. It's driving Alistair up the wall."

"You're very devoted to him, aren't you?"

"Yeah," she said, squinting at me, her tone suddenly hostile. "What of it?"

"It was just a statement."

"Oh." We sat there and watched the smoke from the barn twist into the sky. "I guess I'm just not used to not fighting with you."

"It's weird," I said, hugging my knees and resting my head on them. "I guess we'll both have to adapt. Especially since, you know...you're spending so much time with Lock." I had to push those last words out. Nobody likes to admit when they're acting childish, and I was no exception.

Bianca mirrored the way I was sitting, her cheek resting on her knee so she could see me. "That really bothers you, doesn't it? Sharing your friend?"

I wanted to say no. Deny it and act cool and nonchalant. Not just because I thought it might be the mature response, but also because I didn't want Bianca to feel like she'd stolen him. It would be so easy to say that, think that. But it wasn't the truth. Simple as that. And even if it made my insides feel empty and made a panicked part of my brain yell that we were being replaced, I knew that Bianca wasn't going to take my spot.

"Yeah," I said. "It's hard. I'm used to it being just me, him, and Ezra. And now there are all these other people, and I'm having to make room and share . . . and I guess I'm not good at it. I'm not used to it." I thought on that for a second. "I've never really had to share people before. Until them, I didn't really have people to share."

Bianca didn't respond right away. She stared at me until I wanted to ask if there was something on my face. "So it's not because it's me he's spending time with?"

I snorted. "Geez, Bianca, think pretty highly of yourself, do you?"

She smacked my leg with the back of her hand.

"No, it's not you. I would be grouchy over anyone." Maybe not entirely true. If I had liked Bianca, would that have made it more painful or less? I wasn't sure. Then I realized that part of the equation didn't matter. "Actually, you made it easier. You're nice to him. He seems . . . happy around you. And I'd be a shitty friend if I didn't put that first."

"Just because you take the high road on something doesn't keep it from sucking," Bianca said with a smirk.

I groaned, leaning back against the house. "That is the truest thing I've ever heard. You're right. It sucks. But I'm still happy you took care of my friend while we were fighting. Seriously."

"The timing thing probably didn't help, either. Because you were being a brat and ignoring him, you didn't get to slowly acclimate to my amazing presence." Bianca grinned at me, then wiped her mouth on her arm, like she was trying to rub the smile away. "If it makes you feel better, I still think you're awful."

"Good," I said. "Because I still think you're a rampaging she-beast."

"As long as we're clear on that."

* * *

WE STOPPED by Duncan's on our drive back from the ogre roast. It was on the way, and Sid and Bianca wanted to borrow some dry clothes. I wanted to check on Katya. Apparently Alistair hadn't been able to find family to take her in, so for now she was staying with the drove. He was too distracted to see to her well-being himself, and he didn't think it was a good idea for someone who'd just lost both parents to be left alone.

Frankly, she was lucky she hadn't been quarantined like the peryton. But she'd shown no signs of whatever was causing this madness, and though we didn't know much about it; we did know that it struck pretty fast. Katya was clean. Besides, Alistair was worried that too much more time by herself would be seriously detrimental. Time to grieve is fine. Time to stew and wallow, less so.

We found her helping Olive string up laundry on the line, mostly cloth diapers for the seemingly endless parade of leverets. Since the drove had settled in on Duncan's land, there had been a bit of a population explosion. Turns out it's a lot easier to raise small ones when you're not constantly on the move. This was probably less exciting for Olive, since she was almost permanently on diaper duty. She just couldn't stay out of trouble for very long.

"I thought you were at the cabin." I helped her get the last few up and then motioned her away from the line.

Olive stepped back, curious. "I caught a ride over with Ikka to check in. Besides, I can only trade off my chores so many times." She folded her arms. "I won't owe anyone."

"I get that," I said. I held my hands out, palms up. It wasn't necessary, but it helped me concentrate and focus, and there were few things worse than an unfocused firebug. I heated up the air around the diapers, keeping it short of actual flame. It was a tricky business. The diapers were cotton, and too much heat and I'd have singed diapers, or a flaming laundry line. I dropped my hands and felt the cloth. Nice and toasty.

Olive picked up the basket and started unclipping the diapers. "That's handy. I should bring you next time I have diaper duty."

"Olive, I'd have to move in."

KATYA SEEMED happy to see us, despite her troubles. She'd piled her hair up in a loose bun on her head, and her skin was pale enough that I noticed a fine mist of freckles across her nose. Well, if her hair was a little greasy and her skin a touch on the pale side, who could blame her? Hygiene hadn't exactly been high on my list after I lost my mom. Kat seemed to be taking it a lot better than I had. Hey, at least she was brushing her teeth and not accidentally setting all the furniture on fire. Cade had really had a hard time with me those first few months after my mom died. We went through drapes, quite a few chairs, and at least two couches.

"You seem to be settling in."

She smiled at me over her shoulder as she stacked the last of the wood she'd been carrying under the overhang of the cabin's roof. Katya didn't even manage to fully turn around before she was accosted by a young leveret, maybe two years old, a streak of dirt across his face, arms up and wide eyes pleading in the universal gesture for *pick me up*. Katya scooped the boy into the air, spinning him in a circle—as she did so, he let out a whoop.

"They've made it very easy." Katya snuggled the small boy, who hugged her back before turning wary eyes on me. They

194

started distrusting strangers young in the drove. Katya had already made it past the stranger phase, it seemed. "They keep me busy, so I don't have much time to think about things. There's a lot to do here. It's nice to feel useful." She gave the boy another squeeze before setting him down. "It's not like at home, where my chores didn't really seem to add much. Here . . ." She shrugged. "Here I feel like my contribution matters. Is that weird?"

"No, it's not." I felt the same way when I did things for Cade.

"And I know it's only a few hours away from home, but it seems like a different world." As we talked, a brown hare shot by, followed by several more. The boy at Katya's feet squealed and took off after them, making good time on his stumpy toddler legs, but he wasn't fast enough to catch the hares. He finally got frustrated enough that he changed, shifting seamlessly from boy to hare. Unfortunately, he hadn't stripped out of his clothes first. He was trapped, flopping around in a panic.

Olive approached, stopping to glare down at the hopping mass of clothes. "Really, Toby. Clothes first."

Katya reached down and carefully untangled him. When drove children were small, they only changed under duress. They can't change at will until they're six or seven.

Katya laughed as the leveret bounded off after the other hares, only slightly less awkward in his rabbit form. "The drove doesn't hide what it is, not here, not in their home. I miss my parents, but not hiding is kind of great." She gave me a lopsided grin. "It probably helps that I already knew a lot about rabbits."

The image of Kat's old 4-H photo where she was hugging a huge lop-eared bunny came to mind, and I laughed.

Sid and Bianca suddenly appeared next to us, both of them jumping at Olive. They must have approached under a veil, because none of us had seen or heard them. Olive dropped into a crouch, sweeping her leg out and knocking both of her would-be attackers on their butts. They hadn't managed to surprise Olive much, but Katya squeaked and jumped six inches. Snowflakes began to fall from the sky, though they instantly melted in the summer heat. Kat frowned at them until they stopped.

Olive scowled at Bianca. "That's what you get for using a veil to sneak up on me." Then she kicked Sid. "And that's what you get for startling Katya." She pitched her voice louder. "And if you drop out of that tree and try to scare us, fox, it will be the last thing you do."

Ezra lowered himself down, bouncing on his toes when he hit the ground. "I let you spot me, you know."

Olive grunted, obviously not believing him.

"At least it's never boring here," Katya said.

"It truly isn't. If you stay, I expect you'll be overfed and coddled within an inch of your life," I said, remembering how much the hares liked to fatten me up. "I mean, you'll work, too. And you'll have to watch Olive. Ezra's been giving her pointers to help her become a better pickpocket. But if you've ever wanted to learn how to throw a knife or a punch, it's a good place to be."

Katya went back to stacking wood. "You could have warned me about Olive before I got here, you know."

"Where's the fun in that?"

Duncan came out then to say hi, and we chatted for a few minutes, though it still felt forced on my end. I'd always thought of Duncan as sort of a fill-in grandpa. He'd been the closest thing I'd had to one, anyway. Kindly, dependable and always there for us. But now things were a bit more complicated. He'd fallen off the pedestal I'd put him on and had gotten a little scuffed on the way down. I still loved him . . . but I didn't like all the things that he did. Despite my misgivings, I gave Duncan a hug anyway. I might not have liked all his choices, but he'd always been there for me, and I couldn't discount that. My uncertainty didn't mean he wouldn't be there for Katya, either. I just didn't trust easy, and so when it was broken, it was hard for me to come back from that.

I made my good-byes and double-checked that Katya had my number and knew that she could text me anytime

I eyed Olive and held out my hand. "Can I have my wallet?"

She sighed and handed it back. Bianca began checking her pockets, a look of chagrin on her face. "Damn it, Olive. My wallet *and* my phone, please."

Olive pulled Bianca's stuff out of different pockets. "I would have given them back. I promise."

We stared at her.

"You know, eventually." Now that I could believe.

Kat started laughing so hard, she hiccuped. "I think," she said, when she caught her breath, "I think I'm going to like staying with you guys."

I nodded. "As long as you watch your valuables, you'll be fine."

16

HE'S A REAL FUN GUY

AFTER A QUICK STOP at the cabin, where we picked up Lock, Bianca had us head out to check in with Alistair. We found him, of all places, in a morgue. Or it would have been a morgue if it had been in a human hospital. All the trappings were there—metal tables, refrigerated drawers, cheap linoleum flooring, bright light, and the pervasive smell of bleach. The differences, however, were both subtle and profound. Human morgues don't have warded drawers, for example. I didn't want to know what kinds of things were being kept on those slabs, or what the wards did. Ignorance can equal bliss, or at least a better night's sleep. Some of the equipment varied—a regular bone saw was not going to make it through an ogre's bones without chipping the blade, and I'm sure the good doctor got more use out of a blowtorch than most medical examiners did. A doctor and an assistant were hovering around the room, and I was positive that at least one of them was a practitioner of some sort—a witch, probably.

"I didn't know Currant warranted such a place."

"It doesn't," Bianca said. "We paid the dwarves overtime to set it up. The way things are going, we're going to need it. We even brought out some of our people from Boston."

Alistair was waiting in the hallway, but he was observing the doctor through a large glass window. Bianca joined him, the rest of us trailing behind. They both watched attentively as the doctor in the room worked; the assistant was now scrubbing tools off to the side. I couldn't tell much about either of them since they were covered in gear.

"What's all that?" I asked.

"Personal protective equipment," Alistair said, not looking at me. "PPE." He had his hand on his chin, and he was absently chewing on his thumb. "Since we don't know how or what this thing is or how it's spreading, we can't chance infection. Which means a body suit, gloves, a respirator, et cetera."

"Is the doctor one of us?" I asked.

Bianca shook her head. "Human. You remember Dr. Wooley?"

It was hard to forget someone who'd helped patch you up post–disinfection shower. "I do remember her, yes."

"We brought her to the Coterie when Alistair took over. She's well paid and loyal, and she'll fake whatever paperwork we need to get Howie buried. Dr. Wesley has been on my personal payroll for a long time. Her assistant is a witch, though."

"Aw, man, that's Howie?" I took renewed interest in the corpse, though I couldn't see anything. The doctor appeared to be finished. She'd pulled up the sheet, covering the body. "I was hoping he'd make it."

Alistair sighed and dropped his hand. "The cold temperature we were keeping him at slowed it down but didn't stop it.

He got aggressive, and it was too much of a risk to keep him alive." He turned away from the window and collapsed into a plastic chair.

"If the doc's human, why bother with the PPE?" I asked.

Alistair rubbed the back of his head with one hand. "Until we have definitive proof that this thing can't be spread to humans, I'm not taking any chances."

"Did you tell him about the ogre?" I asked Bianca.

"I did not tell him about the ogre." Bianca brought him a glass of water from the cooler and took a seat next to him, filling him in on the fight. "We're reasonably sure the ogre was infected."

Alistair had set his water on the table without drinking it and dropped his head into his hands. "Great, wonderful. Did any of you come into contact with it?"

"I try to avoid contact with rampaging ogres," I said drily.

Alistair huffed—it might have been a soft laugh, but I wasn't sure.

"But he sneezed on Sid and Bianca."

Alistair eyed the caulbearer, the alertness in his eyes the only sign that he was panicked at all. "How are you feeling?"

"Like I just took a snot bath," Bianca said with a shrug. "Otherwise I'm dandy."

Alistair considered her, not buying her casual assurance. "You don't leave until the doctor checks you out. You either, Sid."

There was a soft whoosh, and the doors down the hall opened, revealing Dr. Wesley. She was as I remembered her— medium build, her skin a rich, warm brown. Despite her serious appearance, I could see the faintest hint of laugh lines around her mouth. She'd pulled her hair up into a no-nonsense bun, and she was holding a clipboard.

Alistair leapt to his feet, holding out his hand for the doctor to shake. "Dr. Wesley, thank you again for coming in. I know we've kept you hopping this week, and we appreciate your dedication."

"Well, at least you've been interesting. It isn't every day I get to take someone apart and find something new." She had the faint glow of triumph about her.

"So you know what he had?" Alistair looked relieved.

Dr. Wesley held up a hand in a stopping motion. "Not exactly, but since you were able to bring me an intact specimen, I can give you something. The rest will have to wait until I'm able to run more tests, but it looks like your boy caught himself some type of fungus."

"Gross." When everyone turned to look at me, I added, "Well, it is."

"Gross, yes. Fascinating? Absolutely. From what I've learned over the years about were physiology, that fungus shouldn't be possible. Their systems are very efficient at flushing out foreign contaminants: viruses, you name it. But this thing was hale, hearty, and eating away at his brain."

"See?" I said, nudging Lock. "Totally gross."

"Which explains a lot of the symptoms you mentioned," the doctor continued. "There was severe damage to the limbic system—that's the part of the brain that controls things like aggression. With the kind of damage Howie had, I'm not surprised that he'd lost upper-level thought processes. In fact, much longer and I bet he wouldn't have been able to walk."

I suddenly had the mental image of Howie crawling along

the floor, biting everyone's ankles. It should have been funny, but instead I shuddered. Alistair and the doctor kept talking, and I did my best to listen in, but something was tugging away at the recesses of my mind. Something about fungus. Wait. That was it.

"Bats!" In my excitement, I may have yelled it. To their credit, everyone simply turned in my direction and waited for me to finish my thought. "What I mean is, we watched a documentary on bats the other day. And they had this fungus."

"White-nose syndrome," Bianca supplied.

"Yes, that. And they were having a hard time containing it—the bats kept going from cave to cave and spreading it. Well, what if the snails had something? What if the snails have some sort of magical fungus?"

"That seems like a pretty big leap," Alistair said. "And we have no proof."

"No, not yet," I said. "But like Sylvie said, all this stuff showed up at the same time. The two might be connected. So now that we know we're looking for snails and fungus, we could go back to different hot spots and look for evidence."

Dr. Wesley fished a pen out of her top pocket and made a note in the chart. "It is possible, Alistair. While I'm running the samples I collected, I'll see if anything similar has been reported to the CDC, but I doubt it has. I do think this fungus is new and built specifically to go after magical species, for lack of a better term. Your theory would support that." She put her pen away. "In fact, from everything Alistair has been telling me, I'm wondering if it's similar to certain parasites that feast on a host and then encourage behaviors that would bring the host body into contact with other viable hosts and food sources." She pursed her lips. "Like how *Toxoplasma gondii* will infect a rat and then convince the rat that it's attracted to the smell of cat urine. The cat then eats the rat, and the parasite lives on. For some reason, they can only reproduce in the feline gut. There's also a kind of hairworm that infects grasshoppers and then forces them to throw themselves into water. The grasshopper drowns, and the worm is free to continue its life cycle."

"I will literally pay you ten dollars to stop giving us examples," I said. The doctor held out her hand, palm up, and I fished out two fives.

"If that's true," Lock said, "then how is it getting passed along? If the snails eat magic, how is the fungus getting anywhere?"

I frowned. "I'm not sure. Maybe the snail dies before it can eat, forcing the fungus to infect a new host?"

"Someone get me a snail," the doctor said, pointing her pen at us, "and I'll get your answers. I know a biologist we can trust. We need to figure out how the creatures are getting contaminated, or coming into contact with the infected fungus. These things don't just appear. You have a hot zone somewhere. Find it." She pocketed the cash. "As many samples as you can get me—one subject does not generate enough data for me to make sweeping pronouncements." She headed for another set of doors. "Be careful, though. I'm not sure how long this fungus takes to gestate or how it's spread. Could be airborne, could be a more intimate contact." She nodded at Bianca and Sid. "You two—my assistant will be out in a second to fetch you. Give me a few minutes, and then we'll get you both checked out. Good luck." And with that cheery pronouncement, she disappeared through the doors.

"Well," I said, "I certainly feel better. Who's up for some fungus hunting?" Bianca and Lock raised their hands.

Alistair crossed his arms. "Sid, Bianca, you get checked out first."

"But snail hunting," Bianca whined. "Come on, I feel fine."

They stared at each other for a long moment before Alistair folded. "You can't avoid hospitals forever, B."

"But I can for now."

Alistair dropped his arms. "Fine, yes. But before the snail hunt begins, we need to have a quick chat with that witch of Sylvie's. I'm very curious to hear what he has to say." Alistair shooed us along. "All right, class. Let's go. Everyone grab a traveling buddy."

17

SOMETIMES THE WARTS
ARE ON THE INSIDE

THERE ARE FEW THINGS stranger than seeing a kelpie sort and wind yarn, but that's what greeted me when we found Sylvie. A now fully clothed Fitz was preparing the yarn for the table full of knitters. Olive, who had hitched a ride with us, joined him. I think she was curious about the kelpie. I recognized a few faces from around the Inferno and from the drove. The room was packed tight, between them, me, Alistair, Bianca, Sid, Ezra, and Lock. Alistair had commandeered the employee lounge at Broken Spines. The faint odor of new paint hit my nose as we walked in, almost entirely covered by the smell of coffee wafting over from the coffeemaker. Large windows let in streams of sunshine, which combined with the overhead lighting to give the knitters plenty of light to work by.

"Weren't you supposed to be on Team Knit?" I asked Sid.

"They were actually able to round up a fair amount of knitters, so I think I'm supposed to float between Team Knit and Team Get Our Ass Kicked."

"I don't think I care for our team name," Lock said.

Alistair had managed to get ahold of Sylvie's aunt and, through her, the witch. I have a problem with stereotyping witches. Even though I know it's just something you're born with—an inherent power not unlike my own—I still imagine them like something in an old picture book. Warty noses, crazy hair, and bats in the belfry. Not to mention the awful teeth and the cackling. One must never forget the cackling. I've never, not once, met a witch that fit that definition, but the stereotype prevails in my mind. I think I'm secretly hoping to meet a witch like that someday.

Sylvie's witch turned out to be a polite middle-aged man named Thomas. Balding, bespectacled, and a little paunchy, he looked more like someone who would teach history in a high school than a witch. He was bent over Fitz's cardigan, arguing with Sylvie. They were trying to keep their voices hushed, but from the sound of it Sylvie was convinced the witch could figure out something that would adjust the sweater's sizing when the kelpies shifted, but the witch kept saying it wasn't feasible.

I think Sylvie was relieved to see us. She looked frustrated and two seconds from losing it, which was unlike her.

"That man is infuriating," she said, trying to not scowl. "He keeps saying it isn't a reasonable idea—not that it's impossible or anything. He just doesn't think it's worth the time or the energy. Even though the ability to change sizes would make it so the kelpies could share the cardigans more easily." She crossed her arms. "I'm beginning to think he doesn't like helping them, that my aunt talked him into it somehow in the first place."

Fitz and Olive had joined us while she vented. The kelpie considered the still-glowering Sylvie. "This witch, he upsets you?"

In the short time we'd known him, Fitz had become viciously protective of Sylvie. It was kind of a relief, really. I'd been worrying about Sylvie being around all the Coterie folk. It's a dangerous spot for a human. But a devoted kelpie bodyguard? You can't buy that kind of protection.

She sighed and relaxed her stance. "Yes, though I shouldn't be letting it get to me. I've just been trying to talk to him about the sizing issue, and he's being stubborn."

"He is afraid," Fitz said. "I can smell it on him when I am near. This is only right. He *should* fear the kelpie. It's his brain telling him that a better predator is near." He gave Sylvie a little bow. "I will handle this. He will not listen to you because you are young, nice. He is used to pushing such people around. Since your way isn't working, we will try mine." Fitz bared his teeth. I was glad to not be Thomas right then.

"How do you mean?" Sylvie asked, but Fitz was already moving away from us, sidling toward Thomas. Sylvie let out a frustrated huff before grabbing a ponytail holder and yanking her hair back. "Thomas is so frustrating. When I worked with him before, he wasn't like this. He was falling all over himself to help my aunt. It was almost a little uncomfortable, like he had a crush on her or something. He even got some of his friends together to work on the problem. He seemed almost giddy about the whole thing. But now—" She cut herself off, her lips pressed tight.

We all watched quietly as Fitz politely asked Thomas to explain the process and the problem. Thomas sputtered his way through the explanation while Fitz simply stood there. He was relaxed, calm, and attentive. No blustering or veiled threats. Yet when Thomas started listing reasons why he couldn't do what Sylvie asked, he kept glancing over, as if expecting Fitz to bite his head off, probably literally. Thomas offered excuses, and Fitz stood there peacefully, locking him in place with a silent stare. His eyes were dark pools—they reminded me of a bayou at night, right before a gator surfaced and ate something onshore. Deep and dangerous waters. Thomas kept stumbling over his words. Fitz still said nothing. I saw the sweat bead on the witch's brow as the kelpie stared him down. Thomas was definitely uncomfortable, but I guess who wouldn't be with a kelpie standing so close to them?

Finally, Thomas stopped talking and they both stared at each other silently. It wasn't even a contest. Thomas broke first, muttering, "I'm sure I can figure something out." Then he mopped his brow with a handkerchief.

Fitz grinned and clasped the witch's shoulder, making Thomas wince. "Aye, that sounds grand. I knew you'd come up with something. And the kelpies will surely be grateful." He gave Thomas's shoulder a squeeze before letting go. Thomas shuddered.

Next to me, Sylvie pouted. "Why did that work? He just stood there."

"You're not scary," I said. "I take that back. You're not obviously scary. Personally, I find you quite terrifying at times, but Thomas doesn't know that. Whereas, with Fitz, he knows without a doubt that the kelpie would eat him raw and not lose a wink of sleep."

Sylvie's face scrunched up in disgust. "That's stupid. I might not be a witch or anything, but even I know that it's the things that don't look scary that you have to watch out for."

"True, but he knows for sure that Fitz is dangerous. He assumes you're not."

"Assumptions are sloppy and unscientific," Sylvie said, not mollified in the slightest.

I nodded. "You are wise beyond your years, Sylvie. And I agree. I think it's safest to just keep your eye on everyone."

"Well, I'm about ready to punch him. I might see if I can leave the group to it for a bit and go back to the cabin with you guys. I need a break. I have a headache from staring at patterns, and Thomas is driving me nuts."

"Might not be much of a break," I said. "We're taking your favorite witch with us. Alistair wants to speak with him about a few things." I looked around for our new favorite person, and I realized I didn't see him. Maybe Thomas had gone to the bathroom or something? Totally plausible, and yet I felt uneasy. Ezra and Lock seemed to pick up on this as they both came closer to me.

"What is it?" Lock asked.

I kept casting around, trying to pinpoint what was making me uneasy. Everything looked normal. The knitters were doing their thing. Sid was keeping an eye on Olive to stop her from "borrowing" things from the knitters. One of the group, an older woman with her gray-shot hair pulled up into a messy bun, was taking a stretch break. The windows were open and a pleasant breeze wafted through, the smell of summer coming in and diluting the tang of fresh paint.

Nothing seemed wrong, and yet I still felt off center. "I don't know."

The lady came up from her stretch and went to the cupboard, probably to get a glass. I heard a rattle, and I was moving before the woman started screeching. The cupboard she had opened was usually full of mugs, but instead there was now a portal into the depths of . . . well, I wasn't sure. It was deep, dark, and foul smelling, the stench of sulfur hitting the back of my tongue as I breathed in. There was a bellow of rage, bottomless and full of pure venom, a primordial base for the thing we evolved creatures call fear. The room grew hot, and a hand issued forth from the cupboard, scaly and red. I got an impression of too many fingers and too many claws, the scales reflecting the light in the room.

My gut clenched as Sylvie walked right up to the horror. I screamed her name, but she ignored me, leaning in to get a better look into the maw of absolute darkness.

She waved her hand right through the whole thing. "Now that is a neat trick." As we all processed what had just happened, our own screaming finally stopped, the room growing quiet except for the hiss of the coffeemaker and the *tick tick* of the fan.

Ezra nudged me. "Though I do admire your enthusiasm, my beautiful petal, you might want to ease off."

I looked to find my hands bathed in flame. I shook them to get the fire to die down before I clenched Sylvie's shoulder and spun her to me. "Don't ever do that again!"

"How did you even know it was an illusion?" Lock asked.

Sylvie reached past the hand and grabbed a mug for the hyperventilating woman who'd opened the cupboard to begin with. "It didn't seem very likely that a portal to some mysterious place would suddenly open up in your brand-new cupboards. And when I looked closer, I could still see the mugs, which seemed even less likely. Therefore, it wasn't real." Sylvie eyed the woman with the mug, who looked ready to faint. "Would you like me to make you some chamomile tea? We could ice it since it's a bit hot out." The woman nodded, gulping air as she did. Lock eased her into a seat.

Fitz joined Sylvie at the cupboard, swishing his own hand through the scales of the beast. "That is one of the best illusions I've laid eyes on in quite a while. Your witch is quite talented."

I looked around, only then remembering that Thomas had taken a powder. "Son of a—"

"Language," Fitz barked. "There are ladies present."

"You *eat* people!" I yelled.

"And some would argue that you are a lady," Lock said, only smiling when I scowled.

"I don't see how diet affects one's manners," Fitz said with a superior tone that I didn't care for.

I threw my arms wide, leaving trails of sparks in the air as I moved. "Don't you get it? That stupid witch was our best lead! And now he's gone." Bianca and Sid ran off, pelting down the stairs, but I doubted they'd find anything. Thomas had a solid head start and motivation.

Thunder crackled in the distance as Alistair glowered out the window. "I don't like this one bit."

Ezra put a hand on my shoulder, which I immediately shrugged off. He simply put it back. "We'll track him, Ava." He waved at the illusion. "He's done what he does best, so now let's do what we do best."

Sylvie joined Alistair at the window, her shoulders slumped.

"It's okay, Sylvie," I said, trying to reassure my friend. "We'll find him. Ezra's right. It's what we're good at." She didn't perk up, so I kept going. "Sure, it's a setback. But have a little faith." Even to my ears it sounded a bit desperate. I tried to think of something more reassuring to say but was distracted by the giant clawed hand coming out of the cupboard. It's just hard to ignore that kind of thing. "And can someone get rid of that?"

Lock reached into the inside of his vest, a gift from Alistair, I knew. The lining was dotted with several tiny hidden pockets. He cupped his hand around a seed, his face serene as he stared down at it. Shoots appeared, rapidly twisting upward. The trunk became brown and almost treelike, tiny leaves popping out, the air filling with the unmistakable bite of rosemary. Lock removed a branch and held it up for me. I lit it with a flick of my fingers, and he waved the smoke under the cupboard. The illusion in the cupboard wavered and broke, dispelled by the rosemary. He sent Olive off with instructions to find Cade downstairs and ask about potting materials. Lock wasn't about to kill off the plant he'd just brought to life. "They're right, Sylvie. We'll track Thomas down and do what we're good at. If he's running, he can't be completely innocent." He turned his head toward me. "And I'm tired of killing things."

Bianca and Sid came back in, their faces flushed. "He's gone," Bianca said, shaking her head, her hands on her knees as she caught her breath. Their faces were both covered in a sheen of sweat. Sid must have really been running. Weres usually have more stamina.

"Anyone else feeling hot?" Sid asked. He didn't notice Bianca nodding as he stumbled toward the fridge and opened up the door. He popped open a Moxie, downing it in several long gulps, before he moved on to another drink. He was halfway through the bottle of sparkling lemonade when he collapsed, the bottle shattering on the floor. Bianca went down a second later, her body rigid, her muscles twitching. Lock dropped the plant as we all converged on our friends. We watched helplessly as Bianca seized, her eyes rolling into the back of her head.

I felt all the blood leave my face. Sid and Bianca were infected. I stood back and watched everyone running around, trying to help. There was nothing I could do. I wasn't a healer. I destroyed things. I didn't know how to put them back together.

Alistair issued orders, shoving me into motion. We cleared the furniture around them and then did our best to flip them onto their sides. That's about all you can do to help someone who's having a seizure. And as I held Bianca gently on her side while her muscles bucked and clenched, I realized that what I'd thought earlier about only being able to destroy wasn't true. Maybe my gift was destructive, but that didn't necessarily mean that I was. I was able to do just as much as anyone else could to help Sid and Bianca. It just wasn't enough. Still, a knot inside me loosened. Not everything I touched had to turn to ash.

Once their seizures stopped, Bianca and Sid were bundled off into a car to be taken back to the clinic. We all tried to follow but were firmly turned away by Alistair.

"You'll do them no good at the clinic." His voice was firm and calm, but his hair was disheveled, and he'd lost the top button on his shirt. "Sitting by their bedsides wringing your hands won't crack this. Find me that witch."

Sylvie reached out and pulled on his sleeve, a childlike gesture. He seemed about to snap at her but then stopped after taking in the big wobbly tears that were about to fall.

"The witch isn't the only lead you have," she said. Her voice cracked, and she took a deep breath and tried again. "You'll need to find him eventually, but until then you also have me."

She looked away, closing her eyes and letting those tears finally fall. "I think I know what's going on . . .. and it's all my fault!" And now she was crying in earnest.

I knew Alistair wanted to leave and take off after Sid and Bianca, but he seemed to sense that what Sylvie had to say was important . . . and that people were starting to stare at the girl sobbing on the sidewalk outside the bookstore. He herded us into the back room of Broken Spines and made her sit down and breathe slowly in through her nose and out through her mouth until she calmed down.

"Feel better?" he asked.

She nodded, though it was clear that she didn't feel great. I handed her Gnarly, the round stuffed narwhal we kept in the back room for Sylvie to hug after she'd had to deal with a tough customer. Okay, so we all had hugged Gnarly a time or two. He was just so . . . squishy.

She hugged Gnarly to her and took one last, deep breath. "Okay. You remember my aunt, the half-siren? Well, the birthday party wasn't the only incident. She does her best, you know. But even humming can cause problems, and people do that without thinking all the time." She rested her cheek on Gnarly. "They've been talking about having a baby, her and my uncle, but she's afraid. You sing to babies. Oftentimes you don't even think about it. And their baby would be mostly human. And she's worried she wouldn't be careful enough." Sylvie squeezed Gnarly tighter. It was a good thing I hadn't given her Horatio, or we'd have had a yowling kitty on our hands.

"I wasn't supposed to know. I overheard them discussing it—my aunt and my uncle—and after the sweaters I thought, well, why couldn't magic help them? Why couldn't we come up with something, some magical googah, to help them? So I talked to Thomas, and he seemed really excited about the idea—coming up with something to dull or remove powers people didn't want."

Oh no. My friend has one of the most brilliant minds in her head, but sometimes . . . well, experiments fail as you perfect them. That's only natural. And sometimes Sylvie failed *spectacularly.* "What did you do, Sylvie?" I asked gently.

She sniffed and Ezra handed her a napkin. "Thomas really thought it was a good idea. He brought in some friends, people he trusted, and we worked on the problem." Her hands were trembling now, and she looked like she was going to cry again, so I handed her another tissue.

"I spent weeks on it. The witch brought me books, and we discussed theory." She sniffed. "I thought about how physicians used to use leeches to drain blood, and I wondered if we couldn't do something similar. Only without the bloodletting. Find something to drain off the magical excess to make normal life possible. Thomas brought up locusts, the magic-eating ones, but they seemed too out of control. We needed something docile and slow. So we tried snails. I mean, who ever heard of killer snails?"

Fitz raised his hand.

"I mean before this."

The hand went down.

"What happened after that?" I asked.

Sylvie shrugged. "I did the theory, but the witch, he was the one who was going to try it out." She tilted her flushed face toward me. "He told me it hadn't worked. That the snails got some kind of fungus and died. It never occurred to me that he was lying. Why would he lie?" She held my gaze, hoping I had an easy answer for her. I didn't.

"Where did you get such big snails?" Lock asked.

"We didn't," Sylvie said, taking another swipe at her wet cheek with the back of her hand. "They were just normal snails. The spells Thomas used must have made them grow bigger."

"The locusts are quite large as well," Ezra said. "Perhaps whatever makes them magic eating also causes gigantism."

"That explains the snails," I said. "But what about whatever is causing the aggression?"

Sylvie slumped into the blankets. "I don't know. That shouldn't be a side effect, but since I wasn't around when the witch tested my hypothesis . . ."

Alistair folded his arms, his face grim. "We need to find that witch."

Sylvie buried her face in Gnarly's plush electric-blue fur.

Alistair reached down and gently tipped her face back up. "Why didn't you come to me sooner?"

"I thought I could fix it. Then maybe you guys would never know how much I screwed up." Her lower lip began to wobble. "I am so sorry. I've killed so many people—"

I squatted down so she had to look at me. "Hey. Don't. Okay, yeah, you screwed up. But would you have released the snails without suitable testing?"

She sniffed. "No. I would have run proper trials, found volunteers—"

"Which Thomas didn't do. So don't take all the blame, Sylvie. It's not all yours to take."

Lock snorted and I looked up at him, ready to argue, but the expression on his face wasn't combative. It had that distinct "you should take your own advice" look to it. Which I, of course, chose to ignore.

Alistair ran a hand through his hair. Bianca's seizure had taken a lot out of our fearless leader. He was rumpled and grim. "I need to get to the clinic. Dr. Wesley is running tests, and I want to be there when the results come in. Ava, Lock, and Ezra, go back to the original scenes and see if you guys can find some snails. I'll put someone else on tracking down the witch. As soon as I have a lead, you'll know it." He pulled out his phone, already texting orders out. "And take Katya with you. We need live samples, and she's the best way to keep them on ice. If she doesn't know how to do that, have her call me. I'm not a frost, but we have some power overlap." He shoved his phone in his pocket. "Sylvie, Fitz—check on the knitters. See if they need anything else or if they can manage the project on their own. Then I want you both down at the clinic. I want you to read over the doctor's findings, Sylvie. See what you can add. If we can tell her where this came from, maybe we can figure out how to stop it."

18

ATTACK OF THE KILLER GASTROPODS

KATYA WASN'T IMPRESSED by the smoke-stained ruins of the warehouse. She kicked aside a chunk of windowpane with her toe, her nose scrunched from the smell. The police had come and gone. The scene had probably been taped off at one point, but really, what was there to tape off?

"So why am I here, exactly?" Katya wiped the sweat off her forehead. The sun was setting, and the air was thick and weighty, despite how close we were to the water. Even the mosquitoes and blackflies were having a hard time cutting through it.

"We need your expertise," I said with a shrug. "And I think we should really pick your brain about what happened at your house." She paled at that and I felt bad, but I'd trade her feelings for anything that would help Bianca and Sid.

"There's not much to look at, is there?" Lock circled to the side of the debris pile. "You really did a number on this place, Ava."

Ezra pinched the front of his shirt, pulling it out to try to get a breeze going. The shirt was tight, and with the humidity it stuck to him like a second skin. Every time he let go, it contoured to his chest and Katya's gaze wandered away from the rubble to Ez's sculpted shirt. I dipped my head so she wouldn't see me smile.

"I don't care if there's nothing here," Ezra said. "I'm just glad to spend five minutes where nothing is trying to eat me or get some sort of goo all over my clothing." He batted away a mosquito. "I'm not against frequent wardrobe changes, but it's becoming ludicrous."

We got our gear so we could check the place out before the oppressive humidity made us all more miserable than we already were. I was very tempted to go and jump in the water that I could see from where I was standing. Seagulls circled over the cool, deep blue of the ocean. Multihued buoys indicating where the lobstermen had dropped their pots bobbed with the current, inviting me in. It would have felt amazing. Then I thought about all the kelpies I'd met recently. Kelpies lived in the water. . . . Nope, I was just going to stay hot and sticky and alive, thank you.

I popped my sunglasses up so I could blot my face before I started exploring. "Look, we're here, so let's just get on with it. Katya and I will walk the perimeter. Ez, Lock, you guys sift carefully through the debris. Alistair wants us gloved and masked." Even though I'd incinerated the place and then the fire department had hosed down what was left, Alistair didn't want to take any more chances that the fungus was still here and viable. Spores are generally very resilient. So we donned latex gloves and face masks. I didn't think it was likely that we'd pick anything up, but after today on top of everything else, well, I was okay with being careful.

To be honest, I would have preferred my own hazmat suit. Images of Howie in the freezer and my fight with the werewolf zombie kept popping into my mind. I could almost smell the burned fat. Of course, that could have been an actual lingering smell. Who knew. But the warehouse wasn't exactly a high-level risk. Besides the fire and the water, time had gone by and the hope was that there wasn't anything left to infect us. And while masks and gloves might warrant a second look, full-on hazmat suits really draw attention. The kind that gets the cops called, though I wasn't sure who would call them out here. So we did our best to stay safe and took the risk.

Katya was watching Ezra, who was now taking pictures of himself in his face mask.

"Doesn't he take any of this seriously?" Her tone spoke of disapproval.

I adjusted my mask. "I can see that, to an outside observer, it might seem like Ezra has no feelings. He doesn't have Lock's furrowed brow, and he's not obsessively checking his phone for news like I've been doing." I left out the part about my hands letting off sparks of frustration at the empty screen every time I did check. She'd seen it. "So I guess it's easy to think he doesn't care that Sid and Bianca are sick. That he thinks of all of this as a game. But everything is a game to a fox, and that doesn't mean he doesn't take it seriously."

I pulled my hair up, twisting it in a knot so it was out of my face. "Ezra watches *us*. He keeps an eye on Lock's jaw to see if it's unclenched. And he always keeps me at the edge of his field of vision, so that every time I check my phone, he can see how I take the news, or lack thereof. We're his emotional barometers." Ezra had never been a worrier. He didn't mother-hen people like Lock did, and to be fair, he didn't really care about a lot of people. But once you had been accepted by Ezra, you were family. And even if he didn't feel that way about Sid and Bianca, he would have been just as vigilant with them, because Lock and I cared, and we were as important to Ez as his own kin.

I left a thoughtful-looking Katya so I could pace along the perimeter, skimming the ground as I walked. Try as I might, all I could find was broken and charred remains of the warehouse, which didn't exactly tell us anything new. The sun beat down on my back, reminding me that it wouldn't be up forever, and I certainly didn't want to do this by flashlight. We moved slowly, scanning the wreckage, pushing larger pieces aside with our shoes or carefully with our hands. After a while, I was more worried about tetanus than anything.

Ezra pulled his mask down in disgust. "Between the mask and the smoke damage, I can't smell a damn thing except the ocean. Can we tell Alistair it's a lost cause yet?"

Lock squatted down to get a better look at something. "You want to be the one who tells him we've got nothing while he's sitting over Bianca's hospital bed?" Ezra thought for a second, then yanked his mask back up. Lock huffed. "That's what I thought."

Far off on the opposite edge of the debris, Katya raised her hand. I decided to take the time to skirt the edges to get to her. Walking over broken glass and rusty nails wasn't my favorite thing. The last time we did that, Lock had to pull shards of glass out of Ezra's back.

Once I was next to Katya, she pointed to what looked to be a crushed shell of some kind.

We both crouched down to get a better look. The mess was

a dark gray husk of something covered in a variegated shell of browns and creams. I poked at it with my finger.

"We came here looking for snails carrying a dangerous and deadly fungus, and I show you something that looks like a snail. Why on earth would you *touch it?*"

"I wasn't thinking!" I snapped. "It's just habit, I guess. Poking things."

"It's a stupid habit."

"Agreed."

The crushed shell was thinner and more delicate than any water-based mollusk I'd seen before. The color wasn't right, either. The shards had housed something at one point—dried and twisted flesh still bound the mess together.

"That looks like one toasted snail," I said, suppressing the urge to sit down. *Tetanus, Ava. Tetanus.* "Fitz said it was large, but stars and sparks." I splayed my hand out over it. "It's bigger than my hand."

"Yes, and *you just poked it.*"

"I get it! Let it go!"

Though her face was obscured by the mask, Katya's forehead was wrinkled as she examined the carcass. "I've seen this before, I know I have. But it's such a mess, I can't figure out where."

"It's like a disgusting puzzle," Ezra said, leaning over us. "A stinky, disgusting, gooey puzzle."

Lock joined him, and they did their own cursory examination. "Well, I know it's not exactly a live sample," Lock said after he was finished looking, "but I say we bag it and take it back to the doctor. Have her examine it."

"Sounds good to me." I held out my hand for a bag. When no one handed me one, I took my hand back and settled my elbows on my knees. This position was going to be comfortable for about another minute. After that, torture. "No one grabbed the collection kit Alistair sent with us?"

Ezra shrugged. "I don't carry things. Sets a bad precedent." We both looked at Lock. He scowled. Ez and I kept staring, our faces expectant. Over the years, we'd perfected the *we're not going to ask you, but clearly we expect you to do this for us* face. I'd learned it from Ezra. I think he was born with it.

Lock's scowl deepened before he stalked off, muttering. I'm not sure what he said, but I'm pretty sure I heard "ingrates," which sounded about right to me.

"He sure is handsome when he scowls." Ezra held up a gloved hand to block the sun from his eyes. "I've never managed the brooding look well, myself. I prefer a more gentlemanly, world-weary, man-about-town sort of approach. Sophistication, Ava. It goes a long way."

"I will get Sylvie to make you an entire batch of whoopie pies if you tell him he's pretty when he scowls," I said. "I bet he'll really like that."

Lock returned, holding out the kit. I took it from him, while Ezra clasped his hands under his chin and fluttered his eyelashes at Lock.

"Do I want to know why you're making that ridiculous face right now?"

"We were just discussing how much you rock the scowl. Your eyes get all stormy and your jaw squares. Swoonworthy, that's what it is." Ezra held out his hand to me and snapped his fingers. I had to set the kit down so I could shake his hand and seal the deal. I now owed him a batch of Sylvie-made heaven in cookie form.

"You are a ridiculous man," Lock said, but his scowl was gone, which was probably why Ezra had started the discussion in the first place.

Ezra adjusted his latex gloves. "Please, it's only one of my many charms."

"Can't argue with that," I said, opening the kit. Once we had the bags, we began the incredibly fun process of trying to pry the sample up without actually damaging it even more. Between the sun and the salt air, it was practically glued to the wooden planks. For reasons I didn't want to examine, the kit included a putty knife, but even with that it was a slow process. Lock and Ezra went back to searching while Kat and I collected. It was slow going until Kat had an idea.

She handed me the Ziploc freezer bag and pushed my putty knife away. "Let me try something." She held her hands out, fingers splayed in a relaxed pose. The air temperature around us dropped, and the area around the carcass frosted. Katya dropped her hands. "I don't want to chill it too much. It might shatter more. But I'm thinking the cold will make it contract and counteract some of the stickiness, so maybe it will be easier to scrape off. You know, like when you have to scrape chewing gum off stuff."

I got back to work with my putty knife. "Can't say I've ever done that, but you're welcome to do your thing at any time today. I'm roasting, and standing next to you is the next best thing to air-conditioning."

Katya gave me a faint smile. "My dad caught me putting my gum under a picnic table once. He made me go back with a putty knife like that one and scrape all the gum off from the underside of the table, even though it wasn't mine. It was disgusting. He took pity on me halfway through and froze the underside of the table. It went a lot faster after that." Telling the story lit up her face, which just made it hurt that much more when the light died and she remembered that her parents were gone now.

I pretended that I didn't notice. Some people liked to talk their grief out. For others, that was the last thing they wanted to do. I'd let Katya choose.

"Does it get any easier?" She cleared a spot and sat down. "I know they say time heals all wounds and all that garbage, but I just can't believe it. It feels like there's this big gaping hole out there and I'm a half step away from being sucked into it at any moment." Her voice thickened and she fell quiet, staring at her gloves. "They were my parents. How will time make anything better? When will it ever stop being the biggest thing in my life?"

I cleared my own spot and sat, tetanus be damned. "I can't tell you how it will be for you. Some people, it rolls right off their backs, like water off a duck. They go on living, and they can talk about their loss in therapy and read some books about grief or the afterlife or whatever and everything seems tickety-boo." A lock of hair fell out of my knot and stuck to my sweaty temple. I shoved it back with my wrist. "That held no appeal for me. Losing my mom . . ." I trailed off, trying to think of how to explain it. "It hurt. I felt gutted and strange. And I couldn't get over the fact that someone so significant was gone and the world kept turning and I was supposed to turn with it. How? How could anyone do that? It was like being a marionette with cut strings, and that was with Cade's help." I pushed the putty knife gently under the snail carcass. The cold really was helping it come away. "I can't say it goes away and everything gets better. There are some days where I feel such an ache for her—her voice, her smell, a hug. I'd kick a sad monkey for a hug from my mother." The carcass slid free, and Katya held out the baggie for me. With gentle hands, I placed it inside and pressed the seal closed.

"And then there are days where I don't think about her. I think that's the biggest change. You go from thinking about them every second, to every few minutes, to every few hours. Then days, if you're lucky. I still miss her. It still hurts, and I don't think the heartache will ever fully go away, but I can breathe now. I can live and not be constantly miserable."

"Doesn't that make you feel guilty?"

I scraped the putty knife off onto the planking. There was a little sticky residue on it. "Sometimes, but she wouldn't want me to live like that. She wouldn't expect me to not miss her, but my mom wouldn't want me to be miserable."

Katya stood up and offered me a hand. I took it, and she hauled me up. "I don't think my parents would want me to feel that way, either." As she stood before me, staring out at the water watching a boat of lobstermen haul in some of their traps, I could see her trying to pull herself together.

I placed my gloved hand on her shoulder. "I never met them, but surely they'd understand that these things take time. Don't let anyone tell you how your grief should run. It's yours. It takes as long as it takes. I think rushing it can be just as wrong as letting it linger."

"Thanks."

I straightened up, trying to unkink my back. "I was lucky

enough to have Cade. He let me miss her but didn't let me turn her into a saint, either. He always stressed remembering her as she was, faults and all."

"Really?"

"Yeah, and let me tell you, I could have done without the story of the first time they skinny-dipped."

Katya laughed. "You're kidding me. Why would he tell you about that?"

I slipped the putty knife into its own bag. "I'm not sure. I think it was to give me an example of something I should avoid doing, but I can't remember what we were actually talking about. He told me Duncan caught them."

Her eyes went wide. "The Duncan I'm staying with? What did he do?"

I snorted. "Said if he caught them again, he'd join in, and nobody wanted that."

"No way!" She shuddered. "Duncan is a really nice man, but I would think that threat would be pretty persuasive."

"It surely was."

"So they never skinny-dipped again?"

I took the sample bag from her. "Are you kidding me? Of course they did. They just got better about being sneaky. I think that's what he really wanted them to learn, anyway. There's a solid life lesson in there somewhere."

"I have a feeling that your upbringing was much different from mine."

"You'd be hard-pressed to find another just like it," I said, shrugging. "Let's go see if the boys found anything else."

We spent another hour searching the scene before we

gave up. The only thing we got out of it was aching backs and dehydration, and I think a mild sunburn for Katya. We piled into the car.

On Alistair's advice, we took the sample straight to Dr. Wesley. I've never seen someone so happy to get a mystery carcass. Her eyes lit up as she took the bag. She handed me a piece of paper and a pen and made me jot down all the info I had on the sample—where we got it, ambient temperature before Katya messed with it, whatever details we could think of. You never know what could prove to be useful, I guess.

The doctor peered into the clear plastic, her fingers gently maneuvering the sample for better visibility.

"It's not fresh, but it was the best we could do," I said, handing my notes to Lock to see if I'd left anything out. Ezra had already lost interest in the proceedings. He was gazing into a vending machine like it might contain the secrets of several universes. Katya stood close to me, anxious to hear the doctor's opinion.

"Obviously I'll have to run some tests and examine it more closely, but with this kind of shell, it's definitely some sort of gastropod, most likely a saltwater-dwelling one. Never seen one this big around here." She squinted. "And for this size, I would have expected the shell to be denser. When you see the large snails that come out of places like Australia, the shell is much thicker."

"Maybe it wasn't very old," Katya said.

"What does age have to do with it?" I asked. I can admit to my snail-based ignorance.

"Baby snails have really thin, almost clear shells. They consume calcium and the shells grow and harden. They gain color. This snail has a hardened shell, but it's not very thick, so maybe it hadn't had much time to grow a better one." When I stared at her, Katya said, "What? We had a snail infestation in my mom's garden one year. I read up on them."

"So you're saying this snail that could easily double for a flattened soccer ball is a teenager?" I shuddered. "I'd hate to see a grown-up."

"From what Sylvie told me, we can't use any of the traditional markers to guess age. The snails might have an accelerated growth rate due to the magic involved."

Katya stilled suddenly, her hand grasping my shoulder, which was quickly and somewhat painfully cold. "Hey, rein it in there, Frosty."

She jerked her hand back. "Sorry! But I remembered where I'd seen the snail before. My dad found one when he went fishing. He brought it home. Thought he could add it to our saltwater tank. My mom threw a fit—she didn't like him bringing home wild creatures and keeping them." She made a face. "The peryton were bad enough, but at least they were never wild."

Totally illegal, but not wild. "What happened to the snail?" I asked. A connection. Finally. It felt good to make some sort of progress.

Katya frowned. "I don't know. It didn't do too well. We put it in the tank, but it didn't thrive. It died, so my dad put it in the compost."

"Did he handle it?" Dr. Wesley asked, her attention focused on Katya.

She thought for a moment. "Yeah. He grabbed it and carried it out. I think in an old newspaper."

"Could he have gone anywhere near the pens from there?" I asked, rubbing warmth back into my shoulder.

"Oh yeah." She walked over to a nearby window and frosted the glass. "The house is here, the pens are here, and the compost is here." She drew little corresponding boxes in the frost. "Dad would often check on the peryton on his way back. Some of them were quite affectionate. You know, before." She smiled sadly at us.

Dr. Wesley made a few notes on her pad. "If your dad handled the snail and came into contact with the mucus, then moved on to the peryton, it's very likely that he could have spread the fungus. We may never be one hundred percent sure if that's what happened."

"Someone needs to go check out your tank," I said to Katya. "Maybe the snail left some spores or something."

Ezra, having finished with the vending machine, came back to us munching on a candy bar. "I have two questions for you. No, wait, make that three." He held up one hand and counted off on his fingers. "One, didn't Fitz mention giant snails in their old hunting ground? If so, that would be a closer collection point. Possible spores and a longer drive versus shorter drive and live snails? Do the math. Second, if all this is true, if the snail is the carrier, and it infected Katya's herd of peryton, why wasn't her family infected? This appears to spread fairly easily, but Katya is fine and she hasn't mentioned her parents going bug-nuts before they died."

Katya shook her head, her eyes wide. "They were fine." What little color she gained drained from her face. "My dad held it. I put my face up to it, but I didn't want to touch it at the time because I'd been baking and I didn't want to wash my hands." She trembled as she turned to the doctor. "Am I going to get sick?"

You would think, with the gravity of the situation and all, the doctor would have looked somber. Instead, she looked like her birthday had come early.

"I'm starting to see why you work for us and not with humans," I said.

Dr. Wesley did her best to tamp down her excitement. "No, Katya, I don't think you're sick. This thing hits fast. Look how quickly Sid and Bianca started showing symptoms, yet you're still healthy. Which means either you never contracted it, or you're immune. Either way, I'd like to run some tests and take some samples from you."

"I don't like needles," Katya whispered.

Lock took her hand. "We'll all be there. You can hold Ava's hand or mine. And I'm sure Ezra will volunteer to distract you. He excels at making a spectacle of himself. Okay?"

Katya nodded, mutely, but her eyes were a little wild.

"Wait," I said. "Ezra, you mentioned three things. That was only two."

He tucked his empty candy wrapper into my pocket. "Yeah, does anyone have any change? I want a soda."

19

COTERIE INSURANCE: IT COVERS THE STRANGEST THINGS

"**W**ELL, I CAN HONESTLY say this is a first." Dr. Wesley stared at the small plastic vacutainer that held Katya's blood. The sample was frozen, and the small alcove we were in was covered in a fine layer of frost. Fat flakes whirled down from the ceiling, and Katya's breath came out in harsh white puffs. Tiny crystals had formed on her lashes.

"I said I don't like needles," Katya said, her voice just this side of hysterical.

"You might have mentioned the possibility of snow," I said. I sat to one side of her, Lock on the other, each of us holding one of her hands. I'd have let go, but I think mine was frozen to hers. I sent a breath of warmth to my hands and Lock's to keep us from getting frostbite. He gave me a grateful look.

Ezra stopped juggling plastic syringes. "Apparently I need to step up my game, because this is clearly not working."

Dr. Wesley set down the tube and placed a Band-Aid on the

cotton ball she'd been holding over the puncture site. The cotton ball made a crunching sound, the blood in it already having frozen. "I hate to tell you this, kiddo, but I'm going to have to do another blood draw. As impressive as this is, freezing the blood cells can damage them. And who knows what it will do to anything currently backstroking its way through your bloodstream."

Katya tensed. "You have to stick me again?"

The doctor nodded. "And you have to turn off the snow machine, and keep it off. I need a regular sample."

Katya let out a shuddering breath. "I'm not sure I can do it."

I squeezed her hand. "Sure you can." I tried to sound positive, but Katya had only lasted about three seconds after the poke before she went nuclear winter. And she'd been relaxed then. Now she was panicked and tense.

Ezra yanked a chair in front of Katya. "Of course we can do this. After all, I'm involved. Therefore, success will follow. It's the natural way of things." He took Katya's hands from us, gently rubbing them in his own. He held her gaze, giving her a reassuring smile. Katya stared back, her focus entirely on Ezra. The snow stopped, and everything began to thaw. I would have tried heating the room up a bit, but with this much medical equipment, I was loath to throw more heat or sparks around. Lots of stuff in clinics goes boom when you do that. A small concentrated surge around our hands was one thing, but I was not comfortable going beyond that.

Ezra leaned forward, his elbows on his knees, his hands holding Katya's, keeping her arms loose and relaxed, with the insides up so the doctor could reach her veins easily.

"Have you ever heard the one about how the stars came to be?" He used his thumbs to squeeze pressure points in her hands, doing what he could to get her to relax.

Katya shook her head again.

"Well, as everyone knows, at first there was only darkness. Darkness is very boring. It lacks a certain appeal, entertainment-wise. So one day, the Great One decided to create the sun. He was very pleased with himself. He turned to his wife, weeping tears of joy, and said, 'Look at this, my love. What a beautiful thing I have made!'

"His wife, the Goddess, agreed that it was indeed lovely. Not to be outdone, she took his tears, stretching them into thin silver strands. She wound them into a tight ball and breathed gently upon them. The silver shone, reflecting the light of the sun back at the Great One. She had made the moon, and he had to admit it was just as skillfully done as his sun.

"Not yet finished, the Goddess pulled at her necklace, a string of precious pearls, a gift from her husband. One by one they spun off, circling around the sun. With that sacrifice, she made the planets. The two of them began to enjoy their game. When they tired of planets, they made mountains, trees, rivers, every-thing down to the smallest squirrel. And they were pleased. But soon, one type of creature, the one called man, began complain-ing. At night these beings were cold. The darkness scared them. And in the darkness they fell too easily to the stronger creatures. The gods had created humankind last, you see, and they'd run out of ideas by then. So men's claws were weak, their teeth almost useless, and they didn't have enough fur to keep warm. But the gods had nothing left to give. So they ignored mankind's pleas.

"One of the younger goddesses took pity on the cold and

naked humans. She thought that, maybe, if they had a bit of the sun, then they would never be cold, and the light would keep them safe. So one day, when the Goddess and the Great One were sleeping, the young goddess changed herself into a fox, because they are the most cunning and the most nimble. The young goddess journeyed to the center of their temple, where the gods kept the great tree, the center of their world. She broke a small limb—the tiniest she could manage—from the great tree, and ran to the sun. Just as the limb caught fire, the other gods woke up, angry at her sacrilege. They chased her away from the sun, but she was too quick for them. As she ran, sparks trailed in her wake, creating the stars. She had brought the sun down to the Earth and given it to the humans, so that they might prosper. As a punishment for her violation, the Great One made her shape permanent. From that day forward, she would always be a fox."

Katya leaned a little closer, her voice a whisper. "And then what?"

Ezra grinned. "And then the joke was on them, because everyone knows that foxes are the pinnacle of creation. Their curse was by far the greatest gift they could have given her."

I patted her shoulder. "You will soon learn that's pretty much how all fox myths end. They think they're the be-all, end-all of everything."

Katya laughed, her cheeks rosy. When she was done, she nodded at the doctor. "Okay, I think I'm relaxed enough now. You can take my blood."

Dr. Wesley held up several small vials. "Already did. I might have to hire Ezra full-time. That was very effective."

Katya blinked and looked down at her arms. Sure enough,

there was a second bandage, a mirror to her earlier one. "How ...?"

Ezra kissed her knuckles. "I told you. Fox. Pinnacle of evolution. We can steal the blood from your very veins and you won't even notice." He gave her a little wink, and she blushed.

Lock and I sighed and double-checked our wallets. Ezra had been holding Katya's hands the whole time, I was sure of it, but with Ezra, better safe than sorry.

I held my hand out. "I had a wallet."

Lock followed suit. "As did I."

"Sorry, Doc, better check your pockets," I said.

The doctor finished labeling the vials and set them on the metal tray. "I don't carry my wallet when I'm working." Her lips pursed as she looked at her arm. "I did have a watch, though."

Ezra sighed and let go of Katya's hands. He dug into various pockets and returned our stuff to us. "You guys are no fun."

"But we're no fun with wallets," Lock said. "And I find my life runs much smoother that way."

THE DOCTOR left to run her tests. There was nothing much we could do at the clinic. We peeked in on Sid and Bianca, peering through a window of thick plastic the only way we could see them. They were officially quarantined and sedated. Sid slept restlessly, tossing in the hospital bed. Bianca looked far more disturbing. She barely moved, her cheeks flushed with the fever. She looked very ill.

I put a shaking hand over my mouth, as if that would contain my horror over the situation. Quarantined with a disease we had no cure for. A fungus that, as far as we know, struck hard and fast and, with the exception of possibly Katya, didn't leave survivors. Of course I'd known all this before now, but there's knowing it in an abstract way and then there's seeing your friends actually suffering, which caused things to really sink in for me. It made it far more real than it had been. And it had already been too real.

What were we going to do? As deadly as everything had been so far, I hadn't really believed us to be in danger. When you dodge things like this your whole life, you start to think you're invincible. With each barely escaped-from scrape, you get a little more cocky. Even after losing my mother, I'd fallen into that trap, and I'd thought that it extended to everyone I knew. With Venus gone, I'd grown even more complacent. She'd been my bogeyman for so long that once she was gone I relaxed. I shouldn't have. Now two of my friends were lying in separate quarantine rooms, both of them marked for a painful death.

I fought things. You wanted someone brought to heel, something to go away, or to inflict a lot of damage, you sent me. I burned things for a living. But what good was I against something like this? You can't fight a disease with your fists, or with fire. I was useless. Sid and Bianca needed a healer, not a destroyer.

Lock took one of my hands. Ezra took the other.

"We'll get them out of there," Lock said.

"Of course we will." Even though Ezra's voice was certain, I knew he was worried. But that was how he worked. If you acted like it was true, you could make it true.

"We just need a direction." Now it was Lock's turn to sound certain.

"Right. Absolutely." It was my turn to fake it. We could do

this. We just needed a little more time. And all Sid and Bianca had to do was hold on that long.

WHEN WE got back to the cabin, Sylvie was already half-asleep on our couch, curled up in a warm blanket.

"I've been trying to make her go to bed," Fitz said, his tone disapproving. "But she won't budge."

"Sylvie, why aren't you in bed?" I asked. "You're knackered."

Sylvie blinked owlishly at me. "How can I sleep while they're in the hospital?"

I snorted, going into my room to grab pajamas for Katya. "What good is your mighty brain if you don't sleep?"

I clambered back down into the living room, handing Katya the pajamas. "Sylvie, when do you need to go home, anyway? Your parents will get worried eventually, and we need to know how long we can stretch their patience. You can only sleep over for so long before they start asking questions."

She blushed, burying herself deeper into the blanket nest. "I can stay for a while longer."

My eyebrows shot up. "And how did you manage that?"

Fitz perched on the arm of the couch. "I don't know why Sylvie is ashamed. Her plan was a cunning one. She has the mind of a kelpie, she does." He patted her head affectionately. "I am sure you have kelpie in your family tree somewhere."

I wasn't sure what to make of that particular compliment, so I ignored it. Leave it to Sylvie to get adopted by a kelpie. "Sylvie?"

"I may or may not have asked my auntie Fi to give my parents a call," she mumbled. "They think I'm staying with her, so I can continue my work here. Well, my mom thinks I'm staying with her. She went a little overboard with dad. When they hung up, he didn't remember he even had a daughter, but Auntie Fi assures me that's only temporary."

"You had your half-siren aunt sing your parents into submission?" I shook my head. "Two days and you're already tricking your parents and operating in morally gray areas."

Lock tousled her hair. "Welcome to the Coterie."

Ezra kissed her cheek. "I knew you'd be a quick study."

I gave up, rolled my eyes, and started helping Sylvie up. "That's it. Time for bed before you really start to spiral down to our level."

I assigned Katya and Sylvie to my bed. Fitz checked the room, looking under beds and in the closet. Once he deemed the place safe for Sylvie, he left to go wherever it was that Fitz slept. With Bianca in the hospital, the couch was free. I tried not to think about that too much. Ezra took a fox bed, and Lock grabbed a sleeping bag and took the floor. We were all exhausted. The rabbit bed was empty; Olive and Ikka had probably headed to the hospital to be with Sid or home with the drove, putting their energy wherever they thought it would be the most helpful.

I woke up when Cade came home, though he tried to be quiet. The bookstore wasn't open long hours, but there were some little things to take care of after it closed. The dwarves were finishing up the last few renovation details, account books had to be gone over. I think it was hard for Cade to spend so many nights alone, and though his house was full at the moment, we'd been running around all the time. So he'd been taking more meals with Duncan and the crew. While it didn't totally remove my guilt at being gone so much, it did lessen it.

He tiptoed through the cabin, leaning down to pull Lock's sleeping bag up and kiss me on the forehead. He paused when he saw I was awake, and sat on the edge of the couch. We chatted quietly, getting the other up to speed.

"Snails?"

"Yup."

"Sylvie?"

"It's less shocking if you think about it," I said. "We both knew Sylvie had the capability to be an evil genius."

"The problem with intelligence like Sylvie's is that if the wrong person guides it, a beautiful gift can be easily twisted into something ugly." He tucked a lock of my hair back. "Like your gift. If we're not careful, Sylvie is going to come out of this afraid to use her ability. She has a good heart. Someone took advantage of that. We need to make sure we get her to understand that it wasn't her doing."

"Yes, it was." Sylvie was perched at the edge of the loft, her bare legs dangling through the wooden bars of the railing. Her hair was tousled and her face flushed from sleep.

"Sorry if we woke you, Sylvie," Cade said. "We were trying to be quiet."

She waved him off. "I was already having a hard time sleeping. Sometimes I can't get my brain to stop, like when it's puzzling over a problem—it will keep cycling and cycling until it's done." She swung her legs back and forth. "Only this time, I thought at first I couldn't sleep because I was upset, but that wasn't quite right, either. And then I figured it out." She gripped the bars. "I'm *mad*. Not angry or upset or a little peeved. I am downright *furious*. How dare that man take my good intentions and turn them into poison!" She balled her fists and got this defeated look, and I knew right then that the problem, beyond everything else going on, was that Sylvie wasn't used to being angry. It was a foreign emotion for her—she didn't know what to do with it, whereas anger was an old friend to me. It was a currency I traded with often. But Sylvie didn't have my practice and she didn't have my gift and she was frustrated.

"You'll find him, won't you, Ava?"

"We sure will," I said.

"Then you and Lock and Ezra will rain fiery vengeance down on him?"

"I think Ikka will want in, but we absolutely will do that if that's what you want."

She leaned into the railing. "What did Cade mean about your gift being twisted into something ugly? Your gift is amazing!"

Struggling to put it into words, I looked to Cade to see if he'd help me out. He very pointedly crossed his arms and stared back. He wanted me to voice my problem myself. Ugh, he'd probably been reading parenting books again. "He meant what I can do. It's pretty much a one-trick pony. I can't grow things, like Lock. Or shift, like Ezra, or start my own impromptu snowball fights, like Katya. My gift can only really hurt."

Sylvie tilted farther into the railing so that I could only see part of her face. "That's not what he said. Cade said it had been twisted into something bad, not that the gift was bad. You're not a one-trick pony, and not everything you can do hurts people." She held up her index finger. "You made the cool fire dragon." She held up another finger. "You thawed Katya's coffee."

"Yeah, but those aren't big things, or even really that helpful."

"You helped me get to sleep and Katya feel better. Those are good, positive, soothing things. I bet if you really think, you'd be able to list more."

"You burned the rosemary for me," Lock mumbled from his sleeping bag on the floor. "And warmed my hands at the hospital after Katya tried to freeze them."

"See?" Sylvie sounded like her usual self now. "You just don't think about these things—you don't agonize or get upset, so you hardly notice them. I want you to promise me you'll think about what I said. I know you too well to expect you to just go along with my obviously superior argument."

I sank into the couch. "Fine, Sylvie. I promise."

She nodded and moved to go back to bed, stopping herself before she pulled her legs all the way back through the bars. "As far as the Thomas thing goes, it's not that I'm a big believer in this kind of thing, you know. I don't believe in revenge. But some evil, it can't be changed or taught. It just has to be stopped. All the kelpies. That ogre. The weres. Bianca. Sid. Katya's family." She shook her head. "He can't come back from that."

"Can we be sure he knew about those things?" Lock asked, his head still buried.

"When you came to confront him, he ran. It wasn't a surprise. He knew what you were talking about. He either did this all on purpose, or accidentally and then decided to not tell anyone. Either way, he knew. He knew and did nothing."

Cade and I stayed silent, letting her work through these thoughts. But that was enough. Sylvie nodded once more to herself, then went back to bed. Cade kissed me good night and took himself off to sleep shortly after that. I sat in the dark and tried to list all the times I'd used my gift where it helped someone instead of hurting them. Since I tended to do it without think-ing, it was hard to remember, but it was still a surprisingly long list.

WE CAUGHT a few hours' sleep before my phone went off, waking me up. It was a short call. Alistair certainly wasn't minc-ing words. "I'm texting you an address. Thomas's houseboat. I want you and your team out there now."

"Aye, aye, Cap'n," I said. "How are Sid and Bianca?"

There was a heartbeat of silence before Alistair answered, his voice a growl. "If that witch has a cure, his death will be quick. That's the best he can hope for."

Okay, then.

I rolled out of bed, making a small flame appear in my hand as I did. I blew on it, sending it up into the air. I needed to find my pants, and I didn't want to wake up Sylvie and Katya in the process. The light from the living room went right into the loft.

Lock crawled out of his sleeping bag and began pulling on clothes. His bleached hair was mussed from sleep, and he'd put his T-shirt on backward. It's one thing to see people when they are groomed and primped and think they are beautiful or hand-some. They've had time to prepare a face they're okay with showing to the public. But when someone just wakes up and their breath probably stinks and their hair is a mess—to see them in that state, well, it's an intimate thing. I've seen Lock in just about every state imaginable during my years with the Coterie, and you can pack a lot of weird into a Coterie year. And I have to admit, as much as I like to see public him, it's messy Lock that makes me pause. Yes, he had bruised circles under his eyes and dark stubble on his chin. But there was a softness to his face, an openness and vulnerability that wouldn't be there when we left the cabin. This Lock, this was mine. My heart creaked as I remembered that wasn't true. He could have been mine if I hadn't screwed it all up.

"Your shirt's on backward."

Lock cursed and turned his shirt around while Ezra sat on the couch and attempted to pull his shoes on. It wasn't going well. There was a muffled sound as the back door opened and Fitz came in from outside, naked except for a damp pair of boxers.

"Why are you in your underpants?" I asked.

"Because the swim trunks chafed." He slipped around me. "I'm here to keep an eye on the girls while you're out. If anyone needs me, I'll be in the tub." He didn't wait for any kind of response before letting himself into our bathroom. "Good night."

"Is he going to sleep in my tub?" I asked.

"Looks like it." Lock settled his shirt back on, this time wearing it correctly.

"Did you guys hear the call?"

"I heard a call," Ezra mumbled before flopping face-first onto the couch. "You guys can handle it. I can tell."

Lock jabbed him with his finger. "You're going. Alistair said the whole team, so we need the whole team. We have a time-line on this, remember?"

Ezra didn't look up from the pillow, just held up one finger to let Lock know exactly how he felt about this field trip, life-or-death situation or not. You can guess what finger he used.

20

I WOULD HAVE MADE A
HELL OF A KELPIE

WE TRIED TO MAKE it out the door without Sylvie and Katya, we really did. Though we got ready quickly and quietly, they heard us. And once they found out what we were doing, they wanted in. At first Fitz was on our side of the argument, until I mentioned that we were venturing onto a houseboat in Portsmouth, and then forget it, because now he wanted to drag in the kelpies as backup. Which was actually a good idea. Which meant Sylvie and Katya were going, too, because though Fitz liked Cade, he didn't see him as much in the way of protection. We argued long enough that Olive and Ikka were able to meet us at the house and pick us up in the drove van. We were going to be lousy with backup, but I understood. Everyone wanted to help. No one was comfortable sitting around.

I'd never seen Olive look scared before. Surly, annoyed, scathing, and blank—these were the faces of Olive. The way she carried herself usually, it was like watching a grown-up in a little girl's body. But tonight, as she gripped Ikka's hand, she looked her age. The jaded facade fell away, revealing a terrified and worried kid.

"Are you sure you guys wouldn't rather be with Sid right now?" I asked. "We'd all understand."

Ikka shook her head. "I'm more useful to Sid helping you guys than I am pacing around that tiny waiting room. Besides, Alistair is handling that just fine on his own. He'll keep us updated. And his pacing will be more efficient without us getting in the way."

"What are we going to do once we get there?" Katya asked, climbing into the van.

It was Olive who answered. "We drag him out from his hole. We find out everything that he knows, by whatever means necessary." He eyes were hard. "Then the drove destroys him and everything that he ever loved."

"We," I corrected. "*We* destroy him and everything that he ever loved. It's not just the drove on this, Olive. We're a team."

She shrugged. "I don't care who does it as long as it's done." There was absolute steel in her voice—I believed her. Olive was going to be one hell of a terrifying adult.

Sylvie clicked her seat belt closed. "To the houseboat. And step on it."

Everyone in the van turned to look at her.

"What? I've always wanted to say that. The step on it part, not the houseboat part. That would be weirdly specific." She shooed us with her fingers. "Now drive."

There was a chill in the night air as we barreled down the road, waiting for the van to slowly warm up. "What I don't understand is why," Katya said, her face an outline in the darkness. "Why would Thomas do any of this?"

Everyone was quiet as we tried to work it out, but again it was Olive who piped up. I wasn't surprised. Olive paid attention. She had a tactician's brain when you could get her to slow down long enough to use it. Her first thought was always to smash her way through, and I couldn't fault her for that. It was always my first thought, too. Talking is great, but sometimes a well-placed uppercut is really more efficient. If you give Olive ten seconds to think things through, however...well, I'm pretty sure she was in line to replace Les when he was no longer able to lead the drove. Yes, Olive was only a kid. But I was learning from Alistair's ability to recognize talent in whatever form it takes, and I wasn't about to brush off a useful resource just because of age or anything like that.

"Whoever is doing this, what's their end goal? If it was happening in Boston, I'd say destabilization. That they want to weaken Alistair's hold so that they, or someone they choose, can come in and replace him. But it's not in Boston. It could be a mistake—an experiment gone wrong." Olive steepled her fingers, like a tiny Machiavelli. "I don't think that's right, either, though." She squinted, her face pinched in deliberation. "After meeting Thomas, my best guess would be that he's a self hater. No, that's not right. I can't think of the word for what he is besides *asshole*."

"While colorful and correct," I said, "it's also vague."

"Do you remember how he was around the sweaters?" Olive asked.

"He's a sweater hater?" Ezra asked sleepily, his head on my shoulder as he catnapped.

247

To Olive's credit, she'd become so used to Ezra that she didn't even get irritated or respond. "I mean how he kept trying to argue with Sylvie without even listening? He didn't actually want to help the kelpies."

"He fears us," Fitz said.

"Then why did he have me help in the first place?" Sylvie asked.

Olive twisted in her seat to stare out the window. "I'm not sure, but it wasn't out of altruism. Sylvie, you said he seemed nice at first, but by the time we met him at the bookshop, he wasn't even trying to pretend to be nice anymore."

I considered this, with Ezra's comforting warmth at my side. I'd have to remember to check for my wallet when we got out. "The sweaters did get the kelpies out onto land more, making them a more available target. Maybe it was just the first part of the plan?"

"There could also be something wrong with the sweaters themselves," Lock said. "I'm going to text Alistair and let him know we need to get another witch to examine them as soon as we can. We shouldn't trust anything from Thomas."

The area we were in didn't have any streetlights, and the limited visibility prevented me from seeing Fitz's face, but his voice had an edge to it. "Thomas's time on this earth is quickly dwindling."

"I don't think the fungus was on purpose. It's too much." Olive waved her hands in frustration as if trying to think of the words. "It's too hard to control. You can't tell it to stop. Even if the jackass has a cure all lined up, that would mean he'd have to be able to get it to everyone. And some creatures are hard to track down. Some are mobile and might have wandered off. It's too likely to spread out of control. Wouldn't he realize he's putting himself in danger, too?" She huffed. "It's stupid and dangerous. And it's not right. He went after Fitz's people. So what if the kelpies are dangerous? They're also part of the what-a-system. The one Lock always talks about."

"Ecosystem," Lock said. "And, yes, creatures like the kelpies are important. People might not like predators, but they are a part of a delicate balance. They keep the other creatures in check."

"See what I mean? He's dumb as a sack of hammers. And I don't particularly like being beat by a stupid opponent." Olive zipped her hoodie up and settled in for a good sulk.

Sylvie leaned forward, straining against her seat belt to put her arms around Olive's neck and hug the young hare. I'm sure she tensed, and Sylvie was lucky she didn't get stabbed for her effort, but Olive was able to rein in her instincts.

"That deserves the last whoopie pie," Sylvie said. "You get it when we get back to the cabin."

"Why does she get the last one?" Ezra sat up, startled, his eyes wide.

"Because Olive helped me understand a little more that this isn't all my fault."

"But . . . but . . ." Ezra sputtered.

Sylvie sighed. "I can make more, Ezra."

THE DROVE VAN was built to carry a lot of people, but our number was pushing it. So by the time we swung by to have a chat with Gwenant, my legs were already feeling cramped. Ikka had driven, since it was her van, and Olive was riding shotgun, but the rest of us were squished into the back. We weren't quite sure where the kelpies were now, though Fitz had a general idea. He wouldn't tell me how he knew. Kelpie secret, I guess.

Fitz directed us to a parking lot closer to parkland than the one we'd been using. The entrance was gated and padlocked, but Ezra and Olive took care of that. Ezra had also been helping her with her lock-picking skills, in addition to her thieving skills, and he wanted to observe her work on this one. So he just supervised. Once we were through the gate, Fitz had us park, and then he disappeared into the brush. He felt he could persuade the rest of the kelpies better on his own.

We got out to stretch but stayed near the van, leaving the door open to let in a breeze. An owl hooted in the distance, followed by other twittering birds, which should have been asleep. Fitz had been gone for twenty minutes. Considering that I was left with a bored Sylvie, it was twenty minutes too long.

"So, that whole business with Ryan, which sounds awful . . . have you seen him since then?" Sylvie leaned on the back of the seat, her eyes alert. Katya was at least pretending she wasn't interested and wasn't listening, I think out of misguided politeness.

When I didn't answer right away, Sylvie continued. She knew how to wear me down. "Rumor around town is that he's in rehab. I bought it, thinking that was maybe why you two were splitsville. You wouldn't stand for a drug habit. But now, after all of this, I'm thinking maybe the rehab thing was a lie."

"I still say we should have just killed him and buried his body in a bog somewhere," Olive muttered.

"Why a bog?" Ezra asked.

"Who hangs out in bogs? No one." Olive dug a candy bar out of her pocket. "Good place for a body."

"You really should be packing better snacks," Ikka chided. "Nuts. Granola bars. Dried fruit."

Olive rather pointedly stared at her and kept eating the chocolate bar. "This has nuts in it."

Ikka gave up. "You know, we should see about making some sort of deal with the kelpies. See if they'd take our bodies. Do you think they eat carrion?"

"It's worth exploring," Lock said.

Sylvie, of course, was still staring at me, waiting for my response, because not even the discussion of hiding bodies could deter her. "I don't really want to discuss it," I said finally.

"I don't see why you don't want to discuss Ryan," Ezra said from his new perch in the passenger seat up front. He'd decided that he needed to ride shotgun for the rest of the trip. "It's such a funny story. I especially like how it ended with me in a bear trap. And Ava almost dead." Sylvie gasped, and then Ezra narrowed in on her soft spot, really going in for the kill. "And Lock. Need I remind you that he was pretty banged up, too?"

The expression on Sylvie's face was pure fury. Her nostrils flared and she balled her fists. "That . . . oh. No whoopie pies for him! Ever! That is just—gah! And I hope he gets . . . really dehydrated! Because that is uncomfortable and dangerous." Then, apparently deciding that wasn't enough, she sputtered a few more vague and outlandish scenarios of comeuppance.

Katya folded her arms on the seat, resting her head. "He got your friends hurt, some of them nearly killed, and the best you have is 'really dehydrated'?"

"That's Sylvie," Lock said, squeezing Sylvie close. "Even when she's being mean, she's too nice." It was too dark to see, but Sylvie was probably blushing.

There was a rustle in the undergrowth, and Fitz appeared. He climbed into the van, taking his seat back and clicking the belt. "Ready to go," he said.

"Where are the kelpies?" Olive asked. She'd been hearing stories, and I could tell she was dying to meet something more deadly than she was. In Olive's mind, that was not to be missed. I mean, think of what she could *learn*. Sure, she'd already met Fitz, but the opportunity to meet an entire deadly herd of creatures? She was there with bells on.

Fitz chuckled, and the malice in it gave me gooseflesh. "Oh, they'll meet us there. We're going on a hunt. Kelpies cannot resist a lovely bit of chase."

It was about an hour to Portsmouth, so those of us not driving or navigating tried to nap. I tried to get comfortable, but I couldn't seem to find a good place to rest my head. Finally fed up with my tossing and fidgeting, Lock twisted me in my seat and pulled me against his chest. He wrapped his arms around me and rested his chin on my shoulder. "Cut it out and rest, okay?" Apparently his familiar scent and the comforting warmth of him were all my restless self needed. I fell asleep a few minutes later.

FITZ HAD PLANNED to meet up with the herd at Sagamore Creek Headlands, though we beat them there. But only by about ten minutes, which meant that the kelpies could swim almost as fast as we had driven, which was a terrifying thought. Gwenant came out of the water first, shaking her mane. She transitioned to her human form, followed by a handful of the others. Only some of the herd had come. From the way Fitz and Gwenant acted about it, I got the impression that they thought five was plenty. None of them were wearing their sweaters. Until we were sure they were benign, they weren't putting them back on.

"Did Fitz explain about the snails?" I asked. When the kelpies nodded, I continued. "The doctor would love a few live samples. We don't want you to get too close, because they will steal magic and we don't want you hurt. If you see one, wave Sylvie over. She has some bags, and she can collect them." Being human was an advantage in this case, since it meant Sylvie was probably the only person who was immune.

"Understood," Gwenant said. Then the kelpies disappeared back into the water, searching for snails and any traps the witch might have left.

Fitz stripped down, folding his clothes and handing them to Sylvie. "I will swim with them for now. That is where I will be the most help. His brow furrowed, and his eyes became dangerous black pools. "While I am gone, you will protect Sylvie." He eyed all of us, like the second his back was turned we were going to chain our friend to a rock and sacrifice her to a kraken.

"She's been our friend for a long time," Lock assured him. "We'd do that anyway."

Fitz stepped up and took Sylvie's hand, holding it in front of Lock's face. "Perhaps. But she has no claws. No teeth to tear." He dropped her hand. "She is not a green man, a hare, or a fox. She can't send fire or ice to do her bidding, and she cannot heal. Her strength is only human." He returned to scowling at Lock. "She has a wonderful mind, but it will not protect her like these things. Those who are used to mighty claws forget what it is like not to have them. So when I say that you will protect her, I am reminding you of this. And you will do so diligently, or fire will rain down upon you, the earth will taste your blood, and you will never know water again."

And with that Fitz turned on his heel and dove into the water.

"That sounded a lot like the speech my dad gave to my last date," Katya said.

"Huh." I watched as the ripples from his plunge eddied out until they dissolved. "I think I've made that speech. I should have been a kelpie." I nudged Sylvie. "Seems like you've made a friend."

Sylvie clasped her hands and held them in front of her mouth, her eyes wide. For a second, I thought she was going to cry. Then she turned to Ezra and said, "You turn into a fox?"

Lock snorted. "Out of all of that, that's the only part she hears."

Ezra tilted his head. "What else would I turn into? Come on. Fox is clearly the only option that makes sense. I am *perfection*."

21

THAT'S GOING TO
LEAVE A MARK

KNOW HOUSEBOATS come in all shapes and sizes, but entering someone's evil lair, I expected something a little more lavish. Or at least seaworthy. From the looks of Thomas's boat, it wouldn't make it ten feet if you unhitched it from the dock. Even in the faint moonlight, the algae growing along the waterline was visible. The wood I could see needed a good varnish or it would rot into oblivion. Cushions and a lobster pot had been tossed around haphazardly.

It was late, so no lights were on—either no one was home or he was asleep. We met the kelpies at the edge of the dock.

Gwenant, her coat almost glowing in the moonlight, popped her head above the surface of the water. "We have spied none of the giant snails." Her lip curled. "And this boat—it is a disgrace. It's poisoning the water. He should be ashamed of himself."

I pulled my jacket closer. Once the sun had gone down, the temperature had dipped into the fifties. Not cold, but not particularly warm, either, and now that we were out of the van I was feeling it. "Did you smell Thomas at all?" I wasn't surprised when she shook her head. "Well, I didn't really expect to find him at the first place we looked. Hoped, yes. Expected, no."

"But we did smell something else," Gwenant said. "We couldn't place the scent."

The run-down houseboat sat off to my right, taunting me. "So you're saying I have to go and investigate the death trap."

"I am saying no such thing. What you choose to do with the information is up to you. Either go inside and decide if whatever is in there is enemy or food, or burn the houseboat down and go on your way. On second thought, don't do that. I don't want the debris in the water. Yes, go inside and investigate. That is the right course."

Kelpies—always looking out for number one. Can't say I blamed them. With the exception of Sylvie, no one else was going to look after them. Probably because most creatures want to live.

I didn't think it was a great idea to have us all tromping around on the houseboat, so only Lock, Ezra, and I went in. Lock pulled out his small flashlight, waiting until we were almost to the door before he turned it on.

"I like this," Ezra whispered, throwing his arm around my shoulders. "Us, getting the band back together. It's been nice to see new faces, but the original team is the best."

"Or you're just stuck in your ways," I whispered back.

Lock slid the door open with a grimace. "I prefer the old team, too, but I don't like the smell coming out of the hull, or that the door wasn't locked."

He flashed the light in, but it was swallowed up by the inky murk. Cautiously, I lit four flames and shaped them like sparrows, then sent them flying into the darkness. I was getting better at this kind of thing, my control having improved over the last few weeks. I thought again about what Sylvie said, and added this to the list of times my power had kept us safe. Someday I wanted that list to be longer than my body count.

The birds flitted about, coming to roost in strategically placed spots in the air. They cast a faint glow on the interior, showing us the ladder down into the hold, the small kitchen and table, and two doors, which I assumed led to the head and the sleeping quarters. Everything was in disarray, but I couldn't tell if there had been some sort of altercation or if that was just the normal state of things. Maybe whoever had been living here was a total slob.

"Those are new," Lock said, indicating the fire sparrows.

"I've been practicing my delicate work," I said. "You know, in my copious amounts of downtime."

"I approve," Ezra said. "Though how you worked without me, your muse, I have no idea."

"It was difficult, but somehow I managed," I said drily. I climbed down the wooden ladder. Since I was directing the fire, I needed to go in before the others. Once we were all down, Lock crept around me and cautiously opened the first door. It was the head, and though it didn't smell spectacular, it wasn't where the odor that we were investigating was coming from. He covered his nose with his elbow and shut the door.

Lock twisted the knob of the second door, the one that led to the living space, but didn't push the door open. Instead, he nudged it with his foot, leaping back as it swung open. The smell that wafted out had us all breathing into our elbows. And this

257

smell I did recognize. I mean, really, there are variations on the theme, but once you smell one dead body, you've kind of smelled them all.

I have no idea how long the man had been there. He was spread-eagle on the bed, fully clothed, though his clothes were tattered like something had shredded them while they were still on him. Thin red welts covered his torso. His head hung off the bed, his eyes white filmed and staring at us. But that wasn't what really caught my attention. No, the thing that really stood out was the silvery sheen of snail tracks. I realized that was what I'd spotted in the warehouse, what felt like eons ago. The snails had been here, and they had feasted well.

And they were still in the room.

We all took a collective step back, moving into the galley. Snails, regular snails, are generally on the sedate side. They take their time getting places. These snails? Not so much. They moved at a pretty good clip.

Ezra hopped up onto the table while Lock scrambled onto the countertop. I started blasting the snails with fire, which— while it did take out a snail or two—acted like a siren call to the snails in the sleeping berth. They streamed out now, along the floor and the ceiling, drawn to my magic.

I threw another fireball. "Guys? A little help? Please don't let my tombstone say 'Death by Gastropod.'"

Ezra grabbed a cribbage board and started whacking them off the ceiling. Their shells gave a loud crunch, and I could tell from the thickness of the shell that these were more mature than the one I'd found at the warehouse. Lock twisted on the narrow counter and threw the cabinets open, tossing out plates and cups and boxes of cereal. I had no idea what he was doing, but I had to have some faith in him and let him go about it. I'd give him a minute. And then I would start yelling.

Dozens of slimy death snails raced toward me. I stomped and kicked, shooting fireballs the whole time, and even though I was making headway, they were moving too quickly and there were too many of them for me to hold them off indefinitely. Especially since more were sliming along the ceiling, despite Ezra's aerial attack.

Lock was still throwing food—boxes of mac 'n' cheese, a jar of jam—and then he must have found what he was looking for, because he spun back around. In his hand was a large container of salt. He popped the spout open and poured it all over the floor. These snails may have been large and magic eating, but they had the same basic biology as regular snails and didn't like salt one bit. The salt got to a few of them before the rest learned and drew back. The snails didn't even pause as they moved to the sides, avoiding the floor and the salty grave awaiting them there.

With more of them coming from the sides and above, Ezra was getting overwhelmed, and he couldn't kill them fast enough.

One landed on his shoulder and I blasted it off. "Don't let them touch you! They're probably carrying that fungus!" I already had two friends in the Coterie clinic doing their best to stay alive. I didn't need Ezra and Lock in there, too.

Lock dug into his pockets and threw a few seeds at the body in the sleeping berth. For a few very long seconds, I didn't see anything happening beyond the snail onslaught. Ezra was swinging and Lock kicked and I threw fire, worried that we'd set the boat alight and not have enough time to escape. Death by snail and death by burning boat sounded equally terrible.

Thick green shoots appeared, their ends flattening as they drew closer to us. Flat mouths appeared and opened, the brilliant pink maws spanning wide before they started snapping up snails with a satisfying crunch. Giant Venus flytraps. I wasn't the only one who'd been working on their game this summer apparently.

Ezra's cribbage board snapped with a splintering crack, making him retreat to the edge of the table. Lock tossed him a cutting board so he'd have something to defend himself with. Snails continued to rain down on us, despite our best efforts.

One managed to get behind me and landed on my back. Panic shot through me at the same time I felt something slimy touch my neck. I felt a weird pull throughout my body as the thing began to feed.

When I was really little, I loved the swings. There was something magical about being able to fly up and almost touch the sky. I don't remember where I was when I first saw a kid jump off midswing, but I instantly saw the appeal. No time-consuming, boring slowdown, but instant flight into the ether. A brief moment of elation hanging suspended in the sky like a bird. I could do that. I *wanted* to do that. So when my mom's back was turned, I took my chance and leapt. Only I didn't fly and land triumphantly on my feet. I dismounted wrong and landed flat on my back, knocking the wind out of me. My lungs contracted and I couldn't draw in breath, and I knew suddenly what a landed fish must feel like.

That's what it felt like to have the snail on me. Like all my air was gone. Like I was dying. I couldn't think, I just reacted. One second, the snail was enjoying his meal. The next, he was vaporized to ash and I could breathe again.

Our fight ended with a final snap of the jaws of Lock's giant flytrap. I listened to the crunch as it chewed, sounding uncannily like me when I'm eating cornflakes.

"I didn't realize Venus flytraps chewed." My voice was strong, but I could feel a fine tremor moving through my body as it tried to process all the unspent adrenaline.

"They don't," Lock said. "I think it's my influence."

I sat on the first step of the ladder leading topside. The floor was littered with smashed shells, scorch marks, and whatever it was that made up the snails' bodies. We stayed like that for a moment, all of us breathing hard and a little bit in shock.

"I'm never eating escargot again," Lock said.

Ezra tossed the cutting board. "Really? I plan on eating it a lot more. Vengeance will be mine, snail-kind."

I carefully examined the wreckage. "I'm assuming we can't just leave now and let this all shake itself out?"

Lock clambered down. "No. We have to call in a cleanup team. These snails need to be disposed of. And unfortunately, we need to look at that guy again and get a picture for identification."

"We are just so lucky." A shell crunched under my boot. Considering how many clothes I'd gone through that month, I was really hoping snail goo cleaned off boots easily.

"And we get the added bonus of worrying about infection. Did either of you come into contact with the snails?" Ezra shook his head, but I had to raise my hand. Lock went pale as I explained and took off my jacket to show him the spot.

He used a butter knife he found in the galley to move my shirt aside so he could look. I'd burned a hole in the fabric since it wasn't warded like my jacket was.

He let out a shaky breath. "I don't even see any residue. I think you burned it clean away. You're probably safe, but Dr. Wesley is going to have to check you out when we get back just in case, okay?" He squeezed my shoulder. "Try to not panic before then."

"I will attempt to not think about the fact that I might have contracted a deadly and incurable disease. Got it."

"If it will help take your mind off it," Ezra said, "I can take off my shirt."

"Your willingness to sacrifice is noted," I said. "But I think I'm all right."

Ezra grabbed my hand. "Okay, but if at any moment you need it, you just let me know."

THE GUY on the bed didn't look any better under the flash of our camera phones. He'd been festering for a day or two, but the snails hadn't bothered him once his magic was gone. "Wait," I said. "How did he die? The snails just wanted magic."

"Pleasant," Ezra said as he leaned over the body and sniffed. "Didn't the snails kill the kelpies that went after them?"

"Yeah, because the snails stole their magic and they drowned. They were used to being able to breathe underwater, and when that vanished, they didn't have time to acclimate. So they drowned." I tucked my face into my elbow again, the smell getting to me. "But he was on land. So why did he die?"

Lock carefully moved the guy's clothes where they were already ripped, looking for any visible wounds. Plenty of scratches, but nothing deadly. "Well, beats me. But I'm with you, Ava. I don't think it was the snails. I think someone killed him and left him for the snails. Not sure why." He went back to the kitchen area and washed his hands. "Ezra, call it in. We'll leave this puzzle for someone else. We have other places to search." He couldn't find a towel, so he dried his hands on his jeans. "After all of this dies down, we'll get someone to come out and get this boat out of the water. Let's keep our kelpie friends happy."

I texted the photo to Alistair and got an address in return. Thomas had another residence.

WE PARKED the van a block away and walked over, stopping just out of plain view of the house. This place was in better shape than the houseboat, probably because, according to the records Alistair had found, it had been a rental until recently. Everything was still neat and tidy, the lawn and bushes probably maintained by a service. Gwenant met us again, this time in human form, and this time the other four kelpies were with her.

"This place reeks of witch and other things. They must have been nesting here for weeks." She spit on the ground. "I can practically taste him. Laziness. They haven't even tried to disguise their scent." The kelpies around her moved restlessly in a pattern I knew well. They were spoiling for a fight. "It is time to hunt."

We made the kelpies hold off as we did a little scouting. And by *we* I mean Olive and Ezra. Ezra piled his clothes behind a bush, and Olive did the same. Light diffused around them, and quicker than you would think, a fox and a hare were in their place. I had to put my hand over Sylvie's mouth to keep her from squealing, she was so excited.

I hoped no one had caught the glimmer as they changed. I hadn't realized how much we'd been relying on Bianca's gift. We really could have used a veil right then. Olive and Ezra darted off, splitting up and heading around different sides of the house. They were quickly out of view.

It felt like they were gone a long time. Ikka kept checking her watch.

"I should have changed," she muttered.

"She's faster," I said. "And good at this sort of thing. You've trained her well. Have faith in that." I peered through the bushes, looking for any sign of movement. "Besides, even if you'd gone instead, she would have waited about ten seconds before following you."

We were all getting impatient, though. The kelpies still wanted to storm the castle. Ikka wanted to go after Olive. I think Katya wanted to go back to the van, but she hid it well. We'd thought about making her and Sylvie stay behind but ultimately decided it would be safer if we could keep an eye on them.

There was a slight rustle in the underbrush, and then Olive stood before us. "There are people inside—I think having some kind of meeting. No sign of Thomas." She pulled on her shirt. "I didn't see any cameras, motion detectors, or security systems." She yanked on the rest of her clothes.

"Geez, Olive, you going to tell us what they had for dinner, too?" Katya's voice was tinged with awe.

Olive slipped into her shoes. "They had cod. With wine and butter, I think, and some lemon. And what smelled like asparagus. Why?"

"Just curious," Katya mumbled.

Ezra popped up right after that and followed suit. Lock repeated what Olive had told us so that Ezra didn't cover the same info. He was clothed by the time Lock stopped. Ezra could get undressed and back again faster than anyone I knew.

"Someone keeps peeking out the window. I've seen the curtain twitch a few times." Ezra left his shoes off, preferring the quiet of bare feet. "If we enter quickly, we should be fine. I don't think we're looking at professionals. If anything, I think we're going in a little overkill here."

"Yes, well, I weep for Thomas." He and any friends he had in there deserved whatever they had coming. "So what's the plan?"

Lock ran a hand over his mouth. "The kelpies will infiltrate from the back of the house, taking out any rear guard on their way. Ezra, Ikka, you take the front. Olive, you stay with Sylvie and Katya. Keep them behind us and keep them safe." Olive made a face as if she were about to argue. "It's important, Olive. They need you. The rest of us will go in the front as soon as Ez and Ikka take down the guards. Let's be as quiet as we can. We don't want them to be alerted until absolutely necessary."

Oddly enough, no one commented on the fact that we were leaving Olive to guard two much older girls. Katya may have had some powers, but we didn't know the extent of what she could do, and since her parents had been in hiding, I doubted she'd had much training. Sylvie, as Fitz had pointed out earlier, was human. Good with books, good with brains, but I didn't want her in a fight.

The kelpies melted into the night, their delicate steps making little noise. Ezra and Ikka went the other direction and, if possible, made even less noise. As someone who can't quite make the transition from drunk elephant to nimble field mouse when it comes to sneaking through bushes in the dark, I was impressed. There was the slightest rustling from the front, and then Ezra peeked around and waved at us. He held a short blade in his hand, and his shirt, chin, and hands were covered in blood. It was best not to dwell on what that meant.

Lock led the way, with Katya and me close behind, then Sylvie, with Olive bringing up the rear. By the time we'd made it to the front door, Ezra was already picking the lock. I could tell when the tumblers fell into place by the smug look on his face.

I could see Sylvie staring at the blood on Ezra's shirt. It's one thing to hear about what your friends do and another entirely to be confronted with the reality of it. "If he could have knocked the person out, he would have," I whispered in her ear. "If Ez had to go that far, it meant the person was a threat and we couldn't afford to have them behind us." Sylvie nodded, but I wasn't sure it had sunk in all the way. It was the best I could do in the situation, so I let it go.

After Ezra peeked in and declared that the entryway was clear, we slipped in one at a time. While the outside of the house was in spectacular shape, the inside was less so. It was clear that several people had been camping out here for days. Clothes everywhere. Magazines strewn on a nearby side table. The TV blared from the other room, and the air held a stale quality that spoke of how long they'd been shut up inside.

Before we could get a proper sneak going, a loud crash erupted from what I guessed was the kitchen, and several people ran our way. I counted six, men and women. Not the best odds, not the worst. Ezra's knife flew through the air, missing one opponent's throat by the barest of margins when he dodged away. Ikka and Lock had been farther into the house, so they both tackled the two people closest to them. Olive had a dagger out, and she was crouched and ready. I threw a fireball, making two of our enemies dance back, while Katya iced the floor, causing the last two to slip and fall, their skulls making thick sounds when they hit the ground.

"Olive, get Katya and Sylvie back!" Now over their surprise, the people in front of us started fighting back. One threw a handful of dust, and a miniature sandstorm broke out, forcing us to close our eyes and fight blind. I kept my eyes squeezed shut, my hands ready, but I couldn't use my powers without seeing. It would be too easy to burn the wrong person. We could really have used Alistair right then. Sand scoured my face, and I had to cover my mouth. The only upside to the spell was that our quarry was similarly blinded. The spell sputtered, and I hesitantly opened my eyes, only to have to abruptly dodge a lamp that was being swung my way. I blocked the woman's wrist, keeping the lamp from coming back toward my head, right before I slammed my other fist into her gut. She collapsed in on herself with a grunt. Ikka ran forward and snapped the woman's wrists. I grabbed a doily and shoved it into the lady's screaming mouth. We were clearly dealing with witches, and whatever kind they were, they needed their hands and sometimes voices to make their magic happen. Snapping her wrists may have been cruel, but it was effective, and at least she'd live. I'd like to say we were being altruistic, but we were just being practical. We needed information, and that was harder to get out of the dead. Not impossible, just more difficult since we didn't have a local necromancer and June had gone home a long time ago.

One of the witches on the floor was regaining consciousness, so I threw a fireball, but it went wide as the witch rolled. Katya leapt forward and stabbed him through the heart with an icicle. It was a fast and ferocious move, making me adjust my assumptions about Katya's upbringing. The man's hands were up, his fingers curled in, words for his next spell fading on his lips. Katya hesitated, her eyes fixed on the dying man. She hadn't thought before acting—the killing move had been a reflex—but now that it was done, she wasn't prepared for the aftermath. And that kind of hesitation can be fatal. Ezra tackled her, spinning her out of the way of an airborne sachet. The sachet hit the wall, and black mold spilled out, devouring paint and drywall until a three-foot hole remained. I could see through to the studs and even clapboard in places. It had taken seconds. What would that have done to Katya?

Lock had his opponent pushed against the wall, one hand covering the man's mouth so he couldn't speak. Lock had managed to pin one arm to the wall, but the other was still free. The witch's hands were blackened and gnarled, spiraling, wicked sharp claws sprouting from the fingertips. As I watched, the witch slashed at Lock's side with his free hand. So I dove in and grabbed the other arm. There was a sharp, burning pain as the witch sliced up my arm, but I managed to pin it. Of course, now we were stuck. The witch was immobilized, but Lock was too close for me to use fire and we couldn't let go.

"Move!" Katya yelled. Instinctively, Lock and I both peeled away, still pinning the man's arms but opening up access to his body. The witch spit a spell, snakes flying from his mouth, but apparently Katya had been prepared for him to make some sort of strike. She'd slid in low on her knees. The snakes flew over her head, spattering against the wall, disappearing into smoke. Illusions. She slammed an icicle up through his gut. Not an immediately killing blow, but what the icicle started the spreading frost finished. His skin blackened with the cold, freezing and curling up on itself. We dropped the body, the palms of our hands red from our own contact with the sudden freeze.

The rest of the group had been doing well without us. Ikka had managed to rip off the arms of her witch. Not her usual move, but I think she had a lot of pent-up rage because of Sid. At least, that was what I inferred as I watched her beat the now-dead witch with his own arms. Ezra threw a screeching woman out the window with one arm. His other arm hung loose, broken or popped out of the socket. I whipped around, searching for the last person. There had been six. I found him gasping for breath at Olive's feet. She whacked him upside the head with a remote control so hard, the remote shattered and the man crumpled, out cold. She got a bit of her revenge, but she wasn't into torture, and she'd managed to leave us another informant. She dropped the shattered remote on the floor, motioning to Sylvie for the bag she'd been instructed to carry. Olive fished out a roll of duct tape and bound and gagged the witch, then regagged the one with the doily in her mouth. She was whimpering over her now-swollen wrists, but I didn't expect any fight out of her. She'd been broken. Olive's movements were quick, precise, and practiced. Drove training—you've got to love it.

Ezra peeked through the front window. "Mine's gone. Maybe she got back up, or maybe she crawled somewhere to die. Either way, the coast is clear." Wordlessly, Ikka came up and grabbed his bad arm. She snapped it expertly back into the socket, causing Ezra to yelp. A fine sheen of sweat appeared, a reaction to the pain, and he panted for a second, but he thanked Ikka nonetheless.

"You okay?" I asked. "Do you need Lock to take off his shirt to distract you from the pain?"

269

Ezra wiped sweat and blood from his forehead with the back of his arm. "I wouldn't say no."

Lock was kneeling, searching the pockets of the dead for ID. "I'm not taking off my shirt."

"You're no fun," I said, stepping over the bound and gagged witches.

We went deeper into the house. The kelpies had surprised the witches in the kitchen. It was a mess of broken cabinets, smashed crockery, and thick black ichor. Spatters of blood could be seen here or there on the floor, but even if you grouped it all together, you could tell it wasn't enough to kill someone. Or at least I could tell. Growing up Coterie, much like growing up drove, adds fun and interesting skill sets to your résumé.

I didn't see any kelpies.

"Where do you think they went?" I asked.

Lock pressed a dishtowel to his side. "More important, where's Thomas?"

22

ONE PERSON'S GLORIOUS NEW DAWN IS ANOTHER PERSON'S HOWLING NIGHT TERROR

WE FOUND THOMAS in the basement. The room was mostly empty except for a large aquarium full of the giant magic-eating snails and a pool. Someone had brought in a large portable swimming pool and set it up. The top was coated in thick green algae, the surface rippling with movement. Something was in there. Thomas was bloodied but upright, huddled in the corner. One witch lay torn open on the floor. The kelpies hadn't made it out entirely unscathed. One was unconscious, his side and stomach slashed open. He was healing slowly. Another, a female, was heaving by the stairs, trying to shake whatever the witches had thrown at her. Gwenant and Fitz were both bloodied and torn, their faces grim. By all accounts, kelpies were amazing fighters. One was deadly and five were a force of nature, and yet Thomas seemed to have them at an impasse. Thomas was no weak power.

But as I stepped closer, I realized his strength hadn't been enough. Thomas had been more seriously wounded in the fight than I'd first thought. One arm was sliced so deep, I could see bone. He wheezed when he breathed, blood-tinged saliva dripping from his mouth. He had a punctured lung at the very least. Between that and the blood loss, if Thomas didn't get medical care soon, his upright days were over.

"You were supposed to capture him alive," I said. Thomas wouldn't have much incentive to tell us anything if he was already dying.

Gwenant turned on me, her eyes glowing with rage. "Two of mine are injured and you are complaining? How many have died from the snails? How many of your people have been lost?"

This is why I'm not a diplomat. I hardly ever say the right thing. "Apologies, Gwenant. I simply meant that it will be hard to extract information from him now."

Thomas laughed, a horrible burbling sound. "Go ahead and ask, firebug. See what tonight has brought you."

It's never a good sign when someone confidently taunts you from his deathbed. "We need a cure for the fungus." I didn't expect him to respond, but he did.

"I don't have one." He cackled like it was a grand joke. "The snails, that was the plan. We were tired of the kelpies and of everything else, tired of sharing our lands with dangerous abominations. Every second that these kinds of creatures exist, they risk exposing us. Do you know what it's like to live in fear every day? To live among humans, an easily scared population that would have no problem reinstituting witch hunts?" He wheezed, overly excited, and we had to wait until he was able to breathe again. "We couldn't take it anymore. Living with that fear. But then your friend thought of the snails, and I saw hope. Safety was a few well-placed gastropods away."

"I'm a firebug," I said. "I already live like that. Where would I fall on your list, Thomas? Am I a danger to you? What about the dryads? Foxes? Hares? Where does your list end?"

"But that's the beauty of it." Thomas's eyes were bright and pleading, trying to get me to understand. He held pressure on his wound, but I didn't think it was doing much. "With the snails, we could free you from all of that. Wouldn't you want that? Freedom? Normalcy?"

The thing is, two months ago I would have been on his offer like Ezra on a whoopie pie. But not now. The kelpies, Lock, Ezra, Katya—what were we if not our powers? What were we without them? They were part of us. My brief moment with the snail had shown me how true that was. Before, convinced that no good could come of my powers, I might have made that sacrifice anyway. Now I knew better—my gift, just like everyone else's, could save just as much as it could hurt. I was no more a monster than your average human, with the potential for good and evil both living inside me. "No," I said. "I wouldn't want that."

Thomas shook his head, insistent. "Maybe not you, but others—the ones that can't pass. The ones that live in fear of the more dangerous creatures—"

I cut him off, because I finally got it. "So someone wakes up with a kelpie in their river, or an ogre next door, and here you come, the cavalry, ready to save them."

"Yes!" he said, ecstatic that I understood at last.

"You don't get to choose who lives and how," I said.

His face crumpled and his shoulders sagged, but his eyes went from shining to banked coals. "Oh, but you do? How am I any different from you and your team, huh? You kill whomever

273

you see fit. What makes it okay for the Coterie to do that and not me?"

I didn't have a quick answer, but Lock did. "Alistair doesn't send us in unless someone has already caused trouble. You're striking preemptively. Assuming that dangerous and different means they will eventually commit a crime."

Sylvie walked up then, her eyes filled with tears, her hands balled at her sides. "I wanted to help people, and you, you . . ." She squeaked, too angry to finish her sentence. Then she slapped Thomas so hard, the sound echoed. I'd never in my entire life seen Sylvie hit someone.

"Do you know anything about the fungus?" she snarled, face close to Thomas's. "How do we stop it?"

He smiled, his teeth bloodstained. "No. Kill me. Raise me back from the dead and interrogate my corpse. But I know nothing about stopping the fungus. It was just a happy accident. One of the snails had a parasitic fungus when we got ahold of it. The spells changed it, and once we saw what it could do, why stop it? That way, even if the snails didn't work, the fungus would finish the job." Bloody spittle gathered at the corners of his mouth. "By themselves the snails can't do much. They will drain you, sure, but they get full. It takes a group of them to drain someone dry. But what the snail can't handle, the fungus can."

I remembered what Dr. Wesley had said about parasites. The fungus lived on the snail, waiting for it to drain the magic off and make the host easier to inhabit. Then it moved in.

"And in the meantime, you make exposure of our world so much more likely, you dumb bastard," Ikka snarled. "Do you know how hard it's been for us to cover up your mess?"

Thomas seemed unconcerned. "Our ends justify our means."

"He could be lying about the fungus," Lock said. His hand was red where it held the towel to his side. He was losing a good amount of blood.

I shook my head. "But he's not. He doesn't care. He's dying and he knows he's unleashed a plague of biblical proportions, and he doesn't care as long as it takes out the creatures he deems unworthy. But you know what, Thomas? The fungus can't tell the difference."

Thomas nodded, his eyes a little glassy. He was fading fast. "Then that's the price we must pay for peace."

"You are insane," I said. "Barking mad."

"You just don't get it." He sighed. "Too bad. You could have been a good ally."

Ezra snorted. "Until you decided Ava was too dangerous to leave running about."

Thomas sagged, sliding down the wall. "Still, I'll get you, won't I?" He flicked his hand out, blood flinging from his fingertips into the pool. "Wake up, my darling." He sang then, a crooning tune with words I couldn't understand. But even though I couldn't grasp the exact meaning, I felt the gist of it. He was summoning something. He treated us all to his crazy stare and laughed one more wet, burbling laugh. "Wait until you meet my security system." The last words came out in a wet wheeze. Then he died.

He dropped to the floor with a thud. After a moment, Lock moved forward and checked for a pulse, shaking his head when he found none.

"Well, that wasn't ominous and creepy or anything," I said. "What do you think he meant?" And that's when the surface of the pool *really* started to move.

The water churned, and we all took a step back as a head emerged. There are a lot of weird creatures on this planet, things that people don't know exist, and a lot of them feature elements found in other creatures. The peryton, for example, blend deer and bird. The vodyanoy combine amphibian, human, and sociopath. It's hard to tell if these blendings are just that—combinations—or if they are simply a new thing that our brains have to piece apart and connect to other creatures so that we can understand what our eyes are seeing.

The creature that crawled out of the pool was like that. The head was reptilian, resembling a crocodile in all its giant-mawed, sharp-toothed glory. It hissed at us as it pulled itself out of the pool. Algae slid off its head, oozing over the yellow slitted eyes. The pebbled skin gave way to thick brown fur and a sturdy body. It fell to the floor with a resounding thud. Instead of a tapered crocodile tail, the creature's tail was flat, like a beaver's. We all backed into the wall, hugging the flat surface.

"What is it?" Katya said, her voice a harsh whisper.

"I don't know," I answered, "but that thing has got to be—what, fifteen feet? At least?" And a third of it was mouth. My knees wanted to buckle. I wasn't an expert at such things, but from the size and the thump that accompanied its watery exit, I was estimating our new buddy at around the three-thousand-pound mark. What were the odds that it wanted to be friends with us?

It slid across the floor on thick, stout legs, heading right for Thomas's body. Its mouth parted, revealing jagged teeth, and it hissed.

A few of us might have made it to the door, but there was no way we would all escape without some of us becoming a late-night nibble. The creature nudged Thomas's body with its nose, its nostrils flaring. Then it ate Thomas.

Have you ever seen a crocodile eat? Sometimes they rub their snouts on their kill, an almost nuzzling, affectionate gesture. Then they clamp down and roll, twisting, tearing, the meat sliding down their throats with a few well-placed moves. The creature didn't roll, probably because it was on land, but the rest was pretty similar. I hadn't liked Thomas, but I liked watching him get torn to pieces even less. He deserved it, but the noises are going to stay with me for a long time.

Gwenant's eyes rounded, her lips slightly parted. I couldn't quite tell if she was scared, awed, or delighted. "It's an afanc." Everything held in stasis for a moment. The monster feasted and we breathed shallowly and nobody moved a muscle, as if one little twitch would break the spell.

Then someone's phone started to vibrate. In the quiet of the room, it was incredibly loud. Heads spun, landing on Sylvie. Her face was sheet white. The monster screeched, bellowing in rage, swinging toward her on instinct. She pressed her back against the giant aquarium, her mouth open. She didn't even try to dodge the freight train of creature coming at her. She was too stunned. My young human friend, who had never even heard of the Coterie until this week.

That might have been the end of Sylvie right there, if it hadn't been for Fitz. He grabbed hold of the afanc's tail and yanked. The crocodile teeth snapped so close to Sylvie that it tore a hole in her shirt, but at least she was still in once piece. Sylvie had her head turned, her eyes squeezed shut, so it took her a minute to realize she was still alive.

Fitz couldn't quite pull the afanc back, but he stalled it with the help of another kelpie who'd joined him. The kelpies were inhumanly strong, but they were losing traction. And the creature was pissed off. It turned, losing interest in Sylvie, its gaze now on Fitz. It barreled toward him, tail swinging out and back legs hurtling into the tank. The tank wobbled. Sylvie, body stiff with fright, was still in danger. She moved, but I didn't think it would be fast enough. Then Fitz, in all his bloody, naked glory, leapt over the afanc's snapping jaws. One foot landed right between the creature's eyes, and Fitz used the resistance to catapult himself right into Sylvie. He curled around her body and took her down to the floor. The aquarium crashed over them, sending shards of glass everywhere.

The noise startled the afanc, and it turned back around only to stop short when it heard a new noise. Gwenant was *singing*. I'd never heard a kelpie sing. Based on their ability to charm people when they spoke, I imagined their singing voices would be ten times better.

I was wrong.

You couldn't even quantify how magnificent their voices were in comparison. Gwenant sang, and I was transported to a green meadow. A cool blue river swelled to my left, curling under an old stone bridge. The sun shone on my face, and the air tasted sweet and clean. The hills rolled emerald up into the mountains, and it was all so beautiful, I wanted to cry. As I moved through the mountains, I saw a lake nestled between them. The water stretched out before me, images of snowcapped mountains rippling in the surface.

When the song stopped, we were all on our knees, weeping. Gwenant was humming now, smiling serenely down at the afanc's head nestled in her lap. As she hummed, she stroked the same spot between his eyes that Fitz had leapt from. "I haven't seen one of these since I left Wales," she said. "And this one is simply stunning. For all his faults, Thomas took good care of him." She cooed, lifting the creature's face up so she could kiss his nose. The afanc answered with a throaty purr.

"Why didn't you do that sooner?" Ikka asked.

Gwenant scratched the afanc under its chin. "It's been so long since I've sung that song. Everything was happening so fast—" The afanc nudged her when she stopped scratching, and she laughed. "I sang as soon as I could, hare."

"Where were we just now?" I asked, wiping my face. My fingers were shaking.

"A lake in Wales. That's where these lovely ones are from." She continued to pet the afanc, who'd gone from being the most dangerous thing in the room to an overgrown puppy. I pulled myself up. It was over, done. We didn't have a cure, but Gwenant had a pet, and we knew there were no ready answers, so we needed to head back.

"Not the best security system." Ezra watched the scene, unable to take his eyes off the afanc. None of us could.

"Oh, likely it would have eaten you all if I hadn't been here," Gwenant said. "Isn't that right, my darling?" I don't know what was more disturbing—Gwenant baby-talking the afanc, or that it was happily wagging its tail in response.

Between Gwenant's singing, fighting for our lives, and a ton of adrenaline, I'd forgotten that the tank we'd busted up held anything. At least, until Sylvie screamed. Snails. The tank had held snails. She was still cradled under Fitz, and he was covered in the wretched things. He wasn't moving.

We would have to take our chances with the fungus. There

was no way we could just leave Fitz there. We didn't have any salt, but we'd gotten much better at killing those things. Katya and I blasted them with fire and ice. Lock and Ezra ran to Fitz, yanking the snails off him. Ikka and Olive were both sporting collapsible batons and were using them with amazing efficiency.

The last kelpie—I didn't know his name—limped over and helped us roll Fitz. He was so still, I thought he might be dead. Sylvie scrambled up, grabbing his hand as she did. She was crying hard now and hiccuping a little. Fitz's color wasn't good, and I didn't like the way his arm hung limply from Sylvie's grasp.

"He's got a pulse," the kelpie said. "Thready and weak, but there. He should see someone. Your doctor, maybe."

"You don't want to take him with you?" I asked. "What do kelpies normally do when they get sick?"

Gwenant walked over, her new afanc friend in tow. "We don't get sick, and if we took him into the water now..." She sighed and pushed Fitz's hair back from his face. "We should be merciful and feed him to my friend, for a kelpie without water..." She trailed off, her expression a mixture of pity and horror.

"Without water?" I stared at her helplessly, hoping I wasn't understanding her correctly.

"His magic," the other kelpie said sadly. "We can't feel it. The snails ate it. If we put him in the water now, he would drown." He made a strange hand gesture, and for some reason, I was reminded of when people cross themselves to ward off bad luck. "I would want someone to take mercy on me."

"We are not feeding him to the afanc," Lock said emphatically.

Sylvie wiped her nose on her sleeve. "But he's a kelpie. They're pretty tough. Won't his magic recover? He'll be up in no time, right?" Her face was pleading as she looked up at us.

The kelpie smiled, close lipped, but didn't answer. He didn't have to. The snails had had a good solid go at Fitz while we dealt with the croc-a-beaver, and there had been a lot of them. We'd asked earlier what a kelpie with no magic would be like. I was worried that with Fitz we were going to find out. He was still alive, so hopefully he wasn't drained. Maybe those other kelpies would have lived if they'd dealt with the snails on dry land. We just didn't know. If he survived, would his magic regenerate? We simply didn't have enough information. And if he had the fungus . . . I shuddered.

Lock put his arm around me. "We have a lot of injured, and Fitz needs to see a doctor. We need to search this house, too. I think Thomas was telling the truth about not having a cure, but it wouldn't hurt to go through his things."

"Who isn't about to keel over?" I projected my voice to the whole room. Ezra, Katya, Ikka, Olive, and Sylvie raised their hands. Lock had a wound on his abdomen from the witch's claws. Fitz was unconscious. The forgotten slice on my lower arm was dripping blood all over the nice concrete floor, and although Sylvie had raised her hand because she wasn't physically hurt, she was definitely in shock.

"Okay," I said. "We'll need to get the injured in the van—including our two new captive witch friends. So that's me, Lock, Fitz, and Sylvie—you're coming, too, so don't argue." The other injured kelpies had no interest in our help. "And we'll need someone to drive, maybe Ezra or Ikka. The rest of you stay here and search the house. See what you can find. We'll call in the cleaners and alert Alistair. He'll find transportation to get the rest of you home. Gwenant, are you and..." I stared expectantly at the other kelpie. He didn't offer me a name. Okay, then. "... your friend and your new pet okay to swim home?"

She nodded serenely at me, her attention still on the afanc. Great. Now we were going to have one of those loose around the Androscoggin riverlands. I'm never swimming again.

THE LONGEST car ride I've ever taken in my life was the time I drove my mom to the hospital after a fight with a Coterie extraction team. I wasn't old enough to drive at the time— I wasn't even old enough for a permit, and I was driving a stolen car that had been rented by the team I'd just helped burn to death. My mom was bleeding out in the back seat from a head wound, and I was in such shock that it took me a full ten minutes to figure out that the awful rattling sound coming from the car was actually my teeth chattering despite the muggy evening heat.

My mom never made it out of that hospital.

Basically, I need to start taking the bus. Or possibly a hot-air balloon.

Even though the trip was the same amount of time driving as it had been to Thomas's, it felt like the hour kept stretching like warm taffy. Fitz was still out, though I could see some movement behind his eyelids, and while his pulse wasn't steady, it was there. The rest of us barely spoke.

Ikka drove us to the clinic. Ezra opted to stay at Thomas's and keep an eye on everyone. Besides, if you want someone to look for information quickly and go through someone's house, you send a fox. Well, a fox and Olive. So they stayed back with Katya to search. We'd thrown the two captive witches in the back. Alistair could question them. I didn't even want to look at two of the people responsible for this whole business. We'd set the Tupperware containing the live snail sample Sylvie had gathered before we left on top of them. I figured they needed a reminder as to why they were back there in the first place. The snail needed direct contact to feed, but I bet that little plastic barrier wasn't giving them much peace of mind.

Lock insisted I bandage my arm before I even looked at his injuries. So after I tied my gauze, I did my best to slow the bleeding coming from Lock's wounds. He'd need a few stitches on one of them, but most were shallow. Still, I didn't like the pale sheen to his skin. Our reserves hadn't been the best when we went in, and they were rock-bottom now. We needed medical care, food, and sleep. If we were lucky, we'd get two out of three. Despite the fear and worry, Lock dozed off on the way, but I think that was partially from blood loss.

We entered through a back door, what had probably been an employee entrance before Alistair had taken the building over. No way were we going to walk through the front covered in blood, carrying a naked, unconscious kelpie wrapped in a thin blanket. For the second time tonight, I was missing Bianca's special brand of magic. And if I was going to be totally honest, I kind of missed Bianca. Not that I was going to admit that to anyone, ever.

Alistair ushered us in, sending someone out to deal with the hostages; he took us straight to the doc. Dr. Wesley, who was starting to look a little worn down herself, went straight to work on Fitz while her assistant took a quick look at us. Her assistant still had on a mask, gloves, and gown, but not the whole hazmat suit anymore. Without the suit I could see that her short hair had been dyed a deep violet. She occasionally tucked a strand behind her ear. Her main communications seemed to be one-word commands and the occasional grunt. Lock was bandaged, stitched, and set up with a saline drip before he was ordered to rest.

My arm was cleaned and rebandaged, and then I was told to keep an eye on it. Who knew what had been on that witch's claws. So I had to keep my bandage dry and look out for the tell-tale red lines that would indicate infection. The assistant left to help the doctor, so after I was taken care of, I was left to put a few Band-Aids on Sylvie. She had some minor cuts from the flying broken glass from the snail aquarium. We'd all had to submit to a blood test, and surprisingly all of us came up clean. Tension I hadn't even realized was there evaporated, and if any of us had still had any energy, there would have been a party. As it was, we had to settle for candy and soda I bought from the vending machine. We wouldn't die of the fungus. At least not today.

"Is Fitz . . . Is he going to be okay?" Sylvie asked, taking in a sharp breath as I dabbed one wound with peroxide.

"I don't know," I said. "I've never seen anyone go through what he's gone through. Right now he's alive and fungus free, and you can't hope for much more than that. The loss of his magic was traumatic. His wounds aren't healing as fast as they normally would, and he got tossed around."

Sylvie's head hung down, her hair falling in her face.

I gently placed another Band-Aid on a long shallow cut on her arm. "Anytime we go out and make it back with a pulse, it's a victory, Sylvie." I spread some antibiotic ointment on one of the deeper cuts. "That's the reality of Coterie life." There was nothing left on my side to bandage, but I used some gauze and

rubbing alcohol to clean some of the dried blood off the sur-
rounding skin. I lifted her chin so I could stare Sylvie right in
the eyes. "You know what I've seen? What the Coterie looks like
to me? Death, pain, and blood." I tossed the dirty gauze in the
garbage can. "I've seen enough to know that as long as Fitz is
breathing, he has a chance, and that's more than some get."

Sylvie let out a shaky breath. "It's my fault."

Her statement could have referred to so many things that
were now her burden to bear, but I knew she couldn't quite
shoulder any of that yet. "Fitz? Yeah, kind of. You froze and he
had to act, but he chose to do that. He's at fault, too. That's the
great thing about Coterie work. Plenty of guilt and recrimination to go around." I smiled at her. "If you're going to stay in
this sandbox, Sylvie, you'd better get used to it. This is what you'd
be signing up for." I felt a little bad about being so blunt, but I
wanted to make sure Sylvie understood what working with her
friends really meant.

I left her with her head resting in her hands as she thought
about what I'd said. Maybe I should have hugged her and told
her everything would be all right. But I wasn't sure that was true,
and I didn't want to lie to her anymore. Besides, I think she
needed time to think more than she needed false comfort. I
could always hug her after her thinking was done and the crying started.

23

SOMETIMES THE PROBLEM
IS ALSO THE SOLUTION

TOOK THE OPPORTUNITY to go check on the other two patients. Bianca was curled sideways on her cot, watching TV. She was naturally pale, and the sickness made her appear waxy. Dark purple bruises had formed under her eyes. Sid had been sedated, and the temperature in his room had been dropped down to almost freezing.

"We needed to slow it down," Alistair said. "And cold seemed to do that with Howie. It's hitting Sid so much faster than Bianca. The doctor thinks it's because of his were biology. The very thing that usually heals them is hurting them in this case. It's helping the fungus replicate at faster speeds." Alistair touched a hand to his mouth, holding it there for a long second before dropping it. "I'm out of ideas, Ava. My people are dying. This *thing* is spreading, and there's nothing I can do." The machines beeped softly in the background. "Gods help us if this thing reaches Boston. With the higher magical-creature density, not only will it spread faster, but the sheer destruction from that many infected..."

I stood next to him by the glass, tempted to give his shoulder an awkward pat. "Maybe they'll find something at Thomas's."

Alistair gave a jaded laugh. "You don't believe that for one second."

"No, I don't." To hell with it. I went ahead and gave him the awkward pat anyway. "Can I go in and talk to them?"

"Wear a face mask, gloves, and whatever else the doctor suggests, and you can visit Bianca. Sid is too dangerous now."

SCRUBS, GLOVES, and a mask donned, I poured Bianca a glass of water from a pitcher and placed it on her small side table even though she didn't ask for it.

"We're screwed, aren't we?" she asked, not taking her eyes off the TV.

"Kind of, yeah," I said. "But at least you've got cable."

That got her attention off the screen. "You can be so terrible sometimes."

"It's part of my charm, or lack thereof." I pulled up a chair. "Honestly, it doesn't look great, and I know you'd kick the crap out of me for saying otherwise. We're doing our best, and there's still time." A commercial came on and the volume went up, a squawking voice talking about car insurance. I muted the TV and took Bianca's hand. "Look, Alistair is trying to move the solar system for you, and I know you don't have faith in the rest of us, but have faith in him. That I know you can do."

She shivered and pulled her blanket close. "How's everyone else? How's Sid?"

I filled her in on the evening's fun, trying to make the story entertaining, if only to distract her from reality for a minute. Then I had to ruin it all by telling her about Sid. She closed her eyes, looking fragile.

"Do me a favor?" she asked, keeping her lids closed. "Have June raise Thomas back from the dead and kill him a second time."

"How about we wait until you're cured and then you can do that yourself? I'll even go in first and get him ready for you."

Bianca snorted. "That implies that I'd need such a thing. I may not be able to light fires, but I can fight." Something unreadable crossed her face, like a shadow underwater. She grimaced. "Ava, just in case, there's something I want to ask you."

"You're not secretly my sister or anything, are you? Because those kinds of revelations are so two months ago."

"Ugh, no. We're not related, I promise."

"Try to not sound so relieved," I said.

She pulled herself upright and took a sip of water. "I know you function under the assumption that the entire world revolves around you, but it doesn't."

"Vicious lies." I helped Bianca arrange the pillows until she was sitting comfortably. This was probably the best hospital bed money could buy, but it was still a hospital bed. Those things are never comfortable.

Bianca nestled back in, her eyelids heavy and drooping already, tired from our short interaction. "If the worst happens, will you take care of Alistair?" Her words were almost a whisper. This conversation was clearly just between us.

I blinked, surprised she'd trust me with the person she held most dear.

She grinned, and I think, if she'd felt better, she would have been howling with laughter at my expense. "The look on your face. I'm not asking you to marry him, Ava, just keep an eye on him. I know you. Once you promise loyalty and protection, you're all in like a bloody Boy Scout. I want him up there at Lock, Ezra, and Cade level."

"But what if I don't stay with the Coterie? And speaking of that, what could I possibly do that he couldn't hire a dozen people to do right now?"

Her brow furrowed, all humor gone, and a faint dew of sweat appeared on her face. I grabbed a paper towel and handed it to her. "That's not the same and you know it. Mercenaries can be bought out. You can't."

"And if I leave the Coterie?"

She examined me then as if really, truly looking at me. "Do you actually think that's possible for you? I don't mean because of your contract. I mean because of you. You're good at this, and I know you don't like to admit it, but when you're in the thick of things, you enjoy your job."

She was right. I didn't want to admit it. I looked out through the thick window and watched Alistair as he talked to Lock and the doctor. Alistair's shirt was unbuttoned at the top and looked like he'd slept in it. His hair was brushed, but sat slightly askew from him running his hands through it. He still looked *GQ*, but for Alistair he looked like a wreck. He was truly, deeply worried. And that right there was the difference between him and Venus. Alistair could be brutal and efficient. He'd make hard sacrifices if he thought they were necessary, but he actually cared about the impact things had on the people the Coterie protected. That might change as the power got to him. He might eventually become corrupt like Venus. But not now. And this Alistair was worth protecting.

"Okay," I said. "You got it."

"One more thing."

"Stars and sparks, I don't even get a thank-you? Man, you are demanding when you are sick. Most people just want soup."

She gave me a lopsided grin, but she was still serious, too. "I want you to give Lock a chance."

"What is in your IV drip, exactly? Because I'm now worried that you think you're hallucinating this whole encounter. Or are you just trying to get me to take your hand-me-downs out of guilt? Was the one date you guys went on that terrible? Is this a weird vengeance game with you?" I took a deep breath and steadied myself. If I sparked, my gloves would melt, and no one wanted that.

"I don't even think that date counted as a whole one. More of a half date. Somewhere between dinner and dessert, he apologized and called things off because of you, saying it wasn't fair to me, and we decided we made better friends."

"Wow, that really sucks." I would say no wonder she didn't like me, but then again, she hadn't liked me before the date.

Bianca waved her hand in a so-so gesture. "Yes and no. It hurt my pride, and I seriously considered shaving your head in your sleep. But then I decided that as great a boyfriend as Lock would have been, I needed the friend I got more." Her voice became bone-dry as she said, "Oddly enough, I don't seem to be very good at making them."

"Wouldn't know anything about that. I'm not awkward with people or anything. Smooth, that's me." I suddenly found the hospital booties on my feet to be really interesting. "Now you can see why I was afraid to screw things up." I was thinking that I could probably slide around in these booties and pretend they were ice skates, especially on the wood floors of the cabin. I'd have to throw these away when I left, but maybe I should steal a new pair on the way out. "You can still shave my head if you want."

"If you figure out a way for me to survive this thing, we'll call it a draw." She closed her eyes, as if the conversation had drained all the energy out of her. "At least think about it, okay?" Her voice was already a half-asleep mumble.

"It's a deal, hoss," I said, tiptoeing across the floor before closing the door softly behind me. Just in case, I'd keep Bianca away from hair clippers if she ever got better.

IT WAS HELL watching our friends get sicker. Alistair tried to send us away, but no one would listen to him. He didn't enforce the decree. Once again I was struck by the difference between him and Venus. We were allowed to disobey. He said "go," we stayed, and no one was hit, tortured, or forced to do anything terrible. We wouldn't be able to stay and observe forever, though. The fungus was going to spread up and down the coast. Alistair's kingdom would fall apart. The other teams he'd put together had been running around dealing with the fallout while we'd been tracking down Thomas, but they couldn't handle it all much longer.

At some point, Alistair got tired of having all of us underfoot and sent us out to at least get some breakfast. Or I guess it was more like brunch now. None of us wanted food, and we weren't fit company for the human populace anyway. What I really wanted was to be home in my cabin, waking up to Cade making me breakfast. I missed the bookstore. I missed having bean suppers with Duncan and the drove. I selfishly wanted to sleep in and watch terrible movies with Sylvie and eat candy until one of us had to vomit. I wanted normalcy. My normalcy, and not anyone else's. It might have taken me a while to realize it, but I liked my weird life, and I wouldn't give it up for anything.

So we ended up going back to the cabin. Judging from the look on Cade's face, that was probably for the best. I looked at our group with new eyes. We were dirty, our clothes were ripped, and most of us had blood on us. We looked like we'd picked a fight with a wild bull and lost. Cade waved us in and got the coffeepot going. No one had the energy to help. We all leaned on the table, quiet, exhausted, and depressed.

"No Veronica and Olive this morning?"

For whatever reason, Cade had really taken to having the hares around. He must really miss having a kid in the house if he was missing *Olive*.

"Everyone met up at the hospital as soon as they were done at Thomas's," I said. "Nothing else useful for them to do right now, so they stayed to keep an eye on Sid."

"If we can," Sylvie added, her cheek resting on the table, "we should bring them some food that doesn't come from a vending machine."

"Of course." Cade got out the bread for toast and grabbed the eggs from the back of the fridge. I stood up to help him, and he shoved me one-handed back into the chair. "You look like you're about to keel over. Sit."

I didn't try to get back up. He was right. I was weary down to my freaking bones. My heart felt worn through, all the energy having leaked out of the resulting hole. I rested my chin on my hands, which were folded on the table.

"I don't think I've ever felt this hopeless," I said. "Even with all the crap we had to wade through with Venus, I never felt like I do right now."

"Not even when you lost your mom?" Katya asked.

"That was different," I said, watching Lock as he rose to grab us all orange juice. Ezra got the glasses. Things had to be bad if Ezra was helping and not complaining about it. "I felt devastated, but I had a goal and a plan, even if it was just to get to Cade. But this . . . I don't even know what to do with this."

Ezra rolled his neck, trying to stretch out the kinks. "I think it's because we were used to how it was before. We might not have liked how Venus ran things, but we knew to expect misery and awfulness. But with Alistair, there's no precedent to follow."

"For a minute, we all tasted change," Lock agreed. "We got to see what the Coterie could become. Then Thomas had to go Attack of the Giant Gastropods all over it." He spilled a little of the orange juice and set the carton down to get a towel. "Also, you hate any situation that can't be solved with fire or a solid uppercut."

I'd have argued, but he was right. That was the scary thing about diseases—you couldn't really fight them. Your immune system had to do that. It didn't matter how healthy and strong you were, either. There was always a tiny organism out there in the world that could take you down. "If we could find a cure, that would be fighting it."

"What do you want us to do, Ava? Put on some lab coats and try to Scooby Doo this problem away?" Lock tossed the towel onto the counter angrily. Cade didn't say anything—didn't even look at him—but two seconds later Lock was straightening it and putting it back on the bar to dry.

"I can't help you with cartoon montages," Ezra said, his chin in his hand. "But I could get us lab coats. I know a guy."

I snorted. "You always know a guy."

Sylvie stared at her orange juice glass, watching the condensation build on the sides. "I've been thinking about that."

"Ezra getting us back-alley lab coats?" I asked.

"I think we've been approaching this wrong again."

Katya drew on the table with her finger, leaving a frost line as her fingertip brushed the surface. "In what way?"

"The doctor's been looking into an antibiotic or some other medicine that can touch this thing. We searched Thomas's house, hoping he had a cure stashed away. Either way, we're going about this medicinally."

"That tends to be how illness is approached," Cade said. The pan hissed as he poured in the eggs.

"But this isn't a normal sickness," Sylvie said emphatically. "It's magic."

"It's still sickness," Cade said. "It's going to act a certain predictable way, and it will react to something. Everything has a cure. You just need to find it in time."

"But that's the thing," Sylvie said, looking up from her glass. "This parasite is predictable, at least so far, but that doesn't mean it's the same as a human illness. We can see that in the fact that Sid's having a hard time with the fungus. If it were a normal disease or parasite, his system would have given it the boot already, right?"

"Where are you going with this?" I asked.

"Magic," she said as Cade put the first batch of toast onto a plate. "That's what's making the fungus act differently."

"They really do remind me of those locusts," Ezra said.

"Then let's start there," Sylvie said. "What made the locusts frenzy?"

I got the jam out of the fridge and placed it on the table. "A high concentration of magic. They're drawn to it." I paused, my hand hovering over the jar after I set it down. "Which is how we baited the locusts. I threw fire to distract them and draw them away from Ezra."

Sylvie tapped the table with her fork. "This fungus is drawn to magic, and it mutated to adapt to the snails' magic. So why wouldn't the cure be magic?"

We all digested this while Cade scrambled the eggs, stopping occasionally to turn the bacon he'd decided to cook in a separate pan. "What we need to do is put all the elements we have together. So what have we learned about the fungus?" Sylvie mused.

"It only affects magical creatures," I said.

"It doesn't seem to like me or my family very much," Katya said.

"It doesn't thrive in the cold," Lock said. "That's why they dropped the temperature in the clinic."

Ezra grabbed a piece of bacon from my plate as soon as Cade placed it there. "What if it hates Katya's family because of what they are? It doesn't like cold. They regularly reach temperatures on the low end. Maybe that's why they were never infected. The fungus finds the cold uninhabitable."

I thought back to the locusts again, and to the snails on the boat—they'd moved toward me even though I was throwing fire at them. "What if we found a way to bait the fungus itself? Draw it out of the host body?"

Sylvie squinted in the bright sun streaming in through the window. "Dialysis. Do you guys know how dialysis works?"

We didn't, but Cade did. "They use an artificial kidney." He scraped the eggs into a large serving bowl. "Your blood goes into the machine and it uses a compound—I can't remember the name—to balance your electrolytes and clean out your blood. Then it goes back in." The pan sizzled and popped as he added new bacon. "I saw a documentary about it."

"So what if we did magical dialysis?" Sylvie asked.

"How? Did you invent a magical artificial kidney this morning before breakfast?"

Sylvie shook her head. "We don't need a machine. Machines aren't magic—you guys are. What we need to do is convince the fungus that its host is no longer viable and it needs to move on. Then we'll need bait to convince the fungus to leave. Once we have it rounded up, we destroy it."

"How would we convince the fungus the host is about to go?" I asked. "It's not like we could send it an invitation or anything."

Lock took over the bacon without being asked as Cade poured pancake batter into a pan. "The doctor mentioned other parasites like this, right?" Lock asked. "They left when they were offered something better or there was a necessary new step, like seeking a breeding ground. Magical creatures offer them food but they also offer them somewhere to breed. We need to ask the doctor if there's some way we could safely make the host body uninhabitable." He turned the pieces of bacon one by one in the pan, making sure they browned evenly. "We need to get back to the clinic and see if we can get anyone on board with this crazy idea."

ALISTAIR WASN'T exactly thrilled with Sylvie's plan, but he listened. I think it was the "make the host's body unappealing" part of things that he found troubling. Because the best idea we had for that was for the doctor to medically induce a coma and use ice packs to cool the body down. We didn't want to use magic to do it because that would be offering the fungus a fuel and would entice it to stay. Once the hosts were cold, we would have to tempt the fungus into exiting. We'd use the snails Alistair's team had confiscated from Thomas's for that. We'd put one into contact with the infected person. The fungus had already shown a liking for them, so it should make its way back into the snail. We would just have to hope that the weakened physical and magical state of the hosts would make the snail not want to feed off them. If not, we'd have to act quickly before the snail got more than a bite or two. Once the transfer had been made, Dr. Wesley or one of our other resident humans could remove the snail. Katya would freeze it, and then we'd bag it up, label it, and hand it off to the doctor to test. We were hoping that she'd eventually be able to manufacture some sort of vaccine or something if we managed to get her enough samples.

It seemed crazy, somewhat dangerous, and I had no idea if it would actually work. So really, not much different from our normal plans.

"We should test it on Bianca," Dr. Wesley said.

"Absolutely not," Alistair said emphatically. I caught a faint whiff of ozone as thunder rolled through the room.

"Cut that out," Dr. Wesley said. "This is a hospital room. Not a good place for a tantrum." The doctor slipped a pen into the pocket of her scrubs. "Remember, Alistair, as the fungus progresses, it destroys the brain. It hasn't gone that far in Bianca, but once it does, there's no coming back from that. Sid is a were. If we get the fungus out of him and give him time, he will heal any sort of brain damage as long as it's not fatal. For her sake, Bianca should go first."

I could tell Alistair still wanted to debate the plan further but couldn't think of anything valid to say. We couldn't put it off if we wanted to save Bianca's brain. She might not have the most charming of personalities sometimes, but better bitchy than vegetable.

Bianca agreed with our logic, though hesitated at the "we're going to put a giant magic-eating snail on your chest" part. Not the forced-coma thing. No, she was cool with that. But the snail? Well, she'd heard what I'd said about Fitz, and he hadn't woken up yet. Bianca's life, like most of our lives, was centered around her gift. What would she do if it were gone?

Dr. Wesley and her assistant hooked Bianca up to a lot of machines that I couldn't identify—things that beeped, hummed, and even went *ping*. The Monty Python boys would have been thrilled. Any machine that wouldn't play well with even the smallest spark was removed if it could be. Cold packs were placed around her body. Sylvie brought in a snail in a cat carrier, which was just weird. Once Bianca was confirmed to be under and cold enough, we needed to offer tempting bait. I, of course, made the best bait.

I created a small fire butterfly, letting it hover above Bianca's chest, keeping it close enough to draw the fungus, but not so close as to warm Bianca up. A rosy stain spread under Bianca's skin directly under the butterfly. The bait was working. Once the stain stopped growing and the doctor thought all the fungus was accounted for, I let the butterfly dissipate, and Sylvie handed the doctor the snail.

The doctor placed the snail on Bianca's chest directly above the pink stain. She held it there, which was harder than it sounds, because the snail wasn't really interested in staying still. We all watched in disgusting fascination as the stain moved up Bianca's chest toward her throat.

Katya stood by, ready to freeze the snail at a moment's notice. Then we waited, a rapt audience observing through the glass. The doctor had insisted that everyone else wait outside unless they were needed. Not a good idea to give the fungus other tempting hosts.

The minutes ticked by.

"How long until we know if it's worked?" Sylvie whispered. Everyone had been whispering, even though they couldn't hear us through the glass and it wasn't like we were going to wake Bianca up.

"Until I'm sure the spores have all moved onto greener gastropod pastures," I said, sounding confident, even though I felt far from it.

Bianca sneezed then. And she kept sneezing, sending a clear fluid out over the doctor and the snail. The snail went crazy for it, and acting on instinct, the doctor let the snail go, letting it clean up all the infected fluid.

"See?" I said. "I told you it would find a way." The fungus was magic, and the snails were drawn to the closest source.

"Nature is disgusting," Katya said.

"I agree." I took another step back, feeling that a little more space between me and the fungus was for the best. "Fighting fungus mucus with snails and vice versa. I am going to be so glad when we can go back to beating things up."

Dr. Wesley removed the snail, holding it up for Katya. The snail shied from her, trying to pull its head into its shell, but you can't run from a Jill Frost. Katya froze it quickly. I doubt the snail had time to suffer. The purple-haired assistant entered as soon as the snail was frozen and the doctor deemed it safe, and held open a collection bag with gloved fingers. The doctor dropped the flash-frozen gastropod inside. It was done. The cold would, hopefully, kill the fungus, leaving the snail for her to dissect and study. Just to be safe, the doctor and her assistant cleared the room so Katya could finish up. We weren't sure that the snail had cleared away all the fungus, so she sent a frost along the walls, blankets, counters, and finally across Bianca's skin. Bianca might end up with some frostbite, but she could recover from that. Katya left the room and the doctor came back in, ready to bring Bianca's body temperature back up. Dr. Wesley kept glancing at the machines, their pings and whirs telling her something that none of us could understand.

After a frenzy of activity involving warm blankets and rapid-fire orders, the doctor stopped. She took off her gloves, tossed them in the garbage can, and pulled down her mask. The doctor came out to go over everything with Alistair. "We've started the wake-up process. Now we'll just have to wait and see."

I crossed my fingers.

24

LIFE BONUS: SOMETIMES THE SELFISH THING IS ALSO THE RIGHT THING

BIANCA DIDN'T just pop right back up after the procedure. Her body had to process the anesthetics she'd been given, and the doctor thought it best to warm her up slowly. While she was sleeping it off, they tried the procedure on Sid. No one wanted to put it off any longer, and the feeling was that if Bianca's procedure hadn't worked, it wasn't like trying the same thing on Sid was going to make him much worse than he already was.

Sid's ride wasn't as smooth. On the one hand, he was already chilled and they didn't have to be as careful with the cold packs, but his body was also more resistant to the anesthetics. He couldn't be dosed as easily as Bianca. The doctor had to take his accelerated metabolism into account and hope that his species wouldn't matter. Weres didn't exactly go to clinics or hospitals usually, so she was essentially flying blind.

After it was done, Alistair sent us all to our beds. No one

had the energy to argue. We'd done what we could, and we were wiped out. Sylvie decided to nap on a pull-out couch in Fitz's hospital room. She thought he'd like to wake up and see someone familiar. I was just hoping he'd wake up at all.

As I was pulling off my boots back at home, I got a text from Cade.

Hope all is well, Rat. The shop is quiet without you and Sylvie. Coming home soon?

My dad would rather poke out his own eye than use textspeak, and he'd have poked out mine if I replied in it.

I am hopeful, which is more than I've been in weeks. At the cabin now. Must rest. Will check in properly later. I hit send, then passed out before I made it under the sheets. I didn't even bother getting out of my clothes.

I felt like I'd just closed my eyes when Ezra sat on the bed with a cup of coffee. "Yes, you're tired and, yes, this is cruel. The fox in me is very angry about being awake. But there is coffee and I'm told the patients are up and Lock feels we should investigate, and he asks for very little, so we're going to indulge him."

I took the coffee he offered. "Bringing me this must go against everything you hold dear."

His head tilted. "Of course not. There are separate rules for family. Sometimes. If I feel like it."

Lock leaned through my doorway, freshly showered and shaved. Like the rest of us, he still looked haggard, but it was an improvement. "'If I feel like it' being the operative part of that statement. We leave in five."

Ezra sighed, staring at my coffee for a long moment right

before he grabbed it back and downed it in one long gulp. "I'll go get you another cup."

"You do that."

BIANCA AND SID were both still hooked to machines, despite the fact that they were sitting up and looking alert. Sid especially looked perky and ready to go and was currently working his way through the entire roast chicken Ikka had brought him. Healing was hungry work. We watched as Bianca threw a veil and Sid demonstrated his shifting skills for the doctor, who was suitably impressed. Their magic was fine, and they appeared fungus free. Dr. Wesley was keeping them under observation for a few more days, though, just in case.

Fitz woke up later that night. The doctor looked him over and declared him physically fit and ready to leave in a few days. She wanted to recheck his blood work. If he was still clear of the fungus, he could go whenever he wanted. Alistair had brought him new clothes, which he'd put on reluctantly, but now he sat despondently on the edge of the bed as Sylvie tried to give him a pep talk. I knocked, and they waved me in.

"It's gone, Sylvie. I can feel the absence of it."

Sylvie's brow furrowed as she gave him a glare I recognized. She was about to argue him into the ground, which I didn't think would go over very well.

"What's going on?" I asked.

"My magic," Fitz said, dipping his head lower in mourning. "It's gone. I am to be stuck in this form forever."

I could think of worse outcomes, but Fitz didn't need to hear that right then. "So you're, what, human now?"

Fitz's head snapped up like I'd slapped him. "Absolutely not. I was born a kelpie, and no matter what is done to me, that's what I'll be when I give myself up to the depths. Nothing you can do will change what I am."

I wasn't sure how I'd feel if I suddenly lost my fire, or if I'd still think of myself as a firebug, but apparently Fitz didn't suffer from the same conundrum. "I didn't mean to upset you."

Fitz waved a hand at me, indicating that all was forgotten, but his eyes were still full of ire.

"We've just been trying to decide where he should go now," Sylvie said.

Fitz ran a hand through his hair. "I cannot stay with the other kelpies now. I've lost my water legs. Besides, I need a fresh start. Somewhere else."

Because it was hard to heal when you had to stare your old life in the face every day. I knew how that was.

"I told him he can stay in Currant," Sylvie said. "But he can't stay with me. I can't think of any excuse to get my parents on board with a strange man moving into our house."

The drove was an option, but not a good one. What would work well for Katya would fail miserably for Fitz. The drove functioned as a whole. Despite the kelpies having recently banded together, they were solitary creatures at heart. They needed quiet. Peace. Like the kind you find in a bookshop. I tried to not think about it, lest I changed my mind. "Fitz, you can come stay with Cade and me until we figure things out. You won't get a real bed, but you'll get a roof and meals. Don't think of it as a forever thing. Think of it as an 'until I get on my feet' thing. If you don't want to stay in the cabin, then there's a nap room above the bookshop."

Fitz considered it, nodding slowly. "I accept. As long as your father agrees, that is."

Now to break it to my dad that we'd have a recovering kelpie staying with us. Good thing he's a flexible guy. Fitz would stay a little longer in the clinic before he came home with me. The doctor wanted a few days of having her patient around for checkups. Sylvie had to finally go to her own home, but she promised to visit him as much as she could. And I still had some fires to put out. Not literally.

With a cure now possible, our assignment shifted. We went from "burn and destroy" to "contain all evidence and bring it in." Ezra got to be a great shot with the tranquilizer gun. Dr. Wesley trained her assistant in the fungus removal procedure so that she could take the occasional break. Since her assistant wasn't human, Sylvie volunteered to do the actual snail holding. She'd screwed up, and this was a concrete way to do something right and make up for her mistakes, however well intentioned they were. With each success, she smiled a little more, and while I was happy for her, I was worried about how much time she was spending with the Coterie. When I realized that there was no way Sylvie was walking away from us, that she was stuck with the Coterie forever now, because there was no way Alistair was letting her go, I felt a heavy sadness settle into my stomach. What could she have become without the interference my friendship had caused? As sad as I felt, I knew it was miles away from what I would have been feeling if this had happened under Venus's watch.

A FEW DAYS passed as the patients got better and the rest of us continued to run around like chickens with our heads cut off. We were making some progress, but we weren't quite keeping up with the demand. Katya was starting to get exhausted and the doctor and her assistant were napping in shifts. And we still couldn't get to everyone in time. Some creatures were solitary and quiet, and we only heard about them when it was too late and they were too far gone.

It was with an entrenched weariness that Ezra and I returned to the clinic from our last task before we went back to the cabin for the night. We needed a break. Katya would have to stay for a bit longer, but she seemed okay with that. Dr. Wesley had set up a cot for her to nap on as well. I think staying busy was helping her, to be honest.

I went to return the tranquilizer gun while Ezra carried an unconscious witch down to the infirmary for quarantine. Despite Thomas and other past experiences, I refused to give witches a bad rap. I'd met a few nice ones and I didn't want to let myself fall into the same trap as Thomas, where I started pigeonholing creatures. Like the body we'd found in the boat, the one Thomas had left for the snails. Turned out he was one of Thomas's group that had started to get cold feet. When he'd tried to back out, he was locked in with the snails. He'd deserved it, surely, but it still made me cringe.

After I turned in the gun to Dr. Wesley's assistant, I went to find Alistair. He sat in a chair in Bianca's room, playing a game of chess with her. Alistair looked more relaxed than I'd ever seen him, and Bianca practically glowed with health.

I pulled up a chair. "They letting you out soon?"

Alistair grinned. "Twenty-four hours and then the doctor is giving her and Sid the heave-ho."

"I think she'll be happy to see the back of us, to be honest," Bianca said. "Well, not so much me as Sid. He's driving her nuts."

Alistair moved his rook, taking one of Bianca's pawns. "We didn't anticipate how difficult sitting still would be for a were."

"Last time Alistair looked, Sid was doing jumping jacks. He's going stir-crazy." She sidled her knight close to Alistair's bishop.

Alistair frowned at the board, seemingly unsure of Bianca's strategy. "Heading home?"

I nodded. "I need a break. Lock, Sylvie, and Fitz are dropping off what finished cardigans they have right now." We'd had an independent witch who Alistair knew from his pre-Coterie days examine the cardigans. He'd shipped them off to Seattle for her to study. I think he wanted to get them as far away from any local witches as he could, and you couldn't get much farther than Seattle. She'd found a suspicious rune after a thorough examination. It needed to be triggered, but once it was, it would wick all the moisture away from the kelpie. If they were close to water, they would be fine, but if the kelpie had wandered too far . . . well, let's just say it's a good thing we had the sweaters checked. Thomas might have been gone, but he clearly hadn't been working alone. All it would take was one witch knowing the spell to end things poorly for the kelpies. Alistair's friend in Seattle had sent a new pattern for Sylvie to follow for the time being and had promised to fly out in a week to work with her on a new size-shifting design.

I didn't ask Alistair what had happened to those two witch hostages from Thomas's group that we'd handed over. Quite frankly, I didn't care. Turns out I have little sympathy for bigots. Who knew?

"We're going to meet back at the cabin when we're done," I said. I'd been thinking on something for a while, back in the recesses of my mind while everything else was going on, and I felt it was ready to present to Alistair. I wasn't sure how he was going to take it, but I needed to try. "About Sylvie, and the possibility of you dangling temptations like college scholarships in front of her..."

"Her choice, Ava." He hesitantly picked up his queen, then set her back down, still thinking. Bianca grinned. Judging from the pile of pieces on her side of the board, she seemed to be winning.

"I know it's Sylvie's choice, but it got me to thinking." I took a deep breath. "I want the same deal."

Alistair frowned, taking his eyes off his queen. "I already told you I would pay for you to go to college. Insisted you pick one, in fact. And you haven't. I know you've been busy, but fall is quickly approaching...."

"Yes, but that's the difference. You insisted. You can order me around. This whole thing, it's illustrated something that Lock told me a long time ago but I'm just understanding now."

"And what's that?" Alistair's tone was wary, but he was listening.

"I always believed the Coterie was bad. Evil. A force for destruction. And on some days that's what it is. But then there are days now when I see what good I can do."

"I'm glad you've decided I'm not an evil despot," Alistair said drily.

"The jury is still out. I haven't decided anything. It's just—I want the option Sylvie has. You don't want to lose an asset, and I get that. No wasting of the resources. So let's renegotiate my contract. I work for you through college—four years minimum, but as an employee. Not a tool you own. There are times when

I'll still have to do the bad bits." I paused, momentarily distracted as I watched Alistair take Bianca's knight with his queen, only to lose his bishop to Bianca's rook.

"Check," she said, a wide grin splitting her face. Alistair scowled at the board.

I took another breath and started up again. "I think my offer is fair. If, after four years, things are still going well, we can move on from there." And honestly, even with my possible education, let's face it, Bianca was right—what would I do besides Coterie work? It was all I knew.

"Ava," Alistair answered, "I'm not even sure I can find a blood witch strong enough to break your contract. The one Venus used was formidable and, unfortunately, is nowhere to be found."

"It doesn't hurt to try."

Alistair leaned back in his chair, and though he was eating and sleeping a little more regularly again now that things were starting to calm down, I could still see the weariness around his eyes and in the way his shoulders rested. "I think that it's an option worth exploring," he said finally

My eyebrows shot up. I hadn't thought it would be that easy. "Really?"

"Really," he said. "Ava, I could trot out all the data that shows happy employees are more productive or state that it's the right thing to do, but all those reasons, while valid, aren't why I'm agreeing to look into it."

"Then what is the reason?" I asked.

Alistair picked up his bishop, moving it decisively on the board. "Checkmate."

Now it was Bianca's turn to scowl at the game, a flush to

her cheeks. Alistair stared back at her, a strange look on his face. It took me a second to realize it was contentment. This is what he looked like when he was happy. Weird.

He turned his attention back to me. "I'm doing it, Ava, because when the Coterie was crumbling, when Bianca was sick, your team—Lock, Ezra, Sid, Ikka, all of them—none of you backed down. It was dangerous work, but you just kept throwing yourselves at the problem until you fixed it. That's not how employees function. That's how family functions. And rather selfishly, I decided that I prefer it."

I swallowed and carefully thought out my response. "Well, as long as you're happy," I said finally.

He nodded, his eyes narrowed. "So I'll do what I can, Ava. For family."

Bianca raised up her ginger ale, the ubiquitous drink of all hospitals. "To family!" she said, raising her glass. "Even if they do cheat at chess."

Alistair stood up, giving her a quick kiss on the forehead. "I never cheat at chess," he said. "I'm just very, very good at it." She grimaced and drank her ginger ale.

To family.

I stopped in to visit Sid. If he had been doing jumping jacks to stay sane, he was in desperate straits. Ikka and Olive were there as well, doing their best to distract him. It wasn't working. Sid grinned fit to bursting when he saw me. He had me in a hug and was spinning me around. "I hear I owe you a thank-you." He put me back on my feet, slinging his arms around me and Ikka. "In fact, I owe all of you." He squeezed us both in, roping in Olive, too, who pretended she didn't want to be hugged, but I saw her lean in when she thought we weren't paying attention. Sid squished us all into a blob of people.

Ezra came in with Katya and the doctor's assistant, whose name was apparently Deena. Sid dropped us and squeezed them as well. "I didn't forget you guys." He kissed both the girls on the cheek, hesitating when he got to Ezra. The fox raised one eyebrow. The hare grinned back, right before he grabbed the sides of Ezra's face and kissed him full on the mouth, slapping one cheek after. "And you, I have to say, will probably be the only fox ever welcomed into a drove of hares."

Ezra gave a half shrug. "I go where I want."

"Yes, but now you're *invited*." And Sid's grin widened at the expression on Ezra's face. On the one hand, the invitation was a bit of a coup for a fox. On the other, it meant he wasn't sneaking and taking what he wanted, which meant it was less fun. He was trying to decide if the two canceled each other out.

Finally, he gave up. "I am honored."

"Great," I said, anxious to get going. "Now return each other's wallets so we can get this show on the road. I am in desperate need of a hot bath and a comfy bed." Both sighed, reaching into their respective pockets.

25

WIBBLY WOBBLY

THINGS SLOWLY shifted back to normal over the next few weeks, even though it wasn't entirely restful. After all, I had a displaced kelpie to keep an eye on. Sometimes explaining the intricacies of being a normal human was harder than I thought it would be. And, yes, I realize that me showing anyone how to be normal was somewhat laughable. But you haven't seen weird until you try to explain to someone Post-its, egg timers, vacuums, and Popsicles.

Thanks to his new ward, Fitz's more kelpie-like features remained hidden. His sharp teeth and pupil-less eyes had been replaced by a nice smile and irises of a warm brown. He still moved too gracefully for a human, but there didn't seem to be much we could do about that. Sylvie ended up telling people he used to be a dancer.

Overall, he was blending in fairly well. Cade even took him to a contra dance—it's sort of like square dancing, only there's no square. Fitz enjoyed the music and the whirling steps, but unfortunately for the girls in attendance, he had no interest in any of his partners. He was light on his feet and picked up the dance quickly, but for the most part, he still saw people as a lesser species, with Sylvie as an exception to the rule. You should have seen the look of horror on his face when I tried to explain why the pretty brunette had handed him her number on a torn slip of paper. I had to stop him from throwing it away where she could see. He still had a lot of learning to do.

Cade was unsure at first how things were going to go, but it helped that Fitz wasn't comfortable just sitting around. Kelpies are independent, and he bristled at the charity offered. So he cleaned, he chopped wood, and he helped mend clothing. Sylvie taught him how to bake, and though the first few tries were akin to hockey pucks in consistency, he quickly learned how to make a passable brown bread. But the thing that really sealed the deal on Fitz staying was when we took him to the bookstore.

Cade and I are very judgmental when it comes to reading. It's not that we care what you read, but there should be a certain reverence for the written word. So I watched Fitz carefully the first time he entered Broken Spines. He stopped in the doorway and took off his hat, a look of awe on his delicate features. I have no idea how old Fitz actually is, but between his kelpie genes and the glamour on the ward, he didn't look much older than me. Until you looked into his eyes. That's when you could see the years stretching out and you'd start to wonder when, exactly, he'd been born.

He marveled at the intricate woodwork. Horatio took one look at Fitz and decided he was better off at the top of the giant stained-glass tree. I made a mental note to go over with Fitz what humans counted as acceptable food sources and to explain that pets, especially a certain shop kitty, were off the menu.

"You've a beautiful shop, Mr. Halloway." We were still working on getting him to call Cade by his first name.

"Thank you, Fitz."

Sylvie grabbed his arm and dragged him around, showing him the layout and explaining how the store worked. After that, he was at the shop more often than not, and we gained a handyman and bookseller in one fell swoop.

Sylvie got her Doctor Who–themed party in the end, though it was belated. She'd wanted to wait until everyone was well. So it was that we found ourselves on a Saturday night with a house full of people. Fitz had helped Cade bake a cake in the shape of the TARDIS. For those who didn't show up in costume, Sylvie had fezzes and bow ties ready. We played board games and charades and watched a few of Sylvie's favorite episodes. Lock, Ezra, Ikka, Sid, Olive, Bianca, and Katya were all there. Katya made an excellent Amy Pond.

Sleeping bags were rolled out—everyone was staying over. The chatter was loud in the cozy space, and it followed me into the kitchen, where I found Lock helping Cade with the pizzas. We'd made the pizza from scratch and had to stop Sylvie before she created a fish sticks and custard pizza. Even if it would have pleased the Eleventh Doctor, we still had to eat it. Party themes can be carried too far.

"You're such a suck-up," I said, pushing Lock out of the kitchen. "Go. Party. Enjoy. I will help with the hosting duties, thank you very much."

"You just want an easy excuse to get away from all the social interaction."

"Vicious lies."

He looked at me for a minute like he was going to argue but then gave up with a sigh and gave my hand a gentle squeeze. "Join us when you're feeling less socially awkward, please."

"Go." I gave him one last shove.

I put away the leftover cheese, getting out some containers for the toppings when I was done. Laughter and conversation filtered in from the living room, but for now it was just Cade and me.

"So," he said, being careful to keep his attention on the pizza he was sliding into the oven, "you and Lock—"

"Haven't even talked to him, Dad. I mean, not about squishy feeling stuff."

"You're going to have to eventually. You obviously like him—"

"This is a conversation we're so not having."

He settled the pizza in the oven. "You realize your denial is just confirming things, right?"

"I don't care as long as I don't have to discuss it."

His shoulders dipped. "Sometimes, you know, you sound just like her. She was never comfortable discussing emotions, either."

My throat tightened. He was right. Mom had hated talking about feelings, but you always knew they were there. She was good at showing them. I left the toppings alone and hugged Cade's back.

He twisted around, pulling me into a proper hug before easing back to look me in the face. "You called me Dad and are embarrassed to talk to me about boys. It's like we're a real father and daughter."

I swallowed hard, willing away any tears. "We are a real father and daughter. I'm sorry if I made you feel like we weren't."

He wiped away a tear from my cheek, letting me know I hadn't been successful in tamping them down. "It was a joke, Rat. Don't worry about it. We'll do this our own way, just like everything else." His nose scrunched slightly as he said, "But maybe without any more of Sylvie's scripts."

"Deal."

He gave me another big bear hug. "I love you, Rat."

"I love you, too." We stayed like that, enjoying the simple fact that I had him and he had me. Nothing else really mattered beyond those two facts.

Sylvie laughed in the other room then, and our quiet spell was broken, but he didn't let go.

I grimaced. "Sorry about the noise."

He laughed. "Don't be. You know, I never had a big family. Growing up, it was just me and my parents, and they were . . ." He struggled for a nice word.

"Awful, even on a basic level?" I'd never met my grandparents, but I was convinced they were emotionless cyborgs.

He frowned but didn't correct me. "It was always a quiet house, and even when we were all home, it felt empty. And then you showed up, and I had a full cabin of my very own, but it was still quiet. This, well, it's loud. And messy. I'm having to get used to finding not just you, but Sylvie and the boys and a displaced kelpie coming and going, and I don't think that's going to stop even when this whole mess is cleared up. Then there's the drove. So the house is loud and full and there are always dishes, and sometimes I don't know whose socks I'm folding, but I like it.

It's just what I imagined a house full of family would feel like."
He tweaked my nose. "And I have you to thank."

I leaned a little so I could see into the living room. Ezra lounged on the couch, his feet up over the arm. Fitz sat hunched against the front cushions, his arms around his knees, his face alight as he listened to Sylvie speak. Her hands flitted through the air as she described something. Lock's head was down as he laughed. Katya was making it snow, but only on Olive's head, which had the young hare scowling, even though you could tell she kind of liked it. Ikka and Sid grinned at her, which made her scowl more. Even Bianca was smiling, her face open and unguarded for once. And I thought about what Alistair had said earlier, about family and what it meant, and what Cade was saying now. None of the people in my living room shared my blood. No one had my genes or my nose or the same eyes. There were no photos of us playing together as children. But each and every one of us would gamble our lives for the others, and all of us had. If that's not family, I don't know what is. So I would hold it close and I would never let go.

"You're welcome, Dad." I leaned my head on his shoulder. "You're absolutely welcome."

ALISTAIR COULDN'T make it to the party, but he sent a gift along—a brand-new Volvo. He gave Sylvie a freaking *car*. The paint matched that of the Doctor Who police box, a deep blue, and the license-plate frame said TIME AND RELATIVE DIMENSION IN SPACE. Bianca handed her the keys, which Sylvie clasped to her chest. "TARDIS," she whispered, reading the frame.

"He thought you might need a reliable car. Something nice

but sturdy. You know, in case you ever want to visit Boston, and as a thank-you." Bianca smiled when Sylvie squeaked and kept staring at the car.

"So it's part thank-you gift, part bribe," I said.

Bianca shrugged. "Two birds, one stone."

Sylvie held up the keys in her fist. "I have my own car! I have my own car! I don't know how I'll explain it to my parents, but I have my own car!" She stopped. "But I almost helped bad people wipe out several magical races."

"Yes, but not on *purpose*."

Sylvie looked hesitant, until Sid grabbed her by the shoulder and said, "We'll figure out something to tell your parents." When she still didn't move, he added, "You have your own car."

"I have my own car!" she crowed, her hand holding the keys thrust into the air. "Who wants a ride?" Then she danced in place until people got in. Personally, I wanted to wait until she calmed down before I got in with her. Sylvie had a lead foot.

Cade tapped on the hood while Sylvie made everyone buckle up. "Cake in twenty minutes?" Sylvie gave him a thumbs-up and then turned the keys, a big, stupid grin on her face.

Ikka had stayed to help Cade with the pizza dishes, and after I picked up the living room mess a little, I took advantage of the quiet moment and snuck up to my loft. Since Fitz was sleeping on our couch until we figured out a better arrangement, I'd closed the curtain we'd hung ages ago so that I could make my open loft private when I needed to. I'd just never really needed it until now. Not that I walked around naked or anything, but sometimes you just want to be alone, and with everything going on, I hadn't really been alone in many weeks.

The curtain was closed as I snuck up to my room. But I

wasn't going to get privacy. Lock sat on my bed, his elbows on his knees, his body tense, though I could tell he was trying to look relaxed.

"I thought you went with everyone."

Lock scratched his side, where I knew his stitches were. Healing is itchy business, and his stitches were about due to come out. "The car was full. Besides, I wanted to talk to you."

"So you waited in my bedroom? Because that doesn't say 'I'm a creepy stalker' or anything." I sat next to him on the bed.

"I promise that I haven't stolen your hairbrush to make a hair doll or anything of that nature."

"I'm both relieved by that and somewhat insulted that you weren't willing to go through the effort. Also, disturbed that those were the first things that popped into your head."

Lock grabbed my hand, and I stopped babbling. I had the urge to bolt. He had a serious expression on his face, which meant the discussion he wanted to have was going to be about big things, and I was scared. It would be so much easier to run, to go downstairs and avoid this talk for as long as I could. As if sensing this, Lock waited, his hold on me loose. I could have sprinted if I'd wanted to. I could have left, and we'd never talk and I could skip to the easy part where we were just friends, but I would also be closing this door. You could only stomp on someone's heart so many times before they stopped leaving it out as a welcome mat for you.

I thought back to Sylvie's script and wished someone could hand me something like that now. Only, I didn't really need it. What I needed to do was be brave. Not the running-into-danger-throwing-punches kind of brave. I was good at that. Emotional bravery was quieter, but so much harder for me. But

I was tired of being afraid and of missing out on things, on important people like Cade and Lock, because I was too chicken. I could do better than this. They both deserved better from me.

So I did the hard thing. I stayed.

"The others will be back soon for cake, so we don't have much time to ourselves."

I nodded, back to that deer-in-headlights feeling I was so fond of in times like these. Lock looked down at my hand, and I thought about how courageous he was to keep putting himself out there even though I kept swatting him down like I was King Kong and he was a teeny airplane circling the Empire State Building. Well, courageous or stupid. I was going with courageous. I was feeling generous.

So I decided that just once, I could be the brave one. Or the stupid one. This time it really was a toss-up. "Okay, let's say we try this. We go out, we have dinner, or see a movie or whatever and it's terrible—or, worse, mediocre—but we try out of sheer will and keep at it until what we do have dies. What then? You and Ezra are my best friends, and I can't handle anything that would jeopardize that. When we weren't talking, I hated every minute of it. It was like a piece of me was missing. And while I love you both, that doesn't necessarily translate over into relationship material." I stopped to examine Lock's face to see if his jaw was twitching, which was one of his "I'm overwhelmingly angry or frustrated with Ava" tells. Instead, he was more relaxed than he had been when I sat down, and if I wasn't wrong, he looked kind of amused.

"I find it funny that you think mediocre is worse than terrible." He rubbed his thumb over my knuckles.

"One abysmal date and we'd move on. Mediocre? We'd keep

320

at it until we suffocated each other, trying to make it work. I don't want that."

"You're really that concerned we'd be a dud, huh?"

I rubbed my other palm on my jeans—I was suddenly a little sweaty. Charming. "Look, it sounds really bad when you say it like that—" I never got a chance to finish my thought. Lock decided that I was only going to accept direct evidence.

He dropped my hand, brushing his fingers up my cheeks instead, stopping with his palms cradling my face as he pressed his lips to mine. Lock was a gentle kind of guy, so when I'd thought about this moment, I'd always pictured a sweet, soft kiss. And I'll admit that, despite all my worries and fears, I had thought of this moment. A lot.

But I didn't get sweet and soft. While his hands were tender, his lips weren't. There was a demand to them. A "you are mine and I'm going to prove it" kind of urgency that the romance novels Sylvie enjoyed so much like to refer to as a claiming kind of kiss. Thought stopped. Worries evaporated into dust and blew away. And my entire body said, *You know, he may have a point here.*

The next thing I knew, I was in Lock's lap, my fingers tangled in his hair, my lips doing their own claiming. One of his arms was wrapped around my waist, pulling me to him, while the other supported my spine, his hand gently cupping my neck. When I finally broke away, we didn't say anything. My breathing was rapid and we were both trembling from the adrenaline rush, but Lock didn't loosen his hold on me. I slid my thumb along his cheekbone. He didn't say anything, just waited for me to sort through my thoughts. Everything inside me slid around, feelings and logic doing a mad dance, each telling me the best thing to do, how to handle this. For that second, everything in me was pure twirling chaos. Then the dancers stopped, collapsing to the floor in exhaustion. All the tumult stilled and solidified, and I realized there had really only ever been one answer to Lock's question.

I held up a finger. "One date. After that, I make no promises."

My breath caught at the slow smile that spread on Lock's face. He pulled me a little tighter. "Not to sound cocky, but didn't I ever tell you one date was all I ever needed?" He rested his forehead on my chin and let out a breath I hadn't realized he'd been holding. "Because you've got to believe I'm going to give it all I've got."

"Boy, do I own you. I mean, we aren't even dating yet, but you're totally in my power. Doesn't that make you sad? It makes me a little sad for you."

"You realize you're on my lap, right?"

I opened my mouth, ready to dredge up a scathing retort, only to realize I had nothing. "Damn." I tilted my head, remembering something he'd said a few months ago. "This date, it's not in a gas station bathroom is it? I seem to remember you saying once that you could take me to a date in one of those and that it would blow anything Ryan ever took me to out of the water." He blinked at me. "What I'm saying is, I don't want this to devolve into a weird revenge date."

"You think I would waste my only shot by trying to get revenge on someone like *Ryan*? Your lack of understanding is troublesome."

"I just wanted to make sure."

"Uh-huh." He pulled me in closer, his face an inch from mine.

He looked so happy and hopeful, I felt I had to be just a little more brave. I cleared my throat. "You know I won't really hold you to just one date, right?" And I tried, as best I could, to show him that I wasn't being glib and that for once in my life I was doing my best to be emotionally honest.

"Well then, our first date will absolutely be in the men's room at a gas station. I have a reputation to uphold."

And that would be the sound of emotional honesty biting me in the ass. I looked at him, my eyes wide. "Stars and sparks, you might actually be the one for me after all."

He grinned and leaned in for another kiss. "Count on it, cupcake. No one else would put up with us."

ACKNOWLEDGMENTS

This book was a beast, and these people helped me take it down, stuff it, mount it, and put it on my wall. To Noa Wheeler, for giving this beast its shape, and to Kate Farrell for gamely jumping in mid-process. Thanks goes to all the amazing people at Macmillan Kids for their continued support. To my agent, Jason Anthony, for not just tolerating my ridiculousness, but encouraging it and supporting me at all times. To the rest of the team at Lippincott Massie McQuilkin, especially Maria Massie for handling my foreign rights. Jill Gillett and Sylvie Rabineau and the RWSG agency also get many thanks for their hard work. April Ward is responsible for my beautiful book covers, and I owe her so many ponies.

Darin and Serafina Carlucci for once again wading through multiple drafts to get my Maine facts right (all mistakes are my fault alone). To my mom for answering all my weird medical questions—you're the best! Huge thanks to Cindy Pon, Kendare Blake, Emily Adams, and Anje Monte Calvo for beta reads. To my writing buddies, Marissa Meyer, Martha Brockenbrough, Jen Longo, Leigh

Bardugo, Jen Bosworth, Sara Wilson Etienne, Jet Harrington, Jolie Stekly, Ayesha Patel, Kim Derting, Rori Shay, and Brenda Winter Hansen. You can blame the kelpies on Claire Addison and ML Brennan. Thanks to Stephen Blackmoore, Juliet Swann, and Team Parkview for all the love. Many thanks to Mel and Anna from University Bookstore. To Sarah Hull for all of the fanart (the sound you just heard was her exploding into a ball of glitter). Many thanks to Dawn Rutherford for holding my baby so I could edit—who knew that was a service Teen Services Librarians offered? And to all you other child wranglers, I love you guys so much. Aaron Carlton and Bradley Bleeker for website shenanigans, and Vlad Verano for designing all of my swag. And I'm just going to assume that Erika and Eric at Imaginary Trends will make shirts or totes for me again for this book. And of course Third Place Books and Team Honeybear for, well, everything.

To my family for the constant, unflinching kindness and support, even when I'm running around the house telling everyone that I'm quitting and becoming a goat farmer. Just so you know, I'm not ruling out Totes My Goats as a business model yet.

To all the booksellers, librarians, and readers who have supported me over the years, thank you for being so mighty and wonderful. You warm the cold, dead cockles of my heart.

I have an overriding fear that I will forget to thank someone for their help during the long, crazy writing process. Between my questionable memory and the quantity of the awesome helpers, it's bound to happen. So if you're one of those people, write your name in the white space below somewhere, and if anyone asks, I'll totally back you up.

ALSO BY LISH McBRIDE:
THE NECROMANCER SERIES

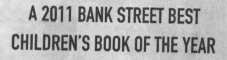

A 2011 BANK STREET BEST CHILDREN'S BOOK OF THE YEAR

"[A] scary and irreverent romp."
—*Publishers Weekly*